CW01084151

GHOSTS
of the
HEART

GHOSTS
of the
HEART

Laurie Button

To order additional copies of this book, contact:
Xlibris
844-714-8691
www.Xlibris.com
Orders@Xlibris.com
834999

Without the support and encouragement of these dear
friends, this novel would have never seen the light of day.
They include my staunchest supporter Marylou, as well as Judy,
Linda, Carol, Celine, Nicole, Ann, Claudia, Paula, Sally, Peni,
Lauren, Kerrie, and my mentor Philip.
Thank you to my musician husband, Joel, who stuck with me while
I sat in front of the computer for days, months, and years writing
and rewriting this book with no apparent end in sight.
I also need to acknowledge our Leonberger puppy, Boji Belle,
who provided love and support by snuggling at my feet
while I worked late at night and in the early hours before dawn.
As for our two cats who exercised their unsolicited editing skills
by walking on the keyboard when I wasn't
looking—the jury is still out.
Finally, thank you to each of the characters who will always be
part of my life and wouldn't let me quit until their
story was finally told.

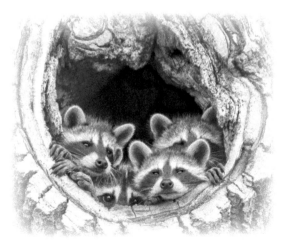

"Paul J. Marcotte Photography."

Cover artwork by watercolorist Janet Graham
Author's photo by wildlife, landscape, and portrait
photographer Paul J. Marcotte
www.pauljmarcottephotography.com

Part One

CHAPTER 1

The Encounter

TARIN GLANCED AT THE FIGURE ONCE MORE BEFORE turning from the window in frustration. Whoever he was, the man had certainly complicated the evening. It was her routine to check the boats every night at dusk, but today she'd delayed the task. Now a trip to the dock would entail an encounter with the uninvited guest.

Not that it's unusual to see someone pause on a calm, clear night at what locals commonly refer to as "The Point." Twinkling stars blanketed the sky and a light breeze rustled aspen leaves in the darkness. Moonlight silhouetted the mountains, sending a swath of diamonds across the rippling water of Ledge Lake. No, it wasn't uncommon to see someone pause to admire the view. This person, however, had been seated on the white Adirondack-style bench for what seemed like an eternity.

"He has to leave eventually," she muttered as if speaking the words might somehow cause the man to follow her instructions. Tarin looked out the window again, shook her head, and scolded herself. During the five years she had lived alone at the lake, she'd come to terms with the apprehension that sometimes accompanies a solitary lifestyle. At this point, she decided, she could handle a short walk to the dock, even when faced with a trespassing stranger.

Tarin suppressed her unease, slipped on a light fleece jacket, reached for a flashlight, and opened the French doors leading to the deck. "Come on, Finn," she called to the black and white border collie napping by the fireplace. "We've got work to do."

She stepped outside and took a deep breath as the canine bounded past her toward the lake. The crisp October air and eerie calls of elk bugling nearby dispelled any thoughts of insecurity. Those familiar sounds, teamed with waves breaking on the rocky shore below, always had that effect upon her.

Tarin's grandfather had brought her to Ledge Lake in a wicker basket when she was just three weeks old. Over time she'd managed to memorize every inch of the lake and knew all the bays, inlets, and beaches by heart. Now, no matter what challenges life presented, she could count on this place to provide serenity and peace of mind.

She stopped a few yards from the stairway leading to the lake and looked toward the lights flickering on the opposite shore. For some inexplicable reason, Tarin felt the need to share her reverence for this special place. She turned toward the bench, directing her words to the silent form seated there. "It's said Ute tribal leaders came to this spot seeking guidance from the spirit world."

For a moment, her words resonated in silence.

"I can understand why," he replied quietly.

Finn introduced himself by planting his front paws on the visitor's lap with his tail wagging and using his nose to investigate this potential playmate. Despite her best efforts, Tarin couldn't call off the overzealous canine.

"I'm sorry. Believe it or not, Finn did go to obedience school."

The stranger massaged the dog's ears. "No worries. He's just being a dog and luckily, I'm a dog person."

With help from an ornamental light at the top of the stairs, her eyes had adjusted somewhat to the darkness. Tarin approached the bench and saw a man in his early thirties—close to her own age, she guessed.

"When I was growing up, my grandmother would bring me here when she wanted to talk. Grammy called it the truth bench."

"Did you always tell her what she wanted to hear?"

She smiled, appreciating his insight. "Usually."

"Have you lived here long?"

"My grandparents bought the property before I was born. I've been at the lake off and on my entire life. Now it's the only place I call home."

Suddenly the man looked troubled, the corners of his mouth turning into an unconscious frown. It was as if he'd remembered something best left forgotten. He started to stand. "I'm sorry. I should be going, and you have things to do."

"Stay if you'd like. This night is much too beautiful to go unappreciated."

Continuing her journey toward the dock, she added, "It only takes a few minutes to check the boats and we'll be out of your way. Don't feel like you need to leave on our account. If you want a place to sit and think, consider yourself invited."

Tarin descended the stairs with Finn scurrying ahead. Reaching the shoreline, she glanced at her beloved boathouse. Perhaps the term boathouse was inappropriate for the small guesthouse built into the rocky bank near the water's edge. In the beginning it was simply a place to store fishing gear and water skis, but as the years passed, she turned it into a small but comfortable getaway. Many nights had been spent in this cozy two-room world close to the water's edge.

Years before, her grandfather had taught Tarin how without warning the early evening calm could turn into an unexpected storm, but tonight there wasn't a cloud in the sky. A brief check confirmed both boats were secure in their lifts alongside the dock. Then, out of the corner of her eye, she noticed the boathouse door was ajar. Finn seemed to read her mind and stopped to sniff at the threshold.

Strange, she thought, moving toward the doorway. *I know I locked it this morning.*

As her fingers touched the handle, the heavy wood door burst open and a dark shape exploded from within, knocking her backward. Tarin lost her balance, and with arms flailing, splashed into the icy water.

She sputtered to the surface in time to see Finn sink his teeth into the man's calf, twisting his jaw from side to side and refusing to let go.

Groaning in pain, the intruder reacted by striking the dog's muzzle before kicking him into the lake.

Her nostrils burned from the water she'd inhaled, and her heart pounded as she watched the man stumble toward the landing and up the steps. Finn wasn't far behind, muscling his way to shore and onto the dock. The canine slipped and slid across the wet planks but regained his footing before disappearing into the darkness. A few seconds later, Tarin heard the unmistakable sound of a struggle on the stairway. And then—nothing. Not a sound.

Tarin waited, shivering in the frigid water. Had it been a few seconds or a few moments?

Suddenly, the sharp punctuation of footsteps on the dock pierced the night air.

Was he coming back?

She tried to remain invisible, stroking through the four-foot-deep water while fighting to keep her balance on the uneven rocks beneath her feet. Tarin's teeth were chattering, and she gripped a moss-covered post in the shadows, bracing for what she feared might happen next.

The footsteps stopped on the weathered planks above her head, and she realized the man from the bench was kneeling on the dock. "Are you okay? What the hell just happened?"

Finn stood nearby—his fur matted, muddy, and dripping with water.

"I'm cold, wet, and terrified," she admitted, her voice cracking. "There was someone in the boathouse. What could he have wanted? There's nothing inside worth stealing." Trembling, Tarin struggled to make her way to shore. The stranger reached down, grasping her hand as she inched along the dock.

"I heard you scream and was coming to see what had happened. About halfway to the lake, some jerk tried to knock me off the stairs."

She stood on the rocky shore—soaked and shuddering in the moonlight.

"You're shaking. Let's sit down so you can catch your breath." Resting his hand on the small of her back, he guided Tarin to the landing at the base of the stairs. "Here, put this on," he said, wrapping his leather jacket around her shoulders.

She watched the man's concerned look turn into an embarrassed grin. He apologized when Tarin met his gaze. "I'm sorry. I know it's wrong to be smiling, but—"

Still shivering, she realized a stringy weed had adhered itself haphazardly across her forehead. Several strands of slimy green moss were tangled in her shoulder-length blonde hair. From head-to-toe, she was dripping wet, clothes clinging to her slender five-foot five-inch frame like a second skin. Wearing but one shoe—the other lost in the fall—Tarin mustered a small smile in return.

"How can I ever thank you?" she asked, still struggling to regain her composure.

"I just wish I'd been able to keep him from getting away, although I don't know what I would have done with him if I had." He untangled a strand of weed from her hair. "Do you have any idea who it might have been?"

"No. It happened so fast, and he was wearing a mask." The intense terror Tarin had felt while hiding under the dock returned. "I never lock the house when I come down to the dock. What if he's gone inside?"

"Don't worry—I promise to check before I let you go in."

She noticed a narrow trail of blood trickling from the corner of his mouth. "What's this?" she asked, lifting her fingers toward his face.

He brushed the back of his hand across his chin. "It's safe to say that guy has one hell of a right hook."

At that moment, Finn wormed his way between the two, using his nose to nuzzle the man's abdomen.

"And what's this?" Tarin saw a tear in the man's shirt was tainted with blood.

"Don't worry. It's not serious. The guy pulled a knife on the landing."

"A knife?" She reached toward the torn fabric. "When were you going to mention that? So much for my litany about lakeshore tranquility. We need to look at the cut, but I'm afraid my flashlight is under four feet of water."

"I'll be fine. It's only a scratch," he assured her. "The important thing is to get you warm and into dry clothes."

Recognizing the urgent look in his eyes, she felt a sudden wave of gratitude. "That man could have killed you and you don't even know my name. I'm Tarin MacGyver. You've already met Finn."

She paused, expecting the man to offer his own introduction.

It took a moment before he broke the awkward silence. "Jonathan Parker. Just Jon to most people."

"Well, Jon—we need to be sure you don't need stitches and give that lip the attention it deserves." She stood and started toward the boathouse. "You know what? I bet we've got a flashlight in there."

He reached to restrain her. "I don't think you should touch anything until the police look around."

"You're right," she admitted. "But I have no idea what to do next. Nothing like this has ever happened to me before."

"That's easy. We need to contact the authorities and get you warm and dry."

Tarin shook her head in amazement. "I don't understand how you can be so calm and collected."

He shrugged. "Trust me—inside I'm probably more traumatized than you are. Later, when I stop pretending to be brave, reality will set in."

Gazing into his eyes, Tarin realized she wanted to know more about Jonathan Parker. But as easily as he'd let his guard down a few seconds before, she watched him become preoccupied once again before following her up the stairs.

CHAPTER 2

The Aftermath

J ON NOTICED TARIN'S HOUSE FOR THE FIRST TIME AS
they approached its expansive porch facing the lake. The two-story
log home was nestled in a thick stand of towering ponderosa and
lodgepole pines. Large windows framed the living room's floor-to-
ceiling moss rock fireplace and the flickering flames dancing within it.
The upper-level exterior was almost entirely glass, with logs defining
the deck that spanned the second story. An identical railing outlined the
porch below, with wide wood steps leading to a pair of French doors.

He restrained Tarin. "Let me go in first."

"Please be careful."

It seemed like an eternity before Jon stepped back onto the porch.

"The house is empty, but be careful when you go inside," he
cautioned.

"Why? What's wrong?" Tarin asked with anxiety embedded in her
voice.

He shook his head. "There are footprints in the kitchen and laundry
room, but I don't think he went any farther, and nothing seems to be
disturbed. Even so, the police will want to take pictures."

"I understand," she replied in an almost inaudible voice.

Watching where she stepped, Tarin hung Jon's jacket on a wrought
iron hook next to the doorway and rubbed her hands together in a

futile attempt to warm them. She moistened a clean hand towel at the sink and instructed him to sit before dabbing at the wound through the tear in his shirt.

He covered her hands with his. "Your fingers feel like ice. Please take a hot shower and change into dry clothes."

"Only if you promise not to go anywhere. I'll be back with antiseptics to clean that cut." Tarin handed him the towel and started up the open stairway to the loft. "When I come back down, I'll need something much stronger to calm my nerves, but if you'd like, there's beer in the refrigerator. There's also hard liquor in the antique icebox in the dining room. Make yourself at home."

"Thanks," Jon called, watching her disappear up the stairs. He put down the towel and opened the stainless-steel door. A quick scan revealed several beers tucked away on the top shelf. Judging from the refrigerator's scant contents, Jon surmised Tarin lived alone.

He grabbed one of the bottled microbrews and turned toward the living room with its vaulted wood ceilings. Drawn to the warmth of the stone fireplace on the opposite wall, he found hundreds of books and photographs lining the built-in shelves on either side of the moss rock. Most of the pictures seemed to be old family photos, while others reflected more recent memorable moments.

A small but familiar device on the coffee table caught his eye, and he cast a quick look toward the stairs before picking up the digital music player. Turning it on with the flick of a finger, he scanned the list of artists cataloged in its playlist.

Toby Keith, Zac Brown Band, Blackberry Smoke, Steve Perry, Journey—so she's mostly into country with a little bit of rock thrown in. Jon was disappointed the band he was looking for was missing from her favorites.

Putting the player back where he'd found it, he surveyed the room and discovered a small piano tucked away in a nook created by the log stairway leading upstairs. He picked at a few keys, unaware that Tarin was standing behind him.

"Do you play?" she asked, tousling her damp hair with a towel.

Startled, Jon turned to face her. "A little. It's a nice piano, but you might want to see about getting it tuned."

"I've been meaning to do that, but it's hard to find someone willing to drive here from Denver." She stepped closer. "Now—are you going to let me take a look at your lip?"

Before he could object, Tarin touched her towel to the corner of his mouth. "I think you'll live. But let's go into the kitchen to check that cut."

Jon followed her to the island where she'd assembled an assortment of over-the-counter medical supplies. There was no room for disobedience when he spoke. "Tarin, you need to call the police."

"I know, but let me take care of this first," she answered, motioning for him to remove his torn shirt.

He pulled the oatmeal-colored Henley over his head, and she caught herself admiring his tan and trim upper body. Feeling awkward, Tarin looked away, opened a packet of antiseptic, and turned her attention to the jagged wound angling several inches across his abdomen. "This may sting."

Jon cringed when she began swabbing his stomach. "You're lucky— the knife just barely broke the skin." She winced, feeling his muscles tighten under her touch. "I'm sorry, but we need to clean it. Who knows where that knife's been."

Tarin cleansed the area several times before applying medicated salve, placing a nonstick bandage over the wound, and then securing it with cotton gauze. She handed him a shirt she'd brought from upstairs. "This was my grandfather's. You won't be making any fashion statements, but I guarantee it's clean."

He began to button the worn denim shirt. "Now, will you please call the police? That guy's still out there, and we already know he's not afraid to come into your house."

"Okay—okay," she replied before picking up a cordless phone tucked away in a corner of the kitchen. "I know you're right."

Chasm Falls' lone dispatcher answered on the first ring. "Marylou? It's Tarin MacGyver. I've been doing well, thank you. But tonight, I need your help. I'd like to report a break-in. Could you send an officer?"

TARIN OPENED THE FRONT door and greeted the first of two uniformed policemen. "Come on in, Mike. I guess you're the lucky one on duty tonight."

"Hi, you." He gestured toward the officer standing behind him. "I'm not sure if you know Deputy Scott Simmons. He came from the West Slope last spring to join the Granite County Sheriff's Department. Tonight, he happened to stop at the station when he went on duty and asked if he could ride along."

The deputy tipped his hat. "Evening, ma'am. I may have seen you around town, but we've never been introduced."

She reached for his outstretched hand. "It's nice to meet you. I'm Tarin MacGyver."

Mike Wilson's trained eyes methodically scanned the living room while continuing the conversation. He noted Jon's presence and nodded. "Good evening, sir."

Tarin glanced at Jon and then back at the officer. "Mike, this is Jon Parker. He was here during the break-in." She paused. "Would you like to go into the kitchen? It might be more comfortable."

"Sounds good," Mike replied as he crossed the living room. "Care to tell me what happened tonight, Tarin? Marylou said something about a man breaking into your boathouse." One of only a handful of police officers in Chasm Falls, Mike had been friends with Tarin since childhood.

"There are footprints in the kitchen and another room you'll want to look at," Jon interjected. "The guy must have gotten into Tarin's house while we were still on the dock."

"Can I get either of you anything? A cup of coffee, water, or a soda?" Tarin asked.

Mike looked at Simmons, who shook his head. "No, we're fine," he answered, pulling a clean incident report from the thin aluminum box in his hand. He walked toward the doorway, looking down at the ceramic tile. "These must be the footprints you mentioned."

The officer turned to the deputy. "Scott, can you get the camera out of my car and a measuring tape?" Kneeling, Mike scrutinized the imprints. "It looks like the man was wearing work boots and not athletic shoes. Unfortunately, most of the men in town wear boots just like this. But we can determine the shoe size and look for any noticeable marks on the soles. Like here, for instance." He pointed to a chip missing in the tread of the right boot. "If we find a suspect who owns a pair of boots with this imperfection, the shoes could become evidence."

Mike finished documenting the prints and sat down at the granite-topped island. "Your assessment that the man stopped in the kitchen area seems to be correct, Mr. Parker. Let's start from the beginning, Tarin."

Standing at one end of the countertop with Jon sitting on a stool at the other, Tarin began to recount the evening's events. "You know my routine, Mike."

Deputy Simmons took careful notes while Tarin described in detail her encounter with the intruder. Then the officers turned to Jon for his version of what had happened.

Mike spoke first. "Let's jump back a bit, Mr. Parker. Tell me where you were when all this was going on." Mike watched for any unexpected expressions on Jon's face.

"I was sitting on the bench near the steps that lead down to the lake."

"Had you been there long?"

"A couple hours, I guess. I wasn't paying attention to time."

"I'm sorry," Simmons interrupted, "but we need to ask. Was it a coincidence you were at the top of the stairs while a break-in was taking place on the dock? Someone might wonder if you were involved in some way—maybe as a lookout."

Tarin reacted without hesitation to the apparent accusation. "You can't be serious. He risked his life to help me, and has a knife wound to show for it."

Retrieving Jon's shirt from the laundry room, she pointed to the bloody tear. "It could have been much worse."

Simmons took the shirt from Tarin. "Like I said, I'm sorry. I wasn't inferring anything, it's just something we need to ask. We'll tag the shirt as evidence and then document your wound."

After removing the wrap Tarin had applied, the deputy snapped a digital photo of Jon's stomach. "You might want to have that cut examined at the hospital and get a tetanus shot. I don't think you'll need stitches, but I'm no doctor."

Jon rewrapped the gauze securing the bandage and buttoned the borrowed shirt while Mike worked on his report.

"Did you see anyone other than Ms. MacGyver go down the steps?" Simmons asked, leaning back on his stool.

"No."

Mike continued to eye Jon. "Do you mind telling us what you were doing there in the first place?" He didn't wait for a reply before asking, "Are you from around here? Can't quite put my finger on it, but it seems like I've seen you somewhere before."

"No, I'm from the West Coast. I was in Denver on business last week and things didn't go as planned. I've been trying to get away from everything for a few days—you know—clear my head." Jon became defensive. "If you'd like to check, I'm staying at the Crescent Lodge. It was a nice night, so I decided to take a walk and wound up here."

"Have you known Ms. MacGyver long?" Mike asked, still taking notes.

"We'd never met before tonight."

"Okay," he replied, making direct eye contact with Jon, and then looking back at his paperwork. "Tell us what you remember."

"Well—I heard Tarin scream, there was a commotion, and then a splash. There were actually two splashes. The second one must have been Finn landing in the water. Thinking someone might be in trouble, I started down to see if I could help. About halfway to the dock, a man coming up the steps nearly knocked me over." Jon stopped for an instant. "I tried to grab him, but he kept pushing me out of the way. Finally, we fell backward onto a landing. He started throwing punches and that's when he pulled the knife."

"Did you notice anything noteworthy about him? Was he tall, short, stocky? Could you tell if he was right or left-handed?" Mike asked.

"The hardest punches came from the right, so I'm assuming he was right-handed. Now that I think about it, he held the blade in that hand, too. As far as size goes, I'd say he was about my height with an athletic build."

"Did you see his face?"

Jon shook his head. "No. He was wearing a mask, and anyway, it was almost pitch black."

"Let's get back to the knife," Simmons suggested, placing a penpoint on the tip of his tongue. "Did you get a good look at it?"

"The blade had a jagged edge," Jon answered. He held his hands out to illustrate the knife's length. "I've never hunted, but it's what I imagine a hunting knife looks like."

"Just for the police report, Mr. Parker, what's your full name?" Mike asked.

"Jonathan Andrew Parker."

"Your address?"

"6100 Camino De La Costa, La Jolla, California."

The officer stopped writing and looked up as though he'd seen a ghost. "Oh, my god. Now I know why you look so familiar. You're *the* Jonathan Parker, aren't you? I knew I'd seen you somewhere but couldn't put my finger on it. My wife has pictures of you all over our house."

Mike noticed the bewildered look on Tarin's face and pointed an index finger in her direction. "Now, don't you get any ideas, my dear. The pictures are on CD covers." He turned his attention back to Jon. "Your band played a concert in Denver last weekend. My wife, Maggie, didn't speak to me for a couple days because I didn't take her. Wait until she discovers you've been in Chasm Falls and we didn't even know it."

Tarin couldn't disguise her confusion. "Am I missing something?" She turned toward Jon. "Should I know who you are?"

He made no attempt to hide his smile. "Actually, it's quite refreshing that you don't."

"Shit. I've been interviewing Jonathan Parker. My wife won't believe this," Mike exclaimed, still shaking his head. Then he sat back, cleared his throat, and worked to regain some degree of professional demeanor. "I'm sorry, sir. I hope we have a chance to talk when I'm off duty, but right now we need to get back to police business." Still somewhat star-struck, he directed a stern look toward his childhood friend. "This is a serious situation, Tarin. We don't know what the intruder was after, and we need to find him before he decides to break in again."

"Do you think he might try, Mike?"

The officer shrugged. "It's possible if he didn't get what he was looking for."

"You keep your doors locked, don't you?" Simmons asked.

Tarin knew she was about to be chastised. "I will now."

Mike closed his eyes and scowled. "We'll talk about security issues tomorrow, Ms. MacGyver. In the meantime, Scott and I will do what we can in the dark. We'll be back in the morning to finish up."

"You didn't touch anything in the boathouse, did you?" Simmons asked.

Tarin looked across the room at Jon. "No. I was about to, but he stopped me."

"Good call," Mike commented as he picked up the incident report. "We'll get what we need out of the car and go down to the dock." He turned to Jon. "We'd appreciate it if you'd stick around, Mr. Parker."

She replied for them both. "We'll be right here, Mike. Let us know if there's anything you need."

Simmons held out his hand to Tarin. "It was nice meeting you, ma'am. I wish it had been under different circumstances, but I promise we'll do everything we can to get to find the person responsible for this. You can count on that."

CHAPTER 3

The Investigation

THE OFFICERS PEERED TOWARD THE LANDING IN the darkness, which was, as Jon had described, about halfway down to the lake. Any illumination from the decorative light at the top of the stairs was lost before reaching the small wood platform.

"I'll do my best with the photos," Simmons said while adjusting the digital camera's settings.

Beaming his flashlight around the area, Mike could see nothing out of the ordinary.

The pair worked their way to where the fight had occurred, scrutinizing the planks at their feet and then the redwood railing outlining three sides of the landing.

"So, you've heard of this guy?"

"Jonathan Parker?" Mike stopped long enough to wipe the back of his hand across his forehead. "Sure. He's the real deal. I've never seen his band Motive play, but my wife Maggie drives me crazy with all their CDs."

"Don't you think it was strange he was sitting on the bench? Especially since he doesn't even know your friend?"

Mike shrugged. "Maybe. But he's not the only one that stops to enjoy that view. And you need to remember, he was a victim, too." The officer seemed to notice something. "Hey, Scott— I've got blood over here. Can I have a swab or two?" He knelt on the platform. "Do you see anything else?"

"Nothing yet."

"A few weeks ago, Parker was on one of those entertainment shows Maggie watches. He's been hanging out with some hot new Hollywood actress." Mike sat up, trying to remember the woman's name. "She's been all over the talk show circuit. I bet you'd know her if you saw her." Just then, something caught his eye. "Well, what do we have here?" he asked, pointing his flashlight at a fresh splinter in the railing.

"It might be fabric snagged in the wood." Simmons examined it in the dim light.

"Shoot it, and then let's take a closer look."

Mike used tweezers to extract a small piece of fleece. "Since Mr. Parker was wearing a light-colored cotton shirt and leather jacket, it looks like our perp must have been wearing a black sweatshirt. Now he owns one with a hole in it." He continued down the steps. "Let's check out the boathouse."

Mike put out his arm to stop the deputy when they reached the bottom of the stairs. He painted the first few feet of the dock with his flashlight. "So much for any hope we had when it comes to finding more footprints. Tarin said her dog, Finn, chased the guy up the stairs. It looks like any evidence we might have found was obliterated when Finn got out of the water. Now, all we have is a smeared mess."

"What kind of dog?" Simmons asked. "I didn't see one when we were in the house."

"Finn? He's a border collie. While you were getting the camera from the car, Tarin told me she'd put him outside in his kennel."

Mike used a gloved hand to push open the boathouse door while Simmons watched from behind.

"Do you think the perp forced his way in?"

Mike nodded. "These are fresh marks from a screwdriver or something like one. The lock is so old I'm sure it didn't take much effort to jimmy." He leaned into the doorway, reaching inside to find the light switch.

Both men peered into the interior of the small structure.

"She must have spooked the guy before he had a chance to do much damage," Simmons observed, stepping over the threshold.

After scouring the two small rooms, Mike stopped in front of a bookcase. "Lucky for us Tarin's a lousy housekeeper. I don't think she's cleaned here in a while. Check this out, Scott."

Mike had noticed a fresh trail left in the dust on one of the shelves. A book had been pulled to the front edge. "We'll need to ask her about this. See if she knows what, if anything, might be missing." He stepped back and walked to the open door. "Take a few pictures and then see if you can lift any prints—but it's doubtful since both Tarin and Parker said the guy was wearing gloves. In the meantime, I'll check out the bank over there."

Mike directed his flashlight toward the rocky shoreline. "If our rock star didn't see anyone go down the steps, the perp must have gotten here a different way. It would have been difficult, but he could have climbed along the bank."

Mike studied the water's edge from his perch on the dock.

"Find anything?" Simmons asked when he emerged from the boathouse.

"I'm not sure but look over there." Mike locked the beam on a small tree. "See those branches? They look like new breaks to me. It's almost like someone slipped and grabbed onto them for support. We'll take a closer look in the morning. For now, let's ask Tarin about the bookcase."

"How long did you say you've known her?"

"I guess since we were five or six years old. Why?"

"Just curious."

"Could it be the new guy in town is looking for a date?" Mike grinned. "Let me tell you about Tarin. She's an intelligent career-driven lady—"

"I can read between the lines, Mike. She's not looking for a relationship or already has one, right?"

"I don't think she's involved with anybody—Tarin doesn't have time for men. But, heck, go ahead and ask her out and see what she says. Find the guy who broke in tonight, and she won't be able to say no."

As they started toward the stairs, Mike put his hand on the deputy's arm. "Would you look at that." Almost invisible in the rocks and brush next to the dock stood a small wood handle.

"Take a picture before I pull it out," Mike said, lowering himself to his knees. After the camera flashed, he reached down to retrieve the tool. "This might be what the perp used to pry open the lock."

Mike felt his cell phone vibrate. Looking at the display, he could tell it was a call from the police station.

"Wilson." Balancing the phone between his chin and shoulder, he put the small chisel into an evidence bag while he listened to the dispatcher. "Thanks. I'll stop over when I finish here."

"Another problem?"

"Naw." Mike smiled. "You've been around here long enough to know one event a night is all we can handle in Chasm Falls. This is more like a welfare check. I'll take care of it when I'm off the clock."

"YOU KNOW, I'M NOT sure if I could even tell you what might be missing. I can't remember the last time I've touched anything in that bookcase. It's full of old paperbacks, photo albums, and board games. Anything of value is here in the house." Tarin was puzzled. "Why would anyone go to so much trouble to steal something that might not be valuable even to me?"

Mike shrugged. "I can't answer that, Tarin. But when someone takes an object, it usually has some kind of importance to the person who steals it. Our job is to figure out who took it and why."

Mike shuffled his paperwork into a neat stack and put it into the aluminum box. "We'll be back in the morning to see if we missed anything. It looks like the perp—that's the perpetrator—got to the boathouse from the rocks along the shoreline. The guy may have been a drifter simply looking for a place to sleep and you surprised him. It's hard to tell. We'll be able to get a better look in the daylight."

He looked at Jon. "Can we give you a ride to the lodge? We're going that way."

"Thanks for the offer, Mike, but I'm taking him to the after-hours clinic to have that cut looked at." Tarin noticed the look of disappointment on her friend's face. "Don't worry. I'm sure there will be another opportunity for you to talk. Maybe you and Maggie can take Jon to lunch."

"We'll figure out who's responsible for this, Ms. MacGyver," Deputy Simmons promised as the two officers turned to leave.

"Call me Tarin, Scott. And thanks for all you do."

"My pleasure, ma'am," he replied before catching himself. "I mean Tarin."

"I BET THIS WASN'T how you planned to spend your evening," Tarin commented when they pulled in front of the lodge.

"Not exactly. Although I do have to admit it's the first time I've been through an attempted burglary, police interrogation, and a trip to the emergency room all in one night. But on the positive side, there was the opportunity to meet you, even if it was under rather unusual circumstances."

The pair sat in the car, each waiting for the other to speak. Jon was first to break the silence. "I feel like we need to get to know each other in—shall we say—a more conventional manner. Maybe I could take you to dinner tomorrow night."

"That would be nice, but how would you feel about a quiet, home-cooked meal at my house? After all, I owe you that and more."

"You know what? That sounds much more inviting," Jon said as he opened the car door. He leaned back through the open passenger window. "What time?"

"Would six thirty work for you?"

"I'll be there."

Long after Jon had disappeared inside the lodge, Tarin continued to reflect upon the evening's events. While she'd been terrified by the intruder, she was intrigued by Jonathan Parker. And she was looking forward to finding out what—if anything—the distant look in his eyes was masking.

MIKE WILSON WAS OFF duty when he fought his way to the bar through the standing-room-only crowd. He had to shout to be heard above the jukebox, and the throng of people standing shoulder-to-shoulder made it almost impossible to navigate the room. He managed to capture the owner's attention and motioned toward the front door. "Can we talk?"

"Any sign of Alex?" Jake Carpenter asked when they were outside.

Mike shook his head. "I couldn't find him. We were finishing a report when they relayed your call to me so I couldn't get on it right away. Alex wasn't in any of his usual haunts. What time was he here?"

"About ten thirty, I think. Late night television had just come on. Did you drive by his house?"

Mike nodded. "Twice. His truck was gone and there wasn't a light anywhere. I even called Rachel at her mom's place. She hasn't seen him today." Reading the look of concern on Jake's face, Mike asked, "Is there a reason you're so uptight tonight?"

"I'm not sure. Everybody knows Alex hasn't been himself since he got back from Afghanistan. But tonight, there was something in his eyes, something I don't think I've seen before."

Mike leaned against the fender of a nearby car. "Do you think the plant closing might have pushed him over the edge?"

Jake shrugged. "Maybe, but he's not alone. Losing the factory hurt most of the families in Chasm Falls. It was tougher for Alex because Rachel took their daughter and moved out about the same time he lost his job. I guess it's no wonder he's a little messed up."

Jake looked out over the packed parking lot and Mike could sense there was something else bothering his friend. "Let's be honest. You've been babysitting Alex since we were in grade school. Maybe it's time he starts managing things on his own and lives with the consequences."

"I know you're right. But damn it. If he doesn't clean up his act, he's bound to get into real trouble one of these days and we won't be able to help."

"I understand, but I can't haul him in just because he needs a lecture on bad behavior." Then, resting an arm on Jake's shoulder, he issued a challenge. "You know what? I bet we have time for at least one game of pool before you close. I'm still mad about the eight-ball shot you made the other night. You owe me a chance to avenge myself."

Mike suddenly remembered the news he'd meant to share with Jake as soon as he had the opportunity. "Hey, I almost forgot. Do you know where we were when you called the station? I couldn't say anything until we filed the incident report. But now that we have—I can tell you. There was a break-in at Tarin's boathouse tonight."

"Are you kidding? Did you catch the person responsible?"

"Not yet but get this. Care to guess who was with Tarin when it happened?" Mike withheld his tidbit of gossip long enough to pique Jake's curiosity. "Jonathan Parker."

Jake looked puzzled. "Jonathan Parker? And that's supposed to mean something to me?"

Mike began strumming his best air guitar.

"Wait a minute—*the* Jonathan Parker? Didn't his band play in Denver a week or so ago?"

"You got it," Mike answered. "He took a couple punches, hit back a few times, and then the perp pulled a knife on him. Parker got cut in the process."

"What was he doing at Tarin's house?"

"Sounds like he's in town to get away for a while and happened to sit down on that bench she has overlooking the lake. That's where he was when it all came down. Whoever broke in and tried to stab him is facing felony charges so it's no laughing matter, but you might find this amusing."

"I'm waiting."

Mike was grinning from ear to ear. "Tarin has no idea who Parker is."

"Should that surprise me? For someone who makes a living interviewing people and covering the news, she leads a sheltered life."

Jake slapped Mike on the back and the two reentered the Sip 'n Strike, trying to banish Alex Davis from their thoughts by discussing Tarin's encounter with a famous singer.

Then the conversation turned back to their down-and-out friend.

"Aw, don't worry, Jake. He'll turn up," Mike reassured. That was one thing about Alex—he always managed to land on his feet and find his way back home.

CHAPTER 4

Anticipation

TARIN SAT STUDYING RECIPES WITH COOKBOOKS strewn across the kitchen island and wireless earbuds tucked in her ears. Holiday parties aside, she couldn't remember the last time she'd entertained a man unless it was Jake Carpenter, and Tarin considered him more like a brother than a gentleman caller.

How sad is that? she scolded herself. When this encounter with Jon Parker was over—and it would come to an end right after dinner—she needed to email that new sportswriter at the newspaper who had been flirting with her the past few weeks. He was intelligent with a good sense of humor and kind of cute, too.

Wait a minute, she caught herself.

When you've passed the age of thirty, potential suitors aren't supposed to be considered cute. At that point, they're handsome or distinguished, but definitely not cute.

Tarin hated the thought of dating a distinguished man. She wanted a guy who looked drop-dead gorgeous in faded jeans, boots, and a black felt cowboy hat. He needed to appreciate the sweet smell of horse manure and be comfortable with the fact she would rather drive her Ford F-150 than the Audi E-Tron held prisoner in the garage. That man wasn't Jon Parker, even if Tarin did feel butterflies when he was nearby.

Curiosity had gotten the best of her earlier in the day, and she'd spent more than an hour downloading songs by the band Motive onto her laptop. Surprised by how many of the tunes sounded familiar, she found herself curled in an overstuffed leather recliner listening to the music with her eyes closed. Backed by lead and bass guitarists, a keyboard player and drums, Jon didn't miss a beat transitioning from hard rock to soft ballads.

She put the earbuds on the counter, closed the cookbooks, and scrapped any ideas of creating a lavish gourmet meal to impress him. Keep it simple, she decided. Lasagna could be made ahead of time. After all, it's hard enough to carry on a coherent conversation with someone you barely know. There was no need to complicate things with the uncharted territory—and potential disaster—of an untried recipe. The main dish and bread could be ready to heat, and with any luck, creating a salad together might serve as an icebreaker.

"It's a plan, Finn," she announced to the dog resting on the floor at her feet, before turning toward the dining room. Dinner in the kitchen where they'd worked with antiseptics and bandages the night before didn't seem to be an option. But with a wall of glass facing the lake and the warmth of family heirlooms, the dining room would be perfect.

The rustic pine table had been crafted of barn wood rescued by her grandfather from an old building on the property. A local carpenter had turned the weathered planks into a table with matching chairs and benches many years ago. The chandelier was made from mule deer antlers with a grapevine garland and red berries woven through the tines to add a dash of color.

She could recite from memory the history of everything in sight. There was her grandmother's milk glass collection and an assortment of antique oil lamps her mother treasured. Stern great-great-great grandparents lorded over the house from their oval wedding photograph on the wall above the oak sideboard. While her mother once said the room—and the entire house for that matter—looked like a museum, Tarin didn't mind the comparison. Instead, she found it comforting.

She carefully lifted her grandmother's Bavarian china from the pie safe and placed two plates across from each other on the ivory lace tablecloth. Then, adding wine glasses and silver to the table, she stood back and smiled. She'd forgotten how enticing the anticipation of entertaining a dinner guest could be. It was then that Tarin realized she'd allowed a newspaper career to become the significant other in her life.

"What do you think about candles, Finn?" The black and white dog tilted his head, looking inquisitively at his mistress.

The doorbell interrupted her thoughts and she turned to find officers Mike Wilson and Scott Simmons standing outside.

Mike grinned, surveying the table and the candles she was trying to hide behind her back. "It looks like you've got big plans for tonight."

Blushing, she poked at Mike's stomach but missed.

"You might want to be careful, Ms. MacGyver. I could charge you with attempted assault on a police officer. That could mean jail time." He continued to grin with his wrists crossed defensively in front of him.

"Give it up, Mike."

"Okay. But seriously, do you have a few minutes? We need to talk."

Slipping the candles back into a drawer, she couldn't miss the look of amusement on her friend's face.

"They were a little over the top," she explained while trying to change the subject. "Did you find anything new this morning?"

Tarin soon learned they'd been able to track the intruder to a dock about one hundred fifty yards from hers. The owners had closed their home for the season and it was vacant. Unfortunately, the two officers couldn't turn up any other clues. Unless they could link the evidence they had discovered to someone, it would be a challenge to find the burglar.

"Please be careful and keep your eyes open. We don't know what this guy had in mind, and like I said last night, he might decide to come back," Mike warned when he opened the door to leave. He leaned over to pick up a long white box from the stone walkway. "I think these are for you. We saw the florist pull out when we were pulling in. I'm surprised they didn't knock. Maybe our squad cars scared them away. Anyway, I need to give that Parker guy credit. He's smooth." Mike grinned and lifted his arm for protection a second time when she reached for the box. "I'll call if we find anything else."

Closing the door behind them, Tarin put the box on the table and untied the satin ribbon. Lifting the lid and folding back the green tissue, she discovered a dozen long-stem burgundy roses and white baby's breath nestled in greenery.

She read the handwritten words on the card with a soft smile lighting her face. "Looking forward to dinner, Jon."

After arranging the flowers in a vase, she touched her nose to the delicate petals and paused to savor the wonderful fragrance. *Who needs candles when you have roses?* Then, glancing at the clock, she realized it was time to figure out what to wear to impress, yet not overwhelm, her guest. That task, she decided, might be the most difficult of all.

JONATHAN PARKER WAS LATE. Not so late Tarin felt she'd been stood up, but he was tardy just the same. Shortly before seven o'clock, her cell phone rang.

"Hi, it's Jon. I'm sorry. I got a call when I was about to leave and had to take it. I'll be on my way in a few minutes, I promise."

"No problem, you're fine," she answered, trying not to expose her relief at hearing his voice.

"You wouldn't happen to have any Jack Daniels in the house, would you? If not, I'll pick up a bottle on my way over. Tonight, I might need a stiff drink or three." Frustration was veiled in his words.

"I'm sure there's some in the cabinet. I'll see you when you get here."

She put the phone on the table and turned toward the vintage wood icebox that had been given new life as a liquor cabinet. Her friend Jake was also a fan of Jon's beverage of choice, and she was sure there was some left from last summer's Fourth of July party.

Relieved to find a half-full bottle, Tarin carried it to the kitchen where she had been sipping a glass of Riesling to calm her nerves. Fifteen minutes later, there was a knock on the door. Taking a deep breath and then exhaling to chase away her mounting anxiety, she turned the handle and unlatched the door.

"LET ME HELP YOU with that," Jon offered, watching her slice cucumbers and tomatoes for the salad. "So, you've heard a little bit about me. And by the way, if you look at any grocery store tabloids, don't believe anything you read." He reached to take the cutting board and knife from her outstretched hand. "Having said that, it dawns on me I know very little about you."

"There's not much to tell," she answered, turning to rinse the lettuce. "My grandparents bought the property in the seventies and lived across the road until they built this house twenty years ago."

"Did you spend a lot of time with them?"

"Every summer when I was growing up. My parents were divorced, and Mom worked two jobs to pay the bills. It gave her a break when I was at the lake, and I didn't mind because Grampa was my hero. He taught me to ride horses, fish, play baseball, and even showed me how to dance. He made me feel like I was the luckiest girl in the world. And before you ask—yes, I was his shadow and aspiring tomboy." She put the crisp lettuce into a bowl. "My mom passed away when I was in seventh grade. That's when I moved here permanently."

"And then?"

"Nothing out of the ordinary. I finished high school, went to college, graduated, and got a job."

"Where did you go to school?"

"College? Columbia University in New York." She filled in the blanks herself before he could continue the quiz. "I have a degree in journalism and found a job working for a newspaper in Virginia. Then, when my grandfather was diagnosed with cancer eight years ago, I moved back to Colorado to take care of him. My grandmother died several years before that."

"It must have been hard for you."

"I was lucky to find work as an editor for *The Denver News*. It was perfect because I could work from home and still take care of Grampa."

She pointed to a corner in the living room where a laptop computer sat buried under loose papers, notebooks, and disheveled newspapers. "That's my office. Sometimes my boss gives me assignments, but not very often. Normally my job is to edit copy and check facts in articles turned in by other staff writers. I also write a column for the paper once a week." She paused long enough to smile. "That's my story. I'm afraid it's not very exciting."

"How big is Chasm Falls?"

She contemplated her answer. "Year-round? Probably five thousand people. Maybe six. The population doubles in the summer because of the mountains and the lake, but most part-time residents leave in the fall and go to Arizona or Florida."

"At the lodge I heard people talking about a big plant closing near here."

"That would be the quarry. Believe it or not, our town used to be a bustling place. We had one of the biggest flagstone plants in the West. But production has been down the past few years and a group of developers bought the company six months ago. They shut it down without warning."

"That couldn't have been good for the town's economy."

"It's been hard on everyone. Now most workers are surviving on unemployment because there aren't enough local opportunities to go around. As a result, quite a few people have been forced to commute to ski areas like Winter Park and Breckenridge to find work. Even more have simply packed up and moved away." She stood up from her stool. "Can I get you another drink?" she asked, reaching for his empty glass.

He nodded. "What keeps you here?"

"I love this place and most of my best friends live in Chasm Falls."

"Any special men in your life?"

She laughed. "Special men? Well, there's my friend Mike—the police officer you met last night. Then there's Jake. He came back a few years ago to take over the local bar and bowling alley from his dad. Mike is married with two little girls, and Jake is the big brother I never had. Alex Davis and I dated through high school, but we broke up when I went to college. Now he's married to my best friend, Rachel. They have a two-year-old daughter named Sarah. Unfortunately, they've had their share of problems." She smiled. "If you're asking if there are eligible bachelors my age in the area, the answer is not many. But to be honest, I'm not looking for a relationship. I'm quite happy with who I am and what I'm doing all by myself."

She handed Jon his glass, and he extended it back toward her. "What about a toast to Chasm Falls' future? Here's hoping your town thrives again very soon."

Tarin met his glass in midair just as the oven timer began to buzz. "Your dinner awaits, Mr. Parker."

LATER THAT EVENING, IT was Tarin's turn to ask questions.

She sat on the porch swing while Jon leaned against the deck's log railing across from her. "Did the phone call tonight have anything to do with what brought you here in the first place and why you're so pensive at times?"

He turned to look over the lake for a moment before replying. "You could say that." Then he sat down next to her. "Our band's been together a long time, and as hard as it is to admit, we're not on the same page anymore. It came to a head last week in Denver. After the show there were fireworks, and we all said things we shouldn't have. But at least now the issues are in the open and we can deal with them."

"Was the call tonight from one of the guys in the band?"

He shook his head. "No. It was our manager. He wanted to remind me that we have a contract to fulfill. I'm sure he called each of us with the same message."

"So now what?"

He shrugged. "I told him I'd be coming back to California in a week, maybe ten days, and then we'd talk. Beyond that, I don't know. That's why I came to the mountains. I wanted to think things through."

"If you planned to remain anonymous, I'm afraid Mike and the staff at the lodge have probably blown your cover. But fear not. Most of the people in Chasm Falls are old-timers, and there's not much chance they would even have a clue who you are."

He was quick with a comeback, "You'd never heard of me, either. Does that put you in the same category?"

"Touché. Now that we've established my lack of exposure to the world of music, would you mind helping me check the boats? After what happened last night, I'm hesitant to go to the dock alone after dark."

Jon surprised Tarin by taking her hand, and with a bounding border collie in the lead, they started toward the stairway leading to the lake.

"You don't plan on any unexpected guests this evening, do you?"

"Let's hope not."

"Even if you are, I'm honored to serve as your bodyguard, Ms. MacGyver."

He smiled and she sensed whatever had been bothering him earlier had, at least for the time being, been pushed from his mind. She hoped the crisp air, the lake, and the snowcapped mountains would help him realize any problems he might be facing weren't as overwhelming as he believed them to be.

Across the yard and disguised by darkness, the man dressed in black leaned against a tree trunk and watched the two descend the steps to the lake. He took one last draw on his cigarette before flicking it to the ground and extinguishing the embers with the heel of his boot. Then he turned and disappeared into the night.

CHAPTER 5

Shuck's

JON WAS DUE TO ARRIVE AT TEN O'CLOCK. TARIN WAS sure that would allow enough time to edit two stories and finish her weekly column. What she hadn't counted on was a bad case of writer's block brought on by thoughts of Jon Parker.

While his entry into her life couldn't be considered anything resembling a potential relationship—sadly, this was as close as she had been to dating anyone since moving back to Colorado. Tarin's avoidance of the opposite sex wasn't intentional, but due to her job and apparent lack of intriguing suitors, the quest for a lasting connection had been sequestered on a backburner. Sure—at staff meetings in Denver—fellow writers would sometimes ask for a lunch date or a quick drink before she drove back up the mountain. But in the end, the relationships never went any further. Plus, as she'd explained to Jon the night before, she was already quite content with her life. Adding a man into the equation would simply complicate matters. Or at least that's the story she liked to tell.

But rationalizing all of this didn't make any of the butterflies disappear. Jon was unlike anyone she had ever met, and she was pretty sure there was more fueling her interest than his fame and fortune.

Tarin stood in the bathroom, staring into the plate-glass mirror. Three hours of sleep hadn't been enough. The red, puffy eyes reflected there betrayed the fact they'd downed a little too much wine while talking well into the early morning hours.

"This won't be easy," she said out loud, using her fingers in a futile attempt to lift and tighten the skin around her bloodshot eyes.

Today's plans included a boat trip to the marina for a late breakfast, so deciding what to wear was a less monumental task than it had been the night before. Jeans and a T-shirt topped with a fleece jacket should be just fine for the five-mile jaunt across the lake.

Tarin glanced at the clock. She was somewhat satisfied that soothing drops and makeup had masked her bleary eyes. Fifteen minutes to spare. There was still time to check email and verify her edits had made it to the copy desk in Denver. A cheery response waited on the laptop, congratulating her on another job well done.

Satisfied, she couldn't help but smile. But while the story-editing tasks were cut and dried, today's column was less than inspired due to her preoccupation with a certain Californian. Fortunately, a bad day for Tarin could be considered a good day for most others in her profession.

She had always given her mother, Lauren, credit for any writing skills she might have inherited. When Tarin's father walked out of their lives, the single mother found herself forced to put food on the table any way she could. Working as a secretary by day and a waitress at night, she was confined to composing mundane letters and guest checks. Only at night, after washing her hands of household duties, could she sit down to write.

Each evening Lauren sat in the kitchen and filled the pages of her spiral-bound notebooks. Tarin loved to sit nearby, crayons in hand, composing her own stories featuring crude but colorful illustrations.

"Always keep a journal," she preached to her daughter. "But don't pack away what you've written. When you look back, the memories will be there whenever you need them. You'll be able to treasure all those experiences you might otherwise forget."

Lauren continued to write long after she was diagnosed with breast cancer. But in the end, the illness took away her ability and then her life.

Tarin didn't follow her mother's instructions to the letter. While she did keep a few journals, she preferred to talk about life through the columns she wrote for the newspaper. But sometimes on cold snowy days, she would curl up in front of the fireplace with her mother's notebooks and relive the stories they told.

A quick rap on the French doors snapped her back to reality. She looked up just in time to see Jon step inside.

"Am I early?" he asked with a degree of hesitation. "I don't want to be blamed for interfering with the flow of creativity."

She closed the laptop and stood to welcome her guest. "I'm finished and the boss has given his blessing. A boat and its driver are now yours."

"Great. What are we waiting for?"

Tarin couldn't help but notice how handsome and almost boyish he looked in well-worn jeans and a navy windbreaker. His brown hair was tucked behind his ears, falling to his shoulders under a denim ball cap embroidered with a mountain scene and the words "Chasm Falls, Colorado."

"What's this?" she teased, reaching for the brim. "Trying to pass for a tourist?"

He intercepted her hand in midair, "What better way to be incognito?" He took both of her hands in his.

As she looked into his deep blue eyes, the butterflies were back, their wings fluttering as fast or faster than her heart was beating.

"I need to thank you for the past few days. Being here was just the break I needed. Meeting you was an unexpected bonus." He grinned and tweaked her nose. "You've even got me believing I can go back to the grind in LA and make it work, at least until we finish this record."

Without warning, he lifted her face toward his and pulled her close. As their lips met, neither could deny the electricity passing between them. He stepped back a few inches, his fingers still resting under her chin.

Savoring the moment but not knowing quite how to react, she glanced away before breaking the silence. She knew her face was flushed. "Would you like to be captain or crew on this maiden voyage?"

Jon ran his tongue over his lips, seeming to savor what remained of the taste lingering there, and then motioned toward the door. "Can

I enlist with the crew until I get my sea legs back? It's been a long time since I've been behind the wheel of anything without wheels."

ONCE ON THE DOCK, Jon marveled at how easily Tarin lowered the vintage eighteen-foot Chris-Craft inboard from its lift. "You've done this before, haven't you?" he asked.

"More than a few times," she answered, monitoring the speed of the boat's descent. "Can I get you to untie the moorings?"

"Aye, captain." Then, holding the fore and aft lines as the boat floated free, he watched her step in, pull the choke, and turn the key in the ignition. After two unsuccessful tries, the boat's engine sputtered small clouds of blue-gray smoke and came to life with a throaty rumble.

"All aboard," she commanded while pushing in the choke and easing the boat into reverse.

He tossed the lines onboard and jumped onto the passenger seat. "I'm impressed. You really know what you're doing."

Calculating the boat's speed while backing to the end of the dock, she turned toward open water, pushed the throttle forward, and sent a confident grin his way. "My grandfather and I spent hours together in this boat. It was his pride and joy, and he was an excellent teacher."

Jon watched her maneuver the speeding vessel as it skimmed across the glasslike surface of the lake and smiled. He couldn't remember being around a woman with as many facets as Tarin MacGyver. Sure, in LA there was no shortage of self-confident women. But she seemed to balance that quality with both beguiling innocence and a crazy kind of vulnerability he couldn't quite put his finger on. While she didn't have the drop-dead gorgeous looks of the models and actresses he usually kept company with, she had a unique beauty all her own.

Maybe it really was time to go back to California. He hadn't come to the mountains to start a relationship he couldn't finish. But studying Tarin, her hair flowing in the wind, he decided to put that thought on hold. He wasn't ready to leave this haven he'd discovered. Not yet.

TARIN TRIED TO HIDE her amusement when Jon saw their destination for the first time. She failed miserably.

Slowing the boat to a crawl, they passed between the aging and yellowed buoys serving as speed signs and she watched him attempt to absorb the scene playing out in front of them.

The marina offered boaters three docks. Two of them were lined with boatlifts in various stages of disrepair—most of them were rusty, bent, and empty. The third dock—the one with gas pumps—was the hub of activity. As for the restaurant and bait shop, they sat on the shore as they had for more than a century. The white clapboard siding wore a fresh coat of paint, but latex alone couldn't bring this building up to date. The porch spanning the entry had settled years ago, but no one seemed to notice.

While Tarin maneuvered the boat to a slip opposite the pumps, Jon jumped onto the dock. He secured the vessel's stern and maintained his hold on the bowline until she turned off the engine, pulled the key, and joined him on the weathered planks above the water.

She adjusted foam fenders into position over the boat's side and together they tied the bow and spring lines. "Ready to take a step back in time?" she asked with a twinkle in her eye.

"Oh, my god," he said under his breath when he turned to survey the one-story structure onshore.

"I thought you might find this place interesting."

"All that's missing from the porch are old men in rocking chairs wearing straw hats and chewing weeds while telling fish stories."

"Colorado natives might take offense to that. First, they're not hillbillies. Secondly, try cowboy hats and pinches of chew." She leaned toward Jon and rested her hand on his arm, "We're just early. The men you're looking for are due to settle in and start rocking about noon."

"How long has this place been here?"

"It feels like forever." Tarin basked in his awe as they walked along the dock. "My friend Rachel's great-great-great grandfather built it after World War I. Now her parents run the business. Believe it or not, they were going to upgrade everything about ten years ago, but there was a big uproar in town. Nobody wanted anything to change, so this remains our own little piece of Norman Rockwell's Americana."

His eyes were riveted on the neon sign mounted on the roof.

"*Shuck's*" it proclaimed in giant, cursive, neon letters. Below in smaller characters, the sign advertised "*Boats, Bait, Breakfast & Gas.*"

"What more could you need?" he whispered in her ear.

"The sign is rather misleading," she whispered back. "Now you can get lunch and dinner here, too. The big question is whether the reference to gas should come before or after the word breakfast, but we'll see what you think after you try the food."

"Come on." She intertwined her arm with his. "The food isn't citified, but it's pretty good. Just don't turn West Coast vegan on me. These are mountain folk and they like their meat."

Once inside, a server seated the pair in a prime booth overlooking the lake. While they were waiting to order, Tarin finally asked the question that had been plaguing her. "What's it like to have people recognize you wherever you go?"

Jon glanced around the small restaurant. "Fortunately, there are still plenty of places where I can find more than enough obscurity." He smiled and sat back against the Naugahyde-covered bench with its vintage horsehair accents.

She held her coffee cup in both hands and continued to quiz him, "Were you born in California?"

"No. I'm New Jersey-born and bred."

"What about your family?"

"It's a big one. I'm the baby of six children—three boys and three girls. Dad met my mom while he was stationed with the Army in Europe. She's Italian and old-school Catholic."

Tarin leaned forward, elbows on the table with her chin resting on her hands. "What made you decide to become a professional musician?"

"My mother was surrounded by music when she was growing up. When the time came to raise her own family, we sang in the church choir and played all kinds of instruments around the house. But I'm the only one that decided to make a career of it."

She watched with interest while Jon seemed to relive memories that hadn't been visited in a long, long time.

"Like a lot of teenage boys, we put together a garage band. We played high school talent shows, dingy bar gigs, and eventually made cheap demo tapes. Then, twelve years ago, I moved to LA to take one last shot at making it. I convinced my friend, Nick, to come along. He can't sing a note, but he's a great songwriter. We were naïve enough to think we could be a good team for somebody."

"And?"

"We wound up going in different directions. Nick wrote a tune called 'Thinking of You.' You may not know the title, but I guarantee you'll know the song if you hear it. It earned him a Grammy. At about the same time, I linked up with Motive. The band was looking for a lead singer and I needed to get my foot in the door. We've been together ever since."

"Where's Nick now?"

"He's still in California. Now and then we do projects together, but he spends most of his time writing songs and working on soundtracks. You'd like him."

She looked into his bright blue eyes, but hesitated before asking, "Will you stay with the band when you go back?"

"I don't have a choice. We're under contract for another album and I need to see it through."

Watching Jon become introspective once again, she attempted to lighten the conversation. "Turnabout's fair play. You asked me about the men in my life. What about the women in yours?"

"We're a sad pair, Tarin MacGyver," he answered. "I almost got married when things were beginning to take off for Motive. She was beautiful and I was impressionable. It wouldn't have lasted. After that, I decided it was better not to get involved. Sometimes it's worked, sometimes it hasn't."

Just then, a voice from across the room interrupted their conversation.

"Tarin?"

Looking toward the source, Tarin sprung up from her seat and sprinted across the room to hug Rachel Davis.

Tarin took her best friend's hand and led her back to the booth. "Got a minute? I'd like you to meet someone. Jon's here for the first time and wanted to check out the best food in town."

Rachel reached out to shake his hand. "I don't know if I'd go that far, but we try," she responded, eyeing the man she had just met. "What brings you to Chasm Falls?"

"I guess you could say a short vacation."

"Well, I hope you enjoy your stay. I'd love to talk, but we're shorthanded today, so I better get back to work." She turned to Tarin. "Mom had to go to Winter Park this morning and I'm filling in for her."

"Where's my girl Sarah?"

"Alex took her for the day. You've probably heard. We're separated again."

"No, I hadn't. I'm so sorry, Rach. We need to get together. I hardly ever see you anymore."

Her friend's warm demeanor seemed to melt, but she managed to paste a smile back on her face. "It was nice meeting you, Jon. Maybe we'll run into each other again." With that, she disappeared behind the kitchen's swinging metal doors.

"Any idea what that was all about?"

Tarin shrugged. "I'm not sure. I've mentioned Alex and Rachel to you before. It's a long, convoluted story." She sighed. "They've had their problems. Alex was a platoon leader in Afghanistan and his unit was caught in crossfire. He lost three of his men and suffered serious wounds himself. Alex almost lost his leg. He hasn't been able to get over the feeling he failed his unit when he didn't get them all out alive."

"What happened when he got home?"

"He had three surgeries to repair his leg and was in rehab for a long time. While he was at the VA Hospital in Cheyenne, doctors diagnosed PTSD."

"How's he doing now?"

"He's been in and out of therapy and has a boatload of prescriptions that are supposed to help. If we go to the Sip 'n Strike, you'll meet him.

I'll let you be the judge if it looks like he's going to counseling sessions or taking his meds. It didn't help when he lost his job at the quarry."

Jon smiled, placing a reassuring hand over hers. "I have a feeling you'll help them make it through this."

"Thanks for the vote of confidence. I'll be there whenever they need me, but this is something they need to work out themselves."

CHAPTER 6

A Fish Story

THEY WERE RETURNING TO THE DOCK AFTER breakfast when Jon stopped to look at Tarin with a mischievous twinkle in his eye. "You go ahead. I'll be there in a minute."

Without waiting for her reply, she watched him dart back into Shuck's as if on a mission.

"Do you need gas today, ma'am?" the dockhand asked while wiping his hands on an already grease-covered towel.

"No, we're fine, but thanks for asking," she answered before starting to work with the lines securing the boat.

Out of the corner of her eye, she noticed the young man lingering nearby. She glanced back toward him, "Can I help you with anything? It's Justin, isn't it?"

"Yes, ma'am." He hesitated. "I was just wondering. Mike—I mean, Officer Wilson— told us the guy you're with is in the band Motive. Do you think you might be able to get his autograph for me?"

Tarin smiled. "Jon's very nice, and if you ask, I'm sure he'd be happy to sign something for you."

Justin pulled a CD case from a shelf by the gas pump, leaned over, and handed it to her. "I got this out of my car while you were eating breakfast. I was hoping he could write something on it. I'd make a bunch of points with my girlfriend. She was at their concert last week."

Holding the jewel case, she realized this was the first time she'd seen a photo of Jon with his band. Somehow it seemed odd to see him in his natural element.

"Hey, Tarin, what if we go fishing? I bought nightcrawlers, grub worms, and crawdads," Jon called as he approached the boat. Noticing the young man standing nearby, he grinned broadly. "Hi, how's it going?"

"This is Justin. He wondered if you might autograph a CD for his girlfriend."

Jon put his treasured bait containers down on a bench nearby, wiped his hands on his jeans, and shook hands with the young man, "Hi. It's nice to meet you. Do you have something special you'd like me to say to this girl of yours?"

Tarin watched Jon transform from a man with childlike innocence hoping to catch a fish or two to a gracious celebrity talking with Justin.

Moments later, she smiled and began to back the boat away from the dock. "So that's what you do. I'm impressed. You're very good with people."

"Thanks, but it's not hard to be nice to kids like that. Anyway, welcome to my world."

"I like seeing another side of you."

"Well," he replied while stretching across the boat to retrieve the plastic containers holding his prized bait. "Now, what I want is to immerse myself into your world for a while. Can we stop and pick up fishing gear at the boathouse? I feel a need to bring home dinner."

"You'll need to buy a fishing license."

"Ha! Thought you had me, didn't you?" He pulled an official-looking piece of paper from his pocket. "I'm one step ahead of you. I got this when I bought the bait."

She couldn't help but laugh at his enthusiasm. "Let's go for it then, but there's something you should know. I've never been able to cut off heads and there's no way I can gut a fish. If you're successful in this quest, who's going to clean them for us?"

Jon looked indignant. "Give me a little credit. I fished a lot with my dad in New Jersey. He made sure I knew how to skin, scale, and gut any fish I reeled in."

She reached for his arm. "Then I stand corrected and I know exactly where I'll take you."

TARIN EASED THE BOAT into a small, secluded bay on the south side of the lake. Her grandfather had introduced her to the spot which was more like a weedy fishing hole than an actual inlet.

"It's time to put out the anchor," she instructed her one-person crew as the boat drifted to a stop.

After completing his assigned task, Jon inhaled and sat down on the seat next to her. "Who needs to fish? Maybe I'll just sit here and soak it all in."

"No way," she teased, "you promised me dinner."

"Hey—nice set-up," Jon exclaimed after baiting his hook and standing the fishing rod in a holder built into the wood deck of the boat. He pulled a cold beer out of the cooler. "This is the life. I can fish, drink, and nap all at the same time." He pulled the brim of his hat down to cover his eyes, rested his feet on the side of the boat, and directed, "Wake me up when I get a bite."

After checking the anchor, Tarin settled onto the seat next to him. "I hope you know real Colorado fishing means you should be standing in a river with a fly rod. Worms are taboo unless you're a flatlander."

"Flyfishing sounds like work. For me, this is just an excuse to be outside in the mountains with you."

"Are you trying to be charming?" she shot back.

"Some things just come naturally." He hesitated before changing his tone. "I hate to bring it up, but have you heard if the police have any leads on who broke into the boathouse?"

She shook her head, trying to untangle a hook at the end of her line. "No. Mike said the only prints they could match from inside the boathouse were mine. They were hoping for more footprints they could work with, but Finn destroyed that evidence when he got out of the lake and jumped onto the dock." She cast her line back into the water.

"I don't want to find myself back in California worried that some guy's going to try and break in again."

While she had heard everything Jon said, the only words ringing in her ears were the ones announcing his impending departure.

"Don't worry. I've got friends around to keep an eye on me." She paused. "Does that mean you'll be going back to La Jolla soon?"

"I was hoping to stay longer, but a family reunion is taking over the lodge beginning tomorrow night. It looks like I'll need to catch a flight back sometime in the afternoon."

Tarin knew where the words came from but wasn't quite sure how they got to her lips. "I've got a guest room sitting empty. You're welcome to stay there if you're not ready to go back to California." She awaited his reply by pulling her line from the water and pretending to check the bait.

When nothing but silence followed, she knew it had been a mistake to make the offer and wanted nothing more than to take it back.

"After what happened the other night, you'd feel safe inviting someone who is almost a stranger to stay in your house? For all you know, I could be a serial killer."

"Somehow, I doubt that. You're more than welcome to stay with Finn and me for a few days."

Just then, the tip of Jon's pole dipped toward the water. She jumped up, pointing at the taut line. "You've got a bite!"

"I can already see it in the frying pan," he coaxed before allowing a little leeway in the line and then tightening it once again.

"You really have done this before, haven't you?"

A few seconds later, Jon pulled a nice-size fish from the water.

"You caught a rainbow trout on a worm and a bobber. The departed fly fishermen of the world are rolling over in their graves," she admonished.

Once his catch was safely on a stringer, Jon paused before asking, "Was that a serious offer?"

"You mean the guest room? Of course, it was."

"Then I'd say you have a house guest."

"But you're going to have to earn your keep and that means you better keep catching fish. I've got a fabulous beer batter recipe my grandmother shared with me that I think you'll like."

After a few seconds of silence, he spoke with sincerity. "Thank you. I'm not quite ready for the studio, my manager, or LA. But if you want to know the truth, I don't want to leave Ledge Lake, or you for that matter."

Suddenly the wake from a speeding vessel caused Tarin to lose her balance. With waves rocking the boat from side to side, she fell onto Jon's lap. He gathered her into his arms to break her fall, but then they both landed awkwardly on the deck. His face was next to hers, his breath warm on her neck. She felt her pulse quicken and her cheeks began to feel warm.

"Excuse me," was the call heard from somewhere in the distance. "Is everything all right?"

They weren't alone.

She sat up and scrambled back onto her seat. A Lake Patrol officer was at the wheel of a boat riding the waves about twenty yards away. All the young man could do was stammer. "Hello there. I saw your boat and it didn't look like anyone was in it. I thought it might have been adrift and I was afraid it was going to hit the rocks. Um, I'm sorry to have bothered you. I'll just be going along now. Have a nice day."

Then they heard an engine revving as the patrol boat made an about-face before speeding across the lake.

Jon began to laugh. "Busted. From the color of his face, I'm guessing he thinks he interrupted something."

She yanked the brim of the hat back down over his eyes. "I think it's time for you to concentrate on catching fish, Mr. Parker. Otherwise, we'll be eating frozen pizza tonight."

"Now wait a minute," he grinned. "You need to have more faith in me."

"We'll see about that," Tarin replied, settling back onto the seat, and casting her line into the water.

At that moment, Jon's line became taut, and the end of the rod curled under the pressure until its tip skimmed the lake's surface.

"Do you have another bite?"

Disappointed, he shook his head. "No. I'm pretty sure I just snagged something. I may have to cut the line. Do you have a knife I can use?"

"I'll check the tackle box."

Struggling to free the line, he looked back to find Tarin staring into the green metal box on the floor at her feet.

"What's wrong?" he asked.

She lifted a long, heavy knife and carefully turned it over several times, appearing puzzled. "I've never seen this before. It's not mine. How do you suppose it got into the tackle box?"

Jon was unable to take his eyes off the jagged blade with its dark, intricate handle.

The tone of her voice suddenly changed. "Jon—I think there's dried blood on it."

He lifted the knife from her hands. "Do you have a towel or something we can wrap it in? I don't want to worry you, but we need to call Mike, that officer friend of yours. I can't be sure, but I think the blood might be mine."

CHAPTER 7

Secrets

WHILE WELL-INTENTIONED, MORE THAN A FEW men have the inborn ability to leave the kitchen in a complete state of disaster after cooking a meal. It didn't take Tarin long to discover Jon was one of those men. Surveying the pots, pans, and plates overflowing from the sink onto the counter, she decided to accept the challenge of cleaning the mess while he retrieved his belongings from the lodge.

The time alone also provided an opportunity to digest what had happened earlier in the day. They had used a cell phone to call the police station from the boat and Mike Wilson was waiting on her dock when they pulled into the lift.

He confirmed their fingerprints would compromise what the lab might find on the knife, but tests would determine if the blood on the blade was Jon's.

"Tarin," Mike advised while laying the wrapped knife on the front seat of his squad car, "you need to install surveillance cameras in your house and on the dock. Whoever this guy is, he's a threat and we need to catch him in the act. Promise me we'll talk about adding a security system as soon as possible."

Tarin glanced out the kitchen window toward the lake and sighed. Someone had planted the knife so she would find it. But why? And how did the weapon get into the tackle box? The box is stored in a compartment on the boat, which means the person responsible had come back. Was this callous intruder trying to prove he could gain access to everything she owned and her emotions at will? If it was the same knife used in the burglary attempt, why would the man leave something police might be able to trace? The only thing Tarin knew for sure was that the events of the past week had left her feeling violated and frightened. She prayed having Jon stay in the house might reestablish some semblance of equilibrium in her life. News that the intruder had been caught and was behind bars would be even better.

POISED TO PUSH THE keyless ignition of his rental car, Jon gazed at Tarin's cozy log home and simply sat in silence. A week in this small mountain town had helped him remember who he was before life got complicated.

Here he didn't have to act. There were no preconceived notions of who he should be and none of the greed that seemed to surround his life in California. Of all the things he'd come to dislike about the music business, the need of some to hoard money at any cost bothered him the most. He understood the reality that those in the entertainment industry need to reap profits while they can. Fame, after all, is fleeting. But greed can make good people do bad things and evil people do inconceivable things. He knew he'd been coerced into doing his share. His most recent transgression was not telling Tarin the complete truth.

Inside his room at the lodge, Jon tossed the key card on the bed and saw the cell phone he'd intentionally left behind. None of the conversations he'd missed would be ones he cared to hear.

Looking at the log, there were two calls from his manager, Tommy, and three from Anna. Of course, he didn't need to listen to her messages—he'd heard them all before.

When are you coming back?

I'm sorry I said what I said.

I wish you'd call. We need to talk.

He didn't want to hear what Tommy had said either, but knew he'd have to call him back at some point and it might as well be now. It was only seven o'clock in Los Angeles, but if this was a day like any other, by now his manager would have downed a quarter-bottle of bourbon.

"Tommy? It's Jon. Do you need something?" He was surprised to hear the voice on the other end sounded crisp and clear despite the hour.

"Think you've got it wrong, partner. It has nothing to do with me. It's what you need, and you need to be in the studio."

"I'll be there when I get there. You know I've never let you down and I'm not about to start doing it now."

"Getting a mind of your own, are you? Maybe it's time to sit back and think about what you're doing. You've got a contract and if you don't follow through, we're both out a lot of money. I could afford to take the hit, but unless you've forgotten, maybe you can't. If I were you, I'd get back here, make amends with the band, and put this new record in the can."

"You know I'll live up to my end of the deal, Tommy, but I'm done with all the bullshit you've attached to it."

"Bullshit is it now? Who pulled you through rehab before rehab was cool and managed to keep it out of the news? And who provided a bankroll when everything was falling apart around you? I've got a serious investment in you Jon, and I'll be damned if you're going to screw it up. You've only got one album left with Clocktower Records, and unless the band can pull something unbelievable out of its collective ass, there won't be another deal. We need to hit it big while we can."

"Fine. I'll get back into the studio and do what I need to do. But I'm finished with the charade you created between Anna and me."

"Oh, give me a break." Tommy's voice resonated with laughter followed by disgust. "You run away to the mountains and rumor has it you've shacked up with some—"

"Watch it," Jon warned.

"Whatever. Anyway, you're out in god's country for a week and suddenly become holier than thou. Unless I'm forgetting something, you certainly didn't mind being linked with Anna a few months ago.

She's still the same pretty little starlet today that she was then. Sorry, Jon. It's nothing personal. But if you want to keep the beachfront house, your stable of cars, and fat recording contracts, you need Anna Haines. She can keep you in the limelight, which means record execs will keep you on their radar. And another thing—all the publicity is putting money in our pockets."

"In your pocket, you mean."

"You get your share, Jon."

Silence.

"I'm sending the jet to pick you up tomorrow. What day is it— Thursday? That'll give you time to say goodbye to this new love interest of yours."

"Saturday, Tommy. I'll fly back Saturday and not a day before."

Jon could sense irritation building on the other end.

"Okay. Saturday it is, but you damn well better be on that plane. Anna's movie premiers on Tuesday and she needs to stick to you like glue. I've got a perfect plan. You're going to ask her to marry you on the way to the opening. That way she'll be all giggly and clingy. It'll make for fantastic footage."

"Haven't you heard a word I said? I'm done leading her on. Forget the fact I don't love her, but for god's sake, she's only twenty-two years old."

"It's just business, Jon. You know that, and you bought into it a long time ago."

"Well, I'm getting out now."

"Don't think so. I own you until you finish this album and deliver on the contract. You got that? I'm not saying you need to go through with it and marry her. Just keep sweet little Anna happy until this record hits the street."

"You're a bastard. You know that don't you?"

"You're not telling me anything I haven't heard a hundred times before. But you know what? You wouldn't be where you are today if I hadn't been in your corner. Chew on that for a little while." There was a pause as Tommy lit a cigarette and blew out the match. "I'll call you with the details when I get the jet lined up. By the way, I bought the ring for you. It's eight karats of bling mounted on a platinum band. That should make little Anna's eyes sparkle for the cameras."

"The day Motive leaves the studio is the day I fire you."

"It's no skin off my teeth. You're on your way out anyway. I'll be in touch. Oh, and Jon. If you decide to fuck that girl in the mountains— use a condom. We don't need any ugly paternity suits complicating things with a new record coming out."

"Son of a bitch," Jon muttered, his voice seething with anger. It took all his self-control to resist launching the phone across the room.

He couldn't talk about this part of his life with anyone, least of all the people he had met in Chasm Falls. What would Tarin think if she knew he had a role in manipulating a young woman's feelings for personal gain? He wouldn't blame her. He hated himself for doing that.

Jon packed his duffle bag and went into the bathroom to see if he'd forgotten anything. He didn't think much of the person he saw in the mirror. The mask was back in place, and there was no reason to believe it would be coming off anytime soon. Tommy Wyndham had made sure of that.

WHEN JON PULLED INTO Tarin's driveway, he glanced toward the lake and realized it looked the same as it had the night of the boathouse break-in. But this time, an unavoidable feeling of helplessness had replaced the adrenaline rush he'd felt trying to stop the intruder.

Maybe Tommy was right. The sooner he got back into the studio, the sooner the band would finish recording. Why put off the inevitable? Staying in Colorado a few more days would simply make it harder to face reality. He dialed his manager's number but couldn't bring himself to complete the call.

"Damn it," he muttered. "Why do I let him get to me this way?"

Instead of going inside, Jon walked to the bench at the Point to gather his thoughts. He didn't want Tarin to sense anything was wrong.

She was on the couch tucked under a chenille throw when he opened the French doors and entered the living room. Finn was sleeping, stretched out on the floor in front of the crackling fire. Soft light from an assortment of candles placed around the room flickered on the walls. A bowl of buttered popcorn, a bottle of white wine on ice, and two glasses were waiting on the coffee table.

He settled next to her, claiming part of the blanket and a handful of popcorn. "What are you watching?"

She smiled. "Do you really need to ask?"

"Let me guess," he pondered while black and white images of Humphrey Bogart and Ingrid Bergman slipped across the screen. "*Casablanca*. Why is it women find this movie so intoxicating?"

"The story is exciting and full of romance. Not to mention the fact Bogie is dashing, daring, and possibly the sexiest man ever born." She poured them each a glass of wine. "I've probably watched this movie a hundred times and I still can't believe Rick sends Ilsa away with Laszlo."

"Tarin—"

She turned to face him and smiled. "Jon?"

"I'll put my bag in one of the guest rooms, but—and I know this may sound strange—would you mind if I sleep in your boathouse tonight?"

Looking puzzled, she hesitated. "Why? I mean of course it's okay, but there's no heat there. It might only be October, but in this part of the country you could be frozen by morning."

"You've got blankets, don't you?" He pushed a few stray hairs from her eyes. "I have some decisions to make and I think being near the water might make it easier. You've told me it helps you."

"You seem so sad and distant—like that first night when you were sitting on the bench."

The worry in her eyes tugged at his heart. "It's nothing you've done. I just need to be alone for a time."

"Okay, if that's what you want. We'll find blankets in the linen closet and set you up in the boathouse. But can we watch Ilsa get on the plane first? As illogical as it might seem, I keep praying they'll change the ending."

"Take your time. I need to get a few things out of my bag anyway." Jon stood and made his way into the guest room, his thoughts turning to the jet scheduled to land Saturday. Unlike the movie they were watching, he would be the one climbing on board, and it wasn't a flight he wanted to take.

JON SPREAD TWO WOOL blankets and a heavy quilt on the bed, his eyes scanning the small rooms of the boathouse. While watching Tarin pull a pair of feather pillows from a closet shelf, he noticed several framed pictures on the wall. "Let me guess. This is your grandfather," he said, pointing to an older man proudly displaying a stringer of trout.

She nodded.

"And your grandmother?"

Again, she nodded.

"This must be your mom. You look a lot like her. Has anyone ever told you how cute you are with a thumb stuck in your mouth?"

"I'm sharing too many stories if you recognize the people in our family photos." She stopped and smiled. "Speaking of talking—you want to be alone—so I'll be on my way. You've got your cell phone, don't you? Promise you'll let me know if you need anything. And please secure the door. I had a new lock installed. My grandfather's shotgun is in the closet. Unfortunately, you'll need to use it like a baseball bat because there aren't any shells."

"I'll be fine, and you'll be the first to know if I need anything at all." He caught her hand when she turned to leave. "Thank you. You keep saving me."

She squeezed his fingers, "If memory serves me correctly, you rescued me first. But just so you know, I'm a good listener when you're ready."

Tarin disappeared up the stairs and putting on a coat, he stepped outside. With hands tucked in his pockets, Jon sat on the wood bench at the end of the dock gazing toward the lights on the opposite shore. The minutes turned into an hour, and before he knew it, the hour became two. The hypnotic rhythm of waves breaking on shore helped clear his head and allowed him to focus for the first time in months. It wouldn't be easy, but he knew how to get his life back on track. Soon Tommy would regret implying he had no backbone.

Jon inhaled a deep breath of crisp mountain air and exhaled as he looked across the water one last time. He turned to find Tarin standing in silence near the boathouse door.

He noticed the timid look on her face. "I'm sorry, I know I shouldn't be here because you wanted to be alone, but I was worried about you."

He brushed his lips across her forehead, hoping to diffuse her fear. "I'm glad you're here and there's no need to worry. There are a few things in my life I need to fix, but because of you, I'm ready to try." He stared into her hazel eyes and made a promise as much to himself as to her. "Tomorrow we'll talk. There are things you need to know about me you may not like, but I'm willing to take my chances." He paused. "But you were right. It's frigid down here, and I'm hoping you'll help keep me warm. No expectations. I just need to have someone close tonight."

Hearing no objections, he took her hand and closed the boathouse door behind them.

CHAPTER 8

Peace and Quiet

TARIN LEANED BACK AND CLOSED HER EYES, lavishing in the hot, steamy water cascading over her body. Drawing a soap-covered washcloth across her skin, she wondered what Jon would think of her body. Her thoughts returned to the events of the night before and she remembered how safe she felt sleeping next to him in the boathouse. As they lay fully clothed side by side, with the curves of their bodies fitting together like three-dimensional puzzle pieces, she could still feel his warmth.

Had she been alone so long she'd forgotten how thrilling the simple proximity of a man could be? She was secretly disappointed that he'd been true to his word and did not attempt to seduce her. Instead, they simply held each other until sunrise.

She tied the belt of her terrycloth robe and grabbed her underwear, jeans, a Western shirt, and a pair of boots.

Moments later, she descended the stairs to find Jon cooking in the kitchen.

He was shirtless, clad in blue jeans with the button at the waist casually left undone, the California glow of his skin emphasizing his well-defined torso.

She noticed his abdomen was no longer bandaged. "How's the cut?" she asked, tracing the knife wound with her finger.

"It's almost healed." He directed a broad smile her way and then pointed to the floor. "But I've got a question for you. Does Finn always pick a spot underfoot or right behind you wherever you're trying to cook?"

The black and white dog stretched and moved toward his mistress' outstretched hand. "Always. I used to think it was because he wanted to be in the middle of things, but now I'm convinced it's a plot to trip me and take over the place."

"Would you like a cup of coffee?" Jon asked while flipping bacon in a cast-iron skillet.

"That would be nice," she answered, settling on a stool at the island and finding she enjoyed the fact a man was taking care of her.

He leaned over and placed a full mug on the countertop. "Do you use training wheels?"

"Training wheels?"

Resting his arm on her shoulders, he brushed her hair with his lips. "My dad always asks that. You know, cream and sugar."

"Black will be just fine."

Back at the stove with a spatula in hand, he issued a challenge. "I hope you and Finn are hungry because I got a little carried away with the amount of food I cooked."

After breakfast, Tarin picked up the satchel she'd packed with a light lunch and gave Finn a quick pat on the head when she closed the door of his kennel. "Next time you can come along, buddy." She found Jon waiting nearby.

Looking mischievous, she grabbed his hand and began pulling him toward the overgrown lane across the road. "Come on, slowpoke!"

He grinned, trying to keep up. "Okay, but where are you taking me?"

She turned and skipped backward until they reached the edge of the forest. "I told you before—it's time you find a little peace and quiet."

The lane wound its way several hundred yards through a curtain of statuesque pines on either side of the abandoned road. Then, without warning, the forest opened into a small meadow filled with the season's last daisies and wildflowers. A weathered prairie-style barn with a gambrel roof stood alone with an assortment of wiry kittens peeking through irregular openings in the siding. The sliding doors at the front of the barn were open, and as the pair approached, several curious horses peered at them from over their stall doors.

"Is this yours?" he asked as they stepped into the ten-foot-wide aisle separating rows of six stalls on either side.

"You mean the barn? Yes. My grandparents' property is almost a thousand acres. Most of the land is in a wilderness corridor extending up the mountain adjacent to the national forest. After my grandfather died, the house, outbuildings, and the land became mine." A big palomino nudged her shoulder when she passed by. "Hey, Babe. How are you doing?" She ran her fingers through the animal's forelock. "Jake—he owns the bar in town—takes care of the barn for me." She unlocked the door to the tack room. "It's a trade-out. He boards his horses here and watches Peace and Quiet for me when I'm on assignment. These two are mine, and it's time to introduce you."

She put several flakes of hay in round buckets in front of each stall door and the pair of horses whinnied to show their appreciation at her arrival. "Good morning, boys. I brought someone to meet you."

She touched the nose of a sorrel paint and then tweaked the upright ears of a tall bay-colored horse in the adjacent stall. "I'd like to introduce you to Peace and Quiet, better known as P and Q." Disappearing into the tack room, she returned with a Western saddle. "Do you ride?" She noted Jon's apprehension in the presence of the thousand-pound-plus animals that seemed to be sizing him up.

"No," he replied, lifting the heavy saddle from her arms. "Wait a minute. I take it back. When I was a kid, we rode ponies at the carnival. You know—the ones that go in circles like they're at the end of spokes on a wheel."

She handed him a pair of leather bridles. Then, going back for saddle blankets, she turned with a twinkle in her eye, "Get ready. Today you become a Colorado cowboy."

After bridling the bay, she secured the horse to an iron ring on the stall door and put a boar's-hair brush into Jon's hand. "While I'm working with P, would you mind brushing the big man?"

Jon timidly touched the soft bristles to the horse's hide. Q responded by raising his head to tighten the reins and then launched his hindquarters toward the stall wall, pinning the newcomer against it.

Tarin was at his side in an instant, cooing to the anxious animal. "It's okay, no need to worry." She pressed her face to the horse's muzzle. "Now, what kind of welcome is that? He's my friend, Q." The bay snorted and seemed to reply by nodding his head up and down in reluctant acceptance. "See, he's getting used to you already."

"Whatever you say," Jon responded warily before raising the brush again. This time he met no resistance. When both horses were saddled and ready to ride, while cautious, he appeared almost comfortable at Q's side.

"Here," she called, tossing a black cowboy hat in his direction. "See if it fits."

He caught it with one hand, took the crown of the hat in the other, dusted it off on his jeans, and using his best John Wayne move, casually placed it on his head. "Well?"

She adjusted the tilt of the brim and smiled. "I think you'll do. But we do need to find you a pair of boots. Those shoes you're wearing just don't cut it."

Once on the trail leading into the mountains, Tarin watched Jon clench the reins and saddle horn for the first mile or so. They rode side by side until the pathway narrowed, and then, sensing her rookie rider was beginning to relax, she took the lead.

Jon watched Tarin ride, admiring how comfortable she seemed to be in the saddle. His eyes traveled from the thick blonde hair below the brim of her straw cowboy hat, along the straight lines of her back, to the small, denim-covered butt rising and falling with each of the horse's strides. Tarin turned in the saddle and he was captivated by her bright smile, but then his unconscious gaze drifted toward her breasts. The lines of her fitted shirt accentuated their firm roundness, and he was teased by the hint of cleavage visible above the placket's buttons. When he lifted his eyes to meet hers, he knew his look had not gone unnoticed. Self-conscious, Tarin turned away.

Without warning the trees thinned once again, and they found themselves about a hundred yards from a rustic log cabin in the shadow of a towering rock outcropping. The horses meandered to a stop and began to graze on the native grass at their hooves.

Jon dismounted, grimaced, and stretched his legs. "What is this?"

"It's my grandfather's hunting cabin. Come on—I'd like to show it to you."

It was apparent the one-room structure wasn't built with comfort in mind. In more than a few places, the chink between the logs was cracked and had broken away, allowing dust-filled rays of sunshine to permeate the room. The cabin featured no indoor plumbing or electricity—not that those amenities were even an option this far into the forest. A woodstove tucked into the corner provided the cabin's only heat and served as a makeshift cooking surface. On the wall opposite the front door stood an old iron bed covered with fatigue-green wool Army blankets. A rectangular table with two chairs offered a place to sit. Next to it, a wood door had been cut in half lengthwise and mounted on the wall as a makeshift counter. Several iron skillets hung on nails and an old graniteware basin and dishes sat underneath them. The floor was hardwood, but the planks were uneven, and a tattered rug covered much of the area. There were two small, curtained windows, one next to the front door and the other on the back wall to the left of the bed.

Jon stood in the doorway, his eyes surveying every inch of the room. "I'm willing to bet your grandmother didn't spend much time here."

"Very true. She only came when it was time to clean up after Grampa and his hunting buddies—once before each of the seasons opened and once after they closed."

He noticed the lack of modern conveniences. "What did they do for a bathroom? Bushes and trees?"

She gestured toward the door. "Don't jump to conclusions. My grandfather spared no expense. There's an outhouse and even a well outside with a hand pump."

"I don't suppose you had any wild, clandestine parties here when you were younger, did you?"

She hesitated before admitting the truth, "Grampa pretended to be oblivious, but I'm sure he knew about the kegs we hauled here from time to time."

Jon rested next to Tarin on the edge of the bed. "What about your boyfriend?"

"You mean Alex? We came here to talk when we were in high school."

"Just talk?" he teased.

Tarin attempted to look indignant. "What are you implying, Jon? And yes—for your information—mostly we just talked. During elk season, he'd spend time here with my grandfather. Sometimes they'd hunt other game if they were lucky enough to get tags."

Still somewhat aroused from watching her on horseback, Jon lowered her onto the bed. His lips lingered near hers before he propped himself on his elbow and twisted strands of her blonde hair between his fingers.

"Jon?"

"Hmm?"

"Last night, you said you wanted to talk to me about something." She turned to look at him. "What was it?"

He hadn't planned on the conversation beginning this way and glanced at her nervously before leaning back against the headboard. She was sitting cross-legged in front of him.

"Are you sure you want to hear all the deep dark secrets that brought me to your bench in the first place?"

She nodded.

He closed his eyes, contemplating what to say next. "So much of what goes on in LA is about staying on top no matter the cost. I got caught up in that rat race a long time ago, and now I'm afraid it's turned me into someone I never meant to be."

"I thought being a musician was your dream."

"It is, but there's more to it than that."

"Like what?"

He avoided her attempt to make eye contact, instead fixing his gaze on the bedspread.

"When you're young, you don't always think about consequences. When Nick and I got to LA, I hired this guy—Tommy Wyndham—as my manager. He took me under his wing, promised me the world, and delivered it on a silver platter. He got me into Motive, negotiated a lucrative contract with a record label, and suddenly I had everything I'd ever wanted—money, fast cars, women, you name it. But what I didn't have at twenty-four was the common sense or maturity to be responsible for my actions. Looking back, I think that's what Tommy counted on. Before long, I'd blown most of the money and experimented with a little too much cocaine." He gazed into her eyes. "Then there was one night that never should have happened."

He paused.

"I'd been with the band about a year, and we had a gig in San Francisco. There was a beautiful girl in the front row wearing a very short denim skirt and a low-cut top. Don't get me wrong. There are always more than enough gorgeous women hanging around the stage, but you couldn't miss this one. And you don't have to be on the road long before you figure out which girls are, well, available. I had the crew invite her backstage after the show. We partied hard, and I took her back to our hotel." His voice trailed into the thin mountain air.

"A few months later Tommy came to me with a picture of the girl. He told me her parents were trying to track me down and asking what I was doing knocking up their sixteen-year-old daughter. He wanted to know what I'd been thinking and why I wasn't smart enough to use protection. Tommy said the parents planned to press charges against me for statutory rape. I could have gone to jail for at least a year, maybe up to four. If the charge became a felony because of the age difference and the fact I'd gotten her pregnant, the sentence could've been a lot longer than that. I would have been a registered sex offender for the rest of my life. Tommy scared the shit out of me."

"Then what happened?"

"He negotiated an arrangement with the parents in exchange for not going to the police." He scrutinized Tarin's face, trying to read her reaction.

"Meaning he paid them off. What about the baby?"

Jon hesitated and then looked back down at the bed. "You can probably guess. An abortion was part of the deal."

"How much did it cost you?"

His voice was subdued, and he grimaced before answering. "Half a million dollars."

Jon sighed, cleared his throat, and watched Tarin look downward with her eyes closed. "Like I said, back then I was blowing through money faster than it was coming in and didn't have anywhere near that much cash in the bank. I gave Tommy two hundred and fifty thousand upfront and he covered the rest. I paid everything back a long time ago, but he's held the whole thing over my head ever since."

Jon took her hands in his. "I know this doesn't change anything, but I swear she told me she was nineteen and could have passed for older than that."

"If she claimed to be nineteen, you could have used that as a defense."

"But it wouldn't have excused me from what I'd done. Anyway, Tommy didn't explain anything to me back then, and he wasn't about to let me wind up in court."

Tarin continued to look away and whispered, "Did you ever see the girl again?"

He shook his head. "I told Tommy I wanted to. You know—just to be sure she was all right. But he wouldn't give me any information. I couldn't even remember her name, so there was no way for me to find her on my own. I only saw her that one night and never talked to the parents. Tommy made sure he took care of everything."

"It sounds like he did his best to protect you."

Jon laughed—his voice filled with cynicism. "Don't give him that much credit. You don't know Tommy. He only thinks about one thing and that's his wallet. If I'd taken a fall, his bank account would have suffered. I'm sure he didn't care about me, the girl, or anyone else for that matter."

"If that's true, why is he still your manager?"

"None of the reasons make me proud. By time, I was hooked on everything he could give me. I got greedy and stuck with him. But after this last album hits the stores, we're finished. I want Tommy Wyndham out of my life once and for all." He pulled Tarin close, and she rested her head against his chest.

A few moments passed before she looked up and met Jon's gaze. "I don't claim to understand anything about the life you were living then or the life you lead now. What I do know is you made a mistake. I can't condone what you did, just like you can't undo it. But I also know that we've all done things we wish we hadn't done. You were young, misguided, and caught up in the moment. And don't forget, part of the guilt lands on the girl's shoulders, too. She intentionally misled you."

Jon felt her fingertips brush his cheek as she continued. "That was a long time ago and I'm sure you're a different person now. I can forgive you, but if you can't find it in your heart to forgive yourself, what happened will haunt you forever."

"I know, but that's easier said than done." He could read the concern in her eyes.

"When you said Tommy has held the incident over your head, do you mean he's been blackmailing you all this time?"

"For cash? No. To encourage me to do whatever he wants—yes— and he's still doing it. Until the past few months, I haven't had the guts to stand up to him, but Tommy's finally pushed it too far. I came here to think about how to deal with him and what I'll do if Motive breaks up. What scares me most is that I've been with the band so long, I don't know if I can make it on my own."

Jon stood, pulling her up alongside him. "You're the only person other than him who knows what happened in San Francisco." He held Tarin for a moment and then—afraid his admission might have overwhelmed her—attempted to lighten the conversation. "Can we talk about this tonight? I'm sure you need time to digest everything I've told you—and that's more than enough seriousness for now. Didn't you say there are some other places you want to show me? Q and I are ready to hit the trail."

Once outside, Tarin handed Jon the bay's reins, but he didn't release her hand right away. "We haven't known each other very long, but there's something you need to know. Meeting you has helped me find the courage to do what I should have done a long time ago." Leaning her against Q's flank, he pressed his mouth to hers, meeting the tip of her tongue with his own.

Pulling away ever so slowly, Jon remembered the look of innocence on Tarin's face when she slept beside him in the boathouse. Chilled that night, she'd nestled close, and he liked the feel of her body next to his.

When their eyes met again, he found something different, something telling him their budding relationship had changed. Tarin had listened to what he'd done and hadn't passed judgment. He needed to explain about Anna, too, but not now. The right moment would present itself.

She lowered her eyes from his and untied P. "Are you ready?"

Taking his hat from its perch on the hitching post, he tipped it her way. "Yes, ma'am. Just lead the way."

CHAPTER 9

———

Mountain Paparazzi

TARIN FELT GUILTY LAUGHING AT HIS EXPENSE, BUT even so, couldn't find a way to hide her amusement. "I'm not sure you can make it back to the house on your own. Do we need to call for a wheelchair?"

"Even if you managed to find one, I'm not sure I'd be able to sit down on it." Jon was inching his way along the lane with more than a great deal of difficulty. "When we started the ride this morning, you didn't tell me I might never be able to walk again. In case you're wondering, you'll find me in the hot tub tonight."

"I'm sorry." She put her arm around his waist, offering support. "I shouldn't have taken you so far on the first ride. But you know what? You're really kind of cute bow-legged."

Then, still laughing when they rounded the last corner, she glanced up and stopped in her tracks. On the road in front of them sat a Granite County Sheriff's Department cruiser. Deputy Simmons was using his body to hold a man against the front quarter panel while he snapped handcuffs around the man's wrists.

"Scott," Tarin sprinted across the road. "What's going on?"

"We may have found your intruder, Tarin," the uniformed officer answered, struggling to catch his breath. "I found this guy in the bushes looking in your living room window. When I called him on it, he took off running. I managed to grab him on the road when he tripped in a rut." He turned the man around to face her. The stranger's terrified face was a ghastly shade of white. "Do you know him?"

She shook her head. "No. I've never seen this man before."

The deputy sent a threatening look the suspect's way. "There was a break-in here a week or so ago, sir, and guess what? Catching you trespassing today makes you a prime suspect."

"But—" the man protested.

"Keep it zipped for now," Simmons commanded, putting one hand on the man's shoulder and the other on his back between the cuffed wrists. "I've called for backup to take him to the station, but Tarin, would you mind if we wait inside for the officers?"

"I guess it would be okay. But Scott—how did you happen to be here?"

The deputy kept walking, pushing the handcuffed man ahead of him while reading him his Miranda rights. "Mike and I have been making regular swings by your place to keep an eye on things and today it paid off."

Once in the living room, Simmons began probing his suspect for answers. "Do you have a name?"

"Matt Carver, sir."

"Okay, Matt. Care to tell me what you were doing outside Ms. MacGyver's house?"

The man's voice quivered. "I'm a freelance photographer working out of a bureau in Denver, sir. Late last night, a man called wanting pictures of this lady and her boyfriend." With wrists still cuffed behind his back, he motioned toward Tarin with his head. "He didn't tell me why he wanted them, and you need to believe me, I don't know anything about a break-in. I didn't get here until this morning." The photographer appeared to be in his late twenties wearing a baseball hat with the brim pointing backward.

Jon protested with the officer. "Scott—he's not even close to the size of the man I fought with on the steps."

Simmons discounted the objection, shaking his head. "He could have been an accomplice. You wouldn't happen to have the name of the man who hired you on the tip of your tongue, would you?"

The young man was more than eager to shift suspicion to anyone other than himself, "No, but I can get it for you, sir. It's written in a notebook on the desk in my hotel room. I was supposed to call him when I had something. I hadn't called yet because I only had a few shots." Suddenly his eyes brightened, "Wait! His number will be on my cell phone. Will that help?" His eyes darted back and forth between Simmons, Jon, and Tarin.

"Where's the phone?"

"In my pack."

The deputy walked to the table and retrieved the phone from a pouch on the side of the backpack. He handed it to the photographer. "Log in for me."

"Look under recent calls. It's the number with a 310 area code."

Jon moved across the room to look over Simmons' shoulder. "That's LA." Scrutinizing the display, he sighed. "Shit. I know that number."

Simmons was perplexed. "Care to explain?"

"The phone number belongs to my manager, Tommy Wyndham."

Simmons redirected the interrogation toward Jon. "Okay. Why would your manager hire someone to take candid photos of you and Tarin?"

"Your guess is as good as mine." He looked at Simmons with apprehension. "Can I call him and ask?"

"No, you can't. This is my investigation and I'll handle it. But if I decide it's okay, you can talk with this Wyndham person when I'm finished. Tarin, may I use your cordless phone?"

Fifteen minutes later, the deputy returned from one of the guest bedrooms and handed the phone to Jon. "He's all yours."

Once outside on the deck, Jon turned his back to the French doors to muffle his anger from the people inside. "Tommy? What gives you the right to hire a photographer to invade our privacy? I don't care what you do to me but keep Tarin out of it."

Lounging by the clear, cool water of his swimming pool, Tommy grinned and reached for a tall glass of bourbon on the rocks. "Tarin . . . Nice name. I'm sorry, Jon. When she started hanging around with you, she became fair game. But relax. It's all just a little misunderstanding. I didn't tell the kid to trespass."

Jon closed his eyes and tightened the muscles of his jaw, trying to maintain control. "Say what you want, but your photographer's handcuffed and being questioned by a sheriff's deputy as we speak. What the hell? How do I get it through your thick head that I don't want you messing around in my private life?"

Tommy remained composed. "I find it curious the cop I talked to was fishing for information about you."

"What did you tell Scott?"

"Interesting. Now you're on a first-name basis with local law enforcement? Because of your past, do you think that's such a good idea? Listen, Jon. The last time we talked, you seemed adamant about dropping Anna. I had to cover my bases."

"Meaning?"

"If you're a no-show at the premiere Tuesday night, people will start asking questions. I'll have pictures to fuel the speculation if I have juicy shots of you and your new love interest. I can see it now: Motive's lead singer dumps beautiful Hollywood starlet for mysterious mountain vixen. I guarantee that would go viral."

Jon glanced back into the living room where Simmons was emptying the young man's bag onto the dining room table. "Stay out of my life, Tommy."

"After all we've been through together, I'm sorry you feel that way."

Neither man spoke for a moment.

"My jet lands at Rocky Mountain Regional Airport near Denver about one o'clock Saturday. Be there. I'll send a car for you in San Diego."

"Don't bother. Nick said he'd pick me up."

"The band is rehearsing at the warehouse Sunday. You know the place and might find it advantageous to show up."

"We'll see," Jon shot back as he ended the call and reentered the house.

"I don't know what to say. I am so sorry, Tarin. Tommy admits he was behind this entire fiasco."

She didn't try to bury her anger. "Doesn't he have anything better to do?"

"You know you can file charges against this guy for trespassing, Tarin. I think you should." Simmons advised.

Her eyes were glued to the frightened young man on the couch. "Take the handcuffs off and let him go, Scott. I won't press charges, but isn't there something we can do to Tommy Wyndham?"

"I wish we could, but probably not." Reluctantly, Simmons unlocked the cuffs, snapped them back on his belt, and directed his attention to the photographer. "You're lucky she's got a good heart. I'd throw the book at you. But remember, I know where you're staying, and we better not catch you within a mile of this place or these two people. In fact, you might want to make it easy on yourself and leave town before there's any more trouble. Got it? Now take your stuff and get out of here."

"Yes, sir."

"One last thing," the officer added. "Hand over the memory card you were using in your camera. Tell the man in LA he owes you a new one."

The young man fumbled with his camera, handed Simmons the card, gathered his things, and disappeared.

The deputy called off the backup and returned to his squad car, but not before taking Jon aside. "You better keep that manager of yours away from Tarin. I don't think I like him much."

"Not many people do," Jon replied. Then he watched Simmons get into his car and pull out of the driveway.

When they were finally alone, Tarin grabbed her jacket and opened the door. "I need fresh air, and since it's getting dark, maybe I'll check the dock. Come on, Finn."

AN HOUR LATER, JON was waiting on the Point when she reached the top of the stairs.

"I know you're angry and I don't blame you, but please sit with me for a minute." He wasn't sure she would even listen to what he wanted to say. Jon fought the urge to reach out when she sat down on the opposite end of the bench.

"There's something else I've needed to tell you but didn't know how to begin. I never dreamed Tommy would pull you into this." He paused, hoping she would acknowledge something he'd said. She didn't.

"About six months ago, Tommy had one of his brainstorms and decided I needed more visibility. He knew the band was in trouble and we didn't have a plan. Then Tommy did what he does best—he started manipulating people."

Tarin sat in silence, stroking Finn's head.

"One of his cronies represents this new actress in Hollywood named Anna Haines. Together he and Tommy decided to manufacture a relationship between Anna and me. They figured her career would benefit from being in the media spotlight Hollywood couples get from entertainment shows. As for me, whether I like it or not, I'm a singer in a band ready to implode. They figured I needed good press even more than Anna did. Tommy and his friend started putting us together in all the right places, with all the right people, and at all the best parties. He turned us into tabloid fodder."

"Does this girl realize what's going on?"

"When they hatched the idea, Anna's manager told her it was a way to get more exposure, meet people in the industry, and snag more film deals. She bought into it. You need to remember Anna's a twenty-two-year-old kid from Kansas with stars in her eyes, and she's just as confused as I was a decade ago."

Jon sensed the disappointment in Tarin's voice. "Knowing how Tommy has manipulated your life, how could you possibly let them start doing the same thing to her?"

"Trust me. If I could do it all over again, I wouldn't."

"Is there anything else in it for you?"

He leaned his head against the back of the bench and looked up at the star-filled sky overhead. "I'll admit it. I get to pretend one of the most beautiful young women in Hollywood is interested in me. That would do something for any guy's ego. Pretty self-serving, isn't it? From a career standpoint, I started to have an identity outside of Motive. But now I know the downside outweighed everything else. I can't get past feeling deceitful."

She looked down and picked at a splinter on the bench. "Tell me about her."

"Anna? She's beautiful, a talented actress, and a good kid, but I don't love her if that's what you're asking."

"Maybe that's how you feel, but does she see things the same way?"

Jon knew he couldn't lie and, more importantly, found he didn't want to. "She understood everything in the beginning. She knew it was just business. But if I'm honest with myself, now I'm not so sure."

Without speaking, Tarin stood and walked to the edge of the bank overlooking the shoreline. He followed, feeling her muscles tighten when he rested his hands on her shoulders. "She has a movie opening Tuesday night. Tommy wants me by her side playing the supportive boyfriend. He's got this wild idea that he can make me propose to her on the way to the premiere. But now you're a threat to his plan."

"How in the world could I be considered a threat to anyone in your world?"

He turned Tarin to face him and looked deep into her eyes. "Because he knows I plan to end it with Anna when I get back to LA. Because he knows you're playing a big part in my decision."

She pulled away. "I'm sorry. I have no right to pass judgment on anything you do. We met how many days ago? It hasn't even been two weeks yet. The last thing I want to do is fall for someone who won't stand up for himself."

"Does that mean there's a chance you could care about me?"

"I'm sorry. I don't know where that came from."

"Your heart, maybe?" He put his arms around her and ran his fingers through her hair. He felt her resist and then finally succumb. "What if I were to tell you I feel the same way?"

"You're going back to California the day after tomorrow."

He smiled. "That's true. But if I have anything to say about it, you'll be on the plane with me. I'm not asking you to stay forever, not this time. Just come for a few days or a few weeks to meet Nick, the guys in the band, and then be there to see the look on Tommy's face when I tell him to go to hell. There's the internet, so you can't use missing work as an out, and it's a private jet, so you could even bring Finn if you want. And if you come up with any other excuses, I'll find a way to vaporize them, too."

He saw there were tears in her eyes. "No need to cry. Just promise you'll think about it." He stretched his legs. "Now, this tenderfoot will either be in the hot tub treating his aches and pains or in the guest room, if you want to talk."

Jon began the short journey to the house, leaving Tarin behind in the moonlight to ponder his proposal.

An hour or so later, she donned a one-piece swimsuit, topped it with a cotton cover-up, and made her way to the hot tub on the deck.

"So, tell me. Is your house on the beach?"

Jon's head was supported by a pillow in the corner of the tub, with powerful jets sending streams of bubbles to soothe his sore muscles. His eyes were closed. "There's a veranda overlooking the ocean, and it's only a few yards to the beach."

She took off the cover-up and lowered herself into the water across from him. "Do you have a convertible?"

"I've got two. One for you and one for me. Your choice."

"What about a boat?"

"No, but Nick's got a thirty-two-foot sloop we can use whenever we want. Unfortunately, we'll need to take him along as the skipper."

"What about a guest room?"

He sat up slowly, opened his eyes, and moved through the bubbling water to face her. "You can sleep anywhere you want." He smiled and touched her lips with his fingertips. "You can even sleep with me."

She linked her fingers behind his neck. "You make it sound very, very tempting, and I want nothing more than to see the look on Tommy's face when you tell him he's finished. But I need someone in my life strong enough to fight his own battles. Someone I can believe in for the rest of my life. Jon, just like San Francisco, these are situations you've gotten yourself into, and you need to be the one that gets yourself out of them. No one can do it for you."

"But—"

"Please understand. I want to see where this relationship might take us—but only after Tommy and Anna are no longer in your life." She paused. "When that's a reality, I'll be on the next plane to California ready to land on your doorstep."

Jon kissed her on the forehead. "I have serious work ahead of me, don't I?"

"It's nothing you can't handle."

He brushed the hair away from her face. "I'm making you a promise. I can't get rid of Tommy until this record is in the can, but he's going to know upfront that I'll be finished with him when it hits the street. As for Anna, when I get back to La Jolla, I'm going to tell her we can't continue this made-for-television relationship. In her heart, she must know it's not healthy for either one of us. Anna deserves so much more. Then, beautiful lady, as soon as I can get a jet in the air, it will be on its way to Colorado. You better be packed and ready to go."

Tarin felt his arm tighten around her shoulders, and she responded by nestling close at his side.

Seventy-five yards away, Tarin's uninvited guest had returned. With binoculars pressed to his eyes, he scrutinized each kiss and every playful embrace. But when the man saw Jon's hand begin to move toward Tarin's swimsuit-covered breasts, he snapped the small branch gripped tightly in his hand. And then, just like before, he was gone.

———

CHAPTER 10

The Intruder

F IGHTING WITH THE KEY FOB TO OPEN THE CAR door, the stranger continued to clench a small piece of the broken branch in his fist. The image of Jon holding Tarin burned in his mind.

"I don't know what she sees in that self-centered prima donna," he mumbled, tossing the branch out the window once he was behind the wheel. "But when he breaks her heart—and he will—I'll be there to pick up the pieces."

He reached toward the passenger seat floorboard and pulled two beers from a brown paper bag. Using an opener stashed in the console, he popped off the first cap before groping in the glove compartment for an almost empty pint of tequila. After downing a lengthy swig, he wiped the back of his hand across his mouth and slammed the first brew. Opening the second, he bent down to retrieve a shoebox from underneath the seat. He lifted the top to gaze wistfully at its contents.

A delicate gold chain was inside, along with a small scrapbook on top of several pieces of meticulously folded clothing. With both hands, he pressed a pair of lace panties to his nose and inhaled. Then, after carefully folding it with care and putting it back, he reached for a bra made of the same delicate material. He'd stolen the underwear from Tarin's laundry basket, and the silk remained infused with her smell—a fragrance that intoxicated him. He'd seen her wear them one night as he peered through her bedroom window. But then she'd lowered the blinds and blocked the view before he could see anything more.

With his eyes closed, he could imagine both the softness of her body and how she would tremble under his touch. Then, gripping the fabric in his fingers, he reached down to where he was growing with excitement.

He flipped open a sterling silver butane lighter and lit the cigarette dangling from his lower lip, a smug smile embedded upon his face. Locking her doors wouldn't keep him out because there wasn't a device he couldn't pick. Maybe it was time for another visit. He would need more of her things for the plan to work, and in the end, she would be at his side forever. That much he knew for sure. And there was no way he was going to let some good-for-nothing, no-talent singer from California get in his way.

Stuffing the butt of his cigarette into one of the beer cans, he pressed the ignition and slammed the transmission into gear.

CHAPTER 11

A Night at the Sip 'n Strike

IT WAS FRIDAY NIGHT AT THE SIP 'N STRIKE. JON maneuvered Tarin's Ford F-150 into the last vacant spot in the pockmarked asphalt parking lot. It was a tight fit, but he managed to lodge the truck between a vintage Mustang convertible and a battle-worn Dodge Ram pickup that had seen better days.

She couldn't resist messing with him a bit. "When was the last time you were in a less-than-hip, smalltown bar like this?"

He grinned. "It brings back memories of gigs Nick and I used to play in Jersey."

"How much did they pay you back then?"

"If we were lucky, we covered our bar tab and could buy enough gas to get home. Sometimes we skipped out owing them money." He hopped onto the blacktop. "Come on. Show me around."

"Hey, Mac!" Jake Carpenter called when he saw them come through the door. He emerged from behind the bar to meet Tarin halfway, smothering her in a bear hug. "What are you up to tonight?"

"Nothing much, but there's someone I want you to meet."

"Girl, you forget this is our buddy Mike's home away from home when he's not on duty. Everybody in town knows about your houseguest." Jake reached out to shake Jon's hand. "I'm Jake, owner of this mecca in the mountains. Can I get you something? It's on me."

"Any beer on tap is fine. I'm not particular."

Chalking his cue, Mike Wilson chimed in from a pool table across the room, "Hey, Parker—feel like losing your shirt?"

Glass in hand, Jon started toward the local pool sharks. "Is that a challenge, Officer?"

"Pick your poison." Mike grinned.

"Eight ball, of course."

"The word around town is that you're going back to California tomorrow. Is there any truth to that?" he asked as Jon racked the balls.

"You heard it right. The rest of the band's ready to start rehearsing and I can't put it off any longer."

"Too bad. I was getting used to you being around here." Mike chalked the tip of his cue. "You're the guest. Go ahead and break."

He nodded his approval when Jon cracked a solid shot, sending two striped balls into corner pockets. "Not bad, but it's early. We'll call it beginner's luck."

Losing the third game by a stroke after splitting the first two, Jon relinquished his spot at the table, opting to watch Mike's next match-up against another eager challenger. Leaning on the tip of his pool cue, he surveyed the room and found Tarin sitting at a table talking with two other women. Continuing to scan the dimly lit area, his eyes passed and then returned to a man walking toward a back booth. While he couldn't quite put his finger on it, there seemed to be something strangely familiar about him.

He leaned toward Mike, who was waiting to take his next shot, "Who's that guy over there?"

"In the blue T-shirt? That's Alex Davis."

"Tarin's old boyfriend?"

"None other," he replied before misfiring a two-ball combination. "Has Tarin told you about him?"

"She's mentioned him a time or two. I met his wife the other day at Shuck's." Jon watched Alex approach a table where an animated poker game was underway.

Mike looked toward Jon. "Let me guess. You're wondering what they ever had in common. Trust me. He's not the same guy we ran around with in high school. He's not even the same person we knew a few years ago. Alex has had his share of hard knocks."

Something continued to nag at Jon. "Has he always had a limp?"

"No. He was wounded in Afghanistan. Why?"

"I don't know. Just curious, I guess." Jon watched Alex start toward the bar. "I'll be back in a minute."

Maneuvering between the crowded tables and throng of bottle-wielding patrons, Jon settled into a space near Alex.

"Ready for a refill?" Jake asked.

Jon nodded and then turned to the man on his left. He attempted to introduce himself by extending his hand, "Hi, how's it going? I'm Jon Parker."

Continuing to stare at his beer bottle, the man absentmindedly rolled it back and forth between his hands. Alex didn't bother to look up, nor did he seem to be in the mood to respond. "I know who you are."

"Here you go," Jake said, setting a fresh beer on the bar in front of Jon. Concerned, he glanced between the two men.

Leaning on his elbows, Jon looked over at Alex. "I hear it's been rough in Chasm Falls since the quarry closed."

"Why should you care? You're not from around here." He turned to face Jon. Despite the weathered lines entrenched in his face and the dull, steel-gray eyes now locked on Jon, Alex could still turn a lady's head with his boy-next-door looks and his muscular, athletic build.

"We see your kind around here all the time. Hotshots with more than their share of money they like to flash around. You come to the mountains from the coast to build your lakeshore retreats and think you're better than the rest of us. But guess what? You're not." His voice reverberated with a wave of anger his lifeless eyes couldn't muster.

He used the empty beer bottle like a fist on the hardwood. Then, pushing himself away from the bar, Alex stopped long enough to direct a dark look Jon's way. "Now, excuse me. I have a poker game to finish."

Jake attempted to apologize for his friend while wiping his hands on a towel. "I wanted to warn you."

"Nice guy, huh?" Jon replied, taken back by the brief encounter.

"Trust me. Alex comes across a whole lot tougher than he is."

"Maybe." Jon sat down on a stool and felt Tarin tighten her arms around his waist from behind.

"Did they take you for all you're worth?"

"No. I gave up my cue before it was too late. I'm pretty sure I still have enough money to get back to the airport in San Diego."

Mike left his game to join them. "Are you flying out of Denver?"

After Alex's pointed comments, Jon was almost too embarrassed to answer the question. "No, my manager's sending a jet to retrieve his prodigal musician. We're meeting the plane at Rocky Mountain Metro Airport."

"Private jet? Nice. Maybe I could arrange a police escort."

Tarin took the off-duty officer's pool cue from his hand. "Sorry, Mike. Something tells me the taxpayers might not buy into that. Anyway, I talked with Jake, and he's coming over at eleven o'clock tomorrow. He'll take us to the airport and then bring me back home."

Mike glanced at Jon. "The way things are going, I thought she might go with you."

Jon rested his arm on her shoulders, "It wasn't for lack of trying. I need to take care of a few things before she'll consider making the trip. But I'm not the type to give up easily."

Doing her best to change the subject, Tarin retrieved a twenty-dollar bill from deep in a jean pocket, waving it in the air to taunt the two men. "Now—who's got enough courage to take me on?"

"Go for it, man," Mike deferred. "You might as well face the inevitable and lose to her now—we all have at one time or another. I'm getting another beer. Does anybody else need one?"

Jake was busy wiping down the bar when Mike turned to the barkeep. "So, you're driving them down tomorrow?"

"Jealous?" Handing Mike, a fresh brew, Jake delivered a Cheshire Cat grin. "Don't worry. I'll give you a full report when we get back. In the meantime, you need to concentrate on finding out who broke into Tarin's place, and we all need to make sure it doesn't happen again."

Alex sat idly rearranging his cards at a table six feet away. His ears perked up at the sound of Tarin's name.

"Sorry, guys. I'm out," he proclaimed before tossing his cards onto the table. "See you later." Alex picked up his winnings and left the bar, almost knocking Scott Simmons over in the doorway.

"Take it easy, fella," the deputy called after him while trying to regain his balance. Alex ignored the warning, got into his car, and burned the tires on the way out of the parking lot. Scott started to follow but decided instead to find Mike Wilson.

"Hey, Scott. How 'ya doing?" Mike asked. "Still on duty?"

Simmons looked at his watch and nodded. "I've got a couple more hours on my shift." He looked toward the empty doorway. "Did you see that guy try to knock me over a minute ago?"

Mike smiled and leaned over to aim his next shot. "Alex Davis. It seems he's popular this evening."

"Meaning?"

Mike smiled. "Nothing. Anyway, he doesn't always watch where he's going. But I kept an eye on him tonight. He wasn't here all that long and only had two beers. He should be okay to drive." After missing the shot, he turned to his fellow officer. "What's up?"

Scott shrugged. "Nothing. I was checking to see if you'd gotten results back on the blood samples we sent to the lab."

"You mean from the landing on Tarin's stairway? Unfortunately, they didn't find anything that will help us. Not that it was a surprise because we knew going in most of the samples were contaminated. The only blood they could identify from the landing belonged to Parker. Everything else is useless."

"What about the knife?"

"Same story. The blood is Parker's, but the only prints were Tarin's from when she took the knife out of the tackle box. We're still trying to trace the manufacturer, but it looks like the knife is custom made and one of a kind, so that's a dead end, too."

"Tough breaks." Scott paused for a moment. "Mike, do you think we could talk?"

"Can't it wait? I'm on the verge of winning fifty bucks."

"Well, it's kind of important."

Reluctantly, Mike handed his cue to another player. "Take over, but don't mess up or you'll owe me later." He turned to the deputy. "Let's go outside."

In the parking lot Scott kicked at the dirt with the toe of his boot.

Mike was curious. "Tell me what's on your mind."

"It's sort of odd that I ran into Davis that way tonight. I had no idea who he was."

Mike was confused. "And that has what to do with anything?"

"Well, rumor has it the welfare check you were on the night of Tarin MacGyver's break-in had something to do with him."

"I don't know where you're going with this."

"The story is that Jake told you he was worried because late that night Davis was acting strange at the bar. I've also heard no one seems to know where he was and what he was up to before that." He looked directly at Mike. "I know he's a close friend, but has it ever crossed your mind Davis might have been the man at the boathouse? Have you even bothered to bring him in for questioning?"

"You're right. He has been my friend for a long time. But I'm a policeman first, and yes, I have asked him what he was doing that night."

"And?"

"He told me he was working on his boat at Shuck's."

Scott leaned against the wall of the building, bending his knee, and resting one foot against the siding. "Can anyone verify that?"

"I talked to several of the employees, and they all said Alex had his boat in a lift under one of the spotlights on the main dock. He had the motor apart and was working on it when the restaurant closed at seven o'clock. He was still there when everyone left twenty or thirty minutes later."

"But from then until he showed up at the Sip 'n Strike, he's unaccounted for, right?"

"What's your point, Scott?"

"My point is that he had enough time after everybody left the marina to get to Tarin's, break into the boathouse, and then be seen at the bar watching late night television."

Mike shook his head. "Under the best of circumstances, it would have been tight." He contemplated the possibilities. "To pull it off, Alex would have needed to establish an alibi at the marina, then put his engine back together and the boat into its hoist before leaving. Let's say all that was accomplished by eight. It would take at least a half-hour to get to the house down the shore from Tarin's, and before that he would have had to hide his truck somewhere. That would take more time. Then he would have to traverse the rocky bank." Mike paused. "What's the clock say now? So maybe it's nine thirty when he gets to the boathouse and that's if he hurried."

"Which is about the time Tarin says she went to check the boats."

An awkward silence descended upon the two men before Scott continued. "In that scenario, there was plenty of time after the fight with Parker to change clothes and get to the bar by ten thirty. Listen. I'm not saying he did it, but you can't discount it as a possibility."

"Give me a motive, Scott."

"From what I've heard, it's common knowledge Davis and his wife aren't happily married. Maybe he's harboring secret desires for his old high school sweetheart."

Mike shook his head. "Okay. Alex and Rachel have had their problems. But they have a beautiful daughter and I know they're trying to work things out. However, I will give you this. Given his current state of mind, I know we can't dismiss him as a suspect." Then his look turned to one of authority. "But it's equally true that I'm not going to accuse Alex on pure speculation and circumstantial evidence. Right now, that's all we've got."

"What if we get a search warrant to look for the torn black sweatshirt and boots at his house?"

Mike remained adamant. "No. I'm not conducting any searches or making any accusations tying Alex to the break-in unless we have tangible evidence. Understand?"

Scott nodded. "Okay. All I'm asking is that you don't allow friendship to interfere with your objectivity."

"Now you're questioning my integrity. Even though you're new to town, you should know me better than that." Mike paused before continuing. "By the way, I'm not sure you're in the loop regarding some new information that's come to light."

Simmons became attentive.

"I've been checking every angle I can think of to find the person responsible for what happened at Tarin's. That means investigating if she had any appliance repair done, landscaping, or anything like that in the months leading up to the break-in. I found one lead. It seems the company that installed Tarin's dock was shorthanded last spring. They hired a man from out of state who just happened to appear one day looking for a job. They told me he was dependable, worked hard, and the owner had no complaints about his job performance. But they could only keep him on for a few months because the work slowed down. As it turns out, he was let go the day before the break-in."

"What are you getting at, Mike?"

"One of the docks he helped put in was Tarin's. He knew all about the boathouse. Without a job, maybe he was simply looking for a place to crash for the night and got caught. I don't know. But it's interesting that the company issues black hooded sweatshirts to all its employees." Mike started back into the Sip 'n Strike. "At this point, I'm not accusing that guy either. Not that we could even find him at this point. What you need to remember is there's more than one possible scenario in this case. Now, I've got a pool game to wrap up and unless I'm mistaken, you have a shift to finish. We'll talk tomorrow."

CHAPTER 12

Don't Go

A WAKENED FROM A DEEP SLEEP, JON OPENED AND closed his eyes, struggling to focus in the darkness. Rolling over in the guest room's king-size bed, he discovered a dim light emanating from the kitchen. Sitting on the edge of the mattress, he glanced at the clock on the nightstand. Three o'clock. It had only been two hours since they'd ended their evening at the Sip 'n Strike.

The sound of a door latch catching on its strike plate broke the silence.

Under normal circumstances, his assumption would be that Tarin had come downstairs and was in the kitchen. But due to the recent chain of events, Jon felt apprehension building in the pit of his stomach. He slipped into his jeans before stepping into the hallway.

Peering around the corner, he noted a single light over the stovetop casting an eerie glow across the empty room. His eyes traveled around the room's perimeter but stopped at the French doors when he saw Tarin's silhouette on the deck.

She turned when he opened the door. "I'm sorry. I didn't mean to wake you."

He put his hands on her shoulders. "What's wrong?"

She shrugged. "I don't know. I just couldn't sleep."

He realized Tarin was wearing nothing more than a flannel nightshirt ending a few inches above her knees. "You're shivering. Let's go inside, light a fire, and talk about whatever it is that's bothering you."

His words brought a smile to her face. "But it's the middle of the night. It would be silly to do that."

"Says who? I may be wrong, but I think we can build a fire and talk anytime we want. Come on, let's get you warm."

Jon held out his hand and she grasped it tightly before following him back into the house.

TARIN STOOD HOLDING TWO coffee mugs, watching Jon puff at the glowing embers. He sat back and brushed his hands together when flames began to leap from the logs. Then, without thinking, she said out loud, "I don't want you to go."

"What was that?" he asked, still intent on the growing fire.

She was thankful he hadn't heard what she'd said. "Coffee?" Tarin handed him one of the mugs and sat on the couch across from the fireplace.

Jon shook his head and patted the floor. "You need to sit closer if you expect me to listen to what's bothering you."

Securely tucked at his side, Tarin couldn't help but feel safe. Feeling his arm around her shoulders, she was determined to fight the unbridled desire she felt growing within. His touch seemed to burn against her skin.

"Now, what made you get up in the middle of the night?"

She bit her lower lip and glanced at Jon's face, unsure how to begin.

"Whatever you need to say is safe with me." He wore that playful grin she'd come to love. "If you're trying to figure out how to get rid of me, just spit it out."

She hesitated for a moment, feeling almost naked under his gaze. "I'm afraid it's quite the opposite. I don't want you to go."

"You know I have to be on Tommy's plane tomorrow, but there's no reason you can't be on it with me."

Tarin smiled. "I must be crazy. There are dozens of women who would give anything for a chance to fly away with you."

"But they don't know me like you do. All they know is the persona Tommy projects of me in the media. To be honest, they would probably be sorely disappointed by the real thing. But you've helped me share the person I really am—the person I want to be. So come to California with me and live dangerously for once in your life."

Live dangerously.

The words echoed in her head and seeing the gentle look in his eyes—feeling the heat of his body next to her own—she did the next best thing: She spoke from her heart. "You know I can't come with you—not yet." Her voice began to trail off. "But there is something I would like to do."

Jon remained silent. Waiting.

Tarin knelt on her knees in front of him. "I don't know how to say this."

"Give it a try."

"Okay, but please be patient." Her voice was filled with apprehension. "Tonight I realized how much I'm going to miss you and I'm afraid that after you leave tomorrow, I'll never see you again."

"You must know I'll be back. We need to find out where this relationship will take us."

Tarin made a conscious decision to continue before her courage evaporated into thin air. "Do you remember when we were in the hot tub after our ride? You told me when I was ready, I could sleep with you." She averted her eyes before looking back toward him. "I know the conversation was all about being at your house in La Jolla, but—"

He put two fingers to her lips. "If I didn't know better, I'd think you were inviting me to take you upstairs."

"Is that wrong?" she whispered.

"It's not wrong, but I don't think we need to go upstairs. We have a beautiful fire and everything we need right here."

One by one, Jon released the buttons of her nightshirt and leaned over to kiss her exposed breasts, moving from one to the other. In turn, she followed the muscled contours of his chest with her fingers before linking her hands behind his neck. His skin was soft, smooth, and warm to the touch.

He brushed her cheek. "Are you sure you want to do this?"

She nodded.

Jon sat up, touching the tip of her nose. "Then wait just a minute."

He disappeared and returned with a down comforter from his bedroom. Spreading it on the floor, he positioned Tarin in front of the crackling fire. Tracing the curve of her breasts with his fingertips, he cradled one while teasing its erect nipple with his tongue. At the same time, his other hand traveled slowly along her abdomen. She felt it come to rest between her skin and the black lace panties she was wearing.

Tarin's nervousness disappeared as she unbuttoned his jeans.

Pushing Jon back onto the comforter, she undressed him. He responded by gathering her into his arms and tenderly rolling her onto her back. Then, with his kisses, he explored the soft recesses of her mouth with the tip of his tongue. At that moment, he met Tarin's body with his own and she caught her breath when he entered her for the first time. Tingling sensations began to pulse through her body, growing in intensity until she climaxed with an uncontrollable throbbing deep within. In an explosion of satisfaction, they lay exhausted, side by side.

Jon pushed the hair from her face and kissed her on the forehead. "You, my dear, are talented in ways I never imagined. You can't be the same shy woman I met wearing one shoe with weeds tangled in her hair."

Tarin followed the lines of his body with her hands, committing every muscle and mark to memory, hoping that would be enough to satisfy her appetite until they were together again. "Would you like to continue this upstairs?" she asked timidly.

Jon leaned over to close the glass fireplace doors and kissed her again. "Lead the way. I can always sleep on the plane."

CHAPTER 13

―――

Departure

TARIN MARVELED AT HOW EASY IT WAS FOR THE trio to make its way through the almost deserted charter terminal. There was none of the hustle and bustle of a commercial airport and no sign of long, patience-testing security lines. The employees working at the counters were relaxed, drinking coffee, and joking with each other. In a matter of moments, the three were outside where Tommy Wyndham's Cessna Citation X sat waiting on the tarmac. The luggage compartment was open and the stairway had been moved into position awaiting their arrival.

Walking around its exterior, Jake took a few moments to examine the jet. "Not bad. This is an impressive machine."

"In Tommy's eyes it's all about putting on a show. He acts like the plane is his, but he's only one of the shareholders." Jon's tone was flavored with distaste for his manager but admiration for the jet. "It flies just under the speed of sound at about seven hundred miles an hour. If the weather is on our side, that should put me in San Diego before you know it. Want to check it out?"

Ducking their six-foot frames to enter the cabin, the two men settled into a pair of the jet's luxurious gray leather seats. Jake stretched out, leaning back, linking his fingers behind his neck. "Yeah, I think I could get used to this."

The pilot emerged from cockpit of the aircraft. "Good afternoon, Jon. We'll be ready to take off in about thirty minutes. Eric's finalizing the flight plan now."

"Sounds good, Joel," Jon said. "By the way, you're looking sharp in your pilot blues—gold stripes and all."

He shrugged. "Hey, when Tommy scheduled this flight, I didn't know who the passengers would be. Now that I know it's you, I can get rid of the uniform and put my jeans back on."

Jon had to laugh. "Okay, but even though I'll be alone on this flight, let's maintain the illusion of grandeur at least until we get into the air. This is Jake Carpenter and behind you in the doorway, you'll find Tarin MacGyver. They brought me to the airport this morning."

"Nice to meet you," Joel acknowledged, tipping his hat before descending the stairs to the tarmac. "Excuse me, ma'am."

Jake leaned over and whispered, "What kind of cut-rate operation is this? No flight attendant at your beck and call?"

Jon shook his head. "Naw, I'm on my own today." He stood and made his way to the galley in the front of the passenger compartment. "But if I know Tommy, there's always a supply of champagne on board. Want to join me?"

Closing the ice drawer, he walked back down the aisle with three crystal flutes in one hand and a chilled bottle in the other. He slid into the seat next to Tarin with Jake facing them.

Popping the cork, Jon offered a toast and filled the stemmed glasses. "Here's to new friends and whatever the future holds."

Tarin took a sip and stood the glass on the teak shelf next to her seat. "If you don't mind, I'd like to go back into the terminal for a minute. There was a brochure about jet charters on one of the counters. I'd love to show it off to my boss, Maury. You know—tease him about the kind of company I'm keeping."

Watching her cross the tarmac, Jon became thoughtful. "Jake, I'm curious. There's no question you're Chasm Falls' most eligible bachelor. You and your family seem to own at least half the town. Plus, you and Tarin have been close friends since you were kids. Why—"

Jake smiled. "Why didn't we wind up together? I'm afraid that's a question you'll need to ask Tarin, but I can tell you this. When I returned to work for my parents and Alex was no longer in the picture, we went out a few times. Let's say it simply wasn't meant to be. She can elaborate if she wants."

"Fair enough. It's just that whenever I turn around, your name pops into the conversation—"

Tarin reentered the cabin and stopped in the aisle, noticing the perplexed look on Jon's face. "Okay, I interrupted something. What?"

Jake grinned. "Would you like to tell this guy why we're not married with three kids and a golden retriever?"

"Because I wanted a border collie." She laughed, dropped onto her seat, and manufactured her best serious expression. "It's like this. Hollywood isn't the only venue with a corner on juicy gossip. We may not have tabloids, but Chasm Falls has its own share of deep, dark secrets." She picked up the bottle and reached for Jon's glass. "You might need a refill to get through this exposé. Anyway, we did date when Jake came back to town. Then one night, his parents sat us down in their living room looking like the sky was about to fall in."

She exchanged a glance with Jake before looking back at Jon. "Remember I told you my parents divorced when I was young? The truth is Mom threw my dad out. We were living near Denver, and he was a beer salesman for an up-and-coming brewing company. One of his accounts was the Sip 'n Strike. He made trips to Chasm Falls every few months and decided to romance a young server who worked at the bar. You can probably guess the rest. She wound up pregnant. When my mom got wind of it, she told my dad in no uncertain terms to get out of our lives. I don't think anybody's seen or heard from him since. It's like he dropped from the face of the earth."

"What happened to the server?"

"Her boyfriend was stationed overseas with the Army. He was a special guy who happened to love her very much. They got married when he came home on leave, and they went back to Germany together. Eventually, when they returned to Chasm Falls with a baby, nobody thought much about it."

Jake finished the story for her. "All things considered, I think they did a good job raising me. The people in town respect my parents enough not to say much, but I'm sure everyone figured out a long time ago that Tarin's my half sister."

Jake's smile faded. "Now that you know about the bastard brother, here's an awkward question for you." He swallowed a swig of champagne. "I need to ask you about something." He pulled a crumpled piece of glossy paper from his back pocket. Unfolding the torn magazine page, he tried to be discreet when he handed it to Jon. "Mike gave me this article last night. His wife had given it to him."

Tarin seemed to sense what was coming. "You don't need to hide the picture. I know about Anna Haines."

Jake looked surprised. Jon simply looked relieved.

She continued her explanation, "What do you want to know? It's a sham devised purely for publicity. Their managers manufactured the relationship a few months ago to promote Jon and Anna through the news media. But Jon's ending the charade when he gets back to California. He's been completely honest with me, so please don't worry."

"Are you sure?" Jake asked, his concern still evident.

Tarin did her best to reassure him. "Really, it's okay."

He shrugged. "Well, if you don't have a problem, Mac, I guess that should be good enough for me. Now I'll get out of here so you can have a few moments alone."

She touched her brother's arm when he turned to leave. "Do you think I could see the clipping?"

Jake handed her the page and was halfway down the steps when Jon started after him. He paused long enough to see her smoothing the wrinkled photo on her denim-covered thigh.

"She's beautiful."

He crouched in the aisle next to Tarin. "True. But you know what? You're the one I care about. Process that while I catch up with Jake."

With one hand on each railing, Jon descended two stairs at a time. "Hey, hold on a minute." He caught up a few feet before they reached the terminal door.

Jake stopped and Jon hesitated. "I'm not sure how to say this."

"I'm listening."

"It's just a gut feeling, but for Tarin's sake, could you keep an eye on Alex Davis? I met him at the bar last night and something about him made me feel uncomfortable, but I can't tell you what it was."

"Are you implying he might be the burglar? I don't mean to disagree, but I can't believe he would do anything to hurt Tarin. Have you said anything to Mike?"

"No, and I won't. But I had a conversation with Deputy Simmons about the case and he's got suspicions, too. For her sake, please watch Davis for me."

"I'll do it, but I think you're wrong."

Tarin met Jon at the door of the cabin just as they heard the pilot's voice. "We've been cleared to taxi and hold for departure."

"Thanks, Joel." Jon gazed at Tarin until their eyes met. "These have been the best two weeks of my life."

She smiled shyly. "Mine, too."

"You don't know how much I wish you were coming with me, but I understand why you're not." He saw tears welling in her eyes.

"I have to go," she whispered.

"Please wait." Taking her hand, he made a solemn promise. "I will be back, Tarin. We need to see what happens next."

"Let me go before I change my mind."

"If there's the slightest chance that might happen, I'll tell Joel to hold the plane." He sensed her resolve was weakening.

"Jake's waiting for me."

Jon could sense the uncertainty in her voice. "When the time's right," she told him, "we will see each other again."

One by one, he felt her fingers slip from his hand as she descended the stairs.

"I'm holding you to that," he called after her.

Then the pilot sealed the door, and Tarin disappeared both into the terminal lobby and for now, out of his life.

CHAPTER 14

End of the Beginning

JON AWOKE WITH A START WHEN HE FELT THE landing gear descend from the belly of the jet. He glanced at his watch to find that with a strong tailwind, they had arrived ahead of schedule. Thanks to the time change, it was midafternoon and the skies over San Diego were bright blue and cloudless.

During the flight, he hadn't stopped thinking about the best way to approach both Anna and Tommy. He didn't care at all about his manager, but Anna was a different story. If what began as a business proposition had turned into something more in her eyes, he didn't want to hurt her. He would need to be careful when choosing his words. Unsure how to live up to the challenges awaiting him once they touched down, Jon remained in a reclined position until the jet began slowing to a stop on the tarmac. His eyes were still closed when Joel made his way down the aisle.

"Do you have any luggage below, Jon?"

He sat up, shook his head, and gestured to the seat behind him. "No. All I have is a duffle bag."

"Okay. Well, hey. It's always nice seeing you." The pilot paused when he opened the cabin door and remarked, "Somebody important must be flying in this afternoon. There are two satellite trucks in the parking lot."

"One thing is certain—it's not me. Tommy has made it quite clear I'm the music industry's next has-been." Jon stretched his arms overhead and prepared to face the inevitable. He was glad Nick would be there to pick him up. The thought of dealing with anyone else today was more than he could handle. Once he was settled at home he would call Anna to arrange a meeting. The sooner he ended the ill-conceived publicity stunt, the sooner Tarin would be back in his life.

Standing in front of the charter terminal, Jon stopped to stare at his reflection in the dark one-way glass. He inhaled deeply and pulled open the door.

He was met by a barrage of flashes and camera shutters, making it necessary to shield his eyes. "What the hell?"

Then Jon saw her.

Anna Haines was flanked by a pair of bodyguards and several airport security employees attempting to keep camera-wielding reporters at a comfortable distance. With dark auburn hair flowing past her shoulders and a designer dress clinging to her flawless figure, the young actress and her bright smile held the entourage captive.

Jon continued to survey the crowd. His eyes locked on Tommy Wyndham who was smirking in the background.

You son of a bitch. What have you done now?

Anna threw herself into his arms. "Yes, Jon! Yes!" she squealed, unable to contain her excitement.

Camera shutters continued to click as he discreetly pushed her to arm's length and whispered, "Yes, to what?"

She put two fingers to his lips before throwing her arms back around his neck and kissing him. "You are so silly. Of course, I will marry you."

Lifting her left hand, he glanced down at the sparkling diamond ring on her finger. "I see you got it," Jon murmured, disguising the anger he felt building inside. He turned to glare at his gloating manager.

Anna giggled incessantly. "It's beautiful, Jon. And I was so worried that you were angry at me for the things I said in Denver. You haven't returned any of my calls. But when the limousine pulled up at my house this morning and a courier came to the door carrying a velvet pillow, I didn't know what to think." She tightened the grip on his arm. "Then I saw the beautiful box tied with a ribbon and the card. You made me feel like a princess. Everything was so perfect—just like a fairy tale."

She continued to chatter nonstop, and while he heard Anna's voice, the syllables ran together like gibberish. Instead, all he could think about was how Tarin would react when she saw the film footage. And she would see it. Unfortunately, in recent weeks there hadn't been enough Hollywood gossip to go around, and that would ensure the engagement would be plastered on every network entertainment show. It wouldn't take long for Tarin to realize his promises meant nothing and he'd betrayed her.

"Come on, Jon. I can't wait to share our news with the reporters, but I'm sure they've already seen the ring. It's so big, how could anyone miss it?" Anna bounced with excitement.

Numb, he followed her like a lost puppy to face the crowd of sharks waiting nearby.

After the media had gotten more than its fill of photos and quotes from his new fiancée, Jon navigated to Tommy's side.

The manager greeted his client with a big grin and a congratulatory pat on the back. "Well, what do you think? I am good, aren't I? I hope you realize it wasn't easy getting coverage on such short notice. They'll be talking about you and Anna for days. And the real reward is you'll have the pleasure of sleeping with one of the most beautiful women in the business when you get home tonight. She'll erase any thoughts of that bimbo in Colorado. I do wish I was in your shoes."

Jon felt the fingers of his hand curling into a tight fist—it was all he could do to refrain from striking the man standing in front of him. His voice was controlled and deliberate. "What the hell do you think you're doing?"

"I'm protecting my investment," Tommy responded. "But then your reaction shouldn't come as a surprise. Now, what do you say we get you back to your beautiful fiancée? I think she's looking for you." He rested his arm on Jon's shoulder as they walked. "Remember—it's like I told you before. I don't expect you to marry Anna. Just string her along and enjoy everything she has to offer until the record's released."

Jon pushed Tommy's arm away. "I'm not doing this. What kind of a bastard do you think I am?"

Tommy stopped in his tracks. "Are you going to make me go over it all again?"

"I made mistakes a long time ago, and you should know better than anyone else that I've learned my lessons. I've been clean for ten years and I'd take back the night in San Francisco if I could."

"But you can't, can you? How do you think the band's fans would react if they found out their golden boy is a sex offender? Who would buy your records or pay to go to your shows? You'd be finished." Tommy patted him on the back and strode away without looking back. "But you know, it's all up to you. The choice is yours."

Jon stood in silence, surrounded by activity, but feeling completely alone. At that moment, he realized Anna was back at his side, "Oh, Jon. Let's go celebrate," she cooed, intertwining her arm with his.

He shook his head. "I'm sorry, but it's been a long day with the flight and all. Nick just got here and if you don't mind, I'll catch a ride home with him. I'll call you tomorrow and we'll talk."

She looked disappointed and pouted. "Okay, but of all nights, it seems like we should be together tonight." Then she giggled and held her left hand in front of her face, "But I'll call and see if Tina and Megan want to go out. I can't wait to show off my ring and tell everybody that soon I'll be Mrs. Jonathan Parker. We'll be just like Nicole Kidman and Keith Urban!"

Anna couldn't contain her squeal as if realizing something for the first time. "We'll need to set a wedding date, won't we? I'll have to pick a dress designer. And I'll need to start packing. When can I move in? Your house is so much nicer than mine—it's on the beach and everything. Just think of the parties we'll have!"

He kissed her on the forehead. "Good night, Anna. Have fun and I'll see you in the morning. We'll work out everything then." Jon turned and grabbed Nick's elbow. "Get me out of here," he mumbled, almost dragging his friend to the terminal exit.

Once in the safety of Nick's SUV, Jon thrust the passenger seat into its reclining position and leaned back in frustration. "Oh, my god. What just happened?"

Nick laughed and eased his car onto the freeway. "Unless I'm mistaken, you're now engaged to one of the most beautiful women in the world. Congratulations, my friend."

"Fuck that."

"What's going on, Jon?" Nick glanced at his friend, waiting for an explanation. "You disappear after the show in Denver and then come back to San Diego two weeks later ready to shuck everything you had when you left. Did I miss something? What happened in Colorado?"

"He's gone too far this time. I can't deal with Tommy anymore."

"Give me a break. That's something new? You've been threatening to ditch him for years but never follow through."

"This time it's different."

"I'm listening," Nick answered, his eyes intent on the road in front of them.

"It's complicated."

"Like I said, I'm listening."

Jon sighed deeply. "Okay, I met someone while I was in the mountains. Someone I care about."

"And?"

"Tommy got wind of it and panicked. He knew I was planning to end the thing with Anna when I got back here, so he decided to control the situation himself. He bought the ring, sent some preposterous limousine, and somehow created the note proposing to her." Jon looked skyward. "Shit. I wanted Tarin—that's her name—to fly to San Diego with me. But she wouldn't come until I straighten things out with Anna and Tommy. Damn him. Now she'll never trust me."

"Okay. What are you going to do about it?"

"What am I supposed to do? Tarin will see the television footage and believe I was lying to her from the beginning. She'll think I'm a total ass and Tommy comes out on top like he always does."

"Wait a minute. Let's back up. How can you give up on this girl when you say she means so much to you?"

"I'll try to explain things, but who knows if she'll even listen. Who am I kidding? I wouldn't." Jon turned to his friend. "She's better off without me, Nick. Nobody knows that better than I do."

"If you go through with this engagement, you're going to hurt Anna, too. Is that what you want?"

"Of course not, but there's more to it than you know."

"Just tell me what's going on."

He shook his head. "I wish I could, but I can't. I need to work through this alone." Resigned, Jon simply stared at the ocean as they drove toward his house in La Jolla. Then he sat up abruptly. "Wait a minute. What time is it?"

Nick looked at the display on the dash's touchscreen. "It's a little after three. Why?"

Jon reached for his cell phone. "I still have time. It's four o'clock in Colorado. If I can get through to Tarin before the shows air tonight, I can explain how Tommy was behind everything. Maybe I can fix things before it's too late."

He drummed his fingers on the console, waiting for her to answer. Then, hearing Tarin's voice, he started to speak before realizing he was reacting to her voicemail. Desperation reverberated in his words. "Tarin—it's me. You may see something on television tonight announcing that Anna and I are engaged. Don't believe it. Tommy arranged it all and you know what he's capable of doing. He knew my plans and decided to take things into his own hands. Please call so I can explain. It's a little after three here. I'll keep my phone with me all night. Please call back."

Nick looked toward his passenger. "I've never seen you like this before. You really do care about this girl, don't you?"

"More than you know."

Nick smiled. "Then, my friend, it's time you take a stand."

"Are you with me?"

"Against Tommy? You damn well better believe it." Nick continued to monitor the traffic in front of them. "But you better hope she gets your message before that film airs tonight."

Jon closed his eyes and leaned back against the headrest. "I know."
Then he picked up his phone and redialed Tarin's number.

Again.

And again.

And yet another time.

Still no answer.

CHAPTER 15

———

Broken Promises

T ARIN TOSSED HER BACKPACK ONTO A SMALL, round table in front of the almost empty bar at the Sip 'n Strike. "Hi, Jake." She turned to greet Mike Wilson, who was sitting a few feet away. "Day off, Mike?"

Neither man replied, and she looked over to see Jake changing channels with the remote.

"What's up, you two?" she asked.

Mike shrugged. "Nothing much. How was your day?"

"My day was fine. After Jake and I got back from taking Jon to Denver, I edited stories most of the afternoon. I lost track of time." Tarin sat on a stool between the two men. "You're awfully quiet. Is there something going on I should know about?"

Jake ignored her question. "Would you like a soda or something?"

"Actually, coffee sounds perfect." She filled a cup from the carafe on the bar and reached for the cream and sugar. "I might even sweeten it up for a change. Mike, isn't this about the time you force Jake to watch *Hollywood Insider*?"

"I guess so, but today's teasers don't look very interesting."

"Let me be the judge of that. As shallow as it seems now that I know a celebrity it's kind of fun to hear all the gossip." She reached to pick up the remote from the bar.

"Why don't we watch something else tonight?" Jake asked, grabbing the device from her hand.

Tarin glanced back and forth between the two men. "All right. What's going on? There's so much tension in this room I could cut it with a knife. You forget I know you both well enough to sense when you're trying to hide something. You know I'll find out what it is eventually. If you don't turn on the show, I will," she commanded.

"And we'll be right back with the news of the day," the commentator announced.

"Why are you making such a big deal about this?" Tarin asked.

"All right," Mike answered. "They're going to show film of Jon arriving in San Diego this afternoon."

"And?"

He hesitated and Jake picked up where his friend had left off. "Inside the terminal that actress Anna Haines announced her engagement to Jon and—"

Tarin held up her hand to silence his words when images of Anna and Jon filled the television screen. There she was in high definition, looking gorgeous and radiant. One minute the young starlet was embracing Jon, while in the next, she was passionately kissing him for the cameras.

"Speculation the couple had gone their separate ways several weeks ago after a confrontation in Denver was squelched when Anna Haines met her boyfriend, singer Jonathan Parker, today at the San Diego airport. An eight-carat diamond ring was on her finger."

Tarin heard nothing after that as images of Anna embracing Jon and holding his hand filled the screen throughout the interview. She tried to make light of the scene playing out in front of her. "Hey, guys— let's be realistic. Did you really think a girl from a small town in the mountains could win Jon's heart over a woman like that?"

Jake came to her side from behind the bar and offered a hug. "I'm sorry. I liked the guy. Parker pulled one over on all of us."

"You know what?" Mike chimed in. "He doesn't deserve you. I'm going home to shred all of Maggie's CDs."

Tarin put an arm around each of them. "Thanks, but you know better than to worry about me. I've been through worse and will rebound from this just fine. But I am embarrassed that I fell for his line." She picked up her backpack and walked toward the exit. "Know what? It's been a long day. Thanks for not saying I told you so. See you tomorrow."

Once outside, Tarin leaned back against the closed door with tears beginning to stream down her cheeks. Slipping behind the wheel of her truck, she glanced at the cell phone resting on the seat and picked it up. A quick look at the log showed Jon had called four times and left four messages.

What could he possibly say that I would want to hear?

For several moments she stared at the phone in her hand in silence. Then, Tarin deleted each of the messages without listening to any of them. It was the first step in erasing Jon Parker from her life. He hadn't belonged there anyway. Putting the truck in gear, she drove home to Finn and an empty house overlooking Ledge Lake.

JAKE SLAMMED A CASE of empty bottles on the counter behind the bar. "That ass better not show his face here again. If he does, I won't be responsible for my actions. I asked him point blank about that actress at the airport today. Tarin said he'd told her all about Anna Haines, that it was all a publicity stunt, and there was nothing to it. She believed he was telling the truth. Lying asshole."

Mike seemed puzzled. "Hold on a minute. I'm confused. Parker wanted Tarin to fly to San Diego with him. If she'd been on the plane, it would have messed up any plans he might have had to get engaged to this Anna Haines woman. Something just doesn't make sense. I don't get it." He swallowed the last of his beer and stood, still shaking his head. "On that note, I think I'll head out."

Alone in the bar, Jake changed channels to a hockey game and went back to work wiping down tables.

Unfortunately, what each of them missed while watching Jon's arrival in San Diego was the fact his smiles were forced and few in number. Jon's detachment was overshadowed by Anna's glowing exuberance. They also weren't aware of the pompous, overweight man lurking in the background wearing a triumphant smile. The man who had, at least for the time being, managed to get his way another time.

CHAPTER 16

━━━

A False Sense of Security

IT HAD BEEN MORE THAN A MONTH SINCE JON'S return to California, and Tarin had buried herself in work to numb the hurt she continued to feel. Jon and Anna had apparently fallen out of favor with Hollywood gossipmongers because they dropped from sight after the engagement. Not that Tarin was watching.

Jon tried to contact her repeatedly the first few days after his departure, but she rejected each call, erasing the voicemails without taking the time to listen. Eventually, the calls became less frequent and finally, they stopped entirely.

On this day, she had agreed to meet Scott Simmons for lunch to talk about security systems. Unable to figure out who had broken into the boathouse, Mike had become relentless in demanding that she install cameras and an alarm. Finally, Tarin had given up the fight.

Scott stood and pulled out a chair as Tarin crossed the restaurant to join him.

"Sorry, I'm late." She seemed out of breath when she sat down at the corner table. "Jake called when I was about to walk out the door. Mike's been talking with him. He wanted to put in his two cents about the importance of installing a security system."

"You know we're right. The alarm can be connected directly to a communication center, and they'll know right away if somebody's trying to breach it. In the military, I worked part-time in security. That was a few years ago, but at least I'm familiar with some of the better companies."

Scott pulled a thick folder from the chair next to him. "Let's order first and then I'll show you what I've found."

With a few recommended systems noted and the dishes cleared away, Tarin turned the conversation to finding out more about her lunch companion.

"If I remember correctly, when Mike introduced us, didn't he mention you're new to the area?"

He nodded. "I moved here in March from Grand Junction."

She poured a packet of sugar into her coffee. "Are you a Colorado native?"

"No. I grew up in Minnesota and moved from the Twin Cities two years ago to work for Mesa County."

"You didn't stay there long." Tarin rested her chin on top of her intertwined fingers. "Didn't you like Grand Junction?"

He shrugged. "I don't know. It didn't turn out to be the opportunity I thought it would be. This department seems to be a better fit."

She smiled. "Well if what I've seen is any indication, Chasm Falls is lucky to have you." Tarin cradled her almost-empty coffee cup. "So—have you met anyone here? Surely local girls know a good catch when they see one."

Scott looked a little uncomfortable, "No, but that's another reason I left Grand Junction. I was, well, in a relationship that didn't work out."

"I'm sorry." Tarin smiled and rested her hand on his. "Trust me. The right girl will come along."

"Thanks for the vote of confidence, but I'm in no hurry." Their eyes connected for an instant before he looked down to glance at his watch. "Well, maybe we should go to your house so I can get an idea what size system you're going to need."

Scott reached for the check, but Tarin picked it up first.

"This one's on me. It's the least I can do to say to thank you for all the research you've done."

TARIN HEARD HER HOME phone ringing when she opened the front door. "Come on in, Scott. I may need to take this call." She dashed toward the kitchen, motioning for him to enter.

"Hi, Maury. What's up? Hold on a second." She turned to the deputy. "This is my boss in Denver, so I'll be tied up for a bit. If you want to start gathering information, I'll be with you in a few minutes."

Scott nodded. "Sure. I just need to check out how many doors and windows there are. You know, things like that. Is it okay if I go upstairs?"

"Absolutely."

"Is your dog going to be upset with a strange man wandering around your house?"

She laughed before sitting down at her desk with the phone pressed to her ear. "Finn's outside in his kennel. I always put him there when I'm going to be gone for a few hours, so you'll be fine. Anyway, you're far from a stranger." She returned to her phone call. "Okay, Maury. I'm back. What's up?"

Tarin opened her laptop while listening to the man on the other end of the call. "No, Maury. Listen to me. I will not cover a charity ball for you tonight. You know I hate those things. Plus, it's already almost one o'clock, the event is in south Denver, and I'm sorry—I already have plans."

"You know I wouldn't ask unless there was no alternative, kiddo," the editor countered from his desk in the newspaper office.

"Don't call me kiddo, Maury. You're not earning any points when you do. I've told you that before," she shot back.

The gray-haired man leaned back in his chair, grinning from ear to ear. "We seem to be venting a fair amount of hostility today. So—what are your plans anyway? It wouldn't be doing laundry, would it?"

There was a noticeable pause.

"Well, it is Monday, and please don't make fun of me. You know I always wash clothes on Mondays. I'm a creature of habit."

"We need to find you a man."

"I don't need a man. They're nothing but trouble."

"Point well taken, but please think about tonight. You're my last hope. I'll even do your laundry myself. The guys upstairs want us to be there because this charity raised more than ten million dollars for the performing arts in Denver schools. Debbie was set to cover everything from start to finish. Unfortunately, I can't help it she shattered her leg skiing." He paused, allowing Tarin to experience a full dose of conscience.

"Why was Debbie skiing in the first place? She can't walk across the room without tripping." Tarin closed her eyes, realizing she was destined to lose the battle.

"Could this be considered a pregnant pause?" he teased.

"Just a minute, Maury." Tarin put the phone down and took a breath. Then, after a resigned sigh, she repositioned the receiver on her ear. "Okay. But if I do this for you, you'll owe me big time. Just remember that fella."

"Don't be calling me fella. You know how I hate that." He paused. "But thank you. My back was up against the wall if you weren't willing to do it. Besides, it's the holiday season. Think about the points you just earned with Santa."

"You don't even celebrate Christmas, Maury. Stop groveling." Tarin found it hard to believe she had agreed to be at a formal event more than a hundred miles away in less than five hours. "So you win. Where do I have to be and when?"

"The Golden Peaks Golf Club at six o'clock for cocktails, dinner at eight, and dancing until the cows come home."

"Those in high society do like to party, don't they?"

"Tarin—"

She smiled. "I know. Lighten up."

"Hey—like I said, the people you're referring to work very hard to keep the arts alive in our schools. That's a good thing. They deserve to be recognized for their contributions. Just don't forget—six o'clock at the Golden Peaks Golf Club. And—"

"I know. Don't embarrass the newspaper by wearing inappropriate attire, which means no leggings, big sweaters, or ripped jeans. Believe it or not, I do have taste and very nice clothes stashed away in my closet.

For you, I'll pull out one of those innocent garments and subject it to the scrutiny of society."

"One of those always the bridesmaid but never the bride dresses you've got?" he teased.

"Goodbye, Maury." Looking up, she saw Scott coming down from the loft.

"I'm sorry about that. Did you get everything you need?"

He held up a yellow notepad covered with notes and smiled. "Think so. I'll call the alarm company when I get home and place the order. With any luck, they'll be able to install the system in a week or so, and then you'll be safe and secure."

Tarin walked toward Scott to hug him. "Thanks. I appreciate all the time and energy you've put into this."

"No problem. I was glad to do it." He turned toward the door. "Now I better get going. I'll give you a call when I know more about the order. Thanks for lunch."

"My pleasure." Tarin watched Scott pull out of the driveway and then trudged upstairs to ponder what she could wear to keep up with Denver's social elite. Ten minutes later, she was still standing in the walk-in closet, staring at the clothes hanging in front of her.

CHAPTER 17

———

Becoming Cinderella

S LIPPING THE COMPACT INTO HER BLACK BEADED
purse, Tarin took one final look at her reflection in the lounge
mirror, then turned and walked back into the lobby.

Couples were already streaming into the building. The women were
dressed in exquisite gowns while the men looked quite distinguished in
black tuxedoes. The towering clubhouse lobby was filled with elegant
holiday finery, causing even the skeptic Tarin to admire the décor. Red
velvet banners accented with thick gold braid were draped from the
vaulted ceiling, while greenery and poinsettias were placed around the
room. A live twenty-five-foot Christmas tree decorated with clear lights
and gold glass ornaments stood in the lobby, while candlelight created
a magical mood.

Captured by the ambiance, she caught herself wondering what it
would be like to be a guest rather than on assignment. Then, amused
by the thought, she snapped herself back to reality. She hadn't been
invited to be part of the celebration. She was simply there to document
it, and with reluctance at that.

Looking across the lobby, Tarin could see ornate tables where
guests were checking in and receiving table assignments. Each person
was handed a festive holiday gift bag upon entering the ballroom.

Twenty yards away, tucked into a corner, she noticed a small card table with a simple white paper sign announcing "MEDIA."

Instead of a lavish gift bag, she was handed a leatherlike portfolio containing a nametag, her seating assignment, a program outlining the evening's events, and a roster of the Denver elite who would be in attendance.

Surveying the other women at the gala, she felt comfortable with her appearance. She'd settled on a floor-length black nylon and spandex dress with a straight, rather low-cut neckline for the evening's festivities. A sheer, satin-trimmed bolero with three-quarter sleeves covered the dress' spaghetti straps. Subtle striping in the fabric and a fitted bodice gave the dress and her trim physique an elegant look.

"Talk about ruining a good dress," she commented as she attached the vinyl clip-on nametag to the bolero and entered the ballroom. "At least I'm not here to impress anyone."

If the clubhouse lobby seemed magnificent, it was nothing compared to the landscape of the fantasy world in front of her.

Full-size carousel horses were placed in strategic places throughout the ballroom. They were harnessed with gold garland and clear lights. Echoing the lobby decor, rich red velvet, poinsettias, and greenery served as backdrops for all the decorations. Round tables with candles and lavish centerpieces filled the center of the room. She calculated there would be about two hundred fifty people in attendance when the meal was served. The most important guests would be seated at long rectangular tables stretching across the front of the ballroom. Thousands of clear twinkling lights illuminated the panoramic glass wall behind them. A string quartet was playing classical music in the background.

Finding her assigned place at a table near the back of the room, she scanned the list of attendees with methodical interest. Tarin had been at her job long enough to know she should seek out not only the perennial regulars but also the up-and-coming socialites. She preferred newcomers because they were friendlier and more eager to make an impression on the news media.

Locating her first subject near one of the cocktail stations, she pulled a digital recorder from her purse and started to walk toward him. A few steps into her journey, she stopped dead in her tracks.

"Debbie, what are you doing here?" she exclaimed, staring at her coworker's uninjured legs.

The other reporter lobbed the question back into her court, "No, Tarin. I think it's more like what are you doing here? This is my assignment."

"When Maury called this afternoon, he said you'd broken your leg in a skiing accident."

"What? You know I'm a klutz. A great ski bunny I might be, but a skier? I don't think so."

"Why would Maury—"

Tarin's heart skipped a beat when she heard a familiar voice. "Could this be the mystery woman who nearly destroyed the rock band Motive?"

Time seemed to stand still. She closed her eyes and turned to find Jonathan Parker standing in front of her.

"I'm confused—why are you here?" she exclaimed, while at the same time trying to fight the uninvited butterflies beginning to flutter in her stomach.

He stood a few feet away. "Two things. My record company donated a fair amount of money to this project, and the execs thought one of their artists should present the check."

"And?"

"It's probably the most important reason of all. I had to see you. I need to explain what happened in San Diego."

"There's nothing to explain. You made your choice and showed your true colors in the process."

Tarin turned away from Jon but then spun around to face him. "Just how did you know I would be here?"

Looking over Tarin's shoulder toward the confused coworker, Jon did his best to shed light on the situation. "I'm sorry—it's Debbie, right? Maury helped me come up with this scheme to be sure Tarin would be here tonight. Trust me. The assignment has always been yours, and I'll prove it by taking away her press credentials." He tossed Tarin's nametag on a passing waiter's tray and kept rambling, "Now she's nothing more than my date for the evening." He extended his hand. "By the way, it's nice to meet you. I'm Jon Parker representing Clocktower Records. Maybe we can talk later."

Placing his hand under Tarin's elbow, he leaned over to whisper, "By the way—you look amazing." He scanned the ballroom. "It's crowded in here. Could we go outside for a minute?"

Tarin pulled away, her heart beating so hard she could barely think. "No. I don't know what you told Maury to pull this off, but I thought he was my friend. I have absolutely no interest in spending another minute with you. You're an insensitive, self-centered, egotistical, spoiled brat, and a liar to boot. Let's leave it at that."

"Tarin, please."

The urgent tone of his voice caused her to look into his eyes. In that instant, she saw the same sincerity she had been drawn to at the cabin two months before. "Jon, I think you have a fiancée waiting for you somewhere or are you married by now? I've lost track. Maybe you brought her along tonight." Her voice was tinged with the kind of edge used to mask deep hurt. "I'd like to meet her."

"Please, let's go outside. I need to explain what happened."

Tarin tried to wipe a tear from the corner of her eye before he noticed it. "You need to explain? Correct me if I'm wrong, but haven't you claimed to do that more than once before? It's a habit with you and I refuse to fall for that line again."

Jon pushed the hair from her eyes, "Please, believe me, I didn't mean to hurt you. It was Tommy—"

"Just tell me, Jon. What would you do if you didn't have Tommy to use as a scapegoat?" She started to walk away but decided to throw one more jab. "You know what? I think you like being manipulated by him. Then you don't have to take responsibility for anything you do."

She was several feet away when Jon admitted almost under his breath, "You have every right to feel that way."

Tarin stopped, her back still toward him.

"She's gone."

"Who's gone?"

"I told Anna it was all a mistake the day after the engagement fiasco at the airport. Somehow Tommy managed to put a gag order on the breakup in the media, but it's over. I tried to call you more times than I can count, but you wouldn't answer. Jake won't talk to me either."

The silence between them was deafening.

"Now," he said, trying to take her hand in his, "can we go outside for just a minute? Then, when I'm finished saying what I need to say, you can tell me to go to hell and I'll never bother you again."

There was no room for discussion in her answer. She pulled her hand away. "You've got five minutes."

Even though there was a December chill in the air, the temperature on the deck was refreshing compared to the stuffy ballroom.

"First, let me look at you."

Tarin felt awkward yet almost aroused with his eyes undressing her in the bright moonlight.

"I thought you looked great in jeans, but you look fantastic tonight," he said, surveying her from head to toe.

Blushing, she fought to maintain her resolve not to fall for this man another time. "Just say what you want so I can go home."

"You need to know, I did plan to end it with Anna when I got back to California, but then—"

"But then what, Jon?"

"Remember when I told you Tommy wanted me to propose to Anna on the way to her movie premier?"

"That's what you said."

"When I told him I was going to end the charade, he decided to take things into his own hands. The day I flew back, he had an engagement ring delivered to her with a proposal I'm supposed to have written. He staged it all. When the plane landed, and the media was there, I felt trapped. How was I supposed to tell her in front of all those cameras that the proposal wasn't real?"

"You could have found a way."

"You're right, and I've spent every minute since thinking about what I should have done. But I did break it off the next day and Tommy's next."

"That's nice, Jon. But I don't see what any of this has to do with me."

"I want you to fly back to California with me. I want to pick up where we left off."

Tarin remained silent.

"I've tried to put you out of my mind, but I can't. After the circus at the airport, I was ready to give up. I didn't see how you could ever forgive me for the mess I'd created. But Nick told me if I care for you as much as I say I do, I need to put up a fight. He told me I might not have any chance of making it up to you, but that I had to try." Jon took a step back and continued as though he was afraid to stop. "He was right. I've spent the last seven or eight years of my life going from place to place and from one meaningless relationship to the next. But you changed all that."

He stepped forward and lifted her chin to look into her eyes. "I need you in my life. Please come to California with me. Say yes this time."

"What makes you think you can walk in unannounced and sweep me off my feet after what you did?" She looked toward the stone tile at her feet before meeting his gaze. "Jon—"

He silenced her objections with a kiss. Then, slowly pulling away, he brushed her cheek with his hand. "I've hired two drivers. One will take us to your house while the other will follow in your car. That means we can celebrate all night if we want."

"You betrayed me, Jon. The last thing I should do is let you back into my life."

He did nothing to convince her otherwise. "I know that."

"I hate you, Jonathan Parker."

He smiled. "No, you don't."

She looked away, realizing she couldn't deny her feelings for this man. "There's one thing I need to know. My boss Maury doesn't come cheap. Just what do you owe him for the part he played in this plot of yours?"

"Not much. All he wants is a trip on Tommy's jet to take his wife somewhere warm and exotic." He pulled Tarin close, holding her so tight she felt as though her breath had been taken away.

"After dinner, may I have the first dance, Ms. MacGyver?"

"This is all wrong, Jon, but I can't say no," she said quietly, feeling a bit like Cinderella and wondering if this night was just a dream.

JON AND TARIN SAT talking at a small table tucked away in the corner, unaware of anything taking place around them. In another part of the ballroom, most of the banquet staff sat at tables with coats buttoned and zipped, waiting for the last guests to call it a night. The cleaning crew was already hard at work filling carts and trays with dirty dishes and abandoned glasses.

Startled by the sound of a loud commercial vacuum, Tarin realized they were almost alone in the ballroom. Smiling, she surveyed the scene. "You know what? I've closed bars before, but never a charity gala. Maybe we should think about going home."

"Good call." He stood, reaching for the tuxedo jacket on the back of his chair. "The drivers should be waiting outside. I don't suppose you remember where you parked your car."

"Details, it's always details with you, isn't it? But you're right. There was valet parking, and I don't have a clue where my car or my keys are," she admitted.

"Well, the crowd's gone and the place is down to a skeleton crew of employees, so it shouldn't be hard to find." He stopped and smiled. "You did drive the car, didn't you? Please tell me you didn't drive the pickup while wearing an evening gown."

Her poke toward him missed and she couldn't help but laugh. "No. Given the opportunity even mountain girls are capable of showing a little class."

"Did you wear a coat?" he asked.

"No."

"I didn't either, which is good since the coat check is locked tighter than a drum." He opened one of the heavy front doors and was greeted by two drivers leaning on a black limo at the curb.

"Good evening, Mr. Parker. Are you ready to leave, sir?" the older of the two asked.

"We are, but we'll need to find Ms. MacGyver's car, which might mean a trip or two around the parking lot. She can't seem to remember where the valet might have parked it."

"That shouldn't be a problem, sir. The staff gave us her keys before they left. If you'd like to get in," the driver offered Tarin with a flourish of his hand.

Jon's assessment of the situation was correct. Due to the hour— the clock was striking one o'clock—parked vehicles were few and far between. It wasn't hard to spot the distinctive profile of her gray Audi.

Jon leaned toward the driver. "You'll have to excuse her. Tarin normally drives a truck and is rather protective of the car."

The older man laughed. "Don't worry, Ms. MacGyver. I drive the speed limit, and we'll be sure my partner stays behind us all the way to Chasm Falls."

Once on the interstate, Tarin nestled against Jon and he rested his arm around her shoulders.

"This has been an incredible night," she whispered.

"What makes you say that?" he asked, caressing her fingers.

"I couldn't take my eyes off the people with their diamonds and beautiful clothes. It was so easy imagining being one of them instead of someone on the outside looking in." She stopped to look up at him. "Promise not to laugh?"

"I promise."

She bit her lower lip. "I imagined myself being whisked into the room by a very handsome man and then dancing the night away in his arms." She paused. "My dream came true."

Without a word, he lowered her to the leather seat and moved closer. Tarin began to feel a warm, tingling sensation sweeping through her body.

"Jon, I can't do this here."

"What's wrong with here and now?" he asked "The driver can't see anything."

"Because I'm still trying to understand what's happening between us. I shouldn't forgive you."

Tracing her thigh with his fingertips, he smothered her words with a kiss. "No, you probably shouldn't." Then, sitting up and repositioning Tarin snugly under his arm, he reassured her. "For you, I can wait."

The pair traveled in silence most of the way to Chasm Falls and she fell asleep with her head resting on his lap. Watching Tarin, he marveled at her innocence and wondered how in the world he had been blessed to find her not once, but twice.

"YOU CAN PUT THIS in the living room for now," Jon told the driver who was lifting the suitcase from the trunk of the limousine.

It was nearly three thirty in the morning, and Tarin was still asleep in the car.

"Do you need help getting her inside, sir?"

"No, we'll be okay. Just give me a minute." Jon placed his hand on her shoulder. "Hey, you, we're home and it's time to wake up."

As Tarin stirred and opened her eyes, Jon eased her into a sitting position before helping her out of the car. "Did I turn into a pumpkin on the way?" she asked, covering a yawn, and reaching for her shoes and beaded bag tucked away on the floorboard.

"Miss, here are the keys to your car. Have a good evening—but at this hour, it would be more appropriate to wish you a good day."

With that, the drivers were on their way back to Denver.

Jon helped her into the house, pausing once they were inside the front door. "I know where the guest room is," his words more a question than a statement.

Tarin glanced toward the loft and her bedroom. Then she reached for his hand and led him upstairs.

CHAPTER 18

—

No Forgiveness

JON WATCHED TARIN PUT THE LAST OF THE DISHES IN the dishwasher. "What's on the agenda today?" he asked.
"After last night, as little as possible. I like the idea of staying here and doing absolutely nothing except taking a lengthy nap."

"That can be arranged." He settled into the recliner with the television remote and began scanning the schedule. "What if I start a fire and we watch a movie or two? You can even pick *Casablanca* if you'd like."

Tarin sat on his lap. "If I'd known that was an option, I wouldn't have gotten dressed today."

He grinned mischievously, reaching for her shirt. "It's not too late for me to take care of that."

She jumped from the chair and struggled to keep Jon from tickling her. "Keep your hands to yourself!"

He stood and started for the deck. "Okay, be that way. I'll get the firewood. You sit here and relax."

"Yes, sir."

Jon had only been gone a minute when there was a knock on the front door. "Anybody here?" Jake called, sticking his head inside.

"Come on in," Tarin answered, standing to greet him. "I forgot you were coming over this morning."

Just then Jon returned with an armful of wood. "Did I hear Jake?"

Tarin's brother froze at the sound of Jon's voice, then moved toward him like a predator ready to pounce on its prey. "What the hell are you doing here, Parker?" His fist was raised. "Get out and leave my sister alone!"

Jake's strike was on target, knocking Jon back against the dining room table. The firewood he was carrying crashed to the floor and he stumbled under the force of the blow.

Tarin was quick to stand between them, but Jake moved forward to attack again.

"Jake—please stop! You don't know what you're doing!" She could see the anger seething on her brother's face. "Calm down." She tried to sound reassuring. "Give Jon a chance to explain."

"Give me one reason why I should."

She put her hand on Jake's arm. "Because I'm asking you to. It's okay. The whole thing was a mistake." She looked toward Jon, who was dazed and trying to stand up. "We're working through it."

Jake cupped his fist with his other hand and flexed his fingers. "Breaking my sister's heart and then showing up on her doorstep a couple months later is just a mistake? Fuck that."

Tarin fought to restrain him.

Jon got up from his knees. "I understand how you feel, Jake, but can we talk about it?"

Jake glared at Tarin before turning to walk away. "I can't believe you'd let this jerk back into your life after what he did to you." He looked back at Jon, "You know—those nights at the bar—I defended you when Alex talked about how rich people come from the coast and believe they're entitled somehow. I thought you were different. But you're not. I'm out of here."

Jon let out a huge sigh of relief when he heard the door slam. "Tarin, he's right—I deserve all his anger. He was on the jet that day when I promised I was going to break up with Anna."

"But Jake didn't give you a chance to tell him what really happened."

"No—but it's still my fault. I should have seen it coming. He has every right to feel the way he does and your friends will have the same reaction. I'm not quite sure how I can regain their trust or if it's even possible." When Jon dropped onto the couch, Finn jumped up beside him.

Tarin sat down next to them both, resting her head against Jon's shoulder. "He doesn't want to see me get hurt again. Have faith. They'll come around—just give it time."

Finn's ears perked up and he dashed to the door.

"Now, who's here?" Tarin popped up to check and found Mike Wilson waiting outside.

"I heard you were back in town, Jon," Mike announced as he entered the house.

"News travels fast."

"Not really. I happened to pass Jake on my way here. He flagged me down and you need to know, I've never seen him this angry."

"All things considered, I can't say that I blame him."

Mike's concern turned to Tarin. "What the hell? This guy has a gorgeous fiancée stashed away in LA and you're letting him hang out here with you? Do you really want to settle for being the other woman in his life?"

Jon moved to her side. "Tarin's the only woman I care about, Mike."

"You need to believe Jon—I do. It's a long story, but he broke off the staged engagement the day after the airport fiasco. He's telling the truth," Tarin pleaded.

"After all he's done, you're buying into that, Tarin?" Mike turned to Jon. "I hope you're ready to give me a complete explanation of what you were thinking with that circus you put us through. Watch your step, Parker. Hurt her again and you'll be sorry you ever met me. I've got my doubts, but I'm willing to abide by Tarin's wishes and give you a second chance. Just don't think you'll be off the hook with anybody else. You've got a lot of convincing to do."

"Trust me, I understand completely."

The silence that followed was broken when Mike continued with reluctance, "Okay. But remember, I'll be watching every move you make; and this discussion is far from over. Now I think I need a beer or a stiff drink. Who else wants one?" When he started toward the kitchen, Mike almost tripped over the firewood on the dining room floor. "What happened here? It looks like there's been an earthquake."

Jon leaned over to pick up the wood and carried it to the fireplace. "Jake shared his dislike for me a little while ago. He packs a pretty good punch." After lighting a fire starter, Jon called toward Mike, "I hate to ask this, but have you had any leads regarding Tarin's break-in?"

"Trying to keep the conversation away from you and that actress, are you?" Mike reentered the living room and handed Jon a bottle of craft beer. He shook his head. "Sorry. But at least Tarin finally listened and is having a security system installed. She's even adding cameras above each of the doors and on the dock."

Jon remained skeptical. "But will she use them?"

Mike shrugged. "That remains to be seen. She better."

"Is the system hard to set up?"

"No. Scott helped her pick it out. It's one of the easiest to operate and the most dependable on the market. There's even a keychain remote to turn it on and off. All she needs to do is get into the habit of using it." He paused for a moment. "Please keep after her. I wish it wasn't true, but even though it's unlikely after all this time, it's possible the guy could come back, and we still don't know what he was after."

"Why do I get the feeling you're talking about me?" Tarin announced, setting a platter of sausage, cheese, crackers, and chips on the coffee table.

The two men became quiet under her scrutiny, looking back and forth between each other.

Mike put his arm around her shoulders. "We care about you, Mac. That's all."

"Thanks, guys, but I'm fine. Now, who's hungry? Football starts in less than an hour if you care to watch."

Jon couldn't hide his concern or his frustration.

"I don't know why you're not more worried, Tarin. This is serious stuff. Someone has been targeting you, and the police can't find a way to snare the creep. I don't mean to alarm you, but what if one of these times stealing things isn't enough? What if he takes you or worse—"

Jon paused and pleaded, "I want you to come to California where you'll be safe."

She tried to reassure him. "I know you're worried and while I might not show it, I am, too. But you need to remember that Mike and Scott are keeping an eye on the house and soon I'll even have that security system. Whoever this man is, if he's around he's bound to make a mistake and they'll catch him."

Mike shook his head. "We're still investigating the case, but like you said, the trail's gotten pretty cold."

Jon hesitated and then asked what was really on his mind. "What's Alex been up to?"

Tarin was quick to answer. "You mean how's he been doing? He and Rachel are back together, and he found a security job in Granby. Things seem to be looking up."

"That's good. I'm glad things are beginning to go his way." Jon paused to turn on the television. "Now—who's playing this afternoon?"

"Denver and the LA Chargers." Mike grinned. "Ten bucks says the Broncos will win by at least two touchdowns."

"You're on, Officer Wilson. Consider it a bet—one I hope you're prepared to lose."

TARIN SPENT MOST OF the next day doing everything necessary to prepare for a vacation. She called Maury Levine, her boss at *The Denver News*, and received both his permission and his blessing to take time off. But before the conversation was over, her long-time colleague teased her without mercy.

The sixty-something editor had hired Tarin when she returned to Colorado from the East Coast to take care of her grandfather. Short and balding with a nose resembling nothing less than a ski jump, Maury was an old-school journalist who came across to most of his staff as uncompromising and demanding. But to Tarin he was simply a big teddy bear at heart. A special bond had grown between them almost instantaneously.

"Let me get this straight," he mocked. "You met this guy during a robbery. A couple days later you invite him to stay at your house. Then he gets engaged to someone else right under your nose, and now you're flying off to move in with him? What's come over my always predictable, never impulsive little Tarin?"

"You've got it all wrong. I'm not moving in with him, Maury. I'll be back in a few weeks and don't worry, you can continue to believe I'll live out my days as an old maid." Speaking the words out loud, she realized her decision was completely out of character. And by making it, she was happier than she could remember being in a very long time. Tarin couldn't quite mask her excitement. "Did I tell you we'll be flying in a private jet?"

"A private jet? My protégé is moving up in the world like I always knew she would. Remind Jon that he still owes me a trip for getting you to that gala." Then Maury became much more serious. "Hey, kiddo. If you like this guy, it's good enough for me. Go have a great time in California. But I want you to know you'll find a pile of work waiting when you get back. And there's that big assignment coming up that we need to talk about."

"Thanks for the warning, Maury." The affection she felt for the man who was more like a father than an employer was evident in her voice. "I'll miss you."

"Right. Like there's a chance I'd ever believe that. But thanks for humoring an old man." He was grinning broadly. "I'll talk with you soon. Be good, darlin'."

TARIN WAS FORCED TO complete the arduous task of packing with Jon lying on her bed and approving or disapproving each garment she pulled from the closet. Eventually tiring of the exercise, he pulled her down next to him and closed the half-filled suitcase.

"I've got an idea. What if I just take you shopping when we get there?"

She teased him with a kiss before standing. "No, there won't be time. You, Mr. Parker, will be in the studio creating an album so you can rid yourself of Tommy once and for all."

Finally satisfied she could clothe herself for almost any occasion, Tarin zipped the suitcase and stood it in the corner of the room. Jon had dozed off and she smiled, sitting down next to him on the edge of the bed.

"Hey, you." She nudged his shoulder. "Tomorrow's a big day. I was going to suggest we go to the Sip 'n Strike for a while tonight, but I'm not ready to face Jake. I think I'll go to bed early. What about you?"

He yawned and stretched before sitting up. "I will too. But packing is hard work. I think I need to take a shower first." He looked at her with a twinkle in his eye. "Care to join me?"

She said nothing, allowing the pillow she tossed in his direction to provide her response to the invitation.

Smiling, he headed toward the master bath. "You can't blame a guy for trying. I'll be back in a few minutes."

CHAPTER 19

A New Beginning

OVERCOME WITH ANTICIPATION, TARIN PEERED through the window with the Pacific Ocean extending as far as her eyes could see. Crowding the shoreline, the San Diego skyline came into full view. Within minutes the jet had skimmed the city's downtown business district to land at Lindbergh Field.

Jon watched the plane taxi to the terminal used by charter flights and private aircraft. "Nick is on time."

Following Jon's eyes, Tarin noticed a man waiting on a wood bench outside the one-story building at the far end of the busy airport. He was dressed in khaki pants and a navy golf shirt. As the whirring jet engines slowed to a stop, Nick Reynolds stood, ran his fingers through his short, spiky blonde hair, and started walking toward them. The stairs had barely touched the ground when he hopped on board.

"Jon, where the hell have you been? Tommy is on the verge of a nervous breakdown and so far, the album sounds like a train wreck. You—"

Nick had no idea anyone was sitting in the seat opposite Jon, and he looked past her once before taking a surprised second look. When their eyes finally met, Tarin welcomed him with a bright smile. "You must be Nick. I've heard a lot about you."

Dumbfounded, Nick stood in the aisle for a moment before speaking. "If you're who I think you are, I've heard a lot about you, too."

"Stop stuttering, Nick. I'd like you to meet Tarin MacGyver. She'll be spending a few weeks with me. Actually, with both of us. I'm going to need your help showing her around until she gets acclimated."

"What's Tommy going to say?"

"I don't really care. That's something he'll need to come to terms with."

Nick shook his head and dropped onto one of the leather seats. "Okay. I admit it. I'm confused. I mean, I'm glad you're here, Tarin. But how did Jon pull this off? The last time I heard, you weren't even accepting his calls."

Jon stood and put a reassuring hand on his shoulder. "It might be easier if we talk while we drive." Walking to the flight deck, Jon leaned into the cabin where the two pilots were busy finishing their flight logs. "Thanks, guys. We'll get the luggage and be out of your way in a few minutes." He turned back toward his friend. "What car did you bring?"

"Not the two-seater if that's what's worrying you. I wasn't sure how much stuff you had along with you. It never crossed my mind the baggage would include a woman." He was still shaking his head. "But to tell the truth, after all these years, why should anything you do surprise me? Anyway, I've got the SUV. It'll be crowded," he announced while counting the number of suitcases piled on the pavement, "but I think we can make it. Barely."

Nick was brought up to speed within minutes of leaving the city behind. And while the two compared notes in the front seat, Tarin was content to watch the ocean and gaze at the lavish homes and beaches while they traveled through La Jolla.

"Now I understand why Tommy's been such a force to be reckoned with the past week or so." Nick issued a warning, "Be prepared. Because of the delay you created getting this project off the ground, he's positioned everybody against you. Don't expect the guys to respond right away to anything we suggest. Drew's having the band work on some rather unorthodox arrangements."

"I'm ready to do battle first thing tomorrow morning. Are we using the same disgusting warehouse for rehearsals?"

"None other. It's hot, dirty, and nasty just like always."

Tarin's eyes widened when Nick turned into a driveway leading toward a large, modern home poised on a low rock cliff next to the ocean. Two stories of tan stucco and glass were visible above ground level. She could only imagine the views from the veranda overlooking the Pacific. Gray marble and polished steel accented the art deco-style front entry. An attached three-car garage angled off to the right of the main house.

Sitting almost sideways with his arm resting on the back of the front seat, Jon turned to Tarin with uncertainty when they pulled into the semicircular drive. "Well, what do you think?"

"It's beautiful," she answered with complete awe. "I can't wait to stand outside and listen to waves crashing on the beach."

By that time, Nick was already unloading suitcases.

Helping her out of the car, Jon put his arm around her shoulders. "Know what? I'm sharing my home with someone for the first time and I like the way it feels."

He pushed a code into the keypad next to the door while Nick struggled with three of the overloaded bags on the sidewalk behind them. "I feel like a bellhop," he muttered under his breath.

"I hope you're not expecting a tip, my friend." Jon laughed, pushed open the front door, and turned on a light in the foyer.

A broad smile crossed his face. "Welcome to California."

THAT EVENING TARIN WATCHED Jon pull out of the driveway. He was meeting with the rest of the band at the warehouse to set a timetable for the new album. His apprehension was real. "I'm not sure how much Tommy has poisoned them against me," he said before leaving.

She turned to look across the sunken living room toward the ocean. The expansive sliding doors leading to the veranda were open, and she could feel both the warm sea breeze and smell the fresh salt air. She stepped down and walked toward the room's focal point: a twenty-foot stainless-steel wall housing a fireplace and a large built-in television. Surprisingly, she found the stark contrast between her own log home and Jon's ultra-modern one more than intriguing. The cool gray tone of the leather couches and the brushed steel found throughout the structure seemed appropriate for Jon. She could imagine him sitting in the living room playing his guitar with friends while Nick sat at the grand piano creating songs for the next project.

Unlike her house, which was overflowing with memorabilia, photographs, and books, Jon's home contained just a few carefully placed accents and a coffee table book she was pretty sure he had never opened. Tarin smiled. The perfection was clearly the result of a well-paid professional designer.

But there was one item she knew belonged to him—a colorful Wurlitzer jukebox that looked out of place, yet strangely at home in one corner of the room. A closer examination proved it was a classic reproduction outfitted with a CD player, USB ports, and Tarin assumed, powerful speakers. The jukebox might fall into her plans for the evening if she decided to follow through with them. Jon's decision to stand up to Tommy by breaking off the phony relationship with Anna Haines had been a big step. She wanted him to know how much that move meant to her.

Tarin walked to the veranda and closed her eyes after settling onto a lounge chair overlooking the ocean. Jon had told her the drive to the warehouse would take at least an hour, so allowing for the meeting and return trip, he didn't plan to be back much before midnight. This time it was Tarin who found herself with thinking to do.

A half hour or so later she gathered her thoughts, walked back into the house, and mounted the steps leading to the upper level. Gold and platinum record albums lined the stairwell, as did black and white concert photos of the band Motive. At the top of the stairs, she found herself facing the master bedroom. Again, the furnishings were contemporary, but at least Jon's presence was evident in this room. A pair of well-worn jeans and a random T-shirt were draped over a chair. Several pairs of mismatched shoes were tucked under a table, and a collection of Billboard magazines was stacked haphazardly on a bench at the foot of his bed. Tarin smiled and closed a dresser drawer that had been left a bit ajar.

Then she discovered the doorway leading to the master bath. Stepping into the room, she couldn't hide her amazement at the sunken six-foot square marble jetted tub. An immense skylight illuminated the space with the glow from an almost full moon suspended in the California sky. There was a steam unit in one corner, and in another an oversized shower encased in glass.

Grabbing the towel and terrycloth robe Jon had found for her before he left, Tarin slipped out of her clothes and into the shower.

Moments after lavishing under the hot, steamy water, she tied the belt of the oversized robe and pondered what to wear. Jon didn't seem the type to choose lavish, lacy lingerie, and that was fortunate because she hadn't brought any.

Opening the door to his walk-in closet, she pushed the garments along the closet rod one by one. Finally, her eyes landed on a long-sleeve Nautica shirt. The fabric was off-white, featuring a gray and black windowpane plaid. She held the garment against her body and looked at herself critically in the mirror.

Slipping her arms into the sleeves and pulling the shirt over her shoulders, she found the tails hit at midthigh. The curves of the shirt at the sides were higher and revealed just a glimpse of the panties she wore underneath. Tarin smiled at her reflection. While it might have been a man's shirt, it was obvious a woman was wearing it.

THE GARAGE DOOR BOUNCED slightly when it met the concrete floor. Once inside the house, Jon could smell the unmistakable fragrance of candles burning.

"Tarin, are you still awake?" he whispered.

Walking into the dimly lit living room, he found her snuggled on one of the couches with a glass of wine in her hand. In addition to flickering candles, there were flames in the fireplace, and he could hear soft music coming from the jukebox.

He sat down and brushed her cheek with a kiss. "You seem to be making a habit of this. What are you up to, my lady?" he asked, masking his curiosity.

"Just waiting for you."

He sat back for a moment, looking at her with a puzzled look. "Is that my shirt?"

"Might be," Tarin teased. She started to unbutton it. "I'm sorry. I can give it back—"

Jon put his hand over hers. "Are you making a move on me?"

"Maybe." Tarin hesitated. "But first, I want to know how things went."

He held her in his arms. "Surprisingly well. Nick was there, too, and by the end of the night, I think we're finally back on the same page."

While he talked, Tarin toyed with the button at the waist of his jeans.

"If I didn't know better, I'd think you have something in mind." Jon moved his hand to rest lightly on the front of the thong that taunted him from under the tails of the shirt.

"Who needs to go upstairs?" Tarin whispered. "As someone once told me, we have candles, wine, an inviting fire, and romantic music right here."

"True," Jon answered while putting her glass on the coffee table and lowering her onto the cushions of the couch.

"It's too bad you have to be up early tomorrow," she teased. "I might keep you up all night."

"Try me," he whispered into her ear.

CHAPTER 20

The Warehouse

SOAKING UP THE SOUTHERN CALIFORNIA SUN while relaxing on the veranda, Tarin put her cell phone on a side table after checking the time. Nick would pick her up in about an hour and a half, then they would drive to the warehouse in Los Angeles that Motive was using for rehearsals. She took a last look at the surf crashing on the beach, reluctantly grabbed her cover-up, and started toward the shower.

An hour later, dressed and waiting for Nick, Tarin couldn't help but think about the events of the day before. First, being whisked away on a private jet, meeting Nick, and then pulling up in front of Jon's beach house had all been surreal experiences for this smalltown girl. Then there was the magical night that followed.

Reentering the house, she heard a car pull into the driveway. Seconds later, there was a knock on the door. "Just a minute, Nick!" she called. Straightening her blouse one final time, she greeted Jon's best friend and chauffeur for the day.

When the door opened, she saw Nick stop in his tracks and the insecurity she felt became real once again. It was evident in her voice. "What's wrong?"

"Ah, nothing really," he said, admiring her appearance. Dressed in slim-cut jeans, an ivory silk blouse trimmed in navy, and wearing heels, she looked both casual yet stylish. The fact the neckline bordered upon being revealing added to the allure. "Under normal circumstances, there wouldn't be a problem. It's just that you've never met the guys in Jon's band."

"What does that have to do with it?"

He fingered his chin, his emerald-green eyes sparkling. "Well, let me put it this way. When they're rehearsing, I don't think I've ever seen them in anything other than torn jeans and T-shirts. Sweaty ones at that."

Tarin picked up the small leather backpack serving as her purse, and he ushered her out the door. "I'll let you draw your own conclusions. As for your attire, it's time a little class entered their lives."

SHORTLY AFTER ONE O'CLOCK, Nick parked the car next to the converted warehouse Motive had rented. She fought the urge to cover her ears when they entered the dim, dusty building. A thin, ghostly trail of cigarette smoke hovered in the air overhead.

Nick laughed, noting the startled look on her face. Leaning toward Tarin's ear, he shouted, "Don't worry—you'll get used to it."

"Do I want to?" She shook her head. "Is it always this loud?"

He responded with a noncommittal shrug. "I guess you're not a rocker, are you? Come on."

Suddenly upon cue from a voice in the darkness, the music came to an abrupt halt.

"Drew, see what you can come up with for the bass part. Whatever you're doing now isn't working with the melody line. The timing's off."

"There was a melody?" Tarin whispered, searching for the origin of the voice. She watched as a short, rotund man holding a clipboard made his way from the opposite corner of the room. His critical comments continued nonstop as he approached the four musicians on the makeshift stage.

Tarin was scanning the room in hopes of finding Jon when a familiar voice exploded from another part of the building. "Reynolds, I should have known you'd show up when the work was almost done."

Nick smiled and turned toward Jon. "Give me a break, Parker. There was no need to get here any sooner. I knew we'd have to start everything all over again anyway."

The scene playing out in front of Tarin was just like Nick had predicted. Each of the musicians was outfitted in torn jeans and a perspiration-drenched T-shirt. Even Jon's white shirt clung tightly to his torso—the result of a long morning's work in a building with poor ventilation. He used its hem to wipe his brow and then took hold of her elbow. "Come on. It's time to meet the new men in your life."

During the hours that followed, Tarin sat alone on a dated and worn plaid couch tucked into a corner near the stage. She watched Nick and Jon walk through fifteen or sixteen songs with the band. At some point, they would weed out the dozen or so tracks that would comprise the final album from this material. Much to her pleasure, most of the songs were quite unlike the loud, unrelenting rock and roll she had heard upon entering the building. She was also pleased to discover Jon's emotion-laden voice sounded exactly like it did in the songs she'd loaded onto her playlist.

Watching Nick work at the piano while Jon orchestrated the musicians on stage, she realized she might like being part of this adventure after all.

Four hours had flown by before Tarin had a chance to think about the time.

She sat down on the piano bench next to Nick and hesitated before speaking. "I'm new to all this, but do you think it would sound better if Jon changed the line 'You should have never called me' to 'You never should have called me?' I'm having a hard time understanding what he's singing. It's coming out like a mushy 'shoulda.' Does that make any sense?"

He nodded. "Good point. I like your revision." Hearing a lull in the music, Nick grinned and called toward the stage. "Hey, Jon. You may have found a natural songwriter in this beautiful lady. You better watch out—I plan to steal her away when you're not looking."

"I wouldn't try it," Jon shot back.

Tarin turned at the sound of a steel door slamming at the back of the warehouse. She saw an overweight, balding man wearing a scowl walking toward them. "Who's that?" she asked.

Nick leaned toward her ear. "Watch your backside. That, my dear, is the infamous Tommy Wyndham."

The disgruntled manager wasted no time in finding Jon. "Nice to see you could make it."

He jumped down from the stage to face Tommy. "Watch your attitude. I told you I'd be here."

"Right." Tommy glanced around the room. "Joel told me there was an extra passenger on the plane. So where is she?"

Jon reached for his manager's arm. "Leave her alone, Tommy."

Pulling away from his grasp, Tommy smirked. "Don't worry, Jon. I just want to welcome the little lady to LA. Now, where is she?"

A confident voice sounded from behind them, "You must be Tommy." She extended her hand and smiled. "Hi, I'm Tarin MacGyver. It's nice to finally meet the man I've heard so much about."

Tommy gripped her hand much longer than necessary. "All good, I'm sure." He turned toward Nick, who was still seated at the piano. "So, Nick. You're the producer of this shindig. How's it going?"

Jon moved to Tarin's side. "Stay away from him whenever possible. Promise?"

"I can take care of myself." She studied Tommy's face as he leaned against the piano and continued his conversation with Nick. The man's thinning black hair had been swept into a classic comb-over in a failed attempt to disguise the large bald spot on the top of his head. The angles of his jaw and cheekbones would have been quite strong were it not for the extra weight that rounded them. With its fleshy jowls, his face could have passed for that of a Prohibition-era mobster.

Jon put his hands on her shoulders. "Just let it go. He'll be out of our lives soon enough."

She reached toward his face to push a strand of hair behind his ear, "Okay. If that's what you want. But I don't trust the man and like him even less."

"Now, I'm going to get back to work so we can go home."

Jon hopped back onto the stage and Tarin watched the pompous, overweight man who had manipulated Jon for so many years. At that moment, she set a goal for herself. She would find a way to expose Tommy Wyndham, no matter what that meant she had to do.

CHAPTER 21

Getting to Know the Landscape

NICK LEANED BACK AND BALANCED HIS CHAIR precariously on two legs. "Are you getting used to the noise?" he asked with a grin.

Tarin returned the smile, still doodling in a notebook on her lap. "I'm either getting used to it or going deaf. Either way, it sounds better than it did yesterday." She picked up her chair and moved it closer to him. "But I am embarrassed. I'm still not sure who is who."

"In the band, you mean?"

She nodded.

"Okay. Over there on the left we've got Drew Michaels on bass guitar. He's the one with the Rasta hair. But he doesn't have any island background, so go figure. Quinn O'Brien is at the back of the stage banging on the drums. He's the band's all-time drama queen. Jimmy Arthur plays the keyboards. He's from New Jersey like Jon and me, but we didn't meet until we ran into each other out here. Finally, there's Bo Jensen. His real name is Robert Timothy Jensen III. But if you value your life, don't call him Bodacious. Of course, we refer to him that way whenever we can, but few people are allowed to get away with it." Nick glanced at Tarin, who was taking notes in her book. "Does that help?"

"I think so. What else can you tell me so I can carry on an intelligent conversation with them? Are they married?"

"Jimmy is. He and his wife have a three-year-old son. The rest of the guys continue to be footloose and fancy-free. Now that I think about it, Quinn was married to a swimsuit model once, but his life was even more complicated than hers, so it didn't last long."

"What about you, Nick?"

He was spared from answering when Jon approached with a towel draped around his neck. "What's going on over here?"

"You might say we're going to school. The class is called Band Mates 101. Tarin's trying to put names with faces."

Jon straddled the seat of a folding chair, resting his forearms on the seatback. "Just wait until we're in the studio. That's when it gets really confusing. We've got sound techs, engineers, label execs, and sometimes even the media."

"Why didn't you start working on the album there instead of in this—"

Jon laughed. "Go ahead and call it as you see it. This place is a dump. But studio time is pricey. Even if you're a successful band, you need to get the basics down and find a direction before you start putting down the final tracks." He looked over at Nick. "Plus, once you get into the studio you need a full-time producer, and the producer expects to get paid. Right now, Nick's just along for the ride, but once we get serious, that's his role. And if you want to know the truth, this guy doesn't come cheap."

"And worth every penny, I might add," Nick shot back.

"Parker! Where the hell are you? How long can a pee break take? You're holding things up."

Jon leaned toward Tarin. "That's Ross. He's a pain in the ass, but he does his best to keep us on task." He got up and threw the towel toward her. "Gotta go."

SHE WAS REACHING FOR a can of Diet Coke in the cooler when Tarin felt a firm hand on her shoulder. "I see you came back for more."

She turned to find Tommy Wyndham standing behind her.

"And why wouldn't I?"

"Oh, I don't know. I thought you might think all this is a little dirty and disgusting. It does get rather hot in this building. Smells like stale beer, sweat, and cigarettes. The acoustics aren't the best, either."

"But the company's good," Nick interjected. "How could she turn down an opportunity to spend time with an accomplished songwriter like me?"

Tommy started toward the stage. "It's getting a little deep in here, Reynolds."

"When was the last time you won a Grammy, Wyndham?" Nick called after him.

Tommy didn't look back, opting instead to lift his hand in the air and extend his middle finger toward Nick.

"Nice man," Tarin said under her breath. But the brief conversation had piqued her curiosity. "You really did win a Grammy, didn't you?"

He nodded. "Once. 'Thinking of You' won Song of the Year not long after we got to California. Call it beginner's luck. Who knows? Maybe I'll win a few more along the way. I've discovered awards make excellent bookends and doorstops."

"You can make light of it, but I'm impressed." She paused when he picked up a stack of music and walked to the piano.

"On another subject, has Tommy always behaved this way?"

Nick looked concerned. "Has he been bothering you? We won't let him get away with it if he's tried to pull anything."

She shook her head. "No, not exactly, but he's so arrogant, rude, and despicable."

"Honestly, from what people tell me, he was a decent guy before his wife left him about twenty years ago. Somewhere I saw a photo of him when he was in his late thirties. He was a very handsome man back then. Slim. Trim. He even had a head of hair."

"How old do you think he is now?"

Nick shrugged. "Late fifties, maybe."

"Any idea why his wife left?"

"I've been told she ran off with some guy in a band Tommy had under contract. That could be why he's so tough on the musicians he's managed since then. He's trying to get back at them for stealing his wife."

She smiled. "I'm glad you didn't get involved with him."

He returned the smile. "There was no need to, thank god."

Tarin hesitated once again. "Nick, could I ask you another question?"

He nodded. "Shoot."

"My mom loved to write poetry. I never really got the hang of it, but I've kept trying and have been tinkering with song lyrics. Sometime could I show you a few things I've written? I've got a notebook filled with song ideas, but I've never shared them with anyone. Writing news releases and articles is a snap. Lyrics I'm not so sure about."

"Sure. Maybe we could look at them tomorrow. Trust me—we'll both need a break from this chaos by then."

CHAPTER 22

Ready to Record

AFTER TWO LONG WEEKS OF DIRTY, PERSPIRATION-filled days in the warehouse, it was finally time for Motive to move into the recording studio.

"Are you ready for the next phase? This is where the fun begins." Nick grinned, pushing open the heavy glass door leading to the studio's sunny reception area. "Hey, Roxanne!" He crossed the room to give the receptionist a quick hug. "I'm guessing they're in Studio One?"

"Just like always, Nick. I think they're almost done miking the drums."

He glanced at his watch. "You must be kidding. They can't be almost finished. It's only ten o'clock, and this is Quinn the Particular we're talking about."

Roxanne smiled. "Have you forgotten they started setting up the drums two days ago?"

"That explains it." He put his arm around Tarin's waist and ushered her toward the counter. "Rox, this is Jon's friend, Tarin. She thinks she wants to sit in on the madness."

"Nice to meet you. But whatever you do, don't listen to this guy. We only keep him around because he's cute, not because he has any talent."

Nick attempted to look disgruntled, putting a fist to his chest. "Ah, your disrespect is a blow to the heart. But at least you admit I'm cute."

He sent a quick grin in Roxanne's direction. "Come on, let's see if we can find Jon."

Traveling through a small kitchen and into the hallway leading to the studio, Tarin noted the décor was much more subtle than the reception area. The walls were either wainscoted with warm hardwoods, painted rich earth tones, or a combination of both. The ceilings echoed the wood treatment, and subdued spotlighting created a calm, soothing atmosphere.

"Let's check the control room first." He took her hand and opened a solid wood door. Inside the spacious room, an engineer was working at one of the console's computers. "Are they driving you crazy yet, Paul?"

The man spun around in his chair and shook his head. "Why do you even bother to ask? These guys always drive me insane. No matter how many times we work together, there's always a new wrinkle." He stood when he saw Tarin enter the room. "And who is this? Have you been holding out on us, Nick?"

"I wish. This is Jon's friend, Tarin MacGyver. Tarin, Paul Fisher." Nick peered through the tinted glass extending across the front wall into the adjacent studio. "Where is he anyway?"

Paul pointed toward the isolation room below them. "We've been trying to get the headphone mix right."

"What microphones did he decide to use this time?"

"They're experimenting with several different models. I think one is a Telefunken and another is a Neumann."

"Good choices. We'll just have to see which ones offer the best dynamics for each song. So—will we disturb anything if I take Tarin down to say hi?"

"You're the producer, Nick."

"Hey, that's right. I forgot. Come on, Mac. I'm the top dog on this project, so that means we can go anywhere we want, whenever we want."

"Mac?" she questioned.

"Yeah. As far as I'm concerned, you will now be referred to as Mac."

"But how did you know that's what my friends call me?"

"I didn't. Maybe the name just fits. Come on. Let's find that guy of yours." Seeing her begin to blush, he continued, "You need to remember I've known Jon a long time and can read his mind. As I see it, he's not letting go of you anytime soon, so you might as well get used to being linked with him."

Once in the studio, they were surrounded by a flurry of activity. Nick pointed toward the back corner of the room where the keyboardist was setting up near a grand piano on an elevated platform. At the opposite corner, a pair of sound techs continued to tweak the drummer's equipment. In the front of the room, another technician worked with the bass and lead guitars. L-shaped wood panels lined with soundproofing material delineated each area.

"Watch your step," Nick cautioned as they made their way through a maze of cords and cables to the vocalist's booth.

Jon was working with Max, the studio's senior engineer.

"I brought you a present," Nick proclaimed when he opened the door to the small soundproof room.

"Hey." Jon laid his headphones on the towel-covered podium, joined Tarin on the studio floor, and rested his arm on her shoulders. "Welcome to my world."

"Wow. This is unbelievable. I had no idea there was so much involved."

He turned to the engineer. "Max, can you give me a couple of minutes? Take a stab at keeping Nick out of trouble."

Jon took her hand. "What if we find you a seat in the control room? There you can watch what we're doing from the comfort of a leather couch. In an hour or so, we should be able to run through a few songs to get a base for our levels."

SITTING ON AN OVERSTUFFED black couch along the back wall, Tarin surveyed the unfamiliar surroundings. The colors in the control room were much like those found in the rest of the studio—deep earth tones with identical dim spotlights providing illumination. The higher-than-normal ceiling angled upward to about twelve feet, where it met a tinted glass wall extending the room's length. Above the console, the ceiling was constructed of richly stained tongue-and-groove planks. Overhead in the back half of the room, soundproofing material was covered with gray fabric. Black carpeting blanketed the floor, except for a rectangle of hardwood installed under the console.

The entire control room was elevated above the sound studio itself, allowing the engineers and others in the room to have a clear view of the activity below.

A forty-eight channel Neve control board stretched across the front of the room, with an angled wing on each side filled with computers and additional effects equipment.

"Want to take a look?" Paul asked.

Interested, Tarin eagerly sat next to him in front of the console. "What are all of these buttons and things for?"

"Let's start with the basics. Each of the musicians has his own track. I won't confuse you with the dials, but the sliders adjust and tweak the levels we're trying to set for each instrument or vocalist. Then we use the computer to do almost anything we want from compressing and adding effects to the vocals, to editing phrases from one take into another."

She pointed to a reel-to-reel recorder tucked away in a corner. "Do you still use tape?"

"Sometimes. You never know what kind of situation you're going to come up against. But to be honest, I just like having the machine around for old time's sake." He turned his chair toward the studio glass and flipped open a mic. "Hey, how's it going down there? Are we ready to try a sound check?"

Tarin stood and put a hand on Paul's shoulder. "Thanks for the short course. You have work to do which means I should get out of your way."

She had settled back onto the couch when a door opened on the other side of the room and Tommy Wyndham made his entrance. He nodded toward the engineer. "Paul. Nice to know we're finally working on this damn record." Then he turned his attention toward Tarin. "Imagine finding you here." Sitting down on the couch, he rested his hand on her knee as if they were old friends. "Are you enjoying yourself?"

Just as casually, she pushed his hand away. "Yes, I am. This is different from anything I've ever experienced. It's fascinating."

Tommy leaned back and smiled. "You know? You're to be commended. I don't need to tell you Jon's a good catch for someone like you."

"And what's that supposed to mean?"

He leaned closer. "I know your type," he whispered in her ear. "You're not the first to try and sink your hooks into him."

There was an unmistakable edge evident in Tarin's voice, even as she tried to maintain her composure. "Are you implying I have an ulterior motive when it comes to my friendship with Jon? You don't know anything about me, and you certainly don't know anything about the relationship we may or may not have."

Tommy grabbed her arm when she started to get up. "Sit back down. I'm sorry—you're right. But do you know how much of an inconvenience you caused by coming between Jon and Anna?"

She shook her head in disbelief. "Tell me something. Do you ever think about anything other than money and controlling people?"

His eyes pierced hers and there was no regret evident in his glare. "That's how I've gotten Jon and all my other clients where they are today, my dear."

"Back off, Tommy. Try being a gentleman for a change. Is everything okay, Tarin?" Nick closed the control room door behind him, his eyes moving back and forth between the two on the couch.

She smiled weakly, trying to hide the anger brewing in the pit of her stomach. "I'm fine, Nick. Mr. Wyndham was simply trying to educate me in music business economics. But having survived my first lesson, maybe it's time to take a break and get a little air. I'll be back in a few minutes."

Once outside, Tarin leaned against the brick wall of the building, closed her eyes, and inhaled. Tommy was every bit as nasty as she had imagined he would be, but to get the information she wanted about that night a decade ago in San Francisco, she would need to earn his trust.

If he wanted a manipulator, it was a manipulator he was going to get. Tarin needed to make him believe she was every bit the self-serving woman he accused her of being. Only then would he feel comfortable enough to tell her what she needed to know. And she would begin spinning her web the next time they met.

CHAPTER 23

The Stage Is Set

JON ROLLED ONTO HIS SIDE AND LEANED ON HIS elbow. He pushed the hair from Tarin's eyes as she nestled next to him in bed. "Nick told me something happened between you and Tommy today. Why haven't you mentioned it?"

"It was nothing to be concerned about."

"Nick said you tried to make light of it, but he thought you were pretty upset."

She saw the concern reflected in his eyes. "Only for a moment or two. He made the kind of accusations we both knew he would. You know—telling me how I'd made his life difficult by coming between you and Anna. How I'm nothing but a gold digger. I thought I was prepared, but he did manage to get under my skin." She tried to reassure him. "Don't worry. He won't affect me that way the next time we meet."

"Promise you'll tell me if he gets out of line again."

Looking into his bright blue eyes, she told him what she knew he wanted to hear, "I promise. Now, let's go to sleep."

TARIN WAS ON HER way to get coffee for Nick and Jon when she felt a strong hand grip her arm. She turned to find Tommy standing behind her.

"You seem to have a talent for sneaking up on people."

"I'm sorry, Tarin. But you know it occurred to me I wasn't very nice when we talked yesterday. Could I make it right by taking you to lunch at one of the clubs down the street? My treat."

Noticing her hesitation, he raised the ante. "If you're going to be part of Jon's life, we need to get to know each other better. The receptionist here—Roxie—takes food orders and brings the guys whatever they want, so they don't even leave the studio. But that doesn't mean you're stuck here. Trust me. I really do want to make up for my bad behavior."

As much as she dreaded the prospect, this was exactly the kind of opportunity she needed to nurture a relationship with Jon's manager. Tarin forced herself to smile. "You don't need to take me to lunch— your apology is enough. But you're right. We do need to get to know each other. With that in mind, I accept. When and where should we meet?"

"THIS WAY, MR. WYNDHAM. Your table is ready," the maître d' announced, pointing to a quiet corner of the room.

Tarin clamped her lips together when she felt Tommy's hand resting comfortably below the small of her back, much lower than necessary or appropriate. She fought the urge to recoil.

Tommy sat in a chair on the opposite side of the table for two. He didn't bother to disguise his fascination with Tarin's cleavage. Noting his attention, she was pleased with the decision to loosen an additional button of her blouse.

"What caused the sudden change of heart? It wasn't hard to sense your dislike for me when we talked yesterday."

Tarin looked down—appearing to be shy—just long enough for him to notice her reluctance to speak. "Maybe I owe you an apology of my own. It's not fair to pass judgment before even getting to know someone, and I was passing judgment on you. For that, I'm sorry but don't get me wrong. I'm still angry about the photographer you hired to spy on Jon and me. You had no right to invade our privacy that way.

But when I stop to look at the big picture, I realize all you want is to be sure Jon is successful. I can't fault you for that."

"I'm glad you're beginning to understand the situation." Tommy reached across the table to rest a hand on hers. "You need to know I've never had anything but his best interests in mind."

She slipped her hand away from his grasp. "But we also know Jon's success means a substantial amount of money in your pocket."

He sat back in the chair with a broad grin on his face. "Care to tell me what's wrong with that?" He paused and then leaned forward on his elbows. "Now, share with me the real reason for your change of heart."

"What makes you think there's more to it than I've already told you?"

He looked directly into her eyes. "Because I know women, and you haven't convinced me you're in this relationship without some sort of motive of your own."

She looked away from his steely gaze. "That's a rather jaded point of view, Tommy. But all right. Maybe I haven't been completely honest." Tarin began to spin her web. "Do you know what I do for a living?"

He shrugged. "I think someone said you work for a newspaper."

"That's true. I'm a journalist. But I've always had this fascination when it comes to writing songs." She reached for a small notebook in her pack and handed it to him. "Here are some of the lyrics I've been working on."

Tarin watched him flip through the handwritten pages. "When Jon and I met, I'm embarrassed to admit I didn't even know who he was. And it was never my intent to use him to meet people who could help me get into the music business. But when he invited me to California, I couldn't stop thinking this might be the break I need." She paused, watching for a reaction on Tommy's face. "I guess when you suggested ulterior motives yesterday at the studio, I became defensive."

He proceeded to smirk and play with the unlit cigar he held between his thumb and index finger. "It's not hard for one manipulator to see right through another—however inexperienced she might be." Tommy turned to catch the attention of a waiter across the room. "Now, what if we have a drink or two and enjoy a good meal? Then we'll talk more about what it is we're both hoping to gain from Jonathan Parker."

Tarin took her notebook from his outstretched hand and— grateful for the distraction— reached under the table to drop it into her backpack.

TOMMY DROPPED TARIN OFF in front of the studio and left to park his car. Once inside the building, she found Nick sitting at the piano in a small rehearsal room.

He greeted her with a smile. "Where have you been, pretty lady?"

She glanced up at the clock—it was already three o'clock. She had been with Tommy for nearly two hours. Tarin hesitated an instant before answering, not knowing what Nick's reaction would be. "You might not believe this, but Tommy took me to lunch." She noticed the bewildered look on his face. "He said he wanted to make up for his behavior yesterday."

"Watch out, Tarin. He doesn't do anything unless it will benefit him one way or another."

"I'll be careful, I promise."

He motioned for her to sit next to him on the bench. "Be honest. Is the studio getting to you? I know it can't be much fun watching us work on the same songs over and over for hours on end."

She shook her head and smiled. "It's not that. I love watching and listening to what you're doing. It's magic. Today I just needed air. As for lunch with Tommy, all I wanted to do was try to figure out this guy for myself." Suddenly Tarin noticed it was her handwriting on the papers strewn in front of Nick. "What are you working on?"

"You know those lyrics you showed me? I've been tinkering around. Let me know what you think."

She was intent on listening to Nick's melody, but her thoughts were interrupted when she felt Jon's arms engulf her from behind. "What are you two up to?"

"Nothing much." Tarin melted into Jon's grasp by placing her hands over his and leaning back against his chest.

"Wrong," Nick chimed in. "Check this out." He began singing the first few lines of Tarin's words meshed with his melody.

"Not bad, especially for a guy who can't sing," Jon announced with genuine appreciation. "When did you find time to write that?"

"I didn't. She did," Nick answered. "I'm afraid your girlfriend's been holding out on you."

Jon stepped back and pushed Tarin away. "You never cease to amaze me." Then he turned his attention to Nick. "Tonight, when we're finished with the band, I'd like to spend a few hours working on it. What do you think?"

"Count me in," Nick replied. "This could be the beginning of an extraordinary collaboration, my friends. Now let's get back to the studio so we can have our own fun later."

It was well past midnight when, with Tarin sleeping on a couch at the other end of the room, Nick and Jon finished the first rough arrangement of her song.

"Hey, you," Jon said, nudging her gently. "It's time to go."

She stirred, stretched, and opened her eyes. "What time is it?"

"It's almost one. You've been asleep for a few hours. Let's go home."

Still half asleep, she nodded. "Okay."

"Guess what? With your permission, we want to make your song the lead cut on my solo album. Now it just needs a title. We were considering 'Ghosts of the Heart.' What do you think of that?"

Tarin smiled. "I think you should sleep on it and listen to the song again in the morning when you have fresh ears." She glanced over at the pyramid of beer cans. "And when you're not under the influence."

"You need to have more faith in what you create, my dear," Jon chided. "Trust me. This song could take us somewhere."

"You should listen to this guy," Nick said, echoing his friend's sentiments. "He speaks the truth. But I need to bail, too. We're supposed to be back here in seven hours, and it'll take me at least an hour to get home and then another one to get back."

Curbing a yawn, Tarin didn't have the energy to fight. "Okay. You win." She linked an arm with each of them. "Let's go, but I'm driving.

And Nick, you can stay at our house tonight." She glanced back at the pile of empty beer cans. "I want to be sure everyone gets home in one piece."

Looking into the studio as Jon flipped off the lights, Tarin wondered what the new day would bring. She'd taken her first step into the world of Tommy Wyndham and there was no turning back now.

CHAPTER 24

Truth Be Told

EVEN THOUGH THEY'D WORKED LATE THE NIGHT before, Jon and Nick were the first musicians to arrive at the studio. Jon was surprised to find Tommy already working at a desk in the control room.

The manager looked up when he entered. "Jon."

"Tommy. I should take a picture. You're never here at this hour. What brings you in so early?"

"Paul planned to be here. We were going to listen to the most recent cuts, but he got hung up in traffic." Tommy sat back in his chair. "The album seems to be coming together nicely. What do you think?"

Jon shrugged. "It'll do, I guess."

"It's better than that and you know it. What do you think about a short tour to promote the project when the album hits the streets?"

"I suppose that would be okay. But don't forget I'm done with the band once this contract is over. Nothing's changed."

Tommy put his headphones on the table. "All the more reason for you to make a big exit. Go out on top. You know—all the clichés. Not to discourage you, but I doubt you'll ever make it to this level again. I'm not saying you're washed up, but Motive is a hard act to follow." He paused to allow time for his words to sink in. "We've been together since the beginning. Be honest. Has it been such a bad ride?"

"There have been a few things I wish had been handled differently." Jon leaned against the counter supporting the mixing board. "I just think the time is right to branch out on my own."

"What's your new girlfriend think about that?" Tommy asked while turning up the volume on the control room monitors.

"What do you have against her? You're not giving Tarin a chance."

"Who says I'm not?"

"I think it's because you can't control her."

Tommy leaned back, locking his fingers behind his head. "Think what you want. But we've been a team for a long time. I hate to lose that."

"Morning, Jon—Tommy," Paul announced as he dropped his backpack on the floor next to the console. "God, I hate LA. The rest of the band is right behind me. Can we start wrapping this thing up? You guys are beginning to get on my nerves."

Nick stuck his head through the studio doorway. "There you are. The band is setting up to try a final take on the title track. You ready, Jon?"

He looked at Tommy before glancing back at Nick. "You're the producer, bud. Let's do it." Jon glanced at his manager one last time before walking out the door.

UNBEKNOWNST TO JON OR anyone else, Tarin continued to meet Tommy for lunch and an occasional dinner while the band was hard at work mixing the album. Today was one of those days when the two sat together at a secluded table in the back of an Italian restaurant near the recording studio.

Tommy poured her a glass of wine and then looked at her inquisitively. "I'm curious. Have you had a chance to consider what we talked about the other day?"

"I'm not sure what you mean."

"You know, I've been watching you with Jon. You're good. I almost believe you care for the guy."

Tarin did her best to remain calm and collected. "What makes you think I don't? He's good-looking, talented, has money, and travels in the right circles. What more could a woman want?"

"I don't know. You tell me."

"For now, let's forget about what I want," she answered, baiting her hook. "I want to hear how you managed to build such a successful clientele. I bet you had to step on a few people along the way to get where you are today."

It hadn't taken Tarin long to realize Tommy loved to flaunt the so-called accomplishments and the triumphs of his career in the entertainment industry. She was usually successful in steering their conversations that direction and soon discovered he was more than happy to sing his own praises for hours at a time. The more encouragement she gave him, the more eager he was to talk. He didn't hesitate to expound upon how he had secretly bilked thousands of dollars from his clients without them having a clue. But despite her prodding, he had yet to admit any wrongdoing when it came to his professional relationship with Jon. And she was running out of time.

Today Tarin was determined to incite the unscrupulous manager into sharing some sort of information that would help build a case against him. On this day she decided to let whiskey be her accomplice. Tommy downed two glasses of Crown Royal on the rocks before lunch arrived and then continued to drink heavily while he ate. Tarin made a point to be sure the waiter brought him another drink as soon as the glass he held was empty. And even though his touch sickened her, she enticed him with a little more freedom as his tongue became looser. At one point, she felt his hand working its way under her skirt. Burying her repulsion behind a smile, Tarin asked the one question she had been waiting to ask.

"You've told me things about all your other clients, but when it comes to you and Jon, the curiosity is killing me. I'm dying to know how much money you've managed to steal without him knowing you've done it."

It took all Tarin's inner strength to maintain her composure when Tommy began to slide his hand upward along her inner thigh. Then, with a sinister smirk on his face, he began to inch his fingers toward her panties. "Forget the money. It's not important. What's exciting is touching the woman Jonathan Parker loves." He washed down his words with a big swig of whiskey. "How about that for an answer?"

Tarin could stand it no longer but tried not to show her disgust when she pushed his invasive hand away. "You need to know something: I don't mix business with pleasure."

He laughed, his speech beginning to reflect the quantity of alcohol he'd consumed. "You can't blame a man for trying." He looked down at his empty glass and motioned to the bar for another. The waiter seemed to question Tarin, who nodded and mouthed the words "I'll get him home." She had a difficult time hiding her emotions. "Other than trying to grope his girlfriend in a public place, how much money have you scammed from Jon over the years?"

Tommy grinned with self-satisfaction. "More than all the others combined. In fact, because he's so damn trusting, he's the easiest mark I've ever—" His face suddenly became flushed, and he stopped in midsentence.

"Tommy, are you all right?"

His speech was slurred. "I think I better go outside."

"Let me get a cab to take you home." Tarin helped the inebriated man to his feet. It was all she could do to keep him upright.

"Do you need help, ma'am?" their waiter asked, rushing to help as Tommy swayed back and forth on his feet. Then, losing his balance, he caught himself on a nearby table, grabbing the tablecloth for support.

She winced as four table settings, salt and pepper shakers, and an oil lamp crashed to the tile floor. Helpless in her attempt to keep Tommy on his feet, she turned to the waiter for help. "I'm so sorry. Do you think you could help me get a cab? I'm afraid he needs to sleep this off."

"There's usually a driver waiting near the front door, ma'am. But if there isn't, I'll call one for you."

Moments later, Tommy was safely deposited in the backseat of a taxi. Tarin tipped the driver enough to ensure he would be taken inside when they arrived at his house. Then she reentered the restaurant to pay the bill. The words she heard behind her sent chills down her spine.

"Would you like to tell me what you're doing here and with Tommy of all people?" Nick's voice trembled with disbelief bordering upon betrayal.

"It's not what you think," she replied, trying not to show the panic she felt. "I can explain."

"That's what people always say when they get caught, but why don't you try me just the same."

She took his hand and led him back to her table. For a moment, they sat in silence, Tarin's heart beating so hard that it hurt.

"I'm waiting." Nick's stare cut through her like a knife.

She looked Jon's best friend in the eyes, and the story began pouring from her lips like a waterfall. She told him about the girl Jon had gotten pregnant and how Tommy had sent a photographer to spy on them in Colorado. She laid out her plan to trap Tommy into admitting all the wrongs he'd done the past ten years. Nick sat and listened, doing his best to absorb it all.

"You're trying to tell me Jon got a sixteen-year-old girl pregnant and paid Tommy half a million dollars to make her go away? If that happened, I'd know about it."

"But that's just it, Nick. Tommy threatened him into secrecy and has held it over him ever since." Tarin paused for a moment before adding, "I'm convinced he made it all up."

"What?"

"Well, maybe not all of it. Jon admits he took her back to the band's hotel. But there's something that doesn't ring true when you hear all the facts." Tarin became animated as she explained her doubts. "After it happened, Tommy wouldn't let him talk to the girl or her family. He told him it was because of her age and that if Jon pushed it, he could land in jail for a long time."

"Well, that's true, isn't it?" Nick asked. "It would have been statutory rape, even if it was with her consent."

"But Jon contends she told him she was nineteen and looked that old if not older. Tommy refused to even listen to his side of the story."

Tarin continued to plead her case. "I know he planted the girl and manipulated the entire situation for his own financial gain. I just need to prove it." Her eyes pleaded with Nick to give the scenario the benefit of doubt.

"Okay," he said, using his elbows to lean forward on the table. "Let's say you're right. What difference will it make? That was ten years ago."

"Tommy's using what happened then to coerce Jon into doing what he wants him to do now. The relationship with Anna is living proof of that. I need to expose what he did so Jon can let go of the guilt he's still carrying around. I want to see that creep face the consequences of what he's done not only to Jon but everyone else along the way."

Nick didn't like the idea and wasn't afraid to tell her so. "Why don't you let me handle it? Tommy doesn't have anything on me and I'm certainly not afraid of him. He's not a nice man, Tarin. If Tommy figures out you've crossed him, who knows what he might do. Especially if he thinks you know something that will ruin his reputation. Now that you've brought me into this thing, I'd never forgive myself if anything were to happen to you."

She smiled. "You need to trust me. I know what I'm doing. Today Tommy was just about to tell me something before he passed out." She held her thumb and index fingers together in front of her face. "I'm this close to getting into his head, and I refuse to quit until I finish what I started."

"I don't like it." He sighed. "I don't like it at all."

"Thanks for worrying, but I can do this." She sat in silence before making one last plea. "Promise me you won't tell Jon. I don't know how he would react."

Nick stood and put his hand on Tarin's shoulder. "All right. I won't say anything. Yet. But you need to promise me you'll be careful. We both know what Tommy's capable of doing." He smiled half-heartedly. "Come on. Let's get back to work before Jon realizes we're missing." With that, they drove back to the studio, trading thoughts of Tommy Wyndham for the work awaiting them.

CHAPTER 25

Deception

TARIN COULDN'T BELIEVE SHE'D AGREED TO MEET Tommy alone at his house. But he wasn't going to take no for an answer, and she couldn't risk the possibility he might question her motives. Not when she'd come this far and was so close to winning his confidence.

Driving Jon's sapphire blue Porsche 911, she arrived at the sprawling house on the beach in Malibu about two o'clock in the afternoon. Tommy greeted her wearing only a white terry cloth robe and a scant Speedo swimming suit. With the front of the robe hanging open, it was impossible to miss the thick gold chain hanging around his neck, the dense carpet of coarse black chest hair contrasting with the bright gold, or the voluminous gut that nearly obscured the front of the minuscule Speedo suit.

Tommy seemed oblivious to his appearance—his arrogance never more apparent. "Let's go to the pool. I've mixed a pitcher of martinis."

Ushering her toward the open wall of glass at the rear of the house, Tarin felt his hot breath on her skin when he leaned to kiss her shoulder. She prayed he hadn't felt her muscles tense under his touch.

"How did you manage to get away from Jon?" he asked, pulling a chair from the table and then in gentlemanly fashion pushing it back as Tarin sat down.

"It wasn't hard," she answered, avoiding eye contact. "I told him I was going shopping to find a dress for a party we're going to this weekend. Every man in the world knows a search like that can take hours. He wanted nothing to do with it. Anyway, the band will be in the studio all day."

"You seem to have him wrapped around your little finger," Tommy announced while he checked the calendar on his cell phone. "As I see it, the album should be finished in the next few weeks." He looked at Tarin, who was holding the stem of her martini glass in both hands. "It's time for you to use your influence and convince him he needs me around. You know, sign a contract extension. After hearing the songs on this latest album, I'm convinced there's more than a little life left in Motive after all. Why look for a new band to promote when I can finish burning this one out and make an easy profit in the process?"

She glanced at him in faux disbelief. "And how am I supposed to accomplish that? He's convinced you're the devil incarnate."

"No thanks to you I might add. Can't you weasel your way in by telling him you've had a chance to get to know me? You know—remind him how important I've been to his career all these years." He placed his hand on her thigh as he spoke.

"You could tell him you understand the entertainment industry better now and my suggestions really are in his best interest." He paused before dealing his trump card. "I'll make it worth your while." Lifting his hand from her leg, he continued, "I've been talking with a friend of mine about you. He wants to look at the lyrics you showed me and is interested in representing you. He's got friends in high places with the biggest labels."

"I don't know, Tommy."

"This is the break you've been looking for and all it's going to cost you is a little innocent deception." He lit a cigar and inhaled, causing the embers to glow. "What do you care anyway? Once you're established in LA you won't need Jon Parker."

She felt her chest begin to tighten while he waited for her response.

Tarin buried her contempt and delivered a convincing smile. "You make a good point. But it won't be easy."

Tommy stood and she became acutely aware of his presence behind her. "Nothing that matters ever is, my dear."

She felt his fingers under the straps of her camisole, pushing them off her shoulders. When his hands began to move downward, she stood abruptly. "Thanks for the martini, Tommy, but I should go."

"What's your hurry, sweetheart?" He pulled her body against his chest and lifted her chin toward his own. "It's a hot day. We should take a swim to cool off."

Tarin struggled to escape but was trapped in his arms. "I don't think so. I didn't bring a suit."

"Who needs a suit among friends?" He pressed his lips hard against hers, forcing his tongue into her mouth.

Using all the strength she could muster, Tarin managed to break his embrace and wiped the back of her hand across her mouth. She glared at her host. "Listen, I'm sorry if I've given you the wrong impression. This is a business proposition, nothing more. I've told you before—I don't mix business with pleasure."

He reached for her, but she stopped him in midair, slapping him with her free hand.

Tommy laughed and walked back to the table for his martini. "You are a little spitfire, aren't you? I like that in a woman."

She was halfway to the house, before turning to face him. "Keep your end of the bargain and I'll see if I can convince Jon that you really are god's gift to musicians. I'll be in touch."

"I like women who play hard to get," he called after her. "You know where to find me. Oh, and Tarin—don't forget to look for that new dress. Make sure it has a plunging neckline."

Moments later and a half mile away, she pulled off the road, thrust the transmission into park, and began digging into the bottom of her backpack. Finding the small bottle she was searching for, she was out of the car in an instant and pouring the mint-flavored contents into her mouth. She swished the liquid around as if she had been poisoned. Spitting the mouthwash onto the grass at her feet, Tarin felt tears begin to cloud her vision. At that moment she didn't know how much longer she could carry on this charade. With her return flight to Colorado booked and just a week away, it was time to put Tommy Wyndham in his place. Filled with renewed resolve, she settled back into the driver's seat, shifted the car into gear and pushed the accelerator to the floor.

CHAPTER 26

The Confrontation

A SOUND TECH STUCK HIS HEAD AROUND THE HEAVY oak door frame. "Nick—got a minute? Paul needs you on the studio floor."

Hesitating, he glanced at Tarin. "Jon told me to keep an eye on you. Will you be okay if I leave for a few minutes?"

She pushed him toward the door. "Go. I'll be fine. I don't know why he's worried."

"Okay, but I'll be right back. I want to concentrate on the song we started today. I need to save the chords we decided on for the bridge. This melody has promise if I do say so myself." He lingered by the door before heading down the hall.

Tarin turned her attention back to the verses they'd been tweaking.

Deep in thought, she didn't see Tommy stride into the room. But she did feel him plant his three-hundred-pound-plus frame next to her. The impact forced her to lean the other way to keep from falling against him. He made a point of stretching his arm behind her on the back of the couch.

"I was hoping to run into you, Tarin. We haven't had an opportunity to talk since the other day at my house. Jon will be working late tonight. I don't suppose you'd like to slip out for dinner and a drink or two. I have a songwriting contract for you. We could get a room at the hotel down the street so you could read through it."

"A hotel room? In your dreams, Tommy."

"Why not? Could it be you're suffering from a sudden burst of conscience? Trust me—it'll pass. It always does with people like us. I'd still like to show you the city. You know, point out where you could be living if you stick with me and keep your sights set on our ultimate goals."

Due to his proximity, she became aware of Tommy's pungent body odor and the beads of sweat glistening on his forehead. He pulled out a linen handkerchief to dab at his face. "It's a hot one out there today. Can't wait until my body catches up with the air-conditioning."

He put his hand on her knee. She ignored it.

"You know, Tarin, I owe you another apology. When I step back and take a good look at the whole picture, Jon couldn't have picked a better time to end it with Anna. The relationship wasn't going anywhere, and the public was getting tired of seeing them together. You know, there wasn't enough intrigue or fireworks to fuel any interest. But when she showed up at the premiere of her new movie alone after her engagement to Jon—"

"The engagement you staged, Tommy."

"Whatever. Anyway, tongues started wagging. I struggled with handling the breakup but called in a few favors and kept the story out of the tabloids. Don't know if you've noticed, but the pictures of you and Jon I leaked last week really caused a stir. The press is scurrying around trying to find out anything they can about you and poor abandoned Anna is the scorned victim. I couldn't have scripted it any better."

She looked at him with disbelief. "People are nothing more than pawns to you, are they?"

"My job is to make sure the clients in my stable are successful and I do it any way I can. If that means a little harmless deceit or manipulation, it's the price they pay to stay on top."

"You call messing with the emotions of a vulnerable twenty-two-year-old woman harmless?"

There was no remorse in his reply. "This is a tough business, my dear. Anna might as well figure it out early. Jon did."

"You're disgusting."

A degree of pride tainted his grin. "Oh, please. I've been described in much more graphic terms than that. Jon's gotten quite good at it since meeting you."

She ignored his response. "Speaking of learning lessons early, tell me about the girl Jon got pregnant in San Francisco."

He was caught off guard and the tone of his voice changed. For the first time, Tarin noticed a degree of insecurity embedded in his words. "I'm surprised he told you about her. She's always been our little secret."

"Jon was pretty darn lucky to have had you around to take care of everything."

Her sarcasm didn't register, and he gave her knee a quick squeeze. "That's what a good manager does. We're more like family than business associates. We take care of each other in times of need."

Moving toward the corner of the couch to put distance between them, Tarin picked up her backpack from the floor. "Would you like a stick of gum?" she asked, digging into the depths of the leather bag.

"No thanks." Quite satisfied with himself, Tommy settled onto the cushions. "You know he could have been in big trouble. The whole episode could have ended his career and landed him in jail. I'm just glad I was there to help."

Tarin placed the open backpack on the couch between them. "I'm puzzled how the parents knew you were the person to help them find Jon."

"Someone must have told them I'm his manager. But I don't see why it matters how they found me. The important thing is that they did, and the cops didn't get involved."

"I'm assuming you needed to create some kind of paperwork."

He fidgeted. "Um, yeah, sure. To do it right, I had to deal with their lawyer." Tommy got up to fill a glass at the water dispenser.

"Did you show Jon any of the documents?"

"I didn't see the need."

Tarin continued to drill him for answers. "Did the attorney practice here in Los Angeles?"

"You know, I think so."

"But the alleged rape happened in San Francisco." Her voice became more animated. "You really can't remember, can you? I don't suppose you can come up with the girl's name, either." She wasn't giving Tommy time to formulate his answers.

"So, what's your point?"

"No point." She watched him sit back down on the couch, clutching his handkerchief in a tight fist. "But I would think that when something so traumatic threatened your biggest client, you might remember more about the situation. Especially when it cost Jon a half-million dollars to get out of it."

"That happened ten or eleven years ago. I don't know how you expect me to remember all the gory details."

"Jon still feels guilty about what happened. Doesn't that matter to you?"

"Why would it? I didn't create the problem, he did. I just fixed it."

Tarin allowed him time to think. "I do wonder why you didn't stand up for him when he said the girl claimed to be nineteen. Of course, that's not a defense, but under the circumstances, it might have made a difference."

"His career was just taking off and we didn't need any adverse publicity. I thought it was best to settle quietly without any potential leaks or possible police intervention."

Tarin stood to get a cup of coffee. "Want some?"

"No, thanks." Tommy's face was beet red, and torrents of sweat streamed down his Godfather-like jowls.

She tossed her gum into the trash and sat back down, cradling the ceramic cup between her hands. "Jon told me he wanted to talk with the girl to be sure she was all right, but you wouldn't let him."

"It would have complicated matters. Jon didn't need to have any kind of attachment to her." Tommy was beginning to glare. "I'm not stupid. If you're trying to accuse me of something, just do it."

From the outside Tarin looked calm, cool, and collected. But on the inside her stomach was churning. "You thought nothing of arranging a relationship with Anna. Who's to say you didn't manufacture a statutory rape charge against Jon? Then you decided to take things one step further and tell him she was pregnant."

"Give me a break. How the hell did you come up with that?"

"You know I'm a writer, but you don't know what my job is for *The Denver News*, do you? I'm a copy editor, but the rest of the time I check facts for a living. And you know what? When it comes to this rape scenario you concocted, some of the details don't fit."

He laughed. "You're crazy. You know that don't you? The guys in the band saw him with her backstage that night and then later at the hotel. They all know what he did. What possible motivation did I have to set him up?"

"I don't know. You tell me."

He turned to face her with anger shooting daggers from his eyes. "Okay, fine. You want to press the point? Just between us, do you know how many of these irresponsible, self-centered, have-it-all musicians I've seen pass through this town? God damn it, I lost my wife to one of them. But the first time I heard Jon sing, I knew he was going to be a star. If we played our cards right, he would be my meal ticket for a long, long time. I couldn't let him blow it—and trust me—he would have sooner rather than later."

Tommy stopped to look for some sort of approval but got none. "He was headed for disaster and about to screw up, so I made it happen on my timetable and under my control. I hired a high-class hooker and paid her ten thousand bucks to sleep with him. She was twenty-one by the way, I checked."

"Let me see if I've got this right. If you gave the girl ten thousand dollars, that means you pocketed a cool four hundred ninety thousand yourself. Not a bad payoff for a day's work."

"It was the best investment Jon ever made. Call it insurance if you'd like. He cleaned up his act after that. Some real-life bitch would have taken him for twice that much and he still could have landed in jail. I've seen it happen."

"You're an ass."

"People call me names all the time. But once again," he snickered, "I have to ask if that's the best you can do."

"No, this is." Tarin reached into her backpack and pulled out a digital recorder. She pressed the rewind key and hit play.

"I hired a high-class hooker to take care of him and paid her ten thousand bucks to sleep with him. She was twenty-one by the way, I checked."

"The tape says it better than I ever could."

Tommy tried to grab the device, but she held it out of his reach.

"Just what do you plan to do with that?"

Tarin smiled. "I've got enough incriminating evidence on this tape to keep you in court for years. Call it insurance if you'd like."

There was a hint of admiration in the dark scowl on his face. "What do you know? Jon finally landed a girl with smarts." He paused as the pieces began to fit together. "The lunches, dinners, the trip to my house—you've been setting me up all along, haven't you?" He shook his head. "I need to give you credit. You're good. No—let me rephrase that. You're better than good. It's too bad you're with Jon. I could have used someone like you in my business."

"I don't think so, Tommy." She stood as if to dismiss him.

"You really love him, don't you?" Tommy asked.

"With all my heart."

"Tell Jon I'll be in touch. Hopefully we can talk through this and find a way to make it right."

"You know what? I think it would be best to keep this conversation just between us for now. I won't tell anyone what I know about you, and you'll let Motive finish the album with no interference. Once that's accomplished, you'll let Jon walk away without a fight. In the meantime, I'd have at least a half-million dollars on hand ready to deposit back into his account."

"You think you've got me cornered, don't you?" Tommy snarled when he finally understood what Tarin meant. "You read the fine print in our contract, didn't you?"

"Are you asking if I know about the option to keep Jon under wraps for another record? Then the answer is yes. But under the circumstances, it's an option I don't think you'll exercise."

Tarin was standing with her face just inches from Tommy's. "Do we understand each other?"

He stormed from the room but spun around to try and get the last word. "Here's one for you. You know those song lyrics you gave me to look at? There's nothing to stop me from selling them. It would be my word against yours as far as ownership goes."

"I wouldn't try it. Before I gave you anything Nick helped me hire a lawyer to begin the copyright process. You wouldn't have a leg to stand on."

Refusing to be defeated, Tommy tried to fire the final salvo a second time. "Would you like to know the best part about that night in San Francisco? Jon passed out before he could get it up. The hooker told me they didn't even screw."

Tommy met Nick in the doorway and thrust him aside.

"What the hell is going on?" Nick demanded.

Jon arrived just in time to see Tarin collapse onto the couch and rushed to her side. "What did he do to you?"

With her head pressed back against the soft leather, she opened her eyes and smiled. "No worries. Tommy and I simply came to a little understanding. I think it's safe to say he won't be bothering any of us anytime soon."

MOMENTS LATER, TOMMY SAT in his Mercedes with a cell phone pressed to his ear.

"Danny-boy? It's Tommy. I need you." He switched the phone into his other hand, jammed the car into reverse, and burned rubber leaving the parking space. "I need to stop at the bank, but I'll see you in about thirty minutes. Be there."

"Shit," Dan Martin muttered under his breath. "Marge? Clear my calendar for the rest of the day."

"Like that's a problem? You don't have anything scheduled until tomorrow and then it's a golf game."

"Disrespectful bitch," he sputtered. Where was the loyalty? He'd kept her on the payroll when he couldn't even cover rent for this seedy little office. When business turned around, he'd find somebody to take her place. Maybe this job would mean his luck was about to change. He usually hated the work Tommy Wyndham sent his way, but the money was always good.

Dan was standing at the window when his office door burst open. He turned, looked at Tommy from head to toe, and exclaimed, "God, you look like hell."

The tails of Tommy's disheveled shirt were hanging out on one side, and the meticulous comb-over he worked so hard to perfect no longer disguised his thinning black hair. He blotted the sweat on his face with a crumpled handkerchief. "I've had better days."

Pulling a photo from his pocket, Tommy quizzed the private investigator. "I've got a question for you. Do you know these people?"

"I think the man is that singer Jonathan Parker. He's one of your clients, isn't he? I've never seen the girl before."

"She's some bimbo he picked up while he was in Colorado. I want you to take care of her."

"Meaning?"

Tommy paced across the room to an open window. "Just what I said. I want you to take care of her. She knows things. Lots of things and I want her out of the picture. A few weeks ago, I overheard Jon talking to Nick Reynolds at the rehearsal warehouse. He's convinced the broad has an old flame stalking her where she lives north of Denver. It sounds like the guy might be unstable, which is all the better for us. I want you to find him. That creep wants her back and I want her gone. If the man is as crazy as Jon thinks, set it up to look like a murder-suicide and nobody will think twice about it."

"Slow down. You're talking cold-blooded murder, Tommy. I've done more than enough things for you that I'm not proud of, but I won't go there. Why do you always assume I'll do your dirty work?"

"Give me a break. Do you even need to ask?" Tommy moved to the investigator's side and rested his arm on the man's shoulder. "I do it because we both know you won't turn me down. If it weren't for me, you'd be making license plates right now."

Unfortunately, Dan knew he was right. "Someday you're going to have to give that up. I can't owe you forever."

"You do this for me and you're free and clear." Tommy reached into a pant pocket. "Here's five thousand dollars to get you settled in Chasm Falls, Colorado. You'll be trying to find property for a nameless investor hoping to retire there. I'll get you more seed money in a day or two, but this should be enough for now."

"If she's out here with Parker, why would I want to go all the way to Colorado?"

"She's flying home in a few days to go back to work."

Dan turned toward the window and took a big breath. Tommy had more than enough information to send him to jail. He felt trapped like a bug under the man's thumb. "All right. But let me go on record telling you I don't like it. If you're sure this is something we need to do, fill me in on what you know."

CHAPTER 27

Wind in the Sails

J ON WAS ALREADY DRESSED AND TARIN COULD SMELL
fresh-brewed coffee when he sat next to her in the semidarkness.

She rolled over in the king-size bed and pulled the comforter over her head. "Jon, what are you doing? Can't you see it's still dark outside? I'm not ready to get up."

"Yes, you are."

She remained unconvinced. "Give me one reason why."

"Because," he answered, pulling the sheets away from her face, "it's going to be a beautiful day in Southern California and we're going sailing."

Tarin's demeanor changed in an instant and she sat up without hesitation. "On Nick's boat?"

"None other."

"But why didn't you warn me? I'll need to get things ready—"

Jon wrapped his arms around her, captivated by her enthusiasm. "That's exactly why I didn't tell you. All you need to do is grab a bathing suit, put on sweats, and get into the car. Nick says he's taken care of everything else."

He couldn't hide his smile when she jumped out of bed and dashed across the room.

"Is it just the three of us?" She called from the bathroom.

"No. I think he's bringing Roxie—you know—the girl from the recording studio. It seems they're in a relationship."

Tarin stuck her head out of the glass shower door. "That's good. I like her. He deserves someone special."

Jon shook his head and began to pack a small duffle bag. "Whatever you say but trust me. No one needs to worry about Nick and his ability with women. He's still got that bronzed, emerald-eyed, surfer look going for him."

Jon wasn't sure if she heard his reply, but it didn't matter. He was content he could give her a taste of the life he hoped they would share someday soon.

"CAN YOU THROW ME the bowline?" Nick called to Jon while Tarin and Roxie situated things in the galley below deck.

"Have you sailed before?" she asked Tarin.

"I have a small sailboat on Ledge Lake back in Colorado," Tarin replied. "But it's nothing like this. This boat is fantastic. My Sunfish is the kind you push to the limit hoping it will tip over. That's half the fun." She handed Roxie several items from the cooler to be put into the small refrigerator. "How long has Nick owned it?"

"About five years. We try to take it out at least once a week." Roxie's voice became more like a whisper. "But don't let that out. Our relationship is sort of under the radar, although I don't know why."

With the lines released and Jon hopping onboard, Tarin felt the auxiliary motor propel the boat from its slip and into the bay.

She quizzed Roxie. "You've been in this business awhile, haven't you?"

"I guess so."

"What's your opinion of Tommy Wyndham?"

"Sleazy. Snakelike. Scumbag. He's a pig." She grinned at Tarin. "Need I say more?"

Tarin returned the smile. "No, I think I know where you stand and apparently, we're on the same page." She paused. "I don't understand why these guys stick with a jerk like him."

"Easy. He gets them what they want and most of the musicians Tommy's got under contract don't bother to ask questions." Roxie's face suddenly took on a glow all its own. "But Nick's different. He didn't sign with Tommy when Jon and Motive did, and he's done just fine on his own."

Topside, the thirty-two-foot boat was passing the last of the piers in the harbor, and Roxie sensed they were ready to set sail toward the open ocean. "Come on. Let's go on deck and see what those two are up to."

At the helm, Nick sent them back to the galley almost as soon as they emerged. "Rox—can you make us a pot of coffee?"

She saluted him. "Yes, sir."

The familiarity in their exchange was evident. Tarin leaned toward Jon's ear. "Why didn't you tell me Nick really does have a significant other?"

Jon returned the whispered message. "Maybe it's because my best friend hasn't realized it yet himself."

After sailing for an hour along the coast, Nick picked a small bay featuring a sandy, secluded beach. With the anchor set and Jon and Roxie snorkeling along the edge of a nearby reef, Nick turned to Tarin and asked the question he'd been dying to ask. "Okay. We both know something went down between you and Tommy yesterday in the control room. I'm sure you finally confronted him. When are you going to tell me what the hell happened?"

She checked to be sure the others were still out of earshot. "Tommy admitted everything. He told me how he hired a hooker to set Jon up. Then he invented the rape charge and pregnancy story to scam him out of the money. Naturally he tried to convince me his motives were honorable."

"And by pretending to take care of everything, Jon came out of it feeling like he owed Tommy more than money. Now what?" Nick asked.

"I'm giving him time to worry about the information I have and what I might do with it."

"Are you telling me you haven't told Jon the truth? I thought the most important thing was to expose Tommy for the devious crook he is."

"And I still feel that way. But trust me, I have my reasons for not saying anything yet. I want him to lose sleep at night wondering what I'm going to do with everything he told me." She looked toward Nick for approval. "Does that make me a bad person?"

"No, but it makes you very dangerous from Tommy's perspective. I'd watch your back."

"I don't think you need to worry, Nick. During those lunches he told me names. He gave me dollar amounts. I can destroy him in the industry and probably put him in jail. He knows that."

"That's what scares me. Exactly what is it you're trying to accomplish?"

"I want Tommy out of Jon's life. I want Jon to know the truth so he can let go of the guilt he's been carrying around for so long."

"But think about it. In the end it's just Tommy's word against yours."

She radiated with confidence. "Not quite. I have everything on my digital recorder. Every despicable word he said, with all his pompous arrogance."

"But you haven't told Jon."

"No."

"Explain to me again why you're waiting."

"Despite everything and as much as I hate him, Tommy can tie up the release of Motive's album, and we all know it's turned out better than anyone thought it would. I need to be careful how and when I use the information against him." Tarin paused, aware that Nick still wasn't buying into her decision to wait.

"Okay. You want me to tell you everything? Jon gave me a copy of his contract with Tommy, and I read it word for word. It's true. For all practical purposes, it ends after this project goes into production. But what he missed is a simple sentence in the fine print that gives either one of them the right to extend the contract for an additional record. I need to have enough ammunition against Tommy to make sure he doesn't exercise that loophole."

"I understand where you're coming from, but you need to be careful. Now Tommy knows you're not afraid to use what you have against him. The bottom line is he's more than capable of making you pay for trying to take him down."

He was surprised by the determination in Tarin's voice. "He doesn't scare me, Nick. I will expose him and make sure he never does anything like this to anyone else. But whether I say something now or wait until the album is finished won't make a difference in what Tommy did to Jon ten years ago. I go back to Colorado this weekend and I'm taking what I know with me. When Tommy is out of our lives for good, I'll play the tape. Not before."

"Am I missing something?" Jon asked as he mounted the ladder at the back of the boat and noted the serious looks on their faces. "We wanted to know if you might like to bring the portable grill to the beach and barbecue lunch. We could use the dingy to get everything to shore and back."

Tarin met him with a smile. "That sounds like a fantastic idea." Glancing at Nick, she was more than happy to end their conversation revolving around Tommy Wyndham.

Sitting on a bench at the stern, Nick did nothing to hide the concern reflected in the look he shot back at her—a look she clearly understood. And she also knew they were far from finishing their discussion.

Climbing the ladder behind Jon, Roxie diverted Nick's attention. "Hey, you two, pick up the pace. Let's go ashore. By the way," she said as she disappeared into the galley, "we're not taking no for an answer. Lunch will be served on the beach in thirty minutes. Be there or go hungry."

Looking at his shipmates, Jon shrugged and grinned. "Who am I to disagree with the studio's office manager? That's a dangerous path to travel if we hope to finish our project on schedule."

Roxie emerged from below deck and draped her arm on Jon's shoulder, "You, kind sir, are perhaps the first person to recognize that undeniable fact. Congratulations. You are now my favorite person on this boat."

Nick attempted to look heartbroken, and Roxie hugged him before kissing his cheek. "Okay. Let me rephrase that. Jon, you're my favorite person on the boat except for Nicholas Alan Reynolds, but that is contingent upon him making sure my steak is medium rare when we get the grill going."

"I own the boat, so you better be careful when it comes to issuing orders, Roxie. I could force you to walk the plank."

"So noted, sir." She snapped to attention and saluted him another time.

Nick stepped onto the boat's teak swim platform and executed a perfect dive into the water below. Coming to the surface, he shook the excess water from his sun-bleached hair and issued an edict. "Now— let's get to the beach. I'm famished."

CHAPTER 28

Fishing for Information

THE NEXT DAY, TOMMY FOUND JON ALONE IN THE control room. He spun a chair around and sat next to him. "We haven't had much time to talk lately. I thought you might want to finish the discussion we started the other day."

"I don't remember casual conversations ever being part of our business relationship, Tommy."

"Do you think that's fair, my friend? You know I've always been in your corner." Tommy was fishing for information. He needed to find out if Tarin had told him any part of what she knew.

"Sometimes your corners are rather self-serving."

"It's business, Jon. Look at the big picture. I know we've had our problems, but have I ever failed you?"

"It depends upon how you define failure."

Tommy exhaled a momentary sigh of relief. Apparently, Tarin was keeping everything she knew under wraps. "It looks like you and this girl may have a real connection."

"And that's any of your business?"

He shook his head. "I thought you would understand where I'm coming from by now. In our business it all has to do with the package. I need to market you to the public in a way they will accept you. No, wait a minute. It's more than that. The public needs to love you. When we put you together with Anna, we had the established rock star smitten by a beautiful young Hollywood starlet. With this woman you brought back from the mountains, I'm not quite sure what direction to take."

"Why does everything in your world revolve around marketability?"

"Because that's where the money is. I don't remember you objecting to my plans or my ideas in the past."

"That's before I realized how manipulative you are."

He met Jon's look with an insightful glance. "Until now, you were perfectly happy benefiting from the profits I brought you. You wouldn't have your beach house or anything else without me."

"What you're saying may be true, but I'm done with that lifestyle."

"Have you listened to yourself? You can be idealistic and expect things to go exactly as planned, but that's not how it works in the real world. We make compromises to get what we want. And as I recall, in the past you've wanted a lot."

"Can't people change?"

"Sure they can, but with guys like you? I don't think so. You want it all and you want it now, especially when you've become accustomed to having it."

"We've been working together a long time, Tommy. I don't want you to think I don't appreciate what you've done for me. But my life is going in a different direction now. I'm tired of the band scene, the tours, and everything that goes along with them. I want a life of my own. Tarin's helped me realize that."

Tommy smiled. "You think you're the first person to feel that way?" He shook his head when Jon started to leave the control room. "Not."

Jon paused in the doorway. "The guys have been working without a break the past couple of weeks, and I had Nick tell them to take a few days off. I've decided to take Tarin to Vegas for the weekend, but I'll be back and ready to work Monday morning."

Tommy turned back to the console. "Why don't you take the jet— it's just sitting there. Consider it a peace offering."

Jon was caught off guard by the uncharacteristic gesture. "Thanks, Tommy. That would be great. See you Monday."

LEFT ALONE, TOMMY PULLED the cell phone from its holster on his belt. "Danny, got anything going on? I think I'd like to stop by. Yeah. I'm losing my hold on Parker. Like I told you the other day, that woman he's hooked up with has planted all kinds of ideas in his head and they don't include me. If the band's album was a bust I wouldn't care, but it's damn good. We could be talking about number one on the charts and streaming platforms. If we can keep the band from imploding, it might mean a rebirth for Motive. That's why we need to pull the plug on this girlfriend of his sooner rather than later."

Dan Martin closed his eyes. "Come over if you want. I'm still not happy with what you're asking me to do, but I'll listen."

"Jon may have given us the opportunity we've been looking for. He's taking the bitch to Vegas this weekend." Tommy lit a cigarette and leaned back in his chair. "It would be tragic if she happened to have an unfortunate accident while they were there. See you in a bit."

Dan hung up the phone. "Damn it. I don't want anything to do with this."

When he'd met Tommy Wyndham, the business dealings were straightforward. Maybe one of his musicians had become involved with a new girlfriend and he wanted a thorough background check done to protect what he called his "investment." Or he needed someone to personally deliver contract documents with a bit of extra incentive to sign them.

And he paid very well.

There had been a time in his life when all of Tommy's questionable deals and ramrod business practices had given Dan a sense of power and control. But now he could see the man for who he was, and the private investigator wasn't particularly proud of the things he'd done to stay in Tommy's good graces.

His relationship with the unscrupulous manager had already cost him his wife. He'd met Jeannie in college. While it was a paycheck-to-paycheck existence, they'd lived an idyllic life until the day Tommy Wyndham appeared in Dan's office the first time. After that, Tommy demanded he be available at a moment's notice—day or night.

Then there was the time Dan had come home with blood on the front of his shirt. Jeannie demanded an answer about what was going on, and he couldn't give it to her. He'd been sworn to secrecy. But she did know one thing: Somehow, Tommy was involved.

Not many wives would stand for that sort of commitment outside their marriage, and Jeannie didn't. In the aftermath, for Dan it seemed easier to stay under Tommy's thumb than try to build a new world without his wife. Working for the entertainment mogul was the easy way out, and that's precisely what he wanted.

Dan continued to make good money digging up dirt about people Tommy wanted to discredit and taught more than a few others it wasn't advisable to disagree with or cross his employer. So, Dan sat in his office waiting for Tommy to call during the day and went home to his cat in an empty apartment at night. Then he did it all over again the next day and the day after that.

The slamming of his office door brought him back to reality. When Tommy landed in the chair across the desk, he sensed an ominous premonition that this time what he was being asked to do would take them both down.

"Okay," Dan said, trying to smile. "Fill me in on what's going on."

CHAPTER 29

What Happens in Vegas

A REPRESENTATIVE FROM THE AUTO DEALERSHIP met Jon and Tarin on the tarmac. "Here's the key fob, Mr. Parker. Any paperwork you might need is in the glove compartment. Enjoy." Then the man shook hands before disappearing into a car waiting nearby.

"Tell me, is this what it's like to be famous?" Tarin was incredulous. "First we fly here on a private jet and then we're met at the airport by a man who simply hands you the keys to a Ferrari convertible—no questions asked."

"You haven't seen anything yet. I plan to spoil you rotten this weekend. You've earned it after spending two weeks in that grimy rehearsal warehouse and then being trapped in the studio for another three." Jon opened the door and helped her into the passenger seat.

"What about our luggage?"

"No worries. It's being delivered to the hotel as we speak."

Tarin had to admit it was exhilarating to drive along the Vegas strip with the top down and Jon behind the wheel. "Do I dare ask where we're staying?"

"I hope the Iconic will do. It's a new hotel and casino with a huge performance venue." He glanced away from the roadway to watch for a reaction. "We have one of the penthouse suites. If the information I've been given is correct, it's about three thousand square feet."

"Jon, that's bigger than my house. What are we going to do with all that space? You should know by now I'm a simple person—all I need is a bed, a couch, maybe a television, and you," she teased.

He continued to grin. "I know and trust me it's much classier than my usual accommodations. But I worked out a deal." He paused. "Did I mention the suite comes with a butler? I thought it might be fun to have one of those at your beck and call."

She leaned over to kiss him on the cheek. "I thought you were going to be the one taking care of me."

"And I will be," he said, pulling into the tree-lined drive leading to the hotel. "Okay, we've arrived."

Tarin put her hand on Jon's arm and exclaimed, "Stop the car!"

"What's the matter?" he asked, stepping on the brake.

"You're huge."

"Thank you, but I thought you might have come to that conclusion before now."

She poked him in the stomach. "That's not what I meant. No, I mean you're really big."

Towering high in the air in front of the Iconic was an immense video marquee featuring a giant photo of Motive with Jon standing front and center.

He leaned over to whisper in her ear. "We play here three nights during the hotel's grand opening. We got a deal on the suite because it wasn't booked, and I agreed with management that Motive would offer a special meet and greet before one of those shows."

Pulling up to the lavishly landscaped hotel entry, Jon pushed a button causing the convertible top to emerge from the deck behind them.

An eager uniformed valet was at Tarin's door in less than a minute. "Will you be checking in, sir?" the regally dressed young man asked as he took Tarin's hand and helped her step onto the tile walkway.

"Yes, we will." Jon handed the young man a sizeable tip. "Thanks."

"Do you have luggage, sir?"

Taking Tarin's arm, he turned back long enough to reply, "We will, but it's arriving separately."

Tarin looked like a small child in a candy store when they entered the grandiose lobby. Jon found himself feeding off her excitement.

"This is gorgeous."

"Just wait. There's more to come."

They were greeted at the registration desk by a young woman standing behind the elegant walnut and granite counter.

"Afternoon. We'd like to check in. The reservation is under Jon Parker."

"Good afternoon, Mr. Parker." The woman scanned the computer monitor and then looked up with a sudden sense of recognition. "It looks like we have a penthouse suite for you. I'll just need a credit card for any incidental charges. We'll bring your luggage to you when it arrives."

After the paperwork was completed, her silent glance signaled a uniformed man at the end of the counter to move to the couple's side. "Cody will show you to your suite." She smiled. "We hope you enjoy your stay with us at the Iconic."

"If you'll follow me, sir," the bellman directed.

Once in the elevator, Cody inserted a key and selected the twenty-fifth floor. When the solid wood doors opened, the look on Tarin's face was transformed into complete awe. The bellman extended his arm, using his hand to direct Tarin toward a short bridge leading to the suites in front of them. It was elevated over a tranquil reflecting pool. She turned to find Jon amused and gazing at her.

She shook her head. "I don't know what to say. This is incredible."

"Cody, could you lead the way?" Jon took Tarin's hand as they followed the young man across the walkway.

Moments later, Tarin was standing in the vaulted living room looking out over the Las Vegas Strip when she heard the ornate gold-trimmed double doors close behind her. She turned to find Jon wearing a mischievous grin. "Well—what do you think?"

Tarin plopped onto one of the soft leather couches. "This is unbelievable. Do people really live like this?"

"We do for the next three days." He took her hand. "Okay. Our Vegas adventure will begin soon enough. But right now, it's tour time. I'd hate for you to get lost and not be able to find me." He scanned the area around them. "Let's see, you're in the living room. Over here we have the wet bar and the solarium. There's a small swimming pool and hot tub on the terrace."

Jon continued to guide her around the suite. He glanced toward a doorway leading into a room on one side of the hall and shook his head. "Don't think we'll need this room unless you want to try being amorous on the conference table."

Still grinning, he kept walking. "Okay. It was just a thought. Here we have the second bedroom in case we want a change of scenery one of the nights we're here."

"Now that you've brought it up, why don't you show me the master bedroom?" She shrieked when he swept her off her feet and started toward the other end of the suite. "Jon—put me down!"

Placing Tarin on the king-size bed, he settled down next to her. "I hope you know how much I love you."

She put her arms around his neck, pulling him close. "And I love you. How would you feel about a late dinner?"

"Only if you'll be my appetizer."

"I think that can be arranged, Mr. Parker."

THE NEXT MORNING TARIN sat cross-legged at the foot of the bed while Jon used pillows to prop himself against the headboard.

"Would you like to go to a show tonight?" he asked, paging through a local entertainment magazine.

She put down the newspaper she'd been reading. "What are my choices?"

"The usual suspects are here—Cirque de Soleil and the ever-present assortment of magicians, ventriloquists, and comedians." He paused while reading a few of the advertisements. "If you're into music, we have Katy Perry, Maroon 5, John Legend, and of course, Wayne Newton. We just missed Cher. Toby Walker is at the MGM Grand."

Tarin didn't let him go any further. "Toby Walker."

"Thanks to Motive, you've experienced an overload of rock music and you're looking for a familiar dose of country, are you?"

She crawled to his side and peered at the magazine. "But the ad says the shows are sold out this weekend."

With a quick hug and a flick of her nose, he left her alone on the bed. "Let's see if I still have any influence with the entertainment industry in this town." Jon smiled. "Finally—a job for the conference room." He disappeared down the hall with the pillow Tarin tossed hitting the floor inches behind him.

Twenty minutes later Jon returned to find Tarin in the bathroom brushing her hair. "It's all set."

She looked at his reflection in the mirror. "You found tickets? How did you pull that off? Oh, I don't even care. I'm just happy you did." Her excitement turned to disappointment.

"What's the matter?"

"I didn't bring anything to wear to a country show."

Jon put his arms around her from behind. "That's simple enough to fix. We'll go shopping."

"WHERE ARE WE GOING?" Tarin asked when the Uber turned onto a narrow service road adjacent to the MGM Grand.

"You'll see," Jon replied with a touch of mystery. "This will be fine," he told the driver when they stopped in front of a gray steel door with dumpsters on either side. It was flanked by several bouncer-sized men.

"Do we have to break in? What kind of tickets did you find?" she asked as the driver helped her from the car.

Jon led Tarin toward the steps leading to the door. "Who buys tickets? I'm relying on my good looks."

One of the guards looked up from his clipboard. "Hey, Jon. It's good to see you. I noticed your name on the guest list. Where have you been hiding?"

"What's up, Andy?" He rested his arm against Tarin's back and offered an introduction, "This is Tarin MacGyver."

"Happy to meet you, miss. But keep an eye on this guy, he's trouble from the word go." The man extended his hand to Tarin before turning to Jon. "Once you get inside, Toby and the band are in the fourth room on the left. Maybe we'll see you after the show."

"Give us a call—we're at the Iconic and plan to have a little get-together later."

With that, Tarin found herself in the bowels of the hotel. "Who was that and how the heck did you get us backstage?"

Jon could sense her growing excitement. "We've played here more than a few times. It's their job to remember people. As for tonight, I might not move in country circles, but I do know Toby. I made a couple calls, and he invited us to stop by before the show." He paused in front of the hospitality room door. "Are you ready?"

All she could do was nod.

Jon knocked and seconds later a T-shirt clad Toby Walker greeted them with a beer in his hand. "Well, if it isn't Jon Parker. Come on in. Who is this beautiful young lady you brought along?" His eyes were bright and his smile even brighter.

Tarin was speechless, leaving Jon to fill in the blanks, "This is Tarin MacGyver. Tarin—Toby."

"Welcome. If you'd like, later I can share some juicy stories about this guy," Toby said, gesturing toward a fully stocked bar and lavish buffet table. "Grab a drink, some food, and then I'll introduce you to the band. You probably remember most of them, Jon. It's the same old crew." Toby had to raise his voice to be heard over the din created by people milling around the room.

"What can I get you?" Jon asked.

"Smelling salts," Tarin replied.

He pointed discreetly to the food. "You'll be fine. I'll get us something to drink while you go check out the spread."

After an hour mingling with the band and VIP guests, Jon leaned over to Tarin and whispered, "I think it's time to find our seats." He walked to the stage manager to shake his hand. "Hey, thanks for the hospitality."

"Hold on a second, Jon. You'll need these to get backstage after the show." He handed the pair all-access credentials.

"Would you pinch me?" Tarin asked under her breath.

"Maybe in a minute, but we're not done yet," he told her, enjoying the curious look on her face. He pulled two tickets from his pocket. "Let's go."

THE FINAL GUEST LEFT their Iconic suite about two in the morning and Tarin collapsed on the couch in front of the fireplace. Jon sat down and pulling her close, rested his arm around her shoulders. "So, what do you think?"

She covered a big yawn with her hand. "What do I think? I just sat in the front row of a concert and watched you be pulled up on stage to perform. If that wasn't enough, I just spent the night with Toby Walker."

"You might want to rephrase that when you tell people about your evening. They might take it the wrong way, particularly Toby's wife." He took her hands in his. "Anyway, I'm looking forward to you spending what's left of the night with me."

Jon couldn't help but notice when Tarin's smile faded. He lifted her chin to look into her eyes. "Hey—what's the matter?"

She hesitated. "I know it's silly, but I kept looking at the young women at the concert tonight, wondering if they might get in over their heads before morning."

"You mean have someone take advantage of them?"

She turned away. "It's just that a few of them looked so star-struck and vulnerable."

Jon ran his fingers through her hair. "In other circumstances, I might worry, but the guys you met tonight are good men. They've been around long enough not to make any silly mistakes. But you know what? You can't save the world, Tarin. Everybody makes their own choices. You've helped me understand that."

He watched her survey the debris left around the room by their guests. "I know you well enough to read your mind. That womanly instinct to start cleaning this mess is running rampant, but let it go. That's why this suite costs what it does. Don't worry—I'll call the butler in the morning and he'll send staff to pick up after us. Right now, I'm taking you to bed."

Tarin brushed his cheek with her hand. "Is this what your life is really like?"

He rested his hand over hers. "You've asked me that before and it's not who I am anymore. I've realized you can destroy yourself if you're not careful. Trust me, I've been there and almost done that." Jon started toward the bedroom. "I don't know about you, but I'm exhausted. What do you say we get some sleep? Tomorrow will be another big day and there's so much I want to show you."

CHAPTER 30

Misstep

JON AND TARIN DISCOVERED THAT WHILE THEY'D been enjoying a late breakfast in bed and lounging next to the pool, they'd missed most of a beautiful Nevada day. The skies were blue, the temperatures moderate, and while the sun was still shining, it was beginning to dip behind the tall structures along the Vegas Strip.

They took the elevator to the lobby and began walking along Las Vegas Boulevard. Tarin linked her arm with his and along with a throng of fellow tourists, they crossed the street to watch the fountains in front of the Bellagio. Almost on cue, the music began and choreographed plumes of water began dancing in the air. She rested her elbows on the ornate concrete railing surrounding the lagoon, while Jon stood behind with his arms around her waist.

"This is beautiful."

He didn't answer, opting instead to watch in silence. When the final drops cascaded from the sky and disappeared into the water below, Jon took her hand and they continued walking along the Strip.

"Has your boss told you anything else about the mysterious assignment he has in mind?"

She shook her head. "All I know is that it's a series of feature articles and I'll need to travel. He made it sound like I could be gone several weeks."

"What am I supposed to do without you?"

"One thing comes to mind—like finishing your album."

"You're pretty good at bringing me back to reality. But you're right. We need to get it done so Motive can hit the road on the mini tour Tommy and the promoters are scheduling. Like I told you, the venue at the Iconic is one of the stops. The record label figures it's a good way to get album sales off and running."

"Maybe we'll wind up in the same city and I can watch you perform."

"You saw me last night."

"Singing one song onstage with Toby Walker doesn't count. I want to see you play with your band knowing I'm the one who gets to take you home at the end of the night."

"I can live with that."

"So where are we going?" Tarin asked.

Jon took her hand. "We'll go anywhere you want. We can even take a trip to the top of the Eiffel Tower."

Continuing their journey along Las Vegas Boulevard, Jon took her hand and pointed toward Caesar's Palace. Come on, let's go inside."

Almost three hours later, the pair emerged from the Forum Shops after window shopping at many of the boutiques, including a lengthy stop inside Cartier. Then they enjoyed a relaxing dinner at Gordon Ramsey's Pub and Grill before continuing to meander along the Strip.

"Don't they annoy you?" Tarin asked as they passed a line of men snapping cards of scantily clad women and thrusting them toward Jon. Several of the men wore full-sized versions of the cards on their backs that were lit like obscene miniature billboards.

"Just ignore them," he replied, passing the men without making eye contact. "If you want to know the truth, the pests hustling timeshares and show tickets bother me more. At least these guys don't talk."

Noting the unmistakable smell of marijuana lingering in the air and the occasional odor of human urine, Tarin asked, "Does it always smell like this?"

Jon shook his head. "City workers do their best to keep the Strip clean, but it's an ongoing battle."

Surrounded by a crush of people on the sidewalk, Tarin changed course to avoid another group of persistent card snappers. Time stood still for Jon when a man in the throng lost his balance and fell against Tarin. Her hand was stripped from his, and she stumbled off the curb onto the boulevard. Hearing the high-pitched screeching of rubber on pavement and brake shoes on metal, he looked up just in time to see the front bumper of a double-decker bus bearing down upon her. In that split second, a uniformed police officer pulled Tarin from the roadway and back onto the sidewalk. The bus stopped precisely where she had fallen mere seconds before.

Jon knelt beside her. "Tarin, are you okay?"

Dazed, she attempted to sit up but instead fell into his arms.

The officer assessing Tarin's condition did his best to hold back the small crowd beginning to squeeze in around them. "Hey, give us some breathing room." He turned toward Jon. "Can you tell me what happened?" he asked.

"A guy stumbled and pushed her into the street," Jon answered, his eyes searching the crowd for the man who had caused Tarin to fall, but he'd vanished. "I can't believe he didn't stick around to see if she's all right."

"Would you like me to call for medical help, ma'am?"

Tarin smiled weakly. "No. I'm embarrassed more than anything else." She took Jon's arm for support and stood on still-wobbly legs. Other than a small tear near the elbow of her sweater, she seemed to have escaped unscathed.

"You're pretty lucky, ma'am," the officer said, looking toward the bus where the driver was leaning against the front bumper attempting to regain his composure. "A second or two later and he wouldn't have been able to stop in time." He picked up Tarin's purse from the pavement and handed it to Jon. "My squad car is around the corner. Are you staying on the Strip? I can give you a ride back to your hotel if you'd like."

The worry in Jon's voice was difficult to disguise. "Thank you. That would be appreciated."

Standing on a balcony above the commotion, Dan Martin felt his cell phone vibrate and reached into his pocket.

"Danny—have you come up with a plan?"

"You're a little late, Tommy. Had a plan and already executed it."

"Make my day. Does that mean our little problem is now a thing of the past?"

Dan grimaced, anticipating Tommy's response. "Unfortunately, no. My timing was a little off."

"Your timing was a little off?" He could hear impatience and irritation building in Tommy's voice. "Care to explain?"

"I tried to throw her in front of a bus."

"You did what?"

"It seemed like a good idea at the time. Vegas was packed tonight. Parker and the girl were walking around and I followed them for a while. A double-decker bus was coming down the street and I helped her get to know Las Vegas Boulevard up close and personal."

"What went wrong?"

"I was a split second early and the bus driver was damn quick. He stopped on a dime. Unfortunately, there was a street cop in the crowd I didn't see until it was too late, and he yanked her out of the way."

"Jon didn't see you, did he?"

"No, but he doesn't know who I am. I pretended like I'd lost my balance and fell into her. It looked like a complete accident. I've been watching everything from a balcony at Margaritaville ever since she went down." Dan hesitated but then asked, "Do you want me to try again?"

"No. We can't take unnecessary chances or arouse any suspicion. Another opportunity will present itself." Tommy pressed the tip of his cigar into an ashtray on his desk. "Have fun for a couple of days on me. I seem to remember you like the tables. Find yourself a woman or two, but then I want you back in LA. We have plans to make. No buses this time."

Before Dan could reply, the cell phone connection went dead.

JON SAT ON THE edge of the bed massaging Tarin's shoulders. "How are you feeling, Mac?"

She turned to face him. "Don't worry, I'm fine. Maybe a little rattled, but that will pass. I need to tell you, though, it's terrifying to look up and have a bus coming at you. I'll blame it on those stupid men and their cards. I wasn't paying attention, or it never would have happened."

"I'm so glad you weren't hurt—you could have been killed. I don't know what I would do without you."

Tarin intertwined her fingers with his. "I don't think that's something you need to worry about."

"Do you want to go back to La Jolla?"

"What? And miss all the excitement in Vegas?" she exclaimed. "No. We're staying and doing everything you planned. Besides," she said fingering the new Cartier pendant hanging around her neck. "I may not be done shopping yet."

With that, he leaned down and kissed her.

CHAPTER 31

He's Back

J ON AND TARIN HAD BEEN BACK IN LA JOLLA FOR
several days when she got the phone call she'd been expecting from
her boss at The Denver News.

"Do you really have to go?" Jon asked, pulling her down onto the bed.

Lying next to him, Tarin kissed him before standing up. "You
know I do. I've been gone too long as it is. This trip to California was
supposed to be for a few weeks, not almost two months. Plus, Maury
called about the assignment he wants me to take. He wouldn't do that
unless it's important."

She saw disappointment cloud his face. "Jon, it's not like I'll be gone
forever, and you've got work to do. You need to finish your album and
I better get back to work before they realize I'm dispensable."

He followed her into the bathroom, continuing to plead his case,
"But Nick and I need your input to be sure we get the editing right.
We're a team."

Tarin leaned back against the marble countertop. She could see
through his feeble attempt to persuade her to stay. "You're being silly.
Trust me, you two will be fine. Now, I need to take a shower," she said,
lifting a towel from the heated rack mounted on the wall.

"Not without me, you don't."

Standing in silence under the spray a few moments later, Jon asked again, "What can I say to make you stay?"

She rested her head against his chest and whispered, "Please don't worry. I'll be back before you know it."

"Promise?"

"Absolutely. Cross my heart and hope to die."

LATE THAT NIGHT, EIGHT hundred miles away, thick clouds obscured both the moon and the stars. Like a ghost in the darkness, a man approached Tarin's front door. He held a long, delicate steel tool and used it to probe the lock until he heard a telltale click in its mechanism.

Once inside, he surveyed the space with a flashlight, deliberately moving around each room in the house. At times he lifted and then fingered photos of Tarin and her friends. One or two of them were stuffed into the backpack he carried.

He glanced toward the loft and mounted the stairway until he stood on the area rug at the foot of Tarin's bed. He inhaled, trying to smell her scent, but she had been gone too long for any trace to remain. Instead, he went to a table where he found an assortment of her favorite fragrances. Putting one after another to his nose, he settled upon the one he liked best and it, too, went into his bag.

Then he began to rifle through her dresser drawers. With gloved fingers, he traced the delicate lace of a bra and managed to find the matching panties. Before he was finished, his acquisitions from her closet also included a pair of jeans, a sweater, two shirts, running shoes, and a light jacket.

Before leaving the house, he made sure nothing looked disturbed. Her dresser drawers were neat and orderly. Shoes were lined up just as they had been. And where framed photos had been removed, shelves were rearranged to hide the fact they were missing.

Then, as silently as he had entered the house an hour or so before, he disappeared back into the darkness. The new alarm system had been installed but hadn't been activated. The cameras above the doorways were in place, but not turned on. It was like the intruder had never been there.

CHAPTER 32

———

Home Again

T ARIN REFUSED TO GIVE IN. "IT'S NOT UP FOR discussion—I'm taking a cab to the airport," she insisted.

"But I want to drive you," he countered.

"Jon, it will be easier if we say goodbye here and then you go to the studio after I leave. Jake will be in Denver to pick me up and I promise to call you when I get to Chasm Falls."

"He's finally speaking to you again?"

She shrugged. "You know Jake. He's stubborn and hasn't forgiven you, but he'll come around. Give him time." She continued to try and reassure him. "Don't worry. You'll finish your album, I'll go on my assignment, and we'll see each other after Christmas. I can't think of a better present from Santa Claus."

He touched her nose. "You know me—I have separation issues. I've gotten used to having you around." Jon paused for a moment. "Has Maury told you anything else about this monumental assignment he's planning for you?"

"A little bit. It's in Paris. There's a young artist from Denver who's been invited to have his work included in a special exhibit at the Louvre. It's an annual event, but this is the first time a Colorado artist has been selected to show his work. He's only eighteen years old, so it's quite an honor. Maury wants me to write a series of feature articles about the exhibit preparation, the show's opening night, and then shadow the artist for a few days. I'll be in Paris for at least two weeks."

"What am I supposed to do in the meantime?" he asked. "I might wither away."

"Give me a break," she teased. "You'll have finishing touches to put on the album and then appearances to promote its release. You'll be so busy you won't have time to think, let alone miss me."

"When do you leave?"

"Sometime next week. Maury hasn't told me the specifics yet."

Hearing a honk in the driveway, Tarin kissed Jon and was out the door. Sitting in the taxi, she turned back to memorize every detail of his house before it disappeared from sight. Then, she gazed absentmindedly toward the ocean. There was so much she had wanted to tell him. But to be sure Tommy didn't exercise a contract extension with Jon, she had to honor the promise she'd made to the man she despised with both her heart and soul.

"IT FEELS GOOD TO be home," Tarin announced when Jake pulled into her driveway at Ledge Lake.

The headlights swept across the front of the log home, a stark contrast to the darkness inside. He put the transmission into park and turned to Tarin. "Well, are you ready to settle back into your ordinary life surrounded by dull mundane people?"

"Actually, I'm looking forward to a little less drama."

Jake noticed Tarin was sitting in silence, staring at the front door. "Is something wrong, Mac?" He could sense she was nervous.

"I know it's silly, but what if someone managed to get into the house while I was away? I'm afraid of what I might find inside."

He walked around to the truck's passenger door. "Mike and Scott have been here—they helped with installation of the security system and didn't notice anything." Jake hesitated. "How about this—I'll go inside with you, and we'll look around. I won't leave until we're sure everything is okay." He reached for her hand. "Come on. It'll be just fine."

At the front door she turned the key and sighed with relief. "The door's locked like it should be. See, I am being silly."

Tarin was already in the living room when Jake flipped on a light in the entry. She was looking for anything that looked out of place.

"I'm sorry, Jake. Would you have time to go upstairs with me?"

He was bringing in the last of her luggage. "Of course, I do. We'll check all the closets and look under every bed. Does that sound like a good plan?"

"Thank you for not laughing at me."

He put his arm around her. "Don't worry. It really is okay. You went to California not that long after the break-in. It's natural you're still a little nervous, especially since they haven't caught the guy."

Standing in her bedroom, she scanned every inch of the room. "Nothing looks different. All the worrying was a waste of time. Everything looks exactly like I left it."

He opted to tease his sister. "Wait." He leaned toward her ear. "Don't forget. We still need to check under the beds." Shaking his head, Jake knelt on the floor, lifted the bed skirt, and looked back at Tarin with a startled look on his face.

"What is it?"

"You really need to clean under here. There isn't room for anyone to hide even if they wanted to."

Twenty minutes later, with the house declared clear of intrusions, Jake climbed into his truck and drove away.

Back in the kitchen, Tarin picked up her cordless phone and dialed Jon's number.

She was quick to reassure him, "Hi. I'm home and everything's fine. Except I wish you were here."

Unfortunately, what she had forgotten is that appearances aren't always what they seem.

JAKE WAS GETTING READY for the nightly after-work rush by washing glasses behind the bar when Mike slid onto a stool. "Did Tarin make it home?"

He handed the uniformed officer a cup of coffee. "I picked her up at the airport last night."

"How's she doing?"

"She looks fantastic and talked nonstop all the way home."

"Do you think she's still hooked on this Parker guy?"

Jake nodded. "But I don't trust him." He dried his hands on a towel. "It was late when we got to her house and Tarin seemed apprehensive, so I went in with her. The front door was locked, and she said everything seemed to be just the way she'd left it."

Mike looked relieved. "That's good. Scott and I have been trying to keep an eye on the place, but we couldn't watch it all the time. Now that she's home, we need to be sure the security system is up and running."

Mike felt his cell phone vibrate. "Wilson. Okay, I'll give her a call." He put the phone back into its holster. "Shit."

"What's up?"

"Tarin just called the station trying to find me. She thinks someone might have been in the house after all." He took one last swig of coffee. "I better check it out."

"Do you want me to come along?"

Mike was almost outside when he called back to Jake, "No. I'll take it from here. Simmons is on duty, so I'll have him meet me at her house. I'll call you as soon as I figure out what's up."

The steel door slammed behind him.

MIKE PULLED INTO THE driveway with Deputy Simmons right behind him. The two officers met Tarin at her front door.

"Okay—so tell me what's going on."

"I know I'm paranoid, Mike, but I think somebody was in the house while I was gone."

He tried to use his most reassuring voice. "Calm down and let's take it one step at a time. What makes you think someone has been inside?"

"You'll think this is silly."

"Try me."

"On the surface, everything in the house looks exactly like I left it, but when I was unpacking, I noticed the hangers in my closet aren't right."

"Okay. Can you tell me what's different?" Mike asked.

"I always point the hook at the top of the hangers toward the wall. I'm anal about it. Right now, one or two of them are pointed toward the front. But that's not all. There's a jacket missing and a pair of shoes, too. I left a lot of my things at Jon's house, but I know I didn't take those to California. Now they're gone."

Concerned, Mike glanced at Deputy Simmons before directing her up the stairs. "Let's go take a look."

After Tarin pointed out the problems in the closet, the officers turned their attention to the rest of the bedroom.

Simmons scrutinized the top of the vanity next to her dresser. He picked up a bottle of perfume and turned it over in his gloved hand. "Have you noticed anything else that's been moved or might be missing in the rest of the house?" he asked.

She shook her head. "I don't think so, but the more I think about it, the less sure I am."

Mike shook his head. "Tarin, you need to take extra precautions. I don't know what this guy is after, but it means you might still be in danger. We need to get the alarm activated and the cameras recording." He turned to the deputy. "Are you on duty tomorrow? I can show her how the system works, but it would be great if you were here to help."

"I'm working the night shift, so I could come over anytime during the day. Just tell me when."

Mike turned to Tarin. "We'll be here right after lunch, okay? Everyone will feel a whole lot better if we know you're protected."

"I'll be ready, Mike."

He stopped to give her a quick hug before following Scott down the stairs. "Hey, it's going to be all right, Mac."

She nodded. "Jake's planning to bring Finn back tonight or tomorrow. I'll feel much safer with my dog in the house. He won't let anything bad happen. I know that for a fact."

CHAPTER 33

No Turning Back

DAN MARTIN RECOGNIZED THE TELEPHONE number and considered letting the call go to voicemail, but reluctantly decided to accept it.

"Martin, here."

"Dan? Did you find out anything?" Tommy sounded anxious.

"You mean about the MacGyver chick? It took some serious sleuthing, but I was able to find out she's got a newspaper assignment coming up. She's about to leave the country, which will delay our plans a bit."

There was momentary silence while Tommy formulated his thoughts. "This could work in our favor. It might give you time to weasel your way into the lives of her friends. Get to know the ex-boyfriend. All we need to do is come up with a believable scenario. Got any ideas?"

Dan swiveled his chair around and looked out over the Los Angeles skyline. "It's like we talked about before. Chasm Falls is a small town in Colorado. What does it have going for it, and why would anyone want to go there?"

"From what I've heard, there's a nice lake and the mountains make it a resort community."

Part Two

CHAPTER 34

The New Man in Town

DAN CARRUTHERS STEPPED UP TO A STOOL AT THE bar and with a quiet nod, caught the bartender's attention. "Afternoon. What can I get you?" Jake asked, placing a coaster on the polished wood in front of the new arrival.

"Got any local brews on tap?"

"Sure. Preferences?"

"Oh, I don't know. Maybe an ale. Just pick your favorite," Dan answered absent-mindedly while he glanced around the almost empty room.

Jake placed a pint glass on the bar. "I don't remember seeing you before. Are you new to town or just traveling through?"

Dan took a long swig before replying. "I'm here to find a piece of property for a client." He smiled. "You wouldn't happen to know of any good real estate buys, would you? It would make my job a whole lot easier. I've never been in this part of the country before and I'm not sure where to begin. You know, I need to find out what areas are good and which ones are less desirable."

"I'd start with the local newspaper." Jake leaned over to rummage through the clutter under the bar. He stood up with something in his hand. "Our paper is weekly, so a new one won't come out until Friday, but I've read last week's issue. You can have it if you'd like. As for real estate, it's a buyer's market around here. Our economy has taken a big hit this past year."

"Thanks," Dan replied, taking the newspaper from Jake's outstretched hand.

"There are a few real estate brokers in town, but they're all friends of mine, so I wouldn't feel comfortable recommending one over another. They're all on Main Street and aren't hard to find."

The two exchanged idle conversation for the next hour or so while watching the five o'clock news on a big-screen television above the bar. Then Dan saw a tall, muscular man enter the bar and sit on a stool five or six feet away. Without hesitating, Jake put a draw and a shot of tequila in front of him.

"What's new, Alex?"

Dan's ears perked up when he heard the name.

Alex handed the bartender a twenty-dollar bill. "Nothing I can think of."

"How's Rachel?"

"Fine, I guess. She moved in with her parents again."

"Have you had any luck in your job hunt?"

Alex shook his head before putting down the empty shot glass and chugging the beer. He didn't need to ask for a refill. Jake exchanged both glasses without comment.

"Where are we supposed to find jobs in this godforsaken town? I'm still caretaking the Schumacher property. That'll have to do for now."

Dan was curious. "What happened to tank the economy around here?"

Alex turned to size up the stranger. "And you are?"

He felt as though the man's dark, piercing eyes were burning through him. "I'm sorry. The name's Dan—Dan Carruthers. I'm here to buy property for a client from out of state."

Alex remained surly. "The only industry we had in town shut down a few months ago. You shouldn't have much trouble taking advantage of our misfortune. A lot of people are more than ready to sell and get the hell out of this dump."

"Sorry to hear that."

"Jake, give the guy another brew. Here's to success in your quest, Carruthers." With that, Alex Davis downed the last of his second beer and left as suddenly as he had arrived.

DAN STACKED ALL THE pillows against the headboard and tossed his briefcase onto the bed. Sitting next to it, he opened the latches and pulled out a thick manila envelope. Pouring its contents on the mattress, he began to place the seven or eight photos he'd found online one by one onto the bedspread.

He recognized the first person immediately. They had already met. *Jake Carpenter. Owner of the Sip 'n Strike Bar and Bowling Alley. Single. A longtime friend of Tarin MacGyver.*

The next photo pictured a man in uniform. *Mike Wilson. Chasm Falls police officer. Married with two kids. Another good friend of the target.*

Then there was the man Tommy seemed convinced would be the perfect fall guy. *Alex Davis. The woman's old boyfriend. Basically unemployed. Married but not happily, according to all reports. One young daughter.*

Dan's first impression was that Alex was cynical and—even for this hardened LA private investigator—had the potential to be threatening. Not a happy camper. The Rachel mentioned must be Alex's estranged wife.

Dan paused and turned over an image of a smiling young woman with shoulder-length blonde hair. *Tarin MacGyver herself. She should have known better. You don't cross Tommy Wyndham without paying for it. He'd learned that firsthand.*

Dan shuffled the photos into a single pile, put them back into the envelope, and stuffed the package into his briefcase. He would need to hang around town a little longer before the other faces made sense. The sound of a cell phone vibrating startled him.

He cradled the phone between his shoulder and neck while he worked with his briefcase. "Yeah?"

"Any progress?" Tommy asked.

"What kind of progress do you expect? I just got here a few hours ago." Dan lit a cigarette and went onto the balcony. "But I did meet the deranged ex-boyfriend, Alex, at a local bar."

"That was quick. And?"

"He's definitely not on an even keel."

"Did you have a chance to lay the foundation for why you're in Chasm Falls?"

"I planted the seeds. Told them I was trying to find property for an out-of-state client. They seemed to buy the story. In fact, the bar's owner, gave me a newspaper to check real estate ads."

"Be the charming guy we both know you can be, Danny. Keep working your way into their lives, gain their confidence, and when the time's right, we'll pull the plug on the bitch. We'll frame the old beau, and no one will be the wiser because they'll both be dead."

Dan took a long drag on his cigarette before asking the question that continued to haunt him. "You've tried to explain it a couple times, but I still don't understand what a smalltown girl like this could have done to make you so determined to take her out and that other guy in the process."

"I told you. Tarin played me and now she knows things. Beyond that, you're working on a need-to-know basis. Right now, the only information you need is what I expect of you, and that's getting rid of Parker's girlfriend. Got it?"

Resigned, Dan shook his head. "Got it, Tommy."

Then the call went dead. Dan put the cell phone on the nightstand, snuffed out the cigarette, and picked up the newspaper to begin his research. Amid the classified ads, he found Chasm Falls' real estate section. It included an assortment of advertisements, many with photos of the agents and an equal number without. Dan's eyes locked on the image of a young woman with long dark hair and the most captivating smile he thought he had ever seen.

"Maria Marshall," read the caption under her photo. "Marshall Realty: Residential properties, lakeshore homes, and vacant land." Next to her picture was that of an older man named Roger Marshall. Due to the difference in age between the two, Dan felt confident the man must be Maria's father and not her husband. That meant it was likely she might still be single. He tore out the ad and put it in his jacket pocket. *Tomorrow I'll make a point of meeting Maria Marshall. If I need to spend time with a real estate agent, it might as well be with a beautiful one.*

Then Dan stripped down to his underwear, pulled back the sheets, and went to bed.

CHAPTER 35

Beginning of the End

JAKE SMILED AS HIS NEWEST PATRON PERCHED himself on a seat at the bar. "How goes the hunt?"

Dan glanced at his watch. "Well, I'm ten hours into it and haven't gotten anywhere. The way it's going I might as well call it quits, admit defeat, and look for another job. Maybe I'll try a beach in the Bahamas. My boss won't welcome me back if I can't find what he wants to buy." He paused, "You see, he's not a patient man."

Jake put a pint draw down on the bar. "Come on. What do you expect on your first day?"

"But I did find an agent," Dan said, glancing toward the silent figure at the far end of the bar. "Afternoon, Alex."

Alex seemed oblivious while watching the replay of a recent Colorado Avalanche hockey game against the Detroit Red Wings.

"What brings you back?" Alex asked. "Carruthers, isn't it?"

Jake reminded his friend, "He's looking to buy property here unless you've forgotten."

"That's right. How could I forget? Take advantage of the down and out here in Chasm Falls."

"Cut him some slack, Alex. Not everyone you meet is an enemy." He turned back toward Dan. "What kind of an investment are you trying to find?"

"My client wants lakefront property."

"Don't they all? The rest of the town is worthless," Alex mumbled.

Jake ignored him. "Are you looking for undeveloped land or something with a house?"

"It would depend on the land and the house."

"How about another beer?" Jake offered.

Dan nodded and put his empty glass on the bar.

"Got a price range?"

Dan smiled, "My client seems to have a bottomless bankroll. He'll pay whatever it takes to get what he wants."

"That should open a few doors for you," Jake answered.

"I just need to find the right property."

"What's your cut?"

Dan shrugged. "Wish I could tell you. Let's just say he takes care of me when I meet his expectations." He picked up the refill and made his way to a vacant seat next to Alex.

"Is there any particular reason why you seem to be so negative about everything?" Dan was chilled to the bone by Alex's piercing stare.

"Aren't you getting kind of personal for a guy who's only been in town one day?"

"I'm not trying to be. Yesterday you said you'd lost your job." Dan hesitated before beginning to weave a tale of his own. "I can identify with that. I haven't been able to keep a regular job since I got out of the Army. I guess seeing everything that happens in a war zone can mess with your head."

Alex tapped a pack of Marlboro Reds on the solid oak bar. "Did you serve in the Middle East?" He'd nibbled but had yet to hit on the bait.

"I was in Desert Storm with the First Cavalry from Fort Hood," Dan replied. "Are you a vet?"

Alex didn't answer.

Jake filled in the blanks for his friend. "Alex did two tours there with the Army—one in Iraq and one in Afghanistan. He came home with a Purple Heart."

"Sounds like you've had it rough since you got back. Sorry to hear that." Dan studied his expression and watched for a reaction.

Alex stood, slapped the bar, and glared at Dan. "Would you like to tell me how the hell you can walk into town and think anyone is even interested in what you think? Try keeping your pity to yourself, find the property you're looking for, and go back where you came from."

Dan was left looking at an empty barstool when he heard the door slam. He smiled reluctantly at Jake. "Sorry. I didn't mean to upset him. It's just that I've gone through some of the same experiences and thought it might help find some common ground. Not that I'm a success or anything, but at least he could see I've managed to move on."

"Don't take it personally."

"What happened with his wife?" Dan asked.

"With Rachel? Which time?" Jake asked. "Their relationship has been a roller coaster ever since they got married. They'll get back together any day now. They always do."

Dan stood and pushed his empty glass toward Jake. "Well, I'm still sorry I riled him." He tried to change the subject. "Maybe I'll have a couple of hot prospects by the time we run into each other tomorrow. Keep your fingers crossed."

Back in his room minutes later, Dan found the light flashing on the hotel phone. It was Tommy and the message was short and sweet.

"Give me a call."

"Shit," Dan muttered when he returned the call. "I wish he would leave me alone and let me finish what he sent me here to do. And why is he using the hotel phone? Stupid."

"Wyndham here."

"What do you want, Tommy?"

"Just checking to see how it's going."

"Give me a break. It's only been twenty-four hours since we talked the last time and there was nothing to report then."

"Time has become an issue. Today, I found out the wench is already back in Colorado. This may be our opportunity. I need to know you've got a plan devised to frame the old boyfriend, leave us in the clear, and send Jon looking for a new love."

"If it makes you feel any better, I did have another conversation with Alex a little while ago. He's more than sour. From talking with the bar owner, it's obvious they think he's unstable."

"What about the MacGyver bitch? Did you talk about her with this Davis guy?"

"No. I didn't want to rush anything for god's sake. He's already wary of me. We need to be patient, Tommy, or it's going to look suspicious."

"Okay, but you either take her out when the timing's right and implicate Alex with a murder-suicide, or you get rid of her, cover your tracks, and hope the police don't tie the murder to you. It's that simple."

"You've made that clear more than once. Now why don't you leave me alone and let me do the job you hired me to do?"

Dan ended the call and grabbed his jacket. Maybe it was time to check out Tarin MacGyver's house to see where she lives when she's not gallivanting around San Diego with Jon Parker. Eventually, he was going to have to break in so he might as well start scoping out the place now.

DAN HAD SPENT THREE long days looking at properties with his real estate agent, Maria Marshall. While he forced himself to act interested in the houses she showed him, enjoying her company came naturally. In her early thirties, Maria was bright, funny, and an attractive brunette. Maria's mother had come to the United States from Mexico, and her daughter had inherited the deep whiskey brown eyes and rich skin color shared by most Latinos.

Without realizing it, he'd asked her to dinner. Dan wasn't sure if she accepted the invitation to talk business, or if she'd agreed because there was always the chance he might be her ticket out of Chasm Falls. Either way, it didn't matter. While she was showing him around the area, he realized he could probably pry more information about the relationship between Alex and Tarin from her than any man he might meet. All the women he'd ever known liked to talk.

Standing in front of the bathroom mirror, Dan continued to wonder what a woman like Maria could possibly see in a man his age. He still had a thick head of hair and worked out enough to have a better than an average physique. Even so, at almost fifty, life had taken its toll. But she had agreed to join him for dinner. Why question a good thing? Just go along with it and enjoy the evening.

Dan grabbed his keys and was out the door.

He picked up Maria at her modest home near downtown Chasm Falls. Her father owned the realty company, and it was apparent he controlled most of the profits.

"What if we drive to a restaurant in Winter Park?" he asked while helping her into the car. "I thought you might like to try something different. If I've done my research, it's only about twenty-five miles away, right?"

Maria nodded her approval. "That would be nice. On the way, we could talk more about the kind of property your client would like to find. I've got a few new ideas."

Dan smiled and told the complete truth for the first time in almost four days. "To be honest, I'm tired of real estate. Could we talk about something else?"

She returned the smile. "Absolutely. Believe it or not, I get sick of the subject, too."

He turned onto the highway heading toward Winter Park and they drove in comfortable silence for several miles before he spoke again. "Do you think you'll stay in Chasm Falls?"

"You mean always?"

Dan nodded.

"Oh, I don't know. It's a nice enough place to live—especially in the summer. The lake is beautiful, and the mountains are spectacular. It's not a bad life. I have good friends here."

"I think I've met a few of them at the bar."

"Like who?"

"Let's see. Jake—he owns the place, right? Then I met some guy named Alex." He watched for any sort of reaction.

She ignored the reference to Alex and her cheeks turned a rosy shade of pink. "I've had a crush on Jake since I was a teenager."

He grinned, enjoying the way she shyly averted her eyes. "He's single, isn't he? Why haven't you made a move?"

Maria looked up and Dan could see she was still blushing. "He works too hard to have a girlfriend. Besides, I've always known he's out of my league."

"Why do you say that?" he asked, not understanding why such a beautiful woman would be intimidated by any man.

She looked toward the floorboard. "My mother immigrated to this country illegally when she was a teenager. She worked very hard and earned her citizenship even before she married my father—" Maria stopped in mid-sentence. "There are some people who think less of our family because of our background."

"Those close-minded people don't know what they're missing." He paused. "If you don't mind me asking, what happened to your mother?"

Maria spoke softly. The memory still visibly painful. "She died in a car accident when I was twelve. My father's taken care of me ever since."

"I'm glad you never pursued Jake—otherwise, I might not be here with you tonight." He paused, "But what about Alex Davis? He's turned a few heads in his lifetime."

"He's married. Plus, even if he wasn't, he's not my type."

"Meaning?"

"Don't get me wrong. He's a legend in town. When he was in high school, he put Chasm Falls on the map. He was the first kid from here to get a full-ride athletic scholarship. But I guess college wasn't right for him. He flunked out his first year and joined the Army." She paused. "Everyone used to see him as a great guy, but he's been different the past few years."

"What happened?"

"Most people think he changed after he went to Afghanistan. I'm not sure I could handle seeing all that death and oppression, either."

"This Rachel that he married. Was she his high school sweetheart?"

"No. Alex was with someone else all the way through school. Her name's Tarin MacGyver. They broke up when she went to a university in New York. Most people think that's the reason he dropped out of college. In the end, Alex married Rachel. She's Tarin's best friend."

"Did Tarin stay in Chasm Falls?"

"She was gone for a while but moved back a few years ago."

"Do Alex and Tarin get along now?"

"I guess so. Tarin works for a newspaper and travels a lot. I don't think they see each other very often." Maria's eyes lit up. "Have you ever heard of the band Motive? Tarin's been dating one of the guys in the band. It's the most exciting gossip to hit our town in a long time."

"How's Alex taken it? Would he be jealous?"

"I don't think so. Alex is really devoted to Rachel and their daughter, Sarah."

"Enough about them. Let's talk about you."

Maria blushed again, and the two shared small talk the rest of the way to Winter Park, throughout dinner, and all the way home.

He walked Maria to her front door, left her with a simple, gentlemanly kiss on the forehead and drove back to the hotel, somewhat surprised with himself. In LA he would have wormed his way into Maria's house to seduce her before leaving in the early morning hours.

It must be the altitude.

Dan didn't look at the pictures in his briefcase that night. Instead, he found himself wondering what it might be like to live an obscure life in a quiet mountain town and have both a wife and family. The peaceful world he imagined disappeared when he thought back to the night Tommy Wyndham had taken control of his life.

In the past, he'd used his muscles for Tommy to make a point with people more times than he cared to admit. The money was always good, and the hours were even better. Most of his time was spent on the golf course or doing whatever else he felt like doing. Eventually, his private detective business was simply a front to conceal his association with Tommy.

But one night, something went wrong.

Tommy had sent him to "convince" a popular musician who had opted not to renew his contract with the overbearing manager to reconsider.

As planned, Dan weaseled his way into the man's house, but a fight ensued in the foyer. He punched him and the man lost his balance, fell backward, and cracked his head on a tile staircase. It didn't take long to realize the man was dead.

The police never linked him to the incident, but after that, Tommy controlled him much like he manipulated Jon and his other clients along the way. He used his knowledge to coerce the detective to do his bidding whenever and wherever he wanted. There seemed to be no way out.

In his hotel room, Dan fell asleep imagining a new life with a smalltown girl in a place far away from Tommy Wyndham. And for the first time in months—maybe years—he slept like a baby.

CHAPTER 36

The Plan

DAN'S BLOSSOMING RELATIONSHIP WITH MARIA Marshall proved to be a blessing when it came to the job at hand. When they were together, she introduced him to people he would have never met otherwise. Her friends seemed to accept him, and at times he even forgot the sinister reason why he was in Colorado.

Each night Dan sat on the bed in his hotel room, surrounded by a growing assortment of pictures and notes, and it was becoming much easier to put names with faces. He had also determined who might pose problems in the final scheme of things.

But try as he might, he couldn't seem to break through Alex's steel facade. He shared that information with Tommy during one of their late-night conversations.

"I'm convinced there's no way to get into the mind of Alex Davis. Not that I'd know what to do if I could," he admitted. "What I do know, however, is the locals would have no problem buying into the notion he was crazy enough to take her out and then kill himself because of what he'd done. It seems to be the consensus around here that he's not only unpredictable but potentially dangerous."

"What about the stalker Jon believes is threatening her? Do you think it's this Alex guy?"

"I've spent time with the officers working the burglary case. They don't have any solid evidence or leads, but Alex is a suspect. They're keeping an eye on him, especially the deputy sheriff. He's convinced Alex is their man. The town cop isn't so sure."

"Go on."

"As I see it, the challenge is to gather incriminating evidence we can plant. We lure Alex to Tarin's house when we're ready, and then take care of them both. Case closed and we get on with our lives."

"Works for me. What's our timetable?"

"First, I need to find a way to get into her house so I can grab a few things to plant in Alex's car for the police to find."

"When you're there, will you leave any evidence to make it look even more likely he's their man?"

Dan shook his head. "No. We don't want them to arrest Alex before we put our plan into motion." He paused for a minute, visualizing how it all might come down. "Anyway, after I have everything, we wait for the right moment to present itself. We need to be patient. And I need to research the alarm system she had installed. That could be my biggest obstacle."

"Whatever it takes. Anyway, I've deposited another three grand in your account. Don't bleed me dry. Just get it done."

"I will, Tommy. Trust me. Everything is falling into place."

He ended the call and leaned back against the headboard. Dan had told the truth. The plan was coming together with one piece missing: The will to carry it out.

CHAPTER 37

Celebrating the Season

MARIA GLANCED AT DAN WITH ANTICIPATION when they pulled into Tarin's driveway and parked near the front of the brightly lit log home.

He had been in Chasm Falls for almost two weeks when the opportunity he needed fell into his lap. Tarin MacGyver was hosting a holiday party, and Maria had invited him to be her date.

Dan smiled. "Whoever lives here must like Christmas."

The pine trees and shrubbery in front of the house were covered with tiny white lights, while a wreath sporting a red plaid bow and sleigh bells welcomed guests approaching the front door. Along the walkway a pair of life-size grapevine reindeer grazed on the snow-covered ground. Visitors could see a towering twelve-foot Christmas tree covered with lights and colorful ornaments through the front window.

"Don't you like the holidays?" Maria asked.

"It's a little different where I live in California. We don't have pine trees and snow to make it seem special." He paused to think about his sparsely furnished apartment and couldn't remember the last time he had bothered with any sort of decorations, let alone a Christmas tree.

"If anyone can throw a great party, it's Tarin. This is the social event of the season in Chasm Falls." Maria looked almost embarrassed.

"She invites me every year, but I've never had anyone to bring. I know it sounds silly, but I didn't want to go alone."

Dan smiled. "Well, you're not alone tonight." He walked to her side of the car. "Come on. What are you waiting for?"

Their hostess met them at the front door.

"Merry Christmas, Maria. You can't know how happy I am to finally have you join us." Tarin gave her a quick hug while extending a hand to the man at her guest's side. "This must be Dan. I'm glad you could come."

"Hey, Mac—where's the corkscrew?" Jake called from the kitchen.

"Hold on a sec. I'll be right there." Tarin glanced around at the other guests. "I'm sorry. He's a man, so there's no way he'll find it without another set of eyes. I think you know almost everyone, Maria, so make yourself at home. I'll be back in a minute."

"Nice place," Dan said as he surveyed the home's interior. He looked toward the digital panel on the wall to his left, barely aware of Maria's response because he was studying the make and model of the security system.

"Her grandparents built the house about twenty years ago." Maria touched his arm to regain his attention. "Dan, do you suppose your client would be interested in a property like this?

He glanced back at her and smiled. "Who wouldn't?"

She became very excited at the prospect. "Why didn't I think of it before? There's a house like Tarin's for sale on the other side of the lake. It's further from town and older, so it needs quite a bit of work, but money doesn't seem to be an issue with your client. Maybe he wouldn't mind the location or the remodeling."

"Anybody need a glass of wine?" Jake asked, approaching them from across the room.

Dan looked at Maria, who nodded. "That would be nice."

"How's the house hunt going?" Jake filled one of the two glasses he held in his hand.

"Not so great, but Maria has another possibility we plan to look at some time this week." Dan put his arm around her waist. "But if I find something, I won't have a reason to stick around. I've gotten quite fond of this little community."

Jake grinned and moved on to the next guests. "You know you'll always have a stool at my bar."

Dan shifted his gaze to the kitchen where Tarin was laughing and talking with Mike Wilson. Suddenly he felt like scum. These people had welcomed him into their world without question and Maria had invited him into her life with blind trust. But his own motives were less than honorable. Much less. If they wanted the truth, the man they thought they knew was nothing more than a figment of their imaginations. At that moment, Dan realized he wanted nothing more than to leave his past behind.

DAN SAW TARIN STRUGGLING with a platter of hors d'oeuvres and a large bowl of chips. "Can I help with that?"

"Thank you. Your timing is perfect. All I want to do is get from here to the table. It shouldn't be such a monumental task." Exchanging the tray for an empty one, Tarin turned to Dan. "I'm sorry. I'm afraid I'm not a very good hostess. We haven't had a chance to talk."

"That's okay. You're a busy lady."

"It's still no excuse."

"Is there anything else I can help you with?" he asked, beginning to feel awkward. *Don't be so fricking nice to me, Tarin. You'll make this much more difficult than it needs to be.*

"No, that should do it for now," she said with a hint of hesitation in her voice. "Dan, I'm thrilled you and Maria seem to have hit it off. She's a charming girl who's had a hard time getting out from under her father's influence. He's a nice man, but he raised Maria by himself after her mother died. He's very protective."

"I've never met him. Should I expect someone to show up at my hotel room door with a shotgun one of these days?"

Tarin couldn't help but laugh. "No. He's not that protective." She turned to put the empty platter on the counter to refill it. "How long do you think you'll be in town?"

Just long enough to kill you. Looking into her sparkling eyes, Dan tried to erase the thought. Then, over his shoulder, he watched someone go into the bathroom near the kitchen and saw the opportunity he needed. "Do you think I might be able to use your facilities? The beer seems to be going right through me."

Tarin turned to point toward the bathroom, but realizing it was in use, gestured upstairs to the loft. "Someone else seems to be having the same problem. You're welcome to use the bathroom in my bedroom. It's upstairs and to the left."

"Thanks. I'll be right back." He smiled and started up the stairs. Once inside her room, he studied its layout, memorizing the location of chairs, dressers, and other furniture that might be obstacles when the time came.

Glancing downstairs, he opened Tarin's jewelry box and lifted a delicate locket. Dan opened it to find a photo of a woman he suspected to be Tarin's mother. He put it in his pocket and continued to scan the room.

Bathroom to the left, bed to the right. Glass across the front leading to a deck.

He walked toward the floor-to-ceiling windows to see if there were steps leading to ground level. There weren't. He would have to come in the front door and up the main stairway.

"Did you find the bathroom?" Tarin asked.

Startled by her voice, Dan's heart skipped a beat. "No—I mean, not yet. I was just admiring your view. Ledge Lake is beautiful."

"Where did Maria tell me you were from?" she asked, walking toward him, and taking in the view herself.

"California."

"What part?"

Think fast. Have I told Maria a city? Shit. I don't think so. But what if I have and tell Tarin something different?

"Near Los Angeles."

Tarin went to her closet, grabbed a sweater, and started back down the stairs. "I've only been to California a few times, but I recently spent time in the San Diego area. I loved it there."

The tightness in his chest began to fade when Dan closed the bathroom door behind him. *That was close. I need to be more careful if I hope to pull this off.*

"ARE YOU READY TO go home?" Dan asked, resting his arm around Maria's shoulders.

"Mmm. I don't know. This is so perfect."

Ten or fifteen other guests were still mingling in various places around the house, but Dan and Maria had settled on an over-stuffed couch opposite the crackling fireplace.

"I'm having a magnificent time," he whispered in her ear. "You have wonderful friends."

"Aren't they great?" She sat up and stretched. "I'm ready to go if you are. Tomorrow morning I need to make an appointment to show a special client a log house across the lake."

He grinned, helping her to her feet. "I wouldn't happen to know that client, would I?"

She took his hand. "You might. Let's say good night to everyone."

Tarin emerged from the dining room and asked, "Are you two leaving?"

"I think so," Dan answered. "Is there anything we can do to help you before we go?"

She shook her head. "No. I'll worry about the mess in the morning. Thanks for coming, and it was certainly nice to meet you, Dan." Pointing to the mistletoe overhead, Tarin kissed him lightly on the cheek. "I'm leaving for Paris the day after tomorrow, but maybe I'll see you again before I go. If not, Merry Christmas."

Once outside, he approached their car in the darkness, brushing the back of his hand across his cheek. Was it his imagination? The place where Tarin's lips had touched his face seemed to be burning.

Moments later, he parked in front of Maria's house and walked with her to the front door. He started to say goodnight, but she silenced his words by placing an index finger to his lips. Then she put her key in the lock, turned the handle, and took him inside.

CHAPTER 38

———

The City of Lights

THE ROCKY MOUNTAINS HAD DIPPED BELOW THE horizon when Tarin reclined her seat and prepared for the seven-hour flight to Reykjavik, Iceland. After a short layover, she would begin the last leg of her journey—the five-hour flight to Paris. The Icelandair 757 had taken off from Denver shortly after five in the afternoon. Due to time changes and a brief layover, she wouldn't arrive in France until the afternoon of the next day. She'd been surprised to learn the newspaper had purchased Saga Class tickets for her—the equivalent of first class with most other airlines. The aisle seat next to her was vacant for both legs of the journey, allowing even more room to relax.

Tarin would be spending the last two weeks of December with Peter Janus, an eighteen-year-old artistic phenomenon from Denver. The college freshman had been invited to show his work at the Louvre in an exhibit spotlighting upcoming artists from around the world. She was excited about being Peter's shadow and sharing his experiences with the newspaper's readership. Tarin feared her reporting skills had gotten a bit rusty and this would be an excellent opportunity to re-hone them. Then, of course, there's always the fact the assignment is in Paris, France. Who wouldn't want to accept it?

WALKING FROM THE CONCOURSE toward the transportation hub at Charles De Gaulle International Airport, Tarin could see blue skies and bright sunshine streaming through the terminal's expansive glass windows. The large, open area was bustling with travelers hurrying to and from their destinations and employees laboring with overloaded luggage carts.

Pushing her suitcase with a carry-on balanced on top, she scanned the placards of the taxi and shuttle drivers hoping to find her name. At the agreed upon location, she found a middle-aged man in a navy wool sweater and black trousers waiting patiently with "MacGyver" written on a small, white eraser board.

"Bonsoir, Monsieur," she said in a relieved voice.

"Mademoiselle MacGyver, I assume?" he asked, taking the luggage handle from her hand. "You have had a long day, no?"

She nodded in agreement, "A very long night and day, thank you."

With his accent wrapped around broken English, the man's warm smile and gentle ways reminded Tarin of her grandfather. "I am Luc, and I take you to your hotel so you may rest. I was told you are staying at the Le Littré."

She nodded.

"Good. We will be there soon."

Tarin watched the sights of Paris flash by from the backseat. It was mid-December and the landscape was dressed in colorful holiday finery.

"It's beautiful, Luc, but you have no snow."

"No," he answered, glancing in the rear-view mirror. "December is our coldest month, but we do not have much snow. Instead, we have cold rain. Today we have sunshine. It is a very nice day."

The rest of the trip was driven in silence while Tarin absorbed the grandeur of the city. They drove along the Avenue de la Grande Armée, under the Arc de Triomphe, and onto the Avenue des Champs Elysées. Then the driver used less-traveled streets to reach their destination on the West Bank.

"How long will you be with us in Paris?" Luc asked as he carried her luggage toward the hotel entrance.

"A couple of weeks," she replied, enamored by the narrow street and the tall buildings lining it.

"Enjoy your stay in our city, Mademoiselle MacGyver." With a tip of his hat, the driver stepped back to his car and disappeared into the afternoon traffic.

Tarin checked in and put her luggage in her room before knocking on Peter Janus' door, which was just down the hall from her own.

"Ms. MacGyver. I wondered when you would get here." The young man stepped aside and invited her in.

She noticed the paintbrush in his hand and the easel standing near the French doors leading to the balcony. She smiled, "You've been painting, I see. May I look?"

His shyness was evident. "I haven't gotten very far."

Tarin stopped a few feet from the canvas and smiled. "It's beautiful, Peter."

With a palette of muted colors, he had recreated the historic architecture, adding bright dabs of color to represent people bustling about on the street below. The narrow roadway was lined with vehicles parked bumper-to-bumper. Looking at the canvas, Tarin could imagine the sounds of a street in Paris at midday.

"This is like a different world," he told her with wide eyes. "Everything is so old."

"It's magical, isn't it?"

"Have you been here before?" he asked.

"No." She turned toward Peter with an enormous smile lighting her face, "Suddenly I'm energized and there's much of the afternoon left. What if we explore a bit of the city together?"

He nodded. "I'd like that, ma'am."

She shook her head and wiggled an index finger in his direction. "Wait a minute. I may be older than you, but I'm certainly not a ma'am—at least not yet. Please, just call me Tarin. Now—have you eaten?"

"No."

"Do you think you can set your paints aside long enough for us to go out for a quick snack? I saw a charming little café down the street."

"I am hungry."

"Good. Put away your paints and let's check it out."

THE PAIR DECIDED TO wander along the Parisian streets and alleyways and found themselves lost at least twice. Opting for dinner rather than a snack, they found a small neighborhood restaurant near the hotel. They spent almost two hours talking and laughing over a traditional French meal of steak and frites.

But after returning to the hotel, the adrenaline she felt upon arriving at the hotel earlier in the afternoon had evaporated. Huddled in a coat, Tarin sat in silence on her balcony and watched the Eiffel Tower's twinkling lights commandeer the night sky. She picked up her cell phone and dialed Jon's number. It was eleven o'clock in Paris, which meant it would be two in the afternoon in California.

"Parker," answered the familiar voice.

"Afternoon, handsome."

"Tarin?"

She could sense the pleasure in his voice.

"I'm sitting on my balcony watching the lights on the Eiffel Tower." She took her time and allowed the vision to sink in. "What are you doing?"

"We're finalizing the album's cover art. What time is it there?"

"It's late and very lonely here without you."

"I could jump on a plane."

"And what would the rest of the band say about that? You stay right where you are and finish that project."

"What have you done so far?"

"I met Peter this afternoon after I got to the hotel. He's a fascinating young man. We had an early dinner at a quaint restaurant down the street."

"Should I be jealous?"

"He's eighteen years old, Jon."

"I know. I'm just teasing. Will there be time to sightsee, or will your days be all work and no play?"

"Mostly work. But spending time in the Louvre is hardly painful. For me it's a dream come true."

"Just don't fall in love with Paris and decide not to come back."

"I wish you could see the holiday lights. They're breathtaking." Just hearing Jon's voice brightened her evening. "What about your day?"

"They've been scheduling guest appearances on talk shows, and we're getting ready to go into production with the album. Can you believe it's almost over, Mac?"

"What's Tommy up to?" She tried to sound nonchalant.

"He's been remarkably mellow. None of us understand why, but we're not asking him to go back to his old ways."

"That's good." She paused for a moment. "I'm getting cold on the balcony. It's time to go inside and let you get back to work."

"Tarin—" He paused. "Could you call and wake me up every morning? I'd like my day to begin hearing your voice."

She smiled. "The time difference might make it challenging, but I bet I can figure it out."

"Promise?"

"I promise. Have a great day."

"I love you."

"Love you, too. Miss you even more. Good night, Jon."

She held the silent cell phone in her hand and looked wistfully at the lights twinkling on the Eiffel Tower. "I really do wish you were here." With that, she walked back into her room and closed the French doors.

CHAPTER 39

Almost Finished

PAUL FLIPPED ON THE MICS IN THE STUDIO. "OKAY, guys—this is it. We've got the tracks down and we're ready to produce the masters. This is when you tell me to go back to the control board or this record will be out there for all posterity. Got it?"

His words were answered with exhausted yet enthusiastic catcalls from members of the band.

"And," he added, "if you're so inclined, there's champagne, beer, and more than enough food in the kitchen to feed an army. It's time to celebrate." Paul smiled at Nick, who was sitting next to him in the control room. "They already know they've got a platinum album, don't they?"

Nick shrugged. "What sounds great in the studio doesn't always live up to the hype."

Paul wasn't buying it. "Give me a break. You know how good this album is."

"Hey, don't take me seriously. I'm just tired. You're right. I think— no, I'm sure—Motive is about to release its biggest album to date. When do you think it will hit the market?"

"If I get right on it, the masters should be ready in less than a week. To be honest, Clocktower isn't going to hold this release. The rumors about Motive breaking up are on every music network and radio station in the country. The label will strike while the iron's hot, and I'd say they'll be hitting the charts in a few weeks." Paul paused before asking the same question everyone in the industry was asking. "Do you really think they'll split up?"

"Looks like it. Let's face it, they've been on the road continuously for more than ten years. Jimmy has a family and the others might want to settle down if they have the chance. We all know where Jon stands. Maybe they're just plain tired of the whole gig. But it doesn't mean they'll disappear. Look at the Stones, Aerosmith, the Eagles, and all the bands from that era. They just keep coming back for more. But one thing's certain—the guys will need to find a new lead singer. Jon's ready to try it on his own."

"Did I hear my name and was it taken in vain?" Jon asked, wiping the sweat from his brow with a towel. Exhausted, he landed in a chair at the console next to Nick.

"It was all good," Paul said smiling. "We were just wondering what you have planned to top this last record."

"Do you have a minute before we join the party?" Jon asked.

Paul was curious. "Sure. What's up?"

Jon pulled a digital tape from his pocket. "Stick this in and see what you think."

The engineer took the tape from Jon's outstretched hand, slipped it into one of the recording units, and hit play.

As the last chords of the first song faded, Paul pressed the pause button and looked over at the two men. "Talk to me."

"You know I've been toying with the idea of a solo album. Something completely different from anything I've ever done. Those are the takes Nick and I have been working on. You don't need to listen to the whole tape to get a feel for where we want to go."

Paul dimmed the control room lights and leaned back in his chair. "I know I don't have to, but I want to."

Thirty minutes later he pressed stop and looked first at Nick, and then at Jon who had been pacing on the other side of the room. "This is good stuff. Even raw the melodies are great and the lyrics are even better." Paul shook his head. "You and Nick are quite a team."

Jon gave his partner a thumbs up.

"All the songs are good, but that third track is dynamite. Sure, we can tighten it up, but it doesn't need much. With that song you'll have every woman who hears it begging for more." Paul stopped, sensing there was something about this tape he hadn't been told. "Okay, guys. What are you keeping from me?"

"First, don't give us all the credit," said Nick. "Jon and I wrote the music, but most of the lyrics aren't ours."

"I guess you found a new collaborator. Feel like clueing me in on who this person might be?"

Jon kept the engineer hanging for a few seconds. "It's Tarin."

"Are you serious?" Paul's response was a mix of admiration and disbelief. "Who knew?"

"Nobody. And for now, we need to keep it that way," Jon instructed.

"My lips are sealed, but at a price," Paul told him. "When the time comes to mix this record, I need to be the man behind the board. Deal?"

Jon extended his hand, "Deal. I wouldn't have it any other way. Keep the tape. We want your ideas and suggestions." He looked intently at his long-time engineer, "Seriously, Paul, put me on your calendar. We don't want to waste any time. I want to start working on the album this spring. Can we make that happen?"

"Absolutely." Paul watched Jon walk to the window overlooking the dark recording studio. "What are you thinking about?"

Jon shrugged before turning from the glass and sitting back down on the edge of the console. He smiled when he heard a burst of laughter from the celebration still going strong in the kitchen. "Do you think I'm making a mistake?"

"By going out on your own? Not a chance. It's the right move at the right time." Paul turned off the power to the board, stood, and stretched. He looked at Jon, "Tarin's in Europe, isn't she? Do you have plans for Christmas? You know you're welcome at our house if you don't. The kids love their Uncle Jon."

"Thank you, but I've got plans and a ticket. I'm flying to Paris to surprise Tarin. I'll be there Christmas Eve."

Paul gave him a high five. "Good for you, man. Now, let's celebrate."

CHAPTER 40

A Christmas Surprise

JON PAID THE FARE, GRABBED HIS BAG AND JUMPED out of the cab. "Merci beaucoup."

Standing on the wet pavement, he surveyed the streetscape through a light mist. This would be a Christmas unlike any other. Jon gathered his thoughts and walked toward the hotel's awning-covered entrance. Once inside, he approached a gentleman behind the desk, "Good evening."

"May we help you, Monsieur?"

"I hope so. I'm here to visit one of your guests."

"And the party's name, Monsieur?"

"Tarin MacGyver."

"Ah, yes, Mademoiselle MacGyver. Is she expecting you?"

Jon smiled. "No. I'm her boyfriend and I'm hoping to surprise her. You know, bring a little piece of home to Paris for the holidays."

"I believe she is upstairs in her room. Would you like me to call her for you?"

"No. If it's all right, I'd just like to go up and see if she's in."

Reaching the top floor, the elevator door opened, and he found a cozy yet elegantly decorated hallway. A vase of fresh flowers graced a table across from the elevator, the fragrant scent wafting through the air. Studying the polished brass numbers on the doors, Jon deduced Tarin's room must be located near the end of the hall.

He tapped softly on her door.

Tarin didn't look up when she opened the door. Instead, she leaned over to pick up a newspaper from the floor at her feet. "Hi, Peter. Come on in. I'm almost ready—" Noticing her guest's shoes, she realized the person standing there wasn't wearing the young artist's trademark sneakers.

"Peter again, is it? That young man seems to come between us every time I turn around." Jon continued to finger his chin, appearing to be deep in thought. "You go to Paris and waste no time falling for another man. I'm devastated."

"Jon?" Tarin's face evolved from astonishment into pure excitement. "What are you doing here? You're supposed to be getting ready for interviews and talk shows."

"So that's how you greet a man who's just flown six thousand miles to surprise you?"

Tarin grabbed his hand and pulled him into the suite. "Come here, you!"

Closing the door with a thrust of her foot, she threw her arms around his neck. "I'm sorry. I never expected to see you here in a million years."

"And?"

"And Peter's the teenage artist I've been writing about for the newspaper—"

"You forget. We've talked about Peter many times before. Even so, I never expected to be replaced by a younger man."

"Jon—stop it."

He lifted her chin to look into her eyes, "You know I'm messing with you. I missed you too much to stay away. After all, it's Christmas."

"It is, isn't it?" She smiled, "I've missed you, too." Then she spun around, "Come here. I want you to see my balcony."

"A balcony, eh? It appears my lady is traveling in style."

"I can see the Eiffel Tower from here." Tarin opened the double doors leading outside and turned to watch his reaction.

"That you can." Jon wrapped his arms around her from behind and squeezed. Then he looked toward the apartments on the other side of the street. The windows were open at a residence across from Tarin's top-floor terrace and a festive holiday gathering was in progress. Christmas lights decorated nearly all the apartments in the tall stucco and brick buildings towering above the narrow street.

She looked up at Jon. "What do you think?"

"I think I'd rather be here with you than anywhere else in the world."

A knock interrupted their thoughts, and Tarin started toward the door. "This must be Peter. We planned to go to dinner."

"Can I tag along?"

She stopped to send a smile his way and invited Peter into the room.

"Hi, Tarin. How are you tonight?" The young man stood a few steps inside the door, glancing at Jon.

"Peter, I'd like you to meet a friend of mine from California. Peter—Jonathan Parker. Jon—Peter Janus." She watched as the men shook hands. "Now, are you two ready to enjoy a wonderful Christmas Eve dinner?"

"I am," Jon said without hesitation. "The food on the plane was skimpy at best, so I'm starving. What about you, Peter?"

The young man nodded in agreement. "I painted along the Seine today without a break. It rained off and on. I was under a shelter, but it was still cold. I'm ready for a hot meal." He turned toward Tarin. "Remember the café around the corner we talked about trying? I made a reservation on my way back to the hotel. I hope that's all right."

"All right?" she approved. "It's perfect."

Peter looked at his watch. "If we leave now, we should have just enough time to get there."

"What are we waiting for?" Jon lifted Tarin's coat from a nearby chair and slipped it over her shoulders. "Let's go."

"I THINK I'LL GO back to the hotel," Peter announced while the trio lingered over dessert. "I even know how to get there—I almost feel like a real Parisian."

Tarin put a hand on the young man's arm when he turned to leave. "Would you like to spend the day with us tomorrow?"

"That would be great, but one of the curators at the Louvre invited me to spend Christmas Day with his family." Peter extended his hand toward Jon, "It was nice meeting you, sir, and Merry Christmas."

When they were alone, Jon reached to take Tarin's hands in his. "He's a very nice young man." He paused. "Did you ever think we would be drinking coffee together in Paris on Christmas Eve?"

"No, but after meeting you, I've realized anything is possible."

Jon looked around the crowded room for their waiter. "Feel like an adventure?"

She noticed his sparkling blue eyes, "Absolutely. Can we take the train into the city?"

"Anything you would like, Mac."

Wearing a black coat with a black and gray houndstooth scarf looped around her neck, Jon watched Tarin pull a black wool hat from her purse. "Come here," he said, taking it from her hand. "Let me." He placed it on her head, carefully angling it just the right way, and then leaned over to kiss her. "You, Mac, look quite European. Black, black, and even more black."

"And you, Jon, look quite American. We need to work on that."

A HALF AN HOUR later, they emerged from the underground train station into the heart of the city. Strolling arm-in-arm, they passed colorful shop windows, bakeries, and butcher shops. Despite the hour, many of the stores were still open for residents scurrying to find last-minute gifts and supplies for Christmas Day.

"Look," Jon said pointing to a quaint antique store. Taking her arm, they maneuvered through the crowd of people bustling along the sidewalk. He brushed the moisture away from the store's plate-glass window so they could see the assorted treasures inside. "Come on," he said, pulling her toward the door.

"Bonne soirée," he said to the clerk who was almost invisible behind the cluttered counter in the tiny shop. "Parlez-vous Anglais?"

"Oui," the woman answered warmly. "May I help you with something, Monsieur?"

Jon motioned toward a display in the window. "If possible, I'd like to see that bracelet."

Reaching across a tray of gold and silver jewelry, the clerk retrieved an ornately engraved, sterling silver bracelet. Mounted in the center was a delicate locket with colorful gemstones mounted on either side.

"This is a beautiful piece," the woman said, placing it in the palm of Jon's hand. "It is very old and—how you say—" She struggled to find the right words. "It can hold a special photo and the memories that go with it."

He looked at Tarin and then back at the clerk. "We would like to buy it."

"Excellent choice, Monsieur."

Back on the sidewalk, Jon handed her the small, tissue-filled foil bag. "Merry Christmas, Tarin."

She blushed with embarrassment. "It's so beautiful, Jon. But I'm sorry—I don't have anything for you."

"Quite the contrary," he answered. "I have you. Now, what's next?"

"Can we go see the decorations on the Champs Elysées? The lights will stay on all night tonight."

"Which way do we go?" he asked, glancing down the street.

"Let's get back on the underground train." She took his hand and helped Jon weave through the holiday throng. Minutes later, they stood surrounded by what Parisians consider the most spectacular holiday light display in the city.

"This is amazing," Jon said, surveying the buildings and storefronts. "See that bakery across the street? I could use another cup of coffee and we could pick out pastries for tomorrow morning."

Sitting next to each other at a small table, Tarin snuggled against Jon, resting her head on his shoulder. "Even though I don't have the slightest idea what they're saying, I love listening to the French speak. Their language is so beautiful." She sat up and looked at him in amazement. "I didn't know you could speak French. I'm impressed."

He laughed and leaned toward her. "You've almost heard my entire vocabulary. Naturally, my mother tried to teach us Italian, but it's not a subject taught in most high schools. Instead, I took French for a couple of years, but never did master it. You know that old saying if you don't use something you lose it? Well, it's true."

"Does your mother still have family in Italy?"

"Her parents are gone, but she has two brothers there with their families."

Tarin sipped on her coffee. "Have you ever met them?"

"No. Mom hasn't even seen them since she married my dad and came to the United States."

"It's decided then. We should take her to see them someday."

Hugging her, Jon couldn't help but smile. "That's why I love you. You're always thinking about how you can make life better for the people around you. I like your idea. My mom would put up a fight saying the trip would be too expensive, but inside she would love it."

Then, while Jon tried his best to disguise it, Tarin couldn't ignore his yawn. She could sense the long flight was beginning to take its toll. "What do you say we go back to the hotel?" she suggested. "I think you've had enough for one day. We can have a glass of wine on the balcony, watch the city lights for a few minutes, and then I'll take you to bed."

He looked disappointed. "But it's Christmas Eve and we're in Paris. However, the thought of you taking me to bed sounds like something I might enjoy immensely."

"You can make it up to me tomorrow. We can go to the Christmas Market at Notre Dame, the Lumières en Seine at Domaine de Saint Cloud, or we could even go to mass at Sacre Coeur Basilica in Montmartre. The church was built on the highest point in Paris." The enthusiasm for the city she'd come to love reverberated in her voice. "There's also a wonderful holiday market we can visit at Hôtel de Ville—the Paris City Hall. Oh, and there's the Roue de Paris. It's a huge Ferris wheel in the Place de la Concorde in front of the Jardin des Tuileries."

"Slow down! How in the world do you know so much about what's happening here during the holidays?"

"I thought I'd be alone for Christmas, so I've been studying," she admitted.

Jon stretched his hands into the air and looked skyward. "What is this?"

Tarin spun around, catching snowflakes on her gloves. "I was told it hardly ever snows in Paris in December. See, you brought magic to the city." She pointed to a narrow side street. "Let's go this way. It's a shortcut Peter and I discovered that will take us back to the underground."

"You keep denying it," he teased, "but I truly am getting jealous of this young man you've been spending so much time with."

She held Jon's arm, leaning against him while they strolled in the crisp night air and the light falling snow. "There's only one man in my life and that's you." She looked toward his face, her eyes twinkling, but then stopped without warning. "How long can you stay?"

He reluctantly admitted the truth. "I have to be back in LA by the weekend."

Tarin's smile turned into a frown. "But that's only three more days, Jon. And you'll spend one of those days at the airport." She couldn't hide her disappointment. "That means we'll just have tomorrow and the next day. I wanted to take you to Versailles, the Louvre, and on a Seine River cruise, too."

"I guess," he said as they began to walk again, "that means we need to make the most of the next forty-eight hours."

CHAPTER 41

The Hunt

ALEX DAVIS WAS FILLING HIS TRUCK WITH GAS WHEN Dan Carruthers pulled alongside the pump opposite him. "Alex," he said, acknowledging the man's presence. "How's it going?"

"Same old, same old," was the monotone reply.

"It's hard to believe we're already almost a week into the New Year."

"Time flies."

Dan was doing his best to engage Alex in conversation and getting nowhere fast. "You know what? Jake told me you're quite the hunter, and I read in the newspaper that because of the elk count, the state has added a short two-week rifle season. In fact, it's due to open tomorrow. There's no way I can get a tag, but I was hoping to ride along if you have plans to go out." Dan pulled a squeegee from its soapy bin and began cleaning his windshield.

Alex glanced over. Dan had piqued his interest. "You like to hunt?"

"A little. Mostly I go for birds. You know pheasants, ducks, and geese. I've never had a chance to try my hand at an elk."

What happened next came as a complete surprise.

Alex put the nozzle back into the pump, tightened the fuel cap, and turned toward Dan. "I was planning on giving it a shot tomorrow. We're supposed to get a little snow and that's good for tracking. You can come along if you'd like. You won't have a tag so you can't shoot, but you can help us if we get an animal."

Score. "Where should I meet you?" Dan asked.

"What about Shuck's on the other side of the lake? My in-laws own it. The food's not bad and they cater to hunters. Be there at four thirty. We'll want to get an early start."

"Sounds great," he answered. "Thanks."

"No problem." With that, Alex got back into his truck and drove away.

Guess I better find some hunting gear so I look the part. Dan took out his cell phone and dialed Tommy. He got his voicemail.

"Tommy? Dan here. We're finally making progress. I ran into Davis while I was getting gas a few minutes ago. This guy really runs hot and cold. Up until now he hasn't been willing to say more than a few unpleasant words to me. Now suddenly I'm going elk hunting with him tomorrow." He got back into his car and pressed the ignition. "This could be the break we need. Don't worry. I'll let you know how it goes."

WHEN DAN PULLED INTO the restaurant parking lot before dawn, Alex's truck was already parked there along with perhaps a dozen or so other vehicles. He quickly discovered an early morning flurry of activity inside the small café and bait shop. Several waitresses were busy scurrying around serving breakfast to an entourage of men dressed in camouflage clothing and fluorescent orange safety vests.

It didn't take him long to find Alex seated in a booth at the far end of the room. "Good morning." He glanced around, shaking his head in amazement. "This is amazing."

Then he noticed something else he hadn't expected: The deputy sheriff he'd met at the bar was seated in the booth across from Alex. He managed to seamlessly cover his surprise. "Good morning. Scott Simmons, isn't it? I think we played pool the other night at the Sip 'n Strike."

Scott moved to the end of the bench when Dan slid in next to him. "Are you ready to try hunting in the Rockies?" the off-duty deputy asked. "The elk herd is pretty big around here, so you're almost guaranteed to see action."

"Rachel," Alex called to one of the waitresses. "Can you get our friend here some coffee?" He looked back at Dan. "That's my wife. Several generations ago, her grandfather built this place."

"Morning," Rachel said politely while setting a steaming cup in front of the latest arrival. "Cream and sugar are at the end of the table. Can I get you anything else?" she asked for what must have been the hundredth time that morning.

"The biscuits and gravy are good," Scott suggested. "Trust me, you'll need food in your stomach, especially if we get a kill. We'll gut it in the field and haul the carcass out. It could be a long, cold day."

Dan took his advice. "I'll try the biscuits. But I'd also like two over-easy eggs on the side. Thanks." He turned back to his hunting partners. "What's next?"

"We'll head around the lake and go into the woods. There's an old cabin there we can use as a base." Alex scanned Dan's attire. "I got the impression you were a city kind of guy. But you're dressed right for the weather. I'm impressed."

Dan shrugged, "Maybe it's my military background. You need to be prepared for anything." *They don't need to know I bought everything yesterday.*

Scott extended his cup to a passing waitress offering refills. "You've been in town what—a month now? Think I heard you were looking for property. It should be a buyer's market around here."

"Maria Marshall's been showing me around, but we haven't found what I'm looking for yet."

Alex laughed and leaned over the table. "From what I've heard, Maria's showing you more than just houses."

There was a protective edge in Dan's reply. "She's a very sweet and kind woman," he countered. "I'm having a wonderful time working with her."

Alex sat back in the booth and lifted his hands in mock self-defense. "Sorry, I didn't mean anything by it. But it is nice to see Maria going out with somebody. She's always been sort of hard to pull out of her shell."

"Here you go," Rachel said placing a heaping platter of biscuits and gravy and a side of eggs in front of Dan. "Can I get you anything else?" she asked, still talking to Dan but looking at her husband.

"No, I'm sure this will be more than enough."

"Will you be late tonight, Alex?"

He shook his head. "I shouldn't be. Tell Sarah I'll be there to tuck her in."

"She'll like that," Rachel smiled and moved to the next booth, picking up a pot of coffee from the table behind her.

Dan hesitated but asked the question anyway. "I heard you two have been separated for a while. It sounds like you're back together. That's good, right?"

Alex tapped an open hard pack of cigarettes on the table. "We're working at it. Now, you need to finish so we can get out of here and onto the trail."

THE THREE MEN DECIDED to take one vehicle, loaded their gear into Scott's Jeep, and drove out of the parking lot. About twenty minutes later, Scott turned the car onto a narrow, snow-covered lane heading toward the mountains. Dan noticed a familiar house in the rearview mirror.

"Where are we going?" he asked.

Alex rested his arm on the seat back and turned to talk. "There's a place up here where a small herd likes to hang out in this kind of weather."

Dan tried to sound nonchalant. "Isn't that Tarin MacGyver's house back there?"

Alex nodded. "This is her land. She's got at least a thousand acres of forest extending from the road by her house up the side of the mountain. It was her grandfather who taught me to hunt when I was a kid. He used to bring me here all the time. Tarin still lets me use the property pretty much whenever I want."

Scott continued to drive along the icy lane, passing Tarin's barn before the road began a steep incline.

"Hold on," Alex advised. "It'll get rough from here on out. I'm not sure how much farther we'll be able to drive, Scott."

"No worries. We can always hike to the cabin."

"The cabin?" Dan asked.

"Tarin's grandfather built a hunting cabin up here. It's rustic, but there's a wood stove, a well, and an outhouse. It offers all the comfort a man needs," Alex explained, pulling his backpack from the floorboard, and placing it on his lap.

Just then the Jeep high-centered on a drift and slid to the side. "Hold on," Scott advised before he shifted into low gear and managed to get the vehicle moving again. "Like you said, I'm not sure how much closer to the cabin we'll be able to get. I don't want to push it, or we won't be able to drive back out when we need to."

"Speaking of Tarin MacGyver, Scott. Jake told me there was a break-in at her house a few months ago. It sounds like there could be a stalker." Dan watched for a reaction from Alex. "Have you guys gotten any leads?"

The deputy shook his head. "No. Whoever's behind it knows what he's doing. No prints. No DNA." Scott glanced at Dan in the rearview mirror. "We found blood, but most of it turned out to be contaminated. The rest belonged to the other guy that was there." He looked at Alex for help. "What's his name?"

Alex's expression didn't change. "Parker."

"Yeah, that's it." Scott revved the engine a bit. "Anyway, we're still working the case, but the trail's gotten cold. Tarin thinks someone's been in her house since then, so maybe we'll catch the creep that way. He's bound to make a mistake at some point."

Dan continued to watch Alex who seemed to simply stare into the windshield until he spoke. "I may never understand what Tarin sees in that guy." He pulled a pack of cigarettes from his jacket and turned his attention to Scott. "Got a match?"

"No, but there should be a lighter in the console."

"Did Jake tell me you two dated in high school?" Dan asked, sitting on the edge of the backseat. He gripped the headrest in front of him for support on the bumpy road.

Alex avoided making eye contact and flipped open the butane lighter. "Yeah, we did. Everybody assumed we'd get married someday. Even me, but she had other ideas."

"Kind of hard to take, I bet."

Alex's response was very matter of fact. "Things always work out the way they're meant to."

With the Jeep's tires spinning and traction non-existent on the icy road, Scott threw the transmission into park. "This is it, guys. If I've got my bearings right, we should only be about a couple hundred yards from the cabin—maybe a little more."

"And the herd, if it's there," Alex added.

"Sounds like you've hunted here before, Scott."

Once out of the car, the deputy put on a heavy parka and then an orange vest over it. "Alex brought me here a couple of times a month or so ago. The road leads right to the cabin, so it's not hard to find."

Unzipping the padded case protecting his Kimber rifle, Alex took out the gun, checked to be sure it wasn't loaded, and hung the strap over his shoulder. He put a box of ammunition into his backpack and smiled at the others. "All right. Now let's see if we can kill something."

Dan wasn't sure if it was what he said or how he said it, but Alex's words sent shivers down his spine. Shaking off the feeling, he walked toward Scott who was still organizing his gear. Alex had forged ahead, giving Dan a chance to question him.

"I'm surprised to see you so buddy-buddy with this guy. Didn't you tell me off the record, you think he's the stalker?"

Scott smiled and leaned close. "What's that old saying? Oh, heck. It doesn't really matter because I'm going to change it up anyway." He whispered in Dan's ear, "Keep your friends close and your suspects even closer."

He straightened up and walked back to pick up his pack and Browning rifle. "Now, let's get going."

And with that, the hunt began.

DAN CALLED TOMMY NOT long after his return from the hunting trip.

"Tell me all about it. Do we have our fall guy?" Tommy's eagerness was evident.

Dan was still trying to warm his chilled bones. A long, hot shower hadn't helped. "It was an interesting day."

"In what way?"

"Davis invited another guy to come along. A deputy sheriff." Dan pulled back the covers on the bed.

"That's an interesting choice. Were you able to bring our target into the mix with the other guy there?"

He crawled into bed and pulled the sheets and comforter toward his face. "If you mean Tarin MacGyver, we talked about her. The land where we were hunting is hers. Guess it's been in the family a long time."

"What do you think?" Tommy probed for information.

"Think about what?"

"Come on—you know what I'm talking about." Tommy wanted answers. "Do you think Davis is the stalker?"

"I couldn't get a read on him," Dan answered without passing judgment. "He's certainly capable of being one. But he seems to have reconciled with his wife. I'm not sure how that plays into our scenario."

"Did the deputy shed any light on the situation?" Tommy paused. "Wait a minute. Do you remember his name?"

"It's Scott something." He tried to recall the last name. "Think it's Simmons. Yeah, that's right. Scott Simmons. Why?"

"Just curious. I hired a photographer to take shots of Jon and his little mountain vixen last fall, but he wasn't very good at staying out of sight. You get what you pay for. Anyway, I'm pretty sure the cop that caught the kid is the same deputy you mentioned." There was silence until Tommy spoke again, "So where do we go from here?"

Dan stretched out under the sheets on the bed and leaned back against the headboard. He muted the television and began to flip through the channels while he talked. "Wish I knew. He seems to have feelings for his ex, but I can't quite figure out what they are. He's usually dark, foreboding, and very unpleasant. But while we were hunting, he was laughing and telling stories."

"What are you trying to tell me?"

Dan shook his head. "I'm not sure. But I wish you could have seen the look in his eyes when he shot his elk. It was like the rifle brought out a completely different person. He scared the crap out of me. I sure wouldn't want him pointing a gun at me."

"You're still not telling me what you think we should do."

Dan sat up, tossed the covers aside, and put his feet on the floor. "As far as I'm concerned, it's obvious. We continue to set him up as the fall guy and make it look like a murder-suicide. Talk about luck. Would you believe the other night I was invited to a party at Tarin's house? I managed to scope out her bedroom and make off with a few things. It won't be hard for me to plant the stuff in Alex's truck to be found after the fact."

"When does it all come down?"

Dan was decisive in his reply. "She's due back from Paris in a few days. I see no reason to wait."

"Keep me posted, Danny."

Putting his phone down on the bed, Dan looked up to stare at the ceiling. The plan was in place. But one big problem remained—he still wasn't sure he could go through with it.

CHAPTER 42

Seeing is Believing

FEELING MORE THAN A LITTLE HOMESICK AND
anxious to share his experiences with family and friends at home,
Peter Janus cut short his stay in Paris. For Tarin, the city had seemed
desolate after Jon had flown back to California. Now, with Peter gone,
there was nothing to keep her in France.

She fingered the silver bracelet around her wrist, remembering the
time they'd spent together in the city. Someday she hoped to return,
but now she was ready to go home.

The overnight flight back to her "real" world was an arduous one.
To pass the time, she watched three in-flight movies, read a book, and
took a long but restless nap. After clearing customs in Denver, she
caught a connecting flight to San Diego. In total, Tarin spent more
than twenty hours in airports and flying at thirty-five thousand feet.
She was exhausted.

But now, behind the wheel of a rental car and approaching the
outskirts of La Jolla, Tarin's energy was renewed. Adrenaline flowed
freely. Soon she would be with Jon, and this time she had no plans to
leave.

Tarin smiled as she approached the long, gentle curve that would
open into a clear view of his home on the ocean. She had played this
scene in her mind more than once. It was a beautiful morning in

Southern California. The sky was bright blue and foam-tipped waves lapped across the sandy beach below his house.

She glanced at her watch. It was almost ten o'clock. By now Jon would have downed at least three cups of coffee and be reading the newspaper on the veranda or tinkering with a new arrangement on the piano. Tarin was arriving three days early, and she would be the last person he expected to find on his doorstep.

She drove slowly, convinced a quiet arrival would offer a more dramatic element of surprise than a strange car pulling into the driveway.

That's when she saw him.

Tarin was about seventy-five yards from the house when her foot slipped from the accelerator and the car drifted to the side of the road. It came to a stop, almost hidden, near an outcropping of trees and shrubbery.

Jon had opened the front door and her heart skipped a beat. He was wearing his favorite gray flannel sleep pants and a T-shirt. It was the classic Jonathan Parker she had come to love.

Then everything changed.

Seconds after Jon stepped outside, a tall, willowy woman emerged behind him. Dressed in form-fitting white jeans, a mauve sweater with a plunging V-neck and spike heels, the woman struggled to pull a wheeled carry-on bag over the threshold. Jon walked to her and helped lift the small suitcase onto the walkway. Then he rested his arm around her shoulders and pulled her close.

Tarin felt her heart sink into the pit of her stomach. Just ten days ago they had been in Paris on Christmas Eve. On Christmas Day, they strolled through the Tuileries Garden, visited the Eiffel Tower, the Louvre, and took a romantic cruise on the Seine. Jon had told her more than once how much he loved her. But now, none of that seemed to matter.

Her eyes traveled to a pearl-colored Porsche convertible parked in the driveway. The two stopped by the driver's door. Jon lifted the suitcase onto the passenger seat and pulled the woman close, kissing her on the cheek. She responded by kissing him on the lips. When they parted, the woman seemed to be gazing into Jon's deep blue eyes—the eyes Tarin thought she knew so well. Watching them, she felt time was standing still. Each smile and kiss stabbed a dagger deeper into her heart.

Jon took the woman's hands in his and held them while they talked. A few minutes later she slipped into the driver's seat and pulled onto the street. Wearing a Mona Lisa-like smile, she sped by Tarin without a glance. Tarin didn't need a second look to recognize the young woman she had seen in a wrinkled magazine clipping many months before. It was Anna Haines.

Tarin rested her forehead on the steering wheel and her eyes begin to fill with tears. But when the first one began its journey down her cheek, all she wanted to do was go home to Ledge Lake. Home to where people are who they say they are. Anger, disappointment, and bitterness would manifest in due time, but now she wanted to be with her friends, her dog, and her horses.

Maybe it was true. She had never belonged in Jon's world. Jake might have been right—she was nothing more than a novelty in the singer's indulgent life. Who knows? Maybe he and Anna had been seeing each other all along. But none of that mattered. Today she had seen them together and she would never allow Jon Parker to betray her ever again.

Tarin shifted the car into drive and drove back the way she had come.

"JAKE? HI, IT'S ME. I'm at the airport in San Diego waiting for a flight home. Please don't ask why."

"You sound like something's wrong, Mac. Are you sure you're all right?" Jake looked at the calendar behind the bar, his fingers tracing the page to find the date. "You weren't scheduled to come back until Wednesday. That's three days from now. And you were flying from Paris to DIA, not California. What's going on?"

Her voice was subdued and hollow. "I know. We finished early. I wanted to surprise Jon." She paused. "I guess I did."

Jake sat on a stool behind the bar. "Hey, you. I don't like your tone. Did he do something I should know about?"

"Don't worry. I'll be okay. We'll talk when I get back to Denver." Tarin hesitated. "I know it's a lot to ask, but my flight lands at eight o'clock tonight. I could find a hotel room, but I need to get home. I want to sleep in my own bed. Do you think there's any way you could pick me up?"

"You know I'll be there. Which airline?"

"United. Thanks, Jake. Thanks for being the one person I can always count on."

He knew from the sound of his sister's voice there was something she wasn't telling him. He prayed Jon Parker wasn't responsible because if he had hurt Tarin again, the singer would regret it for the rest of his life.

JAKE WAS WAITING WHEN Tarin approached from the escalator. Even though she had tried to freshen her makeup, he could tell she had been crying.

"Can we just get my bags, Jake? I'd rather not talk about it quite yet." She turned toward the baggage carousel, watching the swarm of people battling for position to retrieve their suitcases.

Almost thirty minutes had passed, and there were just three bags and two abandoned boxes circling on the belt. Tarin was staring into space and was the only passenger left at the carousel.

Jake leaned toward her and asked, "Hey, you—I'll stand here all night if you'd like, but are any of those yours?"

She looked up at him and smiled. "I'm sorry. I guess I was somewhere else." She pointed toward two of the three desolate bags when they rounded the corner. "Those are mine."

They walked to his truck in the parking garage, an awkward silence hanging between them. He needed to know what had happened but wasn't going to bring it up until she did.

The lights of the airport and the city were miles behind when Tarin finally spoke.

"She was there, Jake."

He glanced toward her, "Who was where?"

Tarin stared out the window. "Anna Haines was at Jon's house." She turned to look at him. "It was about ten in the morning. I saw them in his driveway. He was still in his pajamas, and she had a suitcase."

Then Tarin began to cry. "Jon was hugging her, Jake, and he kissed her. Then she kissed him back." She stifled a sob. "I recognized her when she drove away—it was Anna."

Her brother's anger had been simmering since her phone call, but now he was ready to explode. And he would have if Tarin hadn't been in the truck. "I hope you slapped him silly and told him where to go."

"We didn't talk."

Jake slowed the truck, pulled over on the shoulder of the two-lane highway, and put the transmission into park.

"Let me get this straight. Your so-called boyfriend lavishes you with attention in Paris but he comes home to mess around with another woman—his former fiancée—I might add. Then you come back early and catch him in the act."

He did his best to remain calm, burying his anger deep inside. "You should have confronted him, Mac, and told him what a worthless jackass he is."

She turned from the window to face her brother. "I know I should have, but I couldn't. All I wanted to do was come home."

He could see the tears streaming down her face. "I'm sorry. I know you don't like him, you don't trust him, and you don't want us to be together." Her voice became almost a whisper, "But I love him."

The rest of the trip to Chasm Falls was driven in silence. Jake was imagining what he would do if ever saw Jon again, and Tarin was trying to imagine what life would be like without him. Neither had an answer.

Part Three

CHAPTER 43

Today's the Day

I T HAD BECOME PART OF MARIA'S DAILY ROUTINE TO meet Dan at the Main Street Coffee Shop for breakfast where they scrutinized any new real estate listings. They would settle upon a house or two to look at, make the arrangements, and then visit the properties. On the surface, today seemed no different from any other day.

But when they pulled into the driveway of this lakeside home, Dan felt a strange connection take control of his senses. The two-story log structure certainly wasn't new—he guessed it to be at least seventy years old—but there was something about the house that invited him inside.

"What do you think? Do you like it?" Maria asked, noting his attentive gaze. "This is the house I told you about when we were at Tarin's party. It's older than hers and needs a lot of work, but it's so warm and cozy." She put a code into the lockbox, retrieved the key, and turned the handle.

Inside the front door a large foyer showcased a log staircase leading to the second story. Rather than sheetrock, the interior walls were logs with aging off-white chink sandwiched between them. A large elk antler chandelier hung overhead in the entry.

"Would you like to look around?" Maria asked, noticing Dan seemed frozen where he stood.

He smiled, "This would be a perfect place to raise a couple of kids, wouldn't it?"

"Does your client have children?"

He put his arm around her shoulders. "No. I was thinking about ours."

She blushed at the thought and pretended she hadn't heard his words. "See—it has a big moss rock fireplace with bookcases like Tarin's." Maria looked down at the floor. "I don't know what they were thinking when they installed this shag carpet, but I guess it used to be in style. I've been told there's beautiful hardwood underneath."

She led him into the kitchen. "This room needs a complete makeover. Avocado green appliances may match the carpet, but they're disgusting and I'm not sure the dishwasher even works." She spun around, envisioning the possibilities. "Can you imagine this kitchen with granite countertops, new cabinets, and stainless-steel appliances?"

Dan gathered her into his arms. "I can see you at the stove cooking me dinner when I come home after a long day at work."

She avoided meeting his gaze.

"What's the matter, Maria? There's nothing wrong with admitting you care for someone. And you need to realize you're a gorgeous woman any man could fall in love with."

"Do you mean it?" she asked.

He nodded. "Now, what do you say we go check out the bedrooms?"

"Why don't we take a look at the backyard first?"

"All right," Dan laughed, "if you insist."

They walked to the edge of the frozen lake and Maria pointed toward Shuck's with excitement. "Look—they're ice skating. Could we stop there before we go back to your hotel?"

"Do you skate?"

"Doesn't everyone?" she appeared to be in awe.

He shook his head. "I never quite mastered skating on sidewalks, let alone on ice."

Maria watched the distant skaters with envy. "My mom was a wonderful figure skater. Her dream was to make it to the Olympics. But she didn't have enough money to pay for the training."

"I bet you look just as beautiful on the ice as she did."

Maria shrugged. "I don't know about that, but I do love how free I feel when I'm wearing skates."

"If you'd like, on the way back to town we can stop at Shuck's and you can show me how talented you are."

"We'll rent skates for you, too. It'll be fun. You'll see."

Dan didn't quite share her enthusiasm but knew if Maria asked, he would follow. He was smitten.

LATER THAT DAY, DAN sat on the couch in Maria's living room while she made hot chocolate in the kitchen. He was damp and cold but quite content. Maria was a brilliant skater and had even managed to pull him—not without a fight—onto the frozen lake. With her pushing him from behind, he soon gained enough confidence to venture out alone.

At one point, a toddler who was marching more than skating fell onto the cold, hard ice in front of him. Between sobs, the young boy was trying to find his mother who was a few yards away. Dan knelt, placed him on a knee, and had the child giggling within a matter of seconds. Maria was quite impressed.

"You're good with children, Dan. You would be a good father," she told him.

Without thinking, he had blurted out that he wanted to put an offer on the house she had shown him. Not for his client, but for them.

"What's wrong?" Maria asked as she handed him a cup topped with miniature marshmallows.

He looked into her eyes. "When I came here, I never imagined I would find you. The sad part is that soon I'll be going back to California, and I don't want to leave you behind."

"You could take me with you."

He placed a hand on her cheek and shook his head. "You don't have any idea about the life I lead."

She seemed confused. "What is it you're keeping from me? What are you hiding? Don't you know by now that you can tell me anything?"

"Maybe I'm not the man you think I am."

"I know who you are, Dan Carruthers. You're sweet, kind, funny and thoughtful, among other things. Did I forget intelligent and talented?"

Would you feel the same way if you knew I've been hired to murder two of your friends?

He pulled her close. "Ah, Maria. Thank you for believing in me." He stood and took her hands in his. "But right now, all I want to do is make love to you. Maybe more than once." He wiped a tear from her cheek. "What do you say?"

She took his hand and led him into the bedroom.

THE SUN HAD YET to rise over the mountains when the hotel phone next to Dan's bed rang. It was Tommy.

"She's back."

Dan squinted and leaned toward the nightstand to check the time. "Shit. It's three o'clock in the morning, Tommy. And why did you call me on this phone?"

"You didn't answer your cell. Today's the day, my friend."

"The day for what?"

"The day we get rid of that MacGyver bitch once and for all."

Facing the reality of what Tommy had said caused Dan to roll over and sit on the edge of the bed.

"Okay. Let's back up and start over. You woke me up out of a dead sleep. I need a minute to clear my head."

Tommy sounded frustrated. "Okay. Here's how it came down. I had to cover my bases, so I paid a guy at her hotel in Paris to let me know when she checked out. He wasn't on top of things but came through in the end. She left Paris yesterday."

"Did she fly back to Denver?"

"Jon's been talking about how she was going to come out here this Wednesday. That must mean she flew back to Colorado, but you need to find out for sure. Keep me in the loop, Dan. There's a big bonus if you take her out. I don't think she's shared what she knows with anyone, so I might get out of this clean. Bring me the tape she recorded and I'll double what you've got coming."

"What tape?"

"She carries a digital recorder in her backpack—for interviews, I suppose. Anyway, she's got a recording of me admitting I set Jon up ten years ago and scammed him for a half-million. That's not all. There's a lot more on that damn tape."

"How the hell were you stupid enough to let her record you?" Dan stood and went into the bathroom. He stared at his disheveled appearance in the mirror. "Listen, I'll keep you posted. But I'm not sure how to find out where she is."

"Just drive by her house, you idiot," Tommy chastised. "It's still dark outside. See if any lights come on. Then call me."

Dan put the phone down and splashed his face with cold water. Then he got dressed, jumped into his car, and drove to Ledge Lake. He had made the drive so many times he could almost do it in his sleep. That was good because his thoughts weren't on the road he was traveling.

CHAPTER 44

The Hit

IT WAS ABOUT FIVE IN THE MORNING WHEN DAN parked his car in the parking lot of a motel a quarter mile from Tarin's house. The late-model Toyota Camry would be invisible surrounded by the twenty or more vehicles already parked there. Dressed in black, he walked in the brush on the far side of the road until he was about fifty yards from her house. Then, hiding in a stand of trees with a clear view of her bedroom, Dan settled in for his watch.

It didn't take long to realize he'd misjudged early morning mountain temperatures. His fingers and toes were beginning to stiffen, and a damp cold permeated his body while he sat motionless on the frozen ground or stood leaning against a tree trunk. He kicked himself for not wearing the insulated camouflage gear he had purchased for the elk hunt.

About six o'clock a light appeared upstairs. The darkness returned a few moments later, but then he saw another light downstairs.

Dan pulled out his cell phone and dialed.

"Leave me a message and I'll get back to you when I can."

Asshole. The jerk went back to bed after we talked. How can Tommy sleep when he knows what he expects me to do?

Hearing the inevitable "beep," Dan recounted what Tommy hoped to hear. "You were right. She's here. I'll call you when it's done. Just be ready to come through with everything you've promised."

AS THE SUN BEGAN to peek over the mountains, Dan drove back to his hotel room. Once inside, he tossed his jacket on the bed and pulled a heavy leather case from the closet. He positioned it on the bed and snapped open the latches. Inside was a Glock handgun. Lifting it from the case, he carefully threaded a silencer onto the gun's barrel.

Dan stood, staring down at the weapon. His thoughts were cut short by a sharp knock on the door.

"Housekeeping."

He glanced at his watch. It was a few minutes after eight o'clock. He was usually out of the room by now, giving the housekeeping crew a jump on their daily cleaning duties. Hearing a key card trigger the lock, he stashed the gun behind his back and covered the open case with his coat.

The door opened and a young woman entered carrying a stack of towels. Seeing him, she apologized. "I'm so sorry, sir. I'll come back later."

Dan reassured her with a smile but wasn't sure he managed to disguise the nervousness in his voice. "It's not a problem. I should be gone in an hour or so. Will that work for you?"

She nodded before backing out and closing the door. "Yes, sir. That will be fine. I'm sorry to have bothered you. Have a wonderful day."

Have a wonderful day? Who was she kidding?

He picked up the phone and dialed the number he'd memorized. "Maria? Did I wake you?" He loved hearing her voice. Can I come over for a few hours? No, I don't want to look at houses. I just want to spend time with you. Okay, I'll be there in a few minutes."

Dan went back to the bed, wrapped the gun in his jacket, and put an extra clip into one of the pockets. Then he locked the case and stashed it back in the closet.

Taking the jacket and its contents to the bathroom, he studied his appearance in the mirror one last time. Then, he draped the coat over his arm to disguise the gun hidden in it. Once in the motel parking lot, he opened the car's trunk, put his jacket inside, and slammed it shut.

DAN SPENT MOST OF the day with Maria, pretending it was a day like any other. But it wasn't. He had a job to do and no idea how it would turn out. Things could go according to plan, or they could go terribly wrong. He could find himself in jail for the rest of his life. But there was no turning back now.

It was almost midnight, and he'd been waiting in the cold mountain air for almost two hours when the light in Tarin's bedroom was turned off.

Okay. I'll give her another hour to be sure she's asleep.

He filled the minutes with thoughts of Maria, but then looked at his watch again and sighed. Dan knew whether he was ready or not, it was time to make his move. He tightened the black hoodie around his head, loaded the clip in his gun, checked the silencer, and began to inch toward the house.

What would Maria think if she knew what I'm doing? But if everything goes right, she'll never have to know. And I swear to God I'll never do anything like this again.

He nervously glanced in every direction and then shook his head. Who did he think would be watching at this hour in this remote place?

It took just a few moments to feel the mechanism release when he picked the lock on the front door. He would only have seconds to disarm the alarm to keep it from going off and alerting Tarin. He had studied the schematics of the security system on the internet for days and was certain he could render it useless, but there was no guarantee. If something went wrong, he would have to resort to Plan B—a plan he didn't have. Taking a deep breath, he turned the handle. The door opened a few inches, and after a quick glance over his shoulder, he slipped inside.

He immediately turned to the panel and was surprised to see the alarm wasn't on. The cameras weren't functioning, either.

That's strange. Maybe Lady Luck is smiling at me. Now, let's get this over with so I can fly to LA, collect my money, and in good time I'll come back to be with Maria. We'll buy that house on the lake. Thanks to Tommy, I'll have enough cash to make it happen. I'm sorry, Tarin. Your misfortune will turn my life around.

Treading lightly, he mounted the first step.

Dan was thankful his work would be done in the dark. He would have to watch when he forced her to call Alex. But he didn't want to see Tarin's face when she was dead. Her only crime had been crossing Tommy. She should have known better.

When he lifted his foot to mount the second step, a wall clock chimed the hour, catching him off guard. He felt his heart stop and then begin beating so fast he had to catch his breath.

Calm down. The hard part will be over soon.

Standing in the doorway of Tarin's bedroom, Dan allowed his eyes to adjust to the darkness. Clouds had moved in overnight to obscure the moonlight that normally streams in through the wall of glass facing the lake. While there was enough natural light to see more than just shapes, the room was still shrouded in darkness.

He watched intently, a few feet from the bed, to be sure she was sleeping. She was resting on her side, and he maneuvered his way across the room to loom above her. Somehow sensing his presence, Tarin opened her eyes just as his hand covered her mouth, and he thrust the gun firmly against her rib cage.

"Don't scream and I won't hurt you," he warned. "Now sit up." Dan's lips were clenched and twitching. Despite his resolve to leave behind the life he'd been living, he found himself almost intoxicated by the power he held over her at that moment. "I'm going to take my hand off your mouth and I want you to be quiet. Understand?"

With her heart throbbing like a hummingbird's wings, she nodded. Looking at the man's face, she realized he wasn't a stranger. "You're Maria's friend—Dan—aren't you? What are you doing here? And why do you have a gun?" Tarin whispered. She reached for a switch on the lamp next to the bed.

He stopped her with the barrel of the gun. "No lights." Then he turned his attention back to Tarin's bewildered face. "What do I want from you? Don't you get it? This has nothing to do with what I want. It's what Tommy Wyndham wants. It's always what Tommy wants." He shook his head. "You should know better than to cross a man like him. Anyway, Tommy says you have a digital recorder and a very special tape. He wants them both. Where are they?"

Tarin shook her head. "I don't know what you're talking about."

"Don't make this any harder than it already is. Tell me where they are." Dan watched her point toward the leather backpack on a chair across the room.

"The recorder is in my pack, but the tape you're looking for is in my top dresser drawer."

Dan rummaged through the bag, found the small recording device, and walked to the dresser. "I wouldn't do that if I were you," he warned when he saw Tarin reach for her cell phone on the nightstand.

He walked back, picked up the phone, and handed it to her with the recorder and tape in his other hand. "But there is one call you do need to make. I want you to call Alex Davis." He used the gun's barrel to trace a line from her stomach to her T-shirt-covered breasts, pressing the end of the weapon's cold steel barrel between them.

"But, why—"

"No questions. Just do it," he commanded, forcing the gun harder against her chest. But his resolve was weakening. This wasn't like the times Tommy had sent him to rough up strangers he would never see again. Tarin had opened her home to him. She had treated him like a friend. In his imagination, he could see Maria standing on the other side of the bed, horrified at the scene playing out before her eyes.

Dan looked toward the ceiling in a failed attempt to regain his fortitude. "You're going to tell him you're afraid someone is trying to break into your house. You're scared and want him to come over right away."

"But I'd call the police if that was true. Alex is the last person I'd ask for help."

He raised the barrel and lodged it against her throat. "He doesn't know that. Now do what I say if you know what's good for you. I don't want to hurt you." Looking into Tarin's eyes he saw the terror reflected there and had to turn away. In his mind's eye, Maria was still gazing at him—judging him.

Then staring down at the weapon in his hand, Dan shook his head and exclaimed, "Go to hell, Tommy. I can't do this." He stepped away and lowered the gun to his side. "I'm so sorry, Tarin."

Her look changed to confusion. "Can't do what?"

Before he could answer, an ominous voice rang out from behind them. "Is that you, Carruthers? I don't know what you're doing here but drop the gun and get away from her."

"What the hell?" Dan muttered in surprise as he turned toward the doorway.

The tension in the air was shattered when Tarin heard a gunshot, but the sound was muffled and almost surreal. Struck in the heart, Dan's lifeless body collapsed on top of her. Screaming and feeling warm blood beginning to saturate her shirt, she fought to move the dead weight away.

"It's okay, Tarin. He can't hurt you now."

She recognized the voice and relief washed over her. "Scott? Is that you?"

Thrusting Dan's body onto the floor, Scott Simmons took Tarin's hand and helped her stand. She was trembling and melted against his chest. He closed his eyes and tightened his arms around her. In one of his hands, he gripped a .45 mm handgun with a silencer.

"I don't understand why he was here or what he wanted—" She looked at Scott's face and an unsettled feeling began to overtake her. "You saved my life. But how did you know? Why were you here at this hour?"

She stepped back, breaking his grip.

"Scott—why aren't you in uniform? You're dressed in black, just like him."

Tarin's heart began to race.

He moved toward her, and she took another step back.

"It's nothing to be worried about. I've been watching your house. You know—to see if we could catch the guy that's been stalking you. And I did. Now you're finally safe."

"But Dan told me he was here because of Tommy Wyndham. The stalking began before I'd ever heard of Jon or his manager."

He grabbed her wrist, twisting her arm. "Why does it matter who the stalker is? Can't you just accept the fact I saved your life and I'm the one you can count on to take care of you?"

"Why didn't the alarm go off? I should have known someone was in the house." Tarin's voice was filled with confusion, and fear overwhelmed her once again.

Scott wore a demonic grin and pulled a keychain remote from his pocket. "When I ordered your system, I had them include two remotes. The second one was on a separate order and I intercepted the invoice. All it took to disarm your fancy system tonight was the touch of a button. I turned off the cameras, too."

"But why? I don't understand."

He kicked toward the dead man on the floor at his feet. "Tonight was my night to take you away and this ass got in the way."

Tarin tried to break his hold, but he tightened his grip, his fingers digging into her soft flesh. "Scott, you're scaring me."

Pushing her down onto the blood-spattered sheets, he straddled her hips with his knees, holding her outstretched arms above her head.

"Don't you understand? I'm the one who loves you. Parker doesn't care about you. You're just a toy he'll throw away when another pretty face comes along."

His anger seemed to fade, and Simmons looked at Tarin with tenderness, brushing his hand against her cheek. "I've wanted you since the first time I saw you. Those things missing from your house and the boathouse—I've been taking care of them for you. I've got everything we'll need, and soon you'll understand that we're meant to be together."

His gentleness evaporated. "Now get dressed," he ordered, yanking Tarin back to her feet.

She looked down at the blood covering her hands and then back at Simmons. Her eyes pleaded with him. "Please, can I at least wash my hands?"

He pushed her toward the bathroom. "All right, but I'm going with you."

Trying hard to retain her composure, Tarin watched the warm water cascading over her fingers turn to scarlet in the grey granite basin. She rubbed soap onto her skin as if it could wash away what was happening.

"That's enough." He turned off the faucet, spun her around, and threw a towel in her direction. "Now get dressed."

Scott sat in a chair across the room, gazing in silence, watching Tarin turn her back to him. She lifted the bloodstained T-shirt over her head and began putting on her underwear, followed by a pair of jeans, a flannel shirt, socks, and shoes. He stood and walked to her side. Before she could react, he yanked her hands behind her back, slipped a pair of handcuffs on her wrists, and thrust her toward the doorway. "I'm sorry. I didn't want to use these, but you don't seem happy to see me and I'm afraid you might try to run away. We can't let that happen."

"Scott—"

"Not now." Simmons reached into his coat pocket and pulled out a roll of silver duct tape. "You need to be very quiet." He stretched tape across her mouth and began to drag her toward the stairs. "We need to get out of here before there's daylight and someone sees us."

With that, he pushed Tarin down the stairs toward the front door. She managed to kick him in the crotch, the hall tree falling to the floor in the struggle. But taller and stronger, Scott caught her when she tripped and fell in the front yard. He slammed her face into the snow with his hand and planted a knee between her shoulder blades.

"Please don't try that again. I don't like hurting you." The corners of his mouth twitched. "You're mine now and you'll do what I say."

He lifted her onto the front seat of his Jeep, fastened the seatbelt across her chest, and got behind the wheel. The front door of Tarin's house stood slightly ajar and Dan lay dead upstairs. The private detective's wish had come true: Tommy Wyndham was out of his life forever.

SCOTT EXECUTED A THREE-POINT turn in the driveway and accelerated toward the road. Then, without stopping, he crossed the blacktop and directed his car onto the lane leading to Tarin's barn. Pressing onward, he continued past the building and up the rugged road toward her grandfather's hunting cabin.

Unable to speak, Tarin was terrified as the Jeep forged through the deepening snowdrifts and traveled higher in elevation, traveling much faster than was safe. At one point the car slid sideways and narrowly missed the curtain of pines lining the path.

Minutes later Simmons attempted to pull behind the cabin, but the Jeep slipped into a snow-filled gulley and would go no further. Working his way to the car's passenger door, he sank into the snow up to his knees. Grabbing the cuffed hands behind her back, he pulled Tarin from the vehicle. She fell face-first, and he used the collar of her shirt to pull her to her feet.

"Come on. I have something to show you." He looked skyward, feeling light snowflakes melt on his face. "The news says we're in for a nasty blizzard. Let's go. We need to get moving and start a fire before the weather begins to change."

Simmons kicked open the cabin's front door and led Tarin toward the bed. Fumbling with the key to the handcuffs, he managed to unlock one wrist and secured the device to a rung on the iron headboard.

"You stay here while I bring in wood for the night. We're going to need it."

The door slammed behind him and Tarin collapsed onto the mattress. After resting for a moment, she opened her eyes and began to survey her grandfather's cabin.

"It's been him all along," she whispered, tears filling her eyes.

Simmons had been busy since the elk hunt with Alex and Dan and had completely redecorated the small one-room structure. A new metal clothing rack was tucked into one corner. On it was her missing clothing. Sitting on the floor below was a box without a top. Inside, she could see several pairs of socks, shoes, and underwear stolen from her house.

Hanging on the walls were framed photos she hadn't even realized were missing. One of her high school scrapbooks from the boathouse was sitting on a table next to the woodstove. Then there were four or five pictures of herself she had never seen before. Suddenly she remembered Simmons had confiscated the memory card from the photographer Tommy had hired. He must have printed the photos. Not surprisingly, Jon had been cropped from every image.

Backed by a blast of wind, the door burst open, and Scott thundered into the cabin carrying an armload of snowy firewood. He dropped it without ceremony on the floor next to the stove.

Smiling, he walked to the bed, stripped the duct tape from Tarin's mouth, and sat at her side. "What do you think?" He looked around the cabin with pride. "It's not much, but we won't stay here long—just until the storm passes."

Simmons touched her cheek and she fought to pull away. "This will be a perfect place for us to get to know each other." He rested a hand on her shoulder. "You will fall in love with me, Tarin. You'll see. No one in the world cares for you like I do. I'll give you anything and everything you could ever want."

When she felt him begin to play with the top button of her shirt, Tarin slapped him with her free hand and kicked, struggling to escape his touch. He fumbled to find the key in his pocket and unlocked the empty handcuff he had attached to the headboard. Anchoring the cuffs around one of the iron rungs, this time he secured both her wrists.

"Try to fight me now," he challenged, continuing to release the buttons of her shirt with one hand and fingering the zipper of her jeans with the other.

In that instant, Tarin's thoughts raced back to her bedroom and the memory of warm, sticky blood, and a dead man lying on top of her. She imagined never seeing Jake, her friends, or even Jon, ever again. With a tear traveling down her cheek, she began to fear for her life.

CHAPTER 45

Scene of the Crime

WHEN HE HEARD THE PHONE RING, JAKE RAISED his hand to the man he'd been serving. "Hey, hold on a sec. Sip 'n Strike."

"Jake? This is Jon Parker."

"What can I possibly do for you? Or even want to do for that matter?" he asked coolly, motioning for another server to take his place behind the bar.

"I'm at the airport in San Diego to pick up Tarin, but she didn't get off the plane. I hope you know if I've got the wrong flight or if her plans changed."

"I wouldn't wait too long if I were you." He paused for a moment. "You know what? As much fun as it might be, I'm not going to play games with you. Instead, I'm going to be completely honest and upfront about this. The bottom line is you might as well go home and forget about her. There's no fixing it this time."

Jon was confused, "What? I don't understand."

"I'm telling you she's not coming. Not ever." Jake had been waiting for a chance to confront the man who had broken his sister's heart— not once—but twice. He'd rehearsed the conversation more times than he could count. "Give me a break. How did you think she would react when she found out about you and that actress going at it again?"

There was a deafening silence.

"Jake, I have no idea what you're talking about."

"You don't remember what you and your girlfriend were doing in the driveway last Sunday morning? Or even more importantly, what you and that actress were probably doing to each other the night before."

"What?"

"Tarin finished her assignment in Paris early and rather than come back here, she decided to surprise you in California. She got there just in time to see you and Anna Haines kissing in the driveway. She had an overnight bag. Guess you didn't plan on getting caught, did you?"

"You're telling me Tarin thinks there's something going on between Anna and me?" Jon's voice filled with desperation. "You need to believe me, Jake. Anna stopped at my house to give back the ring Tommy bought for the fiasco at the airport. The day I told her the engagement was a mistake, she threw it across the room at me. I didn't stick around to try and find it. Sunday Anna told me she'd eloped with a guy she met on the set of her latest movie. What Tarin thought was a suitcase was a carry-on bag with a laptop computer and wedding pictures." There was a momentary pause before he continued. "I hadn't spoken to Anna since the day I ended the engagement. Last Sunday we were finally able to make peace with each other. And okay, I did hug and kiss Anna before she left, but it was purely to congratulate her. That's all. God, Jake. Where's Tarin? I need to talk to her."

"Give me one reason why I should believe you."

"Because I love your sister with all my heart. Please, help me prove it to her. If you're honest with yourself, you know she loves me as much as I love her."

While he hated to admit it, Jake could sense the urgency and the sincerity in Jon's voice. "As far as I know, she's at home. She flew back from San Diego late Sunday night. I picked her up at DIA and dropped her off about midnight."

"That was three days ago. I called this morning when she didn't get off the plane. Nobody answered."

"I'm sorry, Jon. I don't know what to tell you. She could be on her way to the office in Denver or maybe buying groceries for all we know."

"Will you do me a favor?" Desperation reverberated in Jon's voice. "Could you call and ask Tarin to please answer the phone? I've tried both her cell and her home phone, but she doesn't pick up either one when she sees it's me. I need to find a way to tell her what really happened with Anna."

"All right, but you damn well better be telling the truth."

"Please believe me—I would never betray her that way. Jake, tonight I was going to ask her to marry me. Promise you'll call me back after you talk with her."

"I can't give you any guarantee she'll even listen."

"Tell her I'm getting on a plane and will be there tomorrow to explain everything in person. If I can charter a plane, I'll be there tonight."

"You might want to hold off on that. There's a bad storm headed our way in the next twenty-four hours. They're predicting record-breaking blizzard conditions across Colorado."

"I don't care. I need to see her."

Ending the call, Jake dialed Tarin. When the answering machine picked up, he turned to the server on duty. "Mel, can you watch the bar for a bit? I need to check on something."

"Sure thing. Take your time," she answered. "I can handle it."

Jake was out the door before he heard her reply. In the parking lot, Mike Wilson was just getting out of his patrol car.

"You look like you're in a hurry. What's up?" Mike called from across the lot.

Jake shook his head and began walking toward him. "I don't know. Something's not right. Jon can't get Tarin to answer the phone. I tried a few minutes ago, and she wouldn't pick up for me, either. I'm going to drive over and check to be sure everything's okay."

"I'm sure she's fine, but why don't you come with me and we'll do a welfare check? I need to talk with her anyway."

Within minutes they were on their way to Ledge Lake.

Mike and Jake weren't surprised when Tarin's unlocked F-150 was in the driveway. But when the front door was ajar, Mike became concerned. "See the coat tree? It's been knocked over." He could sense Jake's apprehension.

"Tarin?" Jake called into the entryway.

There was no answer.

Mike pushed open the door, eyeing the lock. "It doesn't look like there was any kind of forced entry." The officer stepped around the coat tree and shook his head, "This didn't fall over by itself." He took the gun from his holster and released the safety.

Jake's eyes locked on the gun. "Do you think that's necessary?"

"It's just a precaution."

Mike walked toward the alarm panel on the wall. "Shit."

"What's wrong?"

"The system's been disarmed, and the cameras aren't on, either." Mike walked into the dining room. "When was the last time you talked with her?"

"When we got back from the airport Sunday night."

"You haven't called her since?"

"Like I said, I tried today, but there was no answer."

"Any sign of Finn?"

Jake followed Mike into the kitchen. "No, but there wouldn't be. He stayed with me while Tarin was in Paris, and I haven't brought him back yet."

Mike was poised over the answering machine. "Tarin's got twelve messages. She hasn't checked her home phone in a while." He pressed Star 69. "Let's see who called last."

When the number appeared, the two men looked at each other, announcing the same thing simultaneously. "Alex."

"Damn it."

"You don't think he has anything to do with the fact she's missing, do you?"

"Anything's possible. But didn't you say both you and Jon have been trying to reach her? Alex must have called after you did for his number to be the last one in the phone's memory, so my guess is he's in the clear." Mike wrinkled his nose and sniffed. "Do you smell something?"

Jake nodded. "Where do you think it's coming from?"

"Can't tell. Upstairs maybe."

The foul odor became more intense as they approached Tarin's bedroom. At the door, Jake turned his head to look away. "Oh, my god, Mike. What happened here?"

The bloodstained bedspread and sheets were askew on the mattress, and they could see a man on the floor next to Tarin's bed. Stepping toward the motionless body, Mike put the safety back on and holstered his gun. He covered his face with the back of his hand.

"Shit. This guy isn't going anywhere other than the morgue." He avoided the dried pool of blood on the wood floor and knelt beside the man who was lying on his stomach. "Who the hell is he?"

Jake glanced at what he could see of the bloated and distended face. "I can't tell for sure, but it looks like the man who came to town a few weeks ago looking for property. Dan was his name. He's been hanging out at the bar and working with Maria Marshall." All the color drained from his face. "Mike, where's my sister?" He'd seen the bloodstains on the tousled sheets.

Mike pulled out his phone to call Dispatch. "Marylou, this is Mike. I'm at Tarin MacGyver's and need backup from the sheriff and the coroner as soon as you can get them here. There's been a shooting and we've got a dead John Doe. Have them send forensics right away, too. No, there's no sign of her. Oh, and Marylou, have somebody track down Alex Davis. We'd like to talk with him."

Jake peered down at the body, "How long do you think he's been dead?"

"Judging from his condition, at least two maybe three days. The cool temperature in the house probably slowed down the decomposition. Today's Thursday. I'm guessing he was shot sometime Monday, probably Monday night since it looks like Tarin was in bed."

Mike studied the bedroom in detail, his gaze freezing on a chair in the corner of the room. He pointed toward the upended object on its seat. "Do you know any woman who leaves the house without her purse or backpack?"

Jake shook his head. "No. Especially not Tarin. She can't function without it and her cell phone is on the nightstand." Worry clouded his face. "I don't like this, Mike." Then he remembered the call from California. "God. What do I tell Jon?"

"Do you have to call him?"

"He's the one who asked me to check on her."

"Try not to alarm him. Just say Tarin isn't home, and we're trying to catch up with her. If you explain it that way, we're not lying. We really don't know anything at this point."

"But Mike, what was this guy doing here in the first place? Tarin doesn't own a gun, so there must have been someone else in the room. What about the blood on the bed? It looks like there was a struggle and now she's gone."

"I don't think the dead guy came here to be a good neighbor." Mike's eyes locked on the Glock still gripped in the dead man's hand. Then he saw what he couldn't let Jake see—Tarin's bloodstained T-shirt on the floor. He tried to maintain a calm voice but felt a sinking sensation deep in his gut.

"When you call Jon, don't mention the man who was shot. When we find out who else was in the room, we'll find Tarin." The officer paused before completing his thought. "But until then—and I'm sorry, Jake—we have to assume she's been kidnapped, apparently by someone willing to kill to take her." He rested an arm on his friend's shoulder, "Now, let's go downstairs and wait for the lab team. In the meantime, I want you to think back to anything that might give us a clue about what happened. Can you do that for me?"

"Wilson—where are you?"

"Up here, Rick," Mike called back to the county sheriff.

The sheriff grimaced at the bedroom door. "Whew. I'll never get used to that smell." He looked down at the body. "What do we have here?"

"Looks like it might have been a gunshot to the chest," Mike replied. "But we didn't move him to find out. We're waiting for forensics to get here."

"You're in luck. They pulled in right behind us. The coroner is here, too." The sheriff shook his head, "Okay, we might as well get started. Want to fill us in on what you know so far?"

Mike glanced at Jake before answering, "We're pretty sure there's been a kidnapping. The woman who lives here—Tarin MacGyver—is missing."

CHAPTER 46

Into the Storm

JON WAS STANDING OUTSIDE THE CHARTER TERMINAL, cell phone in hand when he got Jake's call. He skipped the formalities. "Did you talk with Tarin?"

"Are you flying in tomorrow?"

He sensed something ominous in Jake's voice. "I'm at the airport now. I chartered a plane, and I'll fly in early tonight. But I need to know, did you talk with Tarin?"

"I don't want you to worry." Jake hesitated. "You know, I'm sure everything's going to be all right."

Jon began to pace. "What do you mean you're sure everything's going to be all right? Don't hold out on me. What's going on?"

"I don't know how to say this. I'm afraid we can't find her."

There was panic in Jon's voice. "What do you mean you can't find her?"

"Just what I said. Mike didn't want me to tell you anything, but I can't lie to you." He paused, reluctant to say the words out loud, "She may have been kidnapped."

Jon dropped onto a bench outside the terminal entrance, a knot growing in his stomach.

"I'm afraid that's not all." There was an awkward moment of silence. "There's a dead man with a gun in her bedroom. Mike thinks the guy may have been trying to kill her, but somebody shot him first."

Jon leaned back with eyes closed, resting his head on the brick wall behind the bench. "I don't understand any of this, Jake. Why would anyone want to kill Tarin? And who shot the man in her room?" His voice was infused with fear, "For god's sake, who would kidnap her? Was it the man who's been stalking her?"

"It's like I said, at this point we don't know what happened."

Jon stood up and began pacing. "Did Alex have anything to do with it?"

"Mike's bringing him in, but he seems to be in the clear. The dead man has been looking at property around here for the past few weeks under the name Dan Carruthers. Seemed like a nice enough guy. We're trying to figure out how he fits into all this."

"Jake, what the hell are they doing to find her?"

"The house is full of investigators and police officers. Trust me, they're doing everything they can."

Jon covered one ear with his hand and pressed the phone firmly against the other, trying to listen as a small Cessna jet approached the terminal. "Jake, my plane's here. I need to go. I'll be there in about two and a half hours." He looked at his watch. "That should put me in Winter Park about five or five-thirty your time. Can you pick me up?"

"I'll be there, but we've got a nasty storm rolling in tonight. Jake glanced toward the lake through the French doors. "The snow's starting to come down now. You and your pilot better keep a close eye on the weather conditions."

"Promise me you'll be at the airport."

"Like I said, I'll be there. But keep me posted if anything changes."

Jake walked back upstairs to find an investigator kneeling next to the body. The man sat up and pointed to the floor next to the bed. "So far, I've found three things. One of them is in the victim's hand."

Mike moved across the room to look.

Jake was inquisitive. "What is it?"

"I've seen this before," Mike remarked, looking at the object gripped in Dan's hand. "It's the recorder Tarin uses during interviews. The tape you found on the floor fits it. Why would this guy have been willing to kill for them? What else did you find?"

The investigator handed Mike a sealed evidence bag. Inside was a silver butane lighter with a hinged lid. On the front was a Marine Corps emblem.

"You won't like what I'm about to tell you," Mike admitted. "I can guarantee this lighter belongs to Scott Simmons. I've seen him with it a hundred times. Check out the engraving."

"SS. Okay, but how did it get here?" Jake asked. The look in Mike's eyes made him feel very uneasy.

"I can only think of one possibility: He must have been the other person in the room."

Jake was perplexed. "But why would Scott have been here? Was he staking out the house to catch the guy stalking Tarin?"

Mike remained silent for a moment. "How did I miss the signs?" He shook his head and looked at Jake. "There were the questions he kept asking about Tarin. Then there was his eagerness to find the stalker, not to mention his attempt to point the finger at Alex Davis. God—he even helped set up her security system." He turned toward Jake. "I hate to say this, but all the evidence points to Simmons as the stalker, and I'd bet my life on the fact he kidnapped Tarin."

"Then what are we waiting for? Get on the radio and bring him in." Jake's frustration surfaced with a vengeance.

Mike shook his head. "Scott planned this damn well. He scheduled a two-week vacation, and I've got a gut feeling we won't find him anywhere. But I'll get a search warrant for his house and send someone over to look for evidence. Hang in there, Jake. We need to figure out if it really was Scott, where he took Tarin, and believe it or not, I have an idea where that might be."

Mike called to the sheriff who was working downstairs. "Hey, Rick. I need a favor. Can you get me anything and everything you have on one of your deputies?"

"Sure, Mike. But which deputy and why?"

"Scott Simmons." Mike looked down at the bloated body on the floor. "He might have something to do with this."

"I'm not sure what you're thinking, but I trust you, so we'll get right on it."

"Thanks, man."

The investigator sat back on his heels. "What did you tell me you thought this man's name was?"

"Dan Carruthers. He said he was from California."

"Well, I've got a wallet and an ID that say his name is Dan Martin and he's a private detective from Los Angeles."

Mike shrugged. "That means Carruthers was an alias."

"Shouldn't we be out there trying to find them?" Jake asked, desperately wanting to do something.

Mike had started down the stairs, looking first at his watch and then at the snow that was growing in intensity. "There are a few things I need to set in motion first. Scott asked a lot of questions about the cabin Tarin's grandfather had in the mountains. I think Alex might have taken him hunting there once or twice a while back. It's a long shot, but facing the storm that's coming, that's where we might find them."

He looked back at Jake who was following him into the living room. "I'll line up a snowcat and snowmobiles to get us to the cabin. In this weather, we're going to need them. Then I'll see if I can get a rescue helicopter on standby in case it's necessary."

Mike turned to Jake. "As for you, get in that truck of yours and bring Jon back here from Winter Park." He looked sympathetically at Tarin's brother. "I have a feel for how you're taking this, Jake, but I can only imagine how he's going to react. Call me when the two of you get to town. We'll organize where the blacktop meets the trail across from Tarin's house. You've got two snowmobiles, don't you? Bring them along."

He glared at his friend. "But promise me: Don't get any wild ideas and go in without support. If they are at the cabin and Simmons is behind this, he's armed and dangerous. You got that?"

"Got it, Mike." Jake mouthed the words, knowing all too well he was making no promises.

JAKE WAS WAITING IN the small terminal building at the airport in Winter Park when Jon's chartered plane touched down on the windswept runway. Air traffic controllers had urged the small jet from San Diego to try landing in Denver instead, but neither the pilot nor his passenger had taken their advice.

Jon couldn't hide his anxiety once he was riding in Jake's truck on the highway leading to Chasm Falls. "God, Jake. Where is she? Are you sure Alex didn't have anything to do with this?"

Jake nodded. "We were all on the wrong track. It looks like it was Scott Simmons all along. They found his lighter on the floor next to the dead man in Tarin's bedroom. She must have struggled with Simmons, and it fell out of his pocket."

The falling snow was limiting visibility to less than twenty feet. Making the situation even more treacherous, it was early evening and the wind-driven flakes swirled around the headlights. Snowdrifts were beginning to form like feathery fingers across the icy two-lane road.

"What's Mike doing to find them?" Jon asked.

"He's putting together a rescue team with a snowcat, snowmobiles, and hopefully a medical helicopter from the Park Service. But in this weather, it would be almost impossible to land the chopper anywhere close to where we need to go."

"Does that mean Mike knows where Simmons has taken her?" Anxiety had evolved into anger.

"He thinks they may have gone to her grandfather's hunting cabin."

"Didn't somebody tell me you have snowmobiles at your house?"

"You know I do. But Mike was specific in telling me we weren't supposed to do anything stupid. If you're thinking we should go in without waiting for them, that would qualify as stupid."

Jon's voice was filled with desperation, "Jake, this is your sister we're talking about. It's also the woman who believes I've lied to her and even worse, cheated on her." He implored her brother to understand. "I can't let anything happen to Tarin. Think about it. It's going to take Mike time to pull all this together. I refuse to wait. Hell, I can't wait. Either we pick up your snowmobiles and go in together or I figure out a way to do it on my own."

"I can't let you do that. You don't know these mountains. In a week they'd find you frozen solid in the forest with your body gnawed by mountain lions."

"So go in with me. If it is Simmons, we can handle him."

Jake glanced toward his passenger. "You aren't going to take no for an answer, are you?"

"No, I'm not."

"I may be sorry when I agree to this, but you win. We'll go in without waiting. Heck, Mike and his team will be right behind us, so what could possibly go wrong?" He met Jon's determined stare. "Next question. Do you know how to shoot a gun?"

"I've been target shooting a few times."

"You better be ready for a crash course, my friend. You might need to defend yourself and we don't have time to practice."

Fifteen miles outside Chasm Falls, with snow falling even heavier, Jake and Jon began to put together a plan. There was only one thing they were sure of: Mike Wilson wasn't going to like it.

"SHIT." THAT WAS THE first word out of Mike's mouth when he turned onto the narrow lane. Parked on the side of the road he saw a pickup and an empty snowmobile trailer. The experienced officer knew immediately who owned both vehicles. "Shit, shit, shit," he repeated under his breath when he stepped out of his squad car. Mike was met by Sheriff Harrington who had pulled in right behind him.

"What's wrong?"

"Tarin MacGyver is the woman who was kidnapped, Rick." Mike pointed across the road. "The man who owns that truck and trailer is her brother and he's got Tarin's boyfriend riding shotgun. They weren't supposed to go in without us."

"Are you sure Simmons took her into the woods?"

"We've issued a regional all points bulletin for him, but the cabin is the best shot we've got locally, and I'm willing to go with my gut."

"What are we waiting for at this point?"

"The town's utility department is loaning us its snowcat. We've got a few more snowmobiles due to arrive any minute and the National Park Service is sending a team. Not sure about the rescue helicopter. The weather's going to force it to be on standby below the ridge on the other side of the mountain."

"Do you think Simmons really is the mastermind behind this?" the sheriff asked.

"The evidence points to him. Why?"

"Just asking. I didn't have a problem with the guy, but there have been more than a few rumors floating around the county. Somebody said he'd left the West Slope under questionable circumstances. I think internal affairs there had started an investigation. Nothing was ever verified, but it sounds like there might have been domestic abuse in his past before he got into law enforcement. I'm not sure how that was missed during background checks."

Just then, two trucks pulling trailers arrived—each carrying a pair of snowmobiles. Following close behind was a flatbed carrying Chasm Falls' only snowcat.

The drivers took a few minutes to compare notes and prepared to head into the darkness. Mike turned to the sheriff on the snowmobile next to him. "We could be in for a long night, Rick." Then he lowered his night vision goggles and motioned for the men to move forward.

Visibility was near zero, and the team soon discovered it was slow going up the windswept mountain. If it hadn't been for the towering pines lining the narrow lane, they would have been lost within a matter of minutes. And even though they were only a mile or so behind Jake and Jon, their tracks had already been erased by the mounting winds.

The search for Tarin was underway.

CHAPTER 47

—

The Escape

TARIN APPROACHED HER KIDNAPPER. "I'M SORRY, Scott. I've been trying to put it off, but I really need to go to the bathroom."

He scrutinized her before answering. "How am I supposed to know you won't try to escape?"

"Just look outside. We're in a blizzard and miles from civilization. Do you think I'm stupid enough to think I can find my way home in a storm like this? Please believe me—I'm not trying to get away from you." She decided to play on his emotions. "Anyway, you told me we need to get to know each other. Maybe I'm ready to see what kind of a connection we might have."

Unconvinced, he looked back and forth between Tarin and the door. "Do you mean that?"

She took one of his hands in hers. Seeing his conviction begin to waiver, Tarin continued, "All I want to do is go outside to the outhouse. Trying to escape would be a death sentence for me. When I get back, I want to hear what you have planned for our future. Where we'll go, what we'll do. It could be a new beginning for both of us."

"Do you mean that?" he asked again.

"Of course, I do. It happened just like you said it would with Jon—he lied and has gone back to his girlfriend in Hollywood. I need to find someone who cares about me and no one else." She turned away, avoiding his gaze.

"Okay. We can talk when you get back. I knew all along he would hurt you." Scott walked to the metal clothing rack and handed her a coat, knit gloves, and a baseball hat. "I'm sorry. I didn't plan on a blizzard when I picked your things, so I don't have any boots, but this should keep you warm until you get back inside. Then I can tell you about the dreams I have for us. You might like them." His eyes brightened at the prospect, and he leaned over to kiss her. "I'll have fresh coffee ready when you get back. It will warm you up. Then we'll talk. I promise you won't be disappointed."

Once outside, she closed the door and scrubbed away the remnants of his kiss with the back of her gloved hand. She was telling Scott the truth: Jon had hurt her. But Tarin was using that fact to try and earn his trust—and as a result, he had decided to let her go outside alone. Bracing herself against the cabin, she stared into the blowing snow. Tarin knew it would take a miracle to live through this blustery night, but she also realized staying with Scott was not an option.

She stepped off the porch and began the dangerous journey she knew offered the best chance to survive. The cave was small, but if she could find it and last until morning, she could elude Simmons and find her way down the mountain. However, locating the small opening she'd played in as a child would be a challenge. She could only see a few feet in front of her, and with no landmarks to serve as guides in the whiteout, she had to trust her memory and instincts alone.

It was hard to maintain any kind of balance on the icy crust, with at least one foot breaking through the surface every fourth or fifth step. She could feel snow seeping into her low-cut shoes.

She slipped, the howling wind catching the brim of her hat, sending it airborne and out of her grasp. Knowing she needed to keep her head covered, she stumbled through a drift to try and recover the ball cap. The wind had blown it onto the branch of a fallen tree and the hat was covered in snow by the time she rescued it. She swept it against her thigh to knock off as much snow as she could. Because she had fallen so many times, her clothing was already damp from head to toe. Finding shelter soon was imperative if she hoped to make it through the night.

Then, out of nowhere, she felt a hand grab her arm from behind. "Did you really think you could get away from me so easily?"

Tarin's heart sank. Saying nothing, she closed her eyes and turned back to Scott.

"You know, maybe I should let you die a miserable death," he warned. "They wouldn't find you until spring and I'd be long gone by then." He lifted her face toward his with a snow-covered glove, "But I can't bring myself to do that, no matter how much you've disappointed me."

"Go to hell," she sputtered through chattering teeth.

Gripping her wrist and dragging her through deep drifts toward the cabin, his grin was filled with malice when she fought to get away.

Tarin wasn't sure where she found the strength, but using every ounce she could muster, she managed to break his grasp. Maybe it was the shift in balance when she broke free, but Simmons lost his footing on a patch of ice and fell backward. Not even the howling wind could silence the sharp crack when his head hit a boulder protruding above the snow. A stream of bright crimson blood began to trail across the frozen ground next to his ear.

He was motionless for several minutes before Tarin had the courage to inch toward him. She stretched her fingers in the direction of the gun she could see holstered under his coat, but he flinched when she touched the cold steel. Frightened, she fell back onto the snow. Scurrying to regain her footing, Tarin stumbled away from the man who had brought her to the mountain that was once her favorite place in the world.

She pulled the coat's collar up to cover her ears and trudged in the direction she prayed would lead her away from Scott and to safety. Finally reaching the mountain wall, she realized she had a fifty-fifty chance of going either toward the cave or away from it. She opted to go to the right, a choice making as much sense as any other at that moment.

Tarin realized she could no longer feel her toes and it was increasingly difficult to pick up her feet and put them back down again. Attempting to establish her bearings, she paused and tried to flex her stiffening fingers. The hair framing her face hung to her shoulders like brittle icicles.

Where is it? She brushed away the frozen tears on her cheeks. Then stumbling again, she landed on her face in the snow. Pushing herself away from the windswept ground onto her hands and knees, she saw the cave opening a few yards away. It was as if there had been some sort of divine intervention.

With newfound energy, Tarin scrambled into the small cavern seeking the shelter she hoped it would provide. Her eyes adjusted to the darkness to discover only a minimal amount of snow had blown past the entrance. She also found remnants of a bale of straw she had left there years before.

Gathering the broken stems with her hands, she spread them on the cold stone and dirt to provide insulation. She found a large pile of aspen leaves and pine needles that had collected in the cave's recesses. They made a perfect layer on top of the straw.

One more challenge remained, and that was to stop the wind from blowing in. To seal the entry, Tarin would use something there was an abundance of—snow. No longer able to bend her fingers, her palms became the only tools she had to complete the task. She left a tiny opening at the top to allow fresh air to flow into the confined space.

Having found refuge, she did her best to nestle into the straw, trying to find relief and seeking any kind of warmth. But a damp cold was penetrating her body and clouding her senses. Tarin found her arms and legs didn't move as she expected them to when she crawled from one end of the cave to the other. Her shivering was now almost convulsive. The knit fabric of her gloves was frozen, and her fingers were rod-like and swollen.

Leaning against the frigid stone, she was suddenly overcome by an overwhelming burst of warmth. Tarin's thoughts had become incoherent. Deciding she needed to cool off, she used her palms to remove her leather shoes. But when she tried to take off her coat, her frozen fingers couldn't hold onto the zipper pull. And when she decided to put the shoes back on, she couldn't remember what to do with the laces.

She was so tired, but something told her she shouldn't go to sleep. It was getting harder and harder to move. But reliving favorite memories helped her stay awake. She could see her mom writing at the kitchen table and her grandpa fishing from the dock. She saw Finn sleeping in front of the fireplace. Then there was Jake teasing her like he always did at the Sip 'n Strike. And she could hear Jon calling her name over and over like he was trying to find her. Remembering the sound of his voice made her feel safe. She wished he would come and take her home. But then she saw him kissing Anna in the driveway. She realized he didn't care after all and now they would never be together. Then she heard Jon's voice again. It was far, far away—almost like it was in the wind. Tarin smiled, closed her eyes, and went to sleep.

CHAPTER 48

Life and Death

THE SNOW WAS SWIRLING PARALLEL TO THE GROUND, whipped mercilessly by a sustained 50 mph wind. Gusts almost double that velocity punctuated the mountain storm. Now that darkness had descended, the blowing snow made flashlights almost useless. Visibility was non-existent and icy crystals in the air became dagger-like projectiles.

If it hadn't been for a swath cut through the trees to define the road, it would have been impossible for Jake and Jon to find the remote hunting cabin. They had abandoned their snowmobiles a hundred yards earlier so there was no chance anyone inside could hear the engines or see the headlights.

Fighting against the wind and snowdrifts had drained their energy. Even with the insulated snowmobile suit and gloves Jake had given him, Jon could feel his fingers beginning to stiffen in the cold. The thermometer had read zero at the beginning of the trek without considering the wind chill factor, and now the temperature seemed to be dropping by the minute. Finally reaching the cabin, the two men positioned themselves behind trees about twenty-five yards from the porch. Through the swirling wall of snow, they could see an occasional flicker of candlelight illuminating a small window next to the front door.

Jon began to make a move toward the cabin, but Jake restrained him. "Hold on. Mike told us not to go in until they get here, and they can't be far behind us."

"You're crazy if you think I'm waiting." He yanked his arm away and surged forward. "I've got to find her."

"Damn it. You know I can't let you go in alone."

Gripping his gun, Jon kicked open the door. He scanned the dimly lit room, his eyes freezing for a moment on the empty handcuffs hanging from the iron headboard. But there was no one inside.

Jake struggled to close the door in the driving wind. "Now what?"

They walked around the room, checking every detail. "Okay. Let's talk it through. There's a fire in the stove that's still healthy. The pot is full of hot coffee. Something tells me they haven't been gone long and that means they can't be far away."

He reached for a framed photo of Tarin. She was smiling at him from a shelf on the wall. "Look at all this stuff. Pictures, photo albums, clothes. He's turned the cabin into a mini shrine with things that belong to her. God damn it. Simmons had every opportunity in the world to grab almost anything he wanted, and no one was the wiser. The creep has been in her house how many times since the burglary investigation started? Hell—he may have even been there before that."

Jon's gaze returned to the handcuffs dangling from the iron headboard. "You don't think he's hurt her, do you?"

"No, I don't think so. He's obsessed with Tarin and the last thing he would want to do is harm her." He paused. "Let's use logic. I doubt they would go for a leisurely stroll together on a night like this. What if she managed to escape somehow? Tarin's resourceful. That would explain why she's not here and why he went out to find her."

"You could be on the right track. But if you are—what should we do next?"

"We go after them. Think. When you were here last fall, did Tarin show you any places where she could hide? Anything at all that could provide shelter?"

Jon sat down, resting his elbows on the table with his forehead in his hands. "Shit. I don't know. We spent most of our time talking and drinking wine on a ridge overlooking the lake."

"Think," Jake pleaded. "Were there any buildings or caves?"

Jon tried to visualize the horseback ride they had taken months before. "She showed me so many things, I'm not sure I can think of anything in particular." But then he remembered something. "Wait a minute. We might be looking for an outcropping that looks sort of like a chimney. There's an opening at the base leading to a small cave in the mountain wall. She told me she played in it when she was a kid." Tears were forming in his eyes. "But what if she's not there? What do we do then?"

"We'll cross that bridge when we come to it. Now let's get the hell out of here before that psycho comes back."

Once outside, the two were trying to get their bearings when Jon noticed several shoe-sized holes in a drift leading away from the cabin. Past that point, the blowing snow had erased any evidence of human beings.

"It's the best shot we've got," Jake said, while taking a few quick readings with his handheld GPS unit.

After what felt like an eternity, Jake and Jon found themselves facing an opening in the forest. Through the blowing and drifting snow, they could see the rock wall ahead.

"But which direction do we go?"

Jake pulled the GPS device back out of his pocket. "Okay. The ridge you were talking about should be to the west. In fact, from these readings, we're almost there. I think we should go east, which would be to the right." Jake glanced at the ground while putting the device away. "God. What happened here?"

Illuminated by his flashlight, the dark red blood on the pointed boulder at his feet was in sharp contrast to the white snow around it. Then, before Jon could respond, they heard the crack of a gunshot and Jake crumpled to the ground.

"Hey, Parker—you're next," Simmons called out in the darkness. Another shot followed seconds after the first. Jon felt a ripple in the air next to his ear as the bullet whizzed by. He knelt beside Jake.

"Where did he hit you?"

Jake bit his lip and grimaced. "In my leg, but I'll be okay. I thought a former Marine would be a better shot than that." He groaned and reached for the gun in its holster. "You've still got the gun I gave you, don't you?"

"Yeah, but we didn't get a chance to practice."

"Necessity is the mother of invention. Get behind those trees before the wind dies down, visibility improves, and he tries again. Jake swallowed hard and closed his eyes. "I'm armed, so don't worry about me. Like I said, I'll be all right. Just be ready when he comes to finish me off. Then we'll take him out."

Jon touched Jake's shoulder before disappearing into the swirling snow.

A moment later, Jake heard boots crunching through the snow from behind.

"Fancy meeting you here, hotshot." Simmons moved in to face Jake and tried to taunt him by waving his gun in the air. "How's that bullet feel? I've got more where that came from."

"You son of a bitch. Where's my sister?"

Simmons smirked, "Tarin's your sister, is she? That explains a few things. It's a shame I'm going to have to kill my prospective brother-in-law." He glanced around the clearing. "Where's that yellow-bellied friend of yours?" The deputy launched into a resonating rendition of a chicken cackling. "Not very nice of him to leave you out here to die."

"You're the one who's going to die, bastard."

Simmons spun to find Jon standing about fifteen yards away. "Trying to be a hero, rock star? Sorry to disappoint you, but there's no chance of that."

"I beg to differ with you, Simmons," Jake said between clenched teeth. "You've got armed men in front and behind you. You may get one of us, but who do you think will come out in the end?"

"I think I still have a little leverage. You want to know where Tarin is, and I can tell you. But it might already be too late."

Jon inched closer. "What do you mean by that?"

Simmons grinned. "More than an hour ago she told me she needed to go to the outhouse. I wasn't too worried. What fool would go out on a night like this the way she was dressed? As I see it, at this temperature with the snow and wind, she might last a couple of hours and that's if she can find shelter." The deputy paused, savoring the hatred directed his way. "Of course, other than the cabin, there isn't any."

"How was she dressed?" Jon moved even closer.

Simmons shook his head, sharing an insincere look of concern. "That could be a problem. She's wearing a light coat, flannel shirt, and jeans. Unfortunately, there weren't any boots, so she's wearing nylon running shoes. But I did manage to find a pair of knit gloves and a baseball hat." He met Jon's gaze. "Do you know anything about hypothermia? The shivering will be the worst part, but in the end, she'll simply go to sleep. You might not even find her body."

"You son of a bitch." Jon raised his gun until the barrel was pointing directly at Scott's chest.

Jake glanced back and forth between the two men, "Jon, if you shoot him nobody would blame you—least of all me. But if he can tell us where Tarin is, we don't want him dead."

The stalemate continued before Jon finally lowered his gun.

Simmons began to laugh hysterically. The sound of his voice was soft at first and then echoed into the darkness. "You really believe I know where she is? Do you think I would still be out here if I did? You idiots. I hope she's frozen solid somewhere. She's not going to love anyone other than me, Parker."

In a calculated motion, Simmons pointed his gun at Jake. Then Jon fired and Scott Simmons fell onto the snow-covered ground. He was motionless.

Mike Wilson and his crew had arrived at the cabin and heard the gun's sharp report.

Jake clenched his lips. His words were weak at best. "You're our last chance, Jon. Find that cave. Mike's team must be close, and I've got a flare to direct them. You've still got yours, don't you?" He paused to look at the man who was still staring at the hot barrel of the gun in his hand. "Jon," he commanded, "get over it and find Tarin."

Fighting through the drifts and using the rock wall as a guide, Jon continued to call her name.

"Give me a sign if you can hear me! Damn it—we know you're here somewhere," he screamed into the darkness.

He punched a tree trunk in frustration. There was a sudden break in the swirling wind, and in desperation Jon looked skyward for encouragement. His prayers were answered. Twenty yards away he saw the chimney rock. Kneeling at its base, Jon began digging for any opening in the frigid wall of ice.

She must have covered the entry to keep the wind out.

One tiny chunk broke away. Then another and another. Jon stuck his flashlight into the small opening. "Tarin? Are you in there? Please answer me!"

From his vantage point, the cave was narrow, about four feet high with a small nook toward the back. Shining the light inside, he saw her lying in a fetal position on what looked like a pile of straw and other debris. "Hey, you—hang on. We're here for you."

There was no response.

She's not moving. I've got to get to her.

Mike had coached Jake and Jon by cell phone during the pair's drive from Winter Park. The police officer's words echoed in Jon's head while he continued to chop at the opening.

If Simmons did take her to the cabin and we find her outside, we'll have a rescue helicopter waiting on the other side of the ridge. That's all the closer the pilot will be able to get in this weather. They'll have EMTs and all the equipment needed to stabilize her condition.

Jon's thoughts raced.

What else did Mike tell us? The officer's warnings reverberated in his head.

Be careful. If she's been outside for any length of time, you need to be gentle. Hypothermia victims are prone to cardiac arrest. Also, don't try to warm Tarin by rubbing her arms and legs. That would pump cold blood back to her heart and could cause it to fail.

The icy wall collapsed, and Jon tumbled into the small cavern. Crawling back outside, he lit his flare to alert the rescue team. Then, returning to her side, he whispered her name, "Tarin, it's me. Please wake up." He took off a glove and placed the back of his hand on her cheek.

Oh, God. Her skin is like ice and turning gray. I can't tell if she's breathing.

Mike's instructions were crystal clear.

Use your body heat to keep her warm.

MIKE HAD ALREADY APPLIED a tourniquet and was wrapping gauze around Jake's leg when he saw Jon's flare burst into the sky. He keyed his radio. "Rescue One, be on standby. It looks like we've found her. We'll keep you posted. Do you copy? Over."

The pilot was quick to respond. "Copy, Mike. We'll have everything ready when you get here and will alert the hospital. Rescue One out."

Mike sat back on his haunches. "You still with me, Jake? Do you think you can make it to the snowcat?"

Jake nodded and stood with the help of another officer. "Then let's get moving."

Within minutes Mike was kneeling at the cave entrance. "Jon— how are you doing?"

There was complete panic in Jon's reply. "I can't tell if she's breathing."

"I'm coming in. Try to stay calm and don't worry. Sometimes hypothermia victims don't seem to have a pulse. We'll get her to the helicopter, and they'll know what to do. But first, we need to get Tarin out of the cave as gently as possible. After we wrap her in blankets, I need you and Jake on either side in the back of the snowcat. Your body heat will be important until we get her to the chopper."

Mike tried to reassure him. "We'll have four snowmobiles in front to open a trail with the rest of us pulling up the rear. It'll be slow going, but the copter's prepared. Are you ready?"

Numb, Jon nodded.

"Then let's get to it."

The two worked together to move Tarin from the small cave to the bed of the snowcat where they did their best to keep her protected from the cold and snow. As the procession began its slow trek to the waiting helicopter, Jake was acutely aware of the worried look riveted on Jon's face and the fear in his eyes.

"There are so many things I need to say to her."

"Go ahead—I have a feeling she'll hear you. But you can tell her everything again later just to be sure." Jake watched him cradle Tarin in his arms. "If we're making confessions, I've got one of my own." He stopped to craft his words. "It's no secret I've never thought you were good enough for my sister. But after today, that's all changed. I misjudged you and I was wrong. I'm sorry."

Jon didn't respond. No words were necessary between them.

Three Park Service rescue team members met the snowcat at the helicopter and took charge of the situation. "Good job, guys. We'll handle things from here."

After a brief conversation with the pilot, Mike approached Jon who was sitting beside Jake's stretcher inside the helicopter door. "I'll be going back to the cabin, but you need to get buckled in for the flight."

"What are they doing?" Jon asked, his eyes glued to the medics.

Jake shifted on the stretcher to look at the medical personnel. His answer was barely audible over the sound of rotors gaining speed. "She's breathing heated air through the mask. That will warm her core—most importantly her heart, lungs, and brainstem. Then they'll remove her wet clothes, put dry clothing back on, and administer warm IV fluids."

"How do you know all that?"

Jake shook his head. "I don't know. You live in the mountains long enough, go on a few rescues, and you learn from situations like this."

"Why did Mike tell us the first thirty minutes are the most critical?"

Jon braced himself when the helicopter lifted off.

Once the chopper was safely airborne, Jake continued, "When the patient's arms and legs begin to warm up, cold blood is pumped back through the body, and it drops the person's core temperature even lower. As a result, ventricular fibrillation can develop. Without getting too technical, when that happens the ventricles don't pump blood into the arteries like they're supposed to. It can be lethal. But I don't want you to worry. These are trained professionals who know exactly what they need to do."

He saw the color drain from Jon's face. "Jake, why are they doing CPR?"

CHAPTER 49

Revelations

D UE TO THE STORM, IT TOOK NEARLY AN HOUR after taking off from the icy mountainside for the rescue helicopter to reach Denver Community Medical Center. An EMT knelt in front of Jon, trying to be heard over the sound of the engine and spinning rotors.

"Mr. Parker, this is how it's going to go when we land." The man grabbed the base of Jon's seat for support when the wind caused the chopper to lurch to the left. "We'll take Ms. MacGyver off first and then Mr. Carpenter. You'll be last, but the Trauma Center staff will want to look at you, too. You're okay to walk, aren't you?"

Jon nodded; his eyes still locked on Tarin.

The medic could see the fear on Jon's face and put a hand on his knee. "She seems to have stabilized. You guys did a great job getting her to us. Hang in there, okay?"

Minutes later, Jon watched the medical team coordinate Tarin's move and then return for Jake.

"Okay, Mr. Parker. Your turn, sir." The medic helped Jon unfasten his seatbelt and put a hand on his shoulder. "It's all going to be fine."

Inside a nurse was waiting to guide Jon toward a curtained examination room. It was then that he saw another nurse and two technicians waiting in front of an elevator with Tarin on a gurney.

"Wait," he called out, rushing to her side.

The nurse was stern when the elevator door opened, "I'm sorry, sir. We need to get this patient to ICU. Please step away."

Jon felt a hand grasp his arm from behind. It was the medic from the helicopter.

"Have faith—it's going to be okay, Mr. Parker. Let them do their jobs."

"But I need to be with her." The steel door closed, leaving Jon feeling helpless.

"Come on, let's get you checked out. Once you've been released, you'll be able to visit the ICU." He paused. "I know you've been through a lot tonight. Like I said before, just hang in there."

"Do you know where Jake is?" Jon searched the area for some sign of Tarin's brother.

"Mr. Carpenter? One of the nurses told me they've taken him into surgery to remove the bullet from his thigh. He was lucky. If it had hit his femoral artery, he could have bled to death." The medic gestured toward the landing pad. "Now I need to get back to the helicopter. You take care."

Upon examination, doctors determined Jon had suffered minor frostbite, but they could treat and release him. Nearly two hours had passed since his diagnosis and he paced like a frightened animal trapped in the ICU waiting room, praying for news of Tarin's condition.

"Mr. Parker?"

He turned, unable to hide his anxiety.

The nurse smiled. "Ms. MacGyver is resting. Normally only immediate family members are allowed in our unit, but her brother made sure you have permission to visit."

Numb, he followed her along the sterile white hallway. Inside Tarin's room Jon could see a doctor adjusting one of the monitors tracking her vital signs. A wall of glass separated the room from the nurses' station. The blinds used to shield the room from view were open.

A gray-haired physician turned and extended his hand, "Mr. Parker? I'm Dr. Byram. I understand you're one of those responsible for getting this young woman to us in time."

"It was a team effort, sir." Jon's face lacked color as he stared at the tubes and wires connected to Tarin. "Is she going to be, okay?"

The doctor spoke in a monotone, "Due to confidentiality laws, I can't tell you much. We'll keep her here overnight, but unless there's a setback, I feel comfortable predicting she'll be moved out of ICU tomorrow or the next day." His bedside manner softened, "I've been provided with a little background information. She's lucky you, her brother, and the others were there to get her out of that blizzard."

"Have you heard how Jake is doing? He was shot in the leg."

"I don't make a rule of tracking surgeries, but under the circumstances I felt it was important. Mr. Carpenter appears to be Ms. MacGyver's only living relative, and if anything were to happen or treatment decisions required, he would need to be involved." The doctor repeated his disclaimer, "Again, I can't say anything other than I've been told he's in recovery."

The doctor glanced at Tarin and then back at Jon. "I've worked in this type of unit for almost thirty years. Don't be frightened by the machines or the noises they make. The equipment is a safeguard so we can track her vitals, anticipate problems, and react quickly if any issues develop." He stopped to put Tarin's chart back into the holder on the wall. "She's sedated and sleeping. At Mr. Carpenter's insistence, I've instructed the nurses you may stay as long as you like. Goodnight, sir."

With that, the doctor was gone.

Jon felt glued to the floor where he stood. Gazing at Tarin, she seemed helpless surrounded by monitors, machines, and IV paraphernalia.

Jon noticed the nurse he met earlier had returned. Her voice was kind and compassionate. "The lights in the hallway are terribly bright. I'll close the blinds so you're more comfortable, plus you'll have more privacy. We'll be across the hall if you need anything."

"Thank you." He pulled a chair next to the bed and held one of Tarin's gauze-covered hands. Then for the first time in as long as he could remember, he cried.

JON HAD FALLEN ASLEEP, his chin resting on his chest when a quiet rap on the doorframe awakened him. He sat up to find Mike Wilson standing nearby.

"Hey, how are you holding up?" Mike asked.

Jon shook his head, trying to clear his thoughts, "Okay, I guess." He looked around the room to find a clock. "What time is it?"

"About four in the morning."

"Why aren't you home in bed?"

"Can't sleep on a night like we just went through. It must be the adrenaline. As for why I'm here, I couldn't be anywhere else. Jake and Tarin are like family to me and now I've added you to the mix. I drove down as soon as we finished at the cabin for the night. The crime scene is under the sheriff's jurisdiction, so they're handling most everything. He's sending one of his men tomorrow to take statements from you and Jake about what happened and asked me to assist."

Mike hesitated. "There won't be any charges filed because it was a clear case of self-defense, but you did shoot and kill a man last night. We need to document the incident."

Jon stared out the window, reliving the instant he had pulled the trigger and the sound of the bullet entering Simmons' chest at close range. Then snapping out of the memory, he turned toward Mike. "Are they going ask Tarin to talk about everything that happened? Is it too soon?"

"Maybe. We'll consult with Tarin and her doctors before that decision is made." Mike paused to take a deep breath and asked the question weighing on his mind, "How is she?"

"She's been sleeping since I got here." There was an unmistakable plea in Jon's voice, "She looks so fragile. I'm scared, Mike."

"Be patient and let the doctors do what they're trained to do." Mike stopped and then forged ahead, "I'm not sure how much more time the nurses will give me—I had to use my badge and uniform just to get in here." He hesitated, "Do you have a minute? There's new information I think you should know."

Jon shook his head. "We can talk, but I don't want to leave her."

Mike was insistent. "I think it would be best if we step outside. I'm not sure how you'll react to what I'm going to tell you."

"What's going on?" Jon asked once the pair stood in the empty waiting room.

"Remember the man Simmons killed in Tarin's bedroom?"

"Yeah. Did you figure out what he was doing there?"

Mike nodded. "Get ready. From evidence found in the man's hotel room, it looks like your manager Tommy Wyndham hired him to kill Tarin. The guy's name was Dan Martin."

Jon crossed the room in disbelief. "Wait a minute. Tommy's done his share of despicable things, but murder? No way."

Mike shook his head, "The evidence doesn't lie." He pulled a small notepad from his pocket. "I took notes. We've got proof Wyndham was depositing large amounts of cash in Martin's bank account. Apparently, they were using burner phones to communicate, but Wyndham slipped up a few times and called the hotel phone. Martin was in Chasm Falls under the alias of Dan Carruthers."

Jon sat down, resting his head in his hands.

"There's more. My guys found an envelope of photos and notes in his room. The pictures were of Tarin, Jake, Alex, and a bunch of others, including me." Mike sat down next to him. "Wyndham wanted Tarin dead, and I'm pretty sure we know why."

Jon stared at Mike, waiting for him to explain.

"When Martin was shot, he was holding something Wyndham was willing to kill to get his hands on."

"What could Tarin have had that was so important?"

"Her digital recorder and the incriminating tape that went with it." Mike turned to look at Jon. "I've listened to the tape. There are probably ten to fifteen conversations on it. All of them are between Tarin and Wyndham."

"What were they talking about and why would she record anything he said?" Jon's confusion was evident, his mind traveling in a hundred different directions. He stood and began pacing.

"On the tape she demonstrates her skill as an investigative reporter by nailing that snake to the wall. More than once he brags about how he's stolen money from clients for years." Mike hesitated, "Unfortunately—and I'm sorry, Jon—one of those musicians was you. The most heated conversation on the tape is about you getting a sixteen-year-old girl pregnant and paying her family a half-million dollars to make the whole thing go away. Wyndham pocketed almost all of that money himself, except for what he paid the hooker to set you up. He admitted to Tarin it was staged from start to finish. There never was a pregnant teenager."

Jon's anger exploded loud enough to elicit alarmed looks from the nurses at their station down the hall. "My god. That's why Tommy came after her? She got him to admit something he did to me ten years ago?"

Mike nodded. "But there's more, a lot more. The names of other clients he scammed. Amounts. She could have ruined his career, landed him in a barrage of civil suits, not to mention criminal charges and jail." He paused for a moment. "A while ago I got a call from the police in Malibu. Shortly after midnight, they found a judge who listened to the district attorney's case. A warrant has been issued to pick up Wyndham. They plan to make an arrest sometime this morning. With the evidence the deputies found last night, it won't be long before he's charged with solicitation of murder for hire and conspiracy to commit murder, among other allegations they're still working on. The DA didn't waste any time."

"Do they usually move that fast?" Jon spoke in a whisper, trying to digest everything he'd just been told.

"They're convinced that once he gets wind of the failed murder attempt and Martin's death, Wyndham might jump on that jet of his and leave the country."

Jon sat down, still trying to fathom how any of this could be real. "How did Tarin get involved in this without me knowing anything about it? And why didn't she let me listen to the tape once she'd gotten his confession? It doesn't make sense." He pleaded for an answer. "Didn't she realize he's not the kind of man you cross?"

Mike shook his head, "Those are questions you'll need to ask Tarin when she's healthy enough to talk with you." He stopped to gather his thoughts. "I understand how you're feeling, but you need to remember Wyndham is only one piece of the puzzle. Don't forget about Simmons, because in the end he's the one who posed the biggest threat. He was obsessed with Tarin and you had nothing to do with that. We're pretty sure he was stalking her even before the break-in. Bit by bit we're learning more about his twisted past."

Jon stood again and Mike moved to his side. "I know Tarin as well as anyone and she wouldn't want you to feel responsible."

"But why would she put herself in the middle of something like this for me?" Jon clenched his lips in a futile attempt to control his emotions.

Mike smiled. "It's simple. She loves you. Now, I'm going home to take a long hot shower and if I can, get a few hours of sleep." He shook his head. "No, on second thought, there's no sleep for me. I refuse to snooze through the moment when Wyndham takes his fall. Seeing photos of him in a police mugshot would make my day. Maybe even my year." Mike started for the door with new energy. "I'll sleep when he's behind bars."

Jon put a hand on Mike's arm before he could leave. "Thank you. You've always given me the benefit of doubt, even when I didn't deserve it."

Mike tried to console the shaken man standing in front of him. "Tarin has excellent instincts. If she believes in you, I have no choice but to believe in you, too." Then a smile crossed his face, "However, now that I think about it, there is one thing you can do for me. If I can call in a favor, my wife would love a new set of Motive CDs. I shredded hers after you got engaged to that actress on national television."

"Consider it done." Jon returned the smile. "You're a saint, Mike."

"No, I'm just someone who likes to see happy endings for people who mean a lot to me. Speaking of those I care about—I checked on Jake a little while ago and he's doing well. I hate to admit it, but even though the two of you disobeyed every order you were given, you turned out to be a damn good team., I'm not sure how things would have turned out without you. Now—see if you can follow instructions for once and get some sleep yourself."

Watching Mike walk toward the elevator, Jon used the back of his hand to wipe away the tears forming yet again and returned to Tarin's side.

Sitting in her room, Jon was drifting in and out of sleep when he heard an almost transparent whisper, "Am I dreaming, or is that really you?"

He leaned toward the bed, combed his fingers through her hair, and kissed her cheek. "It's me."

She struggled to speak, and he moved closer, "I thought I heard you calling my name when I was hiding, but decided it was just the wind."

"It wasn't the wind or a dream. Jake and I were trying everything we could think of to find you."

"But what about Anna?" she asked in a soft voice that was difficult to hear.

He kissed her again and whispered, "Dear, sweet Tarin—there's no Anna in my life. There's only you."

Smiling, she slipped back to sleep. It was a smile Jon would remember for the rest of his life.

CHAPTER 50

———

Justice

NICK REYNOLDS GROPED THE NIGHTSTAND FOR the vibrating cell phone. Finding it at last, he rolled over on his side, leaned on an elbow, and put the phone to his ear.

His answer included a lengthy yawn. "Reynolds."

"Nick, this Jon."

"What time is it?" Nick struggled to get his bearings in the darkness. "Where the hell are you? We had a post-production meeting yesterday afternoon and you didn't show. I know you were supposed to pick up Tarin in San Diego, but we thought you said you could still make it."

"It's almost four o'clock your time and honestly, I don't know where to begin." He paused, "I'm in Colorado."

Nick leaned back against his pillow and Roxie inched closer to his side. "Care to tell me what's going on?"

"Tarin was kidnapped Monday night."

Nick sat up in bed, his heart falling into his stomach like a rock. "God, Jon. Please, tell me you've found her and she's okay."

Jon took a deep breath, "She was taken to a cabin in the mountains but managed to escape. Late last night we found her hiding in a cave in the middle of a blizzard. She's in ICU right now being treated for hypothermia. At this point, it looks like she's going to be all right."

"Please tell me Tommy had nothing to do with it," Nick said under his breath.

"Why did you say that?"

"Say what?"

"The part about Tommy. How did you know he was involved somehow?"

"I didn't," Nick replied nervously, struggling to come up with an answer. "He just always seems to be in the mix when bad things happen." He was relieved when Jon seemed to accept his explanation.

"She was sleeping when a man Tommy hired to kill her got into the bedroom. Before he could finish the job, the man that's been stalking Tarin entered the house. He shot and killed Tommy's guy, then took off with her."

"Was the stalker the old boyfriend?"

"No. We were all wrong. It was the deputy sheriff who's been helping with the burglary investigation."

The color drained from Nick's face. He stood and walked to the bedroom's sliding glass doors. "Damn it. I told her to be careful."

"What was that? Why did you tell her to be careful?"

Nick closed his eyes, reliving the moment he'd agreed to keep Tarin's secret. "I'm sorry, Jon. It has to do with Tommy. One day while we were in the studio, I decided to order carryout from that new Italian place down the street. When I got there, I saw Tarin helping Tommy into the backseat of a cab. He was totally trashed. I followed her back into the restaurant and called her on it. I wanted to know what she hoped to gain by hanging out with him."

Nick paused, remembering the determination he'd seen on her face that day. "Tarin told me she had a tape of Tommy confessing how he'd scammed people for years. But at that point hadn't gotten him to admit to what she really wanted to know. She wanted to nail him for what she believed he'd done to you in San Francisco."

The silence between them echoed.

"Jon, believe me, I told her Tommy was a dangerous man, but I had no idea he would try to have her killed. When she went back to Colorado and then off to Europe, I figured she was away from him and safe."

Jon's words were cloaked in anger, "Let me get this straight. You knew she was putting herself in danger and didn't do anything about it?" His body convulsed when he thought of the things Tommy and his shooter had been capable of doing. "Why the hell didn't you tell me any of this?"

His answer was subdued. "I promised not to say anything until she decided the time was right to expose him. Do you remember the day in the control room when she collapsed on the couch? That's the day she confronted Tommy with the truth. Tarin had more than enough dirt about his early business dealings to fry him, but the only person she cared about was you."

Nick became defensive. "Jon, have you even read your contract? Do you know there's a provision in the fine print giving either you or Tommy the right to extend it for another project? Tarin was holding the tape over his head so he wouldn't exercise that option. She wanted him out of your lives forever."

"He wanted her dead, Nick. You should have told me so I could have protected her. Sorry, I've gotta go." Devoid of energy, Jon looked down at his phone and cut the connection.

Nick sat down on the bed, reached for Roxie, and held her close. "I'm afraid I just lost my best friend. Pack a bag. We're flying to Denver."

TOMMY WAS SITTING WITH Paul, the engineer, in the recording studio's control room. Four members of the band Motive were also there listening to tracks from their newly completed album, along with a trio of entertainment reporters and their videographers. Each one was hoping to get a scoop on what was being hyped in music circles as the band's final project.

At precisely ten o'clock Pacific Time the morning after Tarin was rescued, two plainclothes detectives and three uniformed police officers walked through the studio's front doors. They approached the front desk without fanfare.

"We have reason to believe a man named Tommy Wyndham is on the premises. Could you please direct us to him?"

The startled and speechless receptionist nodded and led them to the control room.

The officers had been provided with photos of Tommy and when they entered the room their eyes went directly to the overweight, balding man sitting at the board. Up until that moment the room had been filled with laughter and celebratory conversations, but in an instant, it became eerily quiet.

"Tommy Wyndham," one of the detectives stated matter-of-factly, his eyes meeting the manager's. "You are under arrest for solicitation of murder for hire and conspiracy to commit murder."

Tommy stared at them without responding. Unfortunately, he had no control over the beads of sweat beginning to dot his face.

Instantaneously, video cameras turned from members of the band to Tommy's flushed face.

"That's absurd," he stuttered. "I have no idea what you're talking about."

Directed by a nod from the lead detective, two of the officers walked toward Tommy and with one on each side, attempted to make him stand. He responded by gyrating his body back and forth to escape from them.

"Get your hands off me. Those charges are insane. Do you know who you're dealing with?" His hands and arms were in perpetual motion while he fought to remain free.

"Mr. Wyndham, it will be much easier for everyone if you come along with us quietly. Don't make it necessary to add resisting arrest to the list of charges already filed against you."

The officers finally found it necessary to use force to lift him from the chair and brute strength to pull his hands behind his back and snap on handcuffs.

Tommy glanced around the room at each of the stunned reporters and musicians. "This is ridiculous!" he growled. "Who in the world do you think I had murdered?"

The detective remained calm when the officers began pushing the struggling man toward the doorway. "You're being charged with solicitation of murder for hire and conspiracy to commit the murder of Tarin MacGyver."

The digital recorders and video cameras pointed toward the action captured it all.

Tommy stopped and turned to look at the detective with a sinister grin on his face. "Does that mean she's actually dead?"

The second detective shook his head. "No. But the man you allegedly hired is."

He motioned toward the door before reciting the Miranda Warning to their prisoner in an expressionless voice, "You have the right to remain silent and refuse to answer questions. Anything you do say may be used against you in a court of law. You have the right to consult an attorney before speaking to the police and to have an attorney present during questioning now or in the future. If you cannot afford an attorney, one will be appointed for you before any questioning if you wish. If you decide to answer questions now without an attorney present, you will still have the right to stop answering at any time until you talk to an attorney. Knowing and understanding your rights as I have explained them to you, are you willing to answer my questions without an attorney present?"

"Go to hell," Tommy responded furiously as he was propelled out the studio's front door and thrust into the backseat of a waiting squad car.

The police cars pulled away from the studio with high-definition cameras recording every second of the unscrupulous manager's demise. The reporters and video crews sped away mere minutes later, cell phones in hand, calling their studios. In what was to become his darkest moment, Tommy Wyndham was about to make national news.

CHAPTER 51

———

Making Amends

J ON WAS RETURNING FROM THE HOSPITAL CAFETERIA
with two cups of coffee when he saw a familiar person lingering in
the waiting room. "Alex? Thanks for being here."

Still in his security officer's garb, he shrugged. "I wanted to be sure
Tarin's getting better, but I also need to talk with you."

Jon motioned toward one of the couches. "Have a seat. Would you
like some coffee? I don't need two cups for myself." He handed one of
the containers to Alex. "She's had a tough time, but you know Tarin's a
fighter. They're still worried about her fingers and toes, but the doctors
are optimistic she'll make a complete recovery. It's just going to take
time. They moved her from intensive care to a regular room a few
hours ago." He paused before looking at Alex. "For what it's worth,
I'm glad you're here because I owe you an apology."

"There's no need to apologize. I know you were convinced I was
the stalker, and I can understand why. But as messed up as I've been,
I could never hurt Tarin."

An awkward silence settled between them before Alex spoke
again. "I'm not going to make any excuses. It's common knowledge
I've been screwed up ever since I came back from the Middle East. I
hit bottom about the time Tarin's boathouse was broken into. But now
I'm doing everything I can to get back on my feet. I've been going to

counseling and following my doctor's orders." He smiled. "It's been a long time coming, but I'm looking forward to the future. Rachel stuck with me through everything, and our daughter Sarah is—"

Jon saw the sparkle in Alex's eyes at the mention of his daughter's name.

"Well—she's the best thing that's ever happened to me. Rachel and I are determined to make our marriage work. We're not about to give up." He stood and turned toward the waiting room door. "Just so you know—I'm glad you and Tarin found each other."

Jon held out his hand to stop him. "Don't you want to see her? She'd want to know you're here."

Alex shook his head. "No. Just tell her she's in our thoughts. That will do for now. We'll talk sometime soon."

"Alex—"

"Yeah?"

"Thanks."

He grinned, "Just promise you'll take good care of her."

"I promise."

Mike entered the waiting room and asked, "Was that Alex?"

Jon nodded. "He wanted to apologize. You could say we apologized to each other. He's not such a bad guy after all."

"I'm glad he finally let you see that." Mike looked down the hall. "Hey, you'll never guess who I found carousing around the hospital."

Jake rounded the corner in a wheelchair, wearing a big smile on his face. "Hey, Parker. What do you say we visit my sister?" He proceeded to scan Jon from head to toe. "Fortunately for everyone in the hospital, Mike found your duffel bag in my truck and brought it with him. You, my friend, are in dire need of a shower, clean clothes, and a toothbrush."

Mike silenced Jon's protests. "I feel no need to be polite. Parker—you're beginning to stink. One of the nurses showed me a shower you can use and that's where you're going." He held his nose and began to propel Jon down the hallway. "Jake, tell Tarin we're fumigating her man, and we'll be back as soon as he's presentable."

Jake spun around in his wheelchair, headed down the hall, and disappeared into Tarin's room.

MIKE AND JAKE WERE sitting next to Tarin's hospital bed recounting childhood adventures to a squeaky clean and rejuvenated Jon, when they heard a soft knock. Mike looked up to see a uniformed officer from the Granite County Sheriff's Department standing in the doorway.

"Hey, Drew. Come on in." Mike stood to shake hands with the deputy. "This is Drew Schaefer. He's here to take your statements about everything that happened." He turned to Tarin, "The doctors have given their okay if you're ready to talk with him today, but there's no pressure if you'd rather give it more time."

Tarin was sitting up in her hospital bed. Color was returning to her skin, replacing the ashen pallor of the day before. "Today is fine. I'd like to get it over with, Mike."

"Okay," Deputy Schaefer replied with a reassuring smile. "It's nice to meet you, Ms. MacGyver. I'm sorry it's under these circumstances." He lifted his briefcase onto Tarin's bedside table, taking out a notebook and a small digital recorder. He turned toward the others in the room. "Mike will be staying, but I'm afraid I'll have to ask the rest of you to leave."

Hearing the door close, the deputy pulled his chair next to the bed. "Is it all right with you if we record this conversation?"

She nodded.

Deputy Schaefer sat down, looked at Mike and Tarin, and pressed record.

THE OFFICER STOOD AND put the equipment back into his briefcase.

"We'll see if the sheriff and DA need anything else. If they do, we can finish this another day." He stopped long enough to rest his hand lightly on Tarin's. "As far as I'm concerned, Scott Simmons kidnapped you, threatened your life, and held you against your will. Simmons is dead, so there will be no trial stemming from those charges. We'll get a statement from Mr. Parker who, from all the evidence, shot him in self-defense. We'll also talk with Mr. Carpenter who was wounded by Simmons. The DA will have the final word, but as I see it, case closed."

"Thank you, Drew," Mike told the deputy. "She's already been through enough."

"If the circumstances were different—if we were facing a trial—we'd need to do more." He paused to put on his coat. "But I can't see any reason to go further at this point. We can always continue the interview later if the DA wants us to."

Schaefer picked up his briefcase and followed Mike into the hallway. "For the hell that man put her through, she's doing really well."

"Tarin's always been a strong person, Drew."

"Mike, there's something you should know. When the recovery team went back to recover Simmons' body, they couldn't find it."

"Everything was happening so fast, and we weren't equipped to take out a body that night," Mike responded. "Normally, we would have had a couple of guys stay with him overnight, but because of the weather, it wasn't possible. We covered Simmons with blankets and a tarp—that's all we had—and used anything we could find as markers."

The deputy nodded. "We completely understand. But so much snow came down that night, by the next morning everything had blown away or was buried with him." He hesitated, "That's not all."

The deputy motioned for Mike to follow him away from Tarin's doorway.

"When we were trying to locate his next of kin, we came up empty except for his almost ex-wife, Ashley."

"Almost ex-wife? Have you talked with her?"

Schaefer shook his head. "Can't. She's dead. She was killed in a one-car accident late at night right after Simmons returned from his last tour of duty." The deputy looked over his shoulder to see if anyone else was nearby. "I guess when he got home, she'd asked him for a divorce because she was involved with another man. It didn't sit well with our former Marine. The divorce wasn't final when she died."

"Did they investigate to see if Simmons had anything to do with the accident?"

"We were told he had an alibi the authorities couldn't crack, so the case was closed as an accidental death. Her family still doesn't buy it."

Leaning closer to Mike, the deputy continued, "There's something else and this is eerie. If you put photos of Ashley and your friend, Tarin, next to each other—except for the hair color, you wouldn't be able to tell them apart."

Mike leaned back against the wall, lowered his head, and the anger he'd buried inside finally surfaced. "You know what, Drew? I hope the mountain lions and coyotes get to his body before the snow melts. As far as I'm concerned, they can devour every ounce of his flesh and then shit it all over the mountain."

"I understand how you feel." Schaefer rested his arm on Mike's shoulder. "But don't let it get in the way of what we need to do. And right now, that's taking statements from Jon Parker and Jake Carpenter. What do you say we find them and get started?"

Mike nodded. "Can we keep this latest information within our departments?"

"That's the plan. There's no need for it to come out now or maybe even ever. But if you have any influence over Ms. MacGyver, please be sure she seeks counseling. I don't care how strong she is. She witnessed a murder, was kidnapped, held hostage, sexually assaulted, and is fighting to recover from the after-effects of hypothermia. Nobody can come to terms with all that alone."

With that, the two started down the hall toward the waiting room to locate their two remaining interviewees and find a pot of strong coffee.

IN THE DIMLY LIT confines of her hospital room, Tarin found herself drifting in and out of consciousness when she felt someone enter the room. "Jon?"

"No, it's me," Maria answered.

"Hi," Tarin whispered, moistening her lips with her tongue. "How are you?"

The young woman shook her head. "How can you ask about me after everything that's happened?" She brushed away a tear from her cheek. "I'm so sorry. I can't believe I fell in love with such an evil man."

Tarin reached for her hand. "Come here for a minute."

Maria pulled a chair to the edge of the bed.

"There's something you need to know. Tommy Wyndham paid Dan to kill me, but when the time came, he couldn't do it." She paused, hoping the words might ease her friend's pain. "Dan may have made some bad choices in his life, but you need to remember the influence you had on him when he came to Chasm Falls. You helped bring out all the good qualities he'd hidden within himself when he worked for Tommy." She winced when a sharp pain shot through her lower legs.

Maria was frightened. "What's wrong? Should I get a nurse?"

Tarin closed her eyes until the pain subsided. "No, it's just something I'll have to live with for a time. Please don't worry about me. There's something you need to know. The night Dan threatened me there was nothing I could do to stop him. But he lowered the gun and started to walk away. I heard him say he couldn't do it." Tarin knew the importance of what she would tell her friend next. "That was when Scott came in. Maria—Dan wasn't going to shoot me. He was going to leave the house." Tarin took her hand. "We both know he was a good man inside and if you'd had more time together, you would have turned his life around. I believe that with all my heart."

Maria buried her head in her hands. "No matter what he'd done or what he had to face, we could have gotten through it. I wish I could have told him that." She looked up with a sad smile. "We were going to buy a house, the one across the lake that's almost like yours. He wanted to have kids."

Tarin ran her fingers through Maria's hair and gazed toward a window across the room. "I know, honey. I know." Then she drifted off to sleep once again.

IT WAS NINE O'CLOCK in the morning when Jon arrived at the hospital after his first complete night of sleep since the kidnapping. He stuck his head inside Tarin's door. "Is it okay if I come in?"

The nurse greeted him with a smile. "Of course. I'm just checking a few things before the doctor arrives. He's talking about releasing her today."

Jon pulled a chair next to Tarin's bed and took her hand. "Are you ready to go home?"

She nodded. "Jake said I could stay at his house for a while. Finn's there to keep me company. I can't go back to the lake. Not yet."

Jon smiled. "I'm pretty sure Jake simply wants you there to cook for him while you both recuperate."

"Why do I get the feeling you're talking about me?" Jake asked as he wheeled in the door.

"Because we are," Jon shook hands with her brother. "How's the leg?"

"Much better. I'm trading this chair for crutches and going home today. How about you two?"

"They might spring her today, too. Tarin told me you've invited her to stay with you until she's ready to go back to her house. I'm hoping she'll come back to California with Finn when she's feeling up to it."

Their conversation was interrupted when a doctor hurried in and took Tarin's chart from the wall.

"Ms. MacGyver, how are you feeling this morning?" He walked to her side and began to unwind the gauze bandage protecting the fingers of her right hand. "Is there any pain?"

She shook her head. "No, not really."

The doctor sat on the edge of her bed. "We won't know for a while if we'll need to amputate any fingers or toes. But we would like to see you every three days to watch for any changes. Possible tissue damage and the onset of gangrene are our biggest concerns." He patted her blanket-covered leg. "Good news, though." He glanced across the room at Jon and Jake. "We're releasing you this afternoon."

The doctor stood and put her chart back in its holder. "I'll start the discharge papers right away."

Jon leaned over to kiss Tarin. "I can't wait to get you home and healthy again."

"Everyone's smiling. That must mean there's good news." Nick and Roxie stood in the doorway.

Jon wasted no time responding. "What the hell are you doing here?"

"Jon—" Tarin protested.

"Don't defend him. He knew you'd put yourself in danger with Tommy and didn't tell me about it." He glared at his friend. "What if his plan had worked and the hired gun had killed you? How would you feel then, Nick?"

"Stop it, Jon." Tarin silenced everyone in the room. "Nick wanted to tell you right away, but I begged him not to. I convinced him I had everything under control. So take your anger out on me, not him." She lowered her voice. "He's been your best friend since you were kids. Don't let something I did come between you."

"I'm truly sorry, Jon. Please forgive me," Nick pleaded.

"I need air. Excuse me." Jon pushed his way past them and down the hall.

Tarin reached toward Nick and took him by the hand. "Give him time. He'll come around. You've always been a team."

Jake attempted to diffuse the tension in the air. "I don't think we've met. I'm Tarin's brother, Jake. Please excuse the wheelchair."

"My name's Nick Reynolds, and this is my girlfriend, Roxie."

Tarin sat up and tried to put her feet on the floor. "I'm glad you're both here. Thank you. If I'm going home today, I'd better take a shower and get dressed." She glanced toward Nick. "I'm still not too good on my feet. Could I get a hand?"

Both Roxie and Nick were at her side in an instant.

"Is it painful?" Roxie asked, providing support with her hand under Tarin's elbow.

Tarin nodded, managing a quick smile. "But it gets better every day." She pointed to a chair across the room. "Having said that, I think I'd like to sit down for a minute."

Nick looked at Tarin first and then at Jake, "If you guys are okay, I need to find Jon."

Jake gestured toward the door. "Go for it. Life's too short not to work things out." He wheeled his chair to where Tarin was sitting. "Well ladies, what do you say we get this one ready to go home?"

CHAPTER 52

The Proposal

I T WAS A PERFECT DAY FOR SAILING IN MID-MARCH with light winds, smooth seas, and bright blue skies overhead. The sound of the hull slicing through the waves was accompanied by sails rustling in the soft ocean breeze. The metal hardware resonating against the mast as the boat rose and then dipped added yet another layer to the soothing sounds onboard.

Jon navigated to a safe spot, eased an anchor to the sandy bottom, and secured the sloop near a small cove they'd discovered along the coast. He turned toward Tarin, who was admiring his new-found sailing skills from the stern of the boat, with Finn resting at her feet.

"Are you the same man who didn't feel comfortable behind the wheel of my grandfather's boat?" she teased.

"When you were in Europe, Nick drafted me to be his first mate a few times. Guess I'm a quick learner. Besides, I was motivated. You love the water and I love you. Now come here."

She met Jon at the railing. "Thank you for making amends with Nick. I could never forgive myself if something I'd done had destroyed your friendship."

"No worries. We worked it out." He felt her shiver. "Are you cold? I can get you a jacket or a blanket."

"No, I'm fine." But sadness lingered in her voice. "I know I haven't been easy to live with since I was released from the hospital. The nightmares won't stop, and I can still feel his hands touching me. I'm so sorry—there have been times I've pushed you away."

Tarin bit her lip and Jon massaged the four remaining fingers of her right hand. "The worst part is every time I look at my hand, I'm reminded of him."

Jon spoke from his heart. "Don't let the actions of one deranged man haunt you. I'm here to help you through this, no matter how long it takes."

She looked into his eyes, "How could I have been so lucky to find you?"

"I think we found each other."

Several minutes passed before either of them felt the need to speak.

Jon hesitated before breaking the silence. "Do you miss Colorado?"

"I miss the way it was before Scott, Tommy, and Dan. We can visit—and we will—but I'm not sure I'll ever be able to live there again." She tried to change the subject. "Alex called. They've torn down the hunting cabin, although if he has anything to say about it, they'll rebuild before the next hunting season."

She paused. "I also talked with Maria today. The family that bought my house moved in last weekend. It's a young couple with a four-year-old daughter They couldn't be a better fit."

"Any word about how Alex is doing?"

"He's counseling veterans with PTSD at the VA hospital in Cheyenne. Rachel says he's never been happier and they're expecting another baby. As for Jake—the builders have started framing his new house by the barn." She smiled, "But the real gossip around town is that Jake and Maria are dating. I guess they connected while selling my house. Mike says the relationship has gotten serious."

"It's about time someone snatched your brother."

"Then there's Mike—would you believe he's running for county sheriff? Rick Harrington, the current sheriff, is term-limited, and he convinced Mike to give it a shot."

There was another break in the conversation.

"Please be honest. You miss your friends, don't you?"

"Sometimes. I'd be lying if I told you that I didn't. But my future is here with you, and I can't imagine anywhere else I'd rather be."

"I was terrified when I thought I'd lost you."

"I'm still here, whether you like it or not."

He held her hands. "I'm serious. I don't ever want to feel that way again."

"I don't plan on going anywhere."

He pressed his index finger to her lips. "Please let me finish."

"Okay, I'm sorry."

"Like I said, I never want to lose you." He was struggling to find the right words. "I didn't think this would be so hard."

"What are you trying to say, Jon?"

"After everything that's happened, I didn't want to put any extra pressure on you. But I can't wait any longer. I'm asking you to marry me."

He was surprised when she stepped away from the railing. When she turned back to face him, he found she was crying.

"I thought you'd never ask. The answer is yes, Jon."

Holding her close, he paused. "Please don't take this the wrong way, but I do have to thank Scott Simmons for one thing. If it hadn't been for his bungled burglary, that night would have been nothing more than an uneventful encounter between a man sitting on a bench and a woman checking her boats. I never would have found you."

"I think you're wrong. In my heart, I believe we would have been led to each other one way or another. That bench has a way of making magic happen."

They settled onto the cushioned seat at the stern, content to sit with the boat swaying in concert with the waves. Enthralled by the gulls overhead and the flying fish nearby, Finn stood guard scurrying back and forth on the bow.

Jon glanced toward the stairs leading to the galley and berth below. He grinned. "Maybe we could seal this engagement below deck?"

His suggestion was rewarded with a poke to the ribs. "Captain Parker, it's getting late, and Nick might be worried about his boat. I'll make it worth your while if you can wait until we get home."

"I guess patience is a virtue." He smacked his forehead with the heel of his hand. "I seem to have forgotten something." Seeing the amusement on Tarin's face, Jon retaliated. "Cut me some slack. I've never done this before."

"What—never gotten engaged?"

Lacking sufficient defense, he admitted defeat. "Alright, I stand guilty as charged. But the airport fiasco wasn't my idea. I've never gotten engaged for real."

Reaching into his jacket pocket, he retrieved a small, polished wood box and offered it in his outstretched palm.

Watching her lift the lid, he explained, "This ring belonged to my father's mother. She passed away when I was a teenager but was very special to me. I could return the ring Tommy bought for Anna and buy you one covered in diamonds, but this seemed more like you, and—"

"Shhh . . ." Tarin placed her hand on his cheek. "Your grandmother's ring is beautiful. But more importantly, it's part of who you are and that makes it even more perfect."

Jon slipped the antique ring with its delicate white gold filigree and solitaire diamond onto her finger. Meanwhile, Finn was busy trying to weasel his way between them to share in the moment. Tarin wrapped her arms around Jon's neck and pulled him close. "Now, can we go home?"

"WHOEVER YOU'VE BEEN WAITING for must be late."

Nick turned to see the comment had come from a man sitting at a picnic table on the grass ten yards or so from where he stood on the wood walkway. He chose to ignore him, but the man was persistent.

"You've been pacing and making phone calls with no luck since I've been sitting here and that's more than an hour."

For some irrational reason, and because he desperately wanted to share his excitement with someone, Nick decided to reply. "It's nothing that can't wait. I'm just anxious because I've got great news to share with the friends who are out on my boat. They should be back any minute."

"Ah, so you're a sailor. What kind of boat?"

"It's a sloop." Nick walked toward the man, surveying him as he approached. He guessed the stranger was younger than his weathered face, scruffy beard, and tattered clothing would lead people to believe. An unkempt fringe of matted and tangled black hair hung below the wool fisherman's cap on his head. Nick noticed a worn surplus store duffle bag propped against the bench next to him.

"Just passing through?" Nick asked.

He shook his head. "No. I'm hoping to find work and stick around for a while. Got some unfinished business to take care of."

When he leaned over to reach into his bag, Nick noticed the man's right arm hung limply at his side.

"You're waiting for somebody, and let's face it—I've got no place to go. Care to join me for a beer? I just bought a six-pack. It's still cold."

Putting two cans on the table, the man pushed a tangled section of wavy hair from his eyes and looked at Nick. "The name's Sam Scofield. And you are?"

Somewhat intrigued, the songwriter tried to mask his curiosity. "My name's Nick."

He extended his hand and Scofield responded by offering his left. "Sorry. The right one doesn't work very well anymore. Nerve damage. Funny," he said with a scathing laugh. "Two stints in a war zone and I lost the use of my arm stateside. Go figure."

Nick sat opposite him and popped the top of his beer. "You were in the military?"

"Two tours in Afghanistan. I was and still am proud to be a Marine. You?"

"Military service?" Nick shook his head. "Sorry, but no."

"No need to apologize. We all do what we're called to do."

The stranger leaned back a bit, finished chugging his beer, and reached down for another. "You ready?" he asked.

Nick put up a hand, "No, I'm fine."

There was a moment of silence. "You said you're trying to find work. What kind of job are you looking for?"

Scofield leaned forward and smiled, "Why? You got one?" He sat back again. "Of course not. You're just making polite conversation. But I've been thinking about working in the shipyards. In the Marines I was an MP. I figure I can get a security job even with a bum arm. I can still make property rounds and shoot a gun. Had some sniper training along the way, too."

He pulled a pack of Marlboro Reds from his shirt pocket and tapped it on the table several times. "Want a smoke?"

Nick shook his head, "No, thanks."

"Mind if I do?" Scofield put the cigarette between his lips and used his good hand to open the lid of a bright silver lighter. He inhaled deeply after striking the flint, then flipped the lid back and tossed it on the table.

"That's nice. Not that I smoke, but may I look at it?" Nick asked, reaching for the lighter.

"Fine with me," was the reply.

Nick ran his fingers over the raised emblem on the face of the silver case. "That's the Marine Corps insignia, right? Is it sterling?"

He nodded. "They don't make many butane lighters like that anymore. A few months ago, I lost the one that carried me through both tours overseas. It was like losing a piece of me. Got this one to replace it. It's not as nice, but it'll have to do."

Nick glanced toward the docks, "Hey, sorry, but I better get going. That's my boat coming in." He took a final swig of beer and tossed the can into a recycle bin. "Thanks for the brew and good luck to you."

The bearded man nodded and watched him trot toward the dock and the boat approaching it. Nick was waiting when Jon cut the engine and the boat drifted into its berth.

"Hey—what's up?" Jon asked, tossing a line to his long-time friend.

"Where have you been? I guess you didn't have cell service where you were, but that's no excuse. I've been calling every fifteen minutes," Nick announced, a mischievous grin plastered on his face.

He had piqued Jon's curiosity. "I had my phone turned off. What could be so important? Tommy broke out of jail and he's gunning for us?"

"That's not funny," Tarin frowned, turning her attention to Nick. "So—what is it?"

"You really want to know?"

"Don't mess with us, Nick." Jon shot back, tossing the spring line toward Tarin.

"Okay. If you really, really want to know. The phone's been ringing off the hook. Motive's album just went double platinum. But that's not the best news."

"You haven't answered my question. What's going on?" Jon demanded, jumping off the boat and onto the dock.

"It's only been out a day and 'Ghosts of the Heart' debuted at number one on both the iTunes and Billboard charts. All the late night and daytime talk shows are battling to showcase the music industry's hottest new solo artist. And you were worried about going out on your own. You did it, Jon."

"We did it, the three of us, and this is just the beginning. By the way," he added. "On a more important subject—I don't suppose you'd be my best man?"

Nick hugged Tarin. "It's about time, Parker. Count me in. I have no idea why a woman of this caliber would pick a loser like you, but you've always been the luckiest guy I've ever known. What am I thinking? I bet you two want to be alone."

"True, but I do have an idea for you." Jon rested an arm on his friend's shoulder. "Why don't you give Roxie a call? Better yet, stop by her condo and surprise her."

Nick smiled. "You know what? That's a great idea. Why didn't I think of it? But forget the condo—she moved in with me last weekend and probably has dinner ready and waiting. Now let's get out of here."

The three were walking toward the parking lot when the unkempt man at the table called out, "Nick—looks like you gave your friends the good news. Treasure the moment. You never know when or even if it'll ever come around again."

Jon glanced toward the origin of the comment and discreetly leaned toward Nick. "Who's your new friend?"

"Some homeless guy," Nick responded. "And a war vet. Wish we could do something to help men like him. They don't deserve to be on the streets begging for work."

Tarin tightened her grip on the leash when Finn strained toward the man at the table with a guttural growl rumbling deep in his throat. She needed to use both hands to restrain him and even then, Finn snarled until they were more than thirty yards away. Unaware of the confrontation, Jon and Nick continued to walk while they talked.

"How did he know your name?"

"I was waiting for you, and he offered me a beer." Nick stopped to explain, "Hey—when have you ever known me to pass up a free beer? You were late and I was thirsty. Anyway, we talked for a while. That's all."

Still trying to reassure Finn, Tarin glanced back toward the solitary man. Acknowledging her look, he touched the brim of his hat, the corners of his mouth turning upward in a faint smile. But it was no ordinary smile. It was the smile of someone who relished the fact he was hiding more than he was telling.

Their eyes met for only a few seconds before she turned away, but in that instant, a frigid chill swept through Tarin's body. She pulled Finn's leash, commanded him to follow, and hurried to catch up with Jon and Nick on the walkway.

"Congratulations you two. I've got a great idea—why don't you sleep in tomorrow? Talk with you both later," Nick called as he sprinted toward his car.

Finally alone, Jon lifted Tarin's chin with his fingertips and gazed into her bright hazel eyes. "I hope you know how much I love you."

"Not as much as I love you."

But Tarin looked away when she spoke, trying to fight the unsettled feeling growing inside.

"What's wrong?" he asked. "Already having second thoughts?"

Her voice was filled with apprehension. "I can't explain it, but I have a terrible feeling something might tear us apart again." Her eyes pleaded with his. "I know you'll think I'm being silly, but can we get married right away? I don't want to miss spending a single day with you."

Jon ran his fingers through her hair, pulling her even closer, "Don't you know by now I won't let anyone, or anything come between us?" He pushed her to arm's length, "You know what? I can't believe I'm talking to a woman who wants to forego an extravagant wedding in some exotic place for a private ceremony with a Justice of the Peace."

"Somehow, I don't see us as the million-dollar wedding kind of couple. I want our ceremony to be small, on the veranda at your house with Nick and Roxie as witnesses."

"Why not Colorado? That's your home and where your friends are."

She shook her head, "I can't go back there yet. My home is here with you."

"Okay, then. Today is Tuesday. This Saturday is too soon. What about a week from Saturday? That gives us a little more time to pull it together. We can charter a plane to fly your friends to San Diego. I'm thinking of Jake, Mike, his wife and kids, Alex, Rachel and Sarah, and anyone else you'd like to invite. Oh, and of course Maury and his wife. I still owe him a private jet adventure."

Her eyes brightened. "Definitely Maria. Finn could be the ring bearer and Sarah the flower girl. Paul, his family, and your band should be there, too. Could your family come? Oh, my gosh, our small wedding just became big. Can we fit everyone on the veranda?"

"I'm sure we can. So, it looks like we've set the date."

She linked her hands behind his neck and their lips met. Tarin stepped back and brushed his cheek. Happier than she could ever remember being, she chose to ignore the dark feeling the stranger at the marina had planted deep in her subconscious.

He kissed Tarin's hand and fingered the diamond ring on her finger. "Now, soon-to-be Mrs. Parker, let's go home."

THE MARINA PARKING LOT was nearly deserted. One by one, flickering lights began to illuminate the harbor as the sun disappeared and was replaced by the moon. Picking up his bag, Sam Scofield pushed himself away from the picnic table. He took one last draw on his cigarette before flicking it to the ground and extinguishing the embers with the heel of his boot.

"This time," he promised under his breath, "she won't get away."

CHAPTER 53

The Search for Answers

MIKE WILSON WAS WORKING IN THE GARAGE AT HIS house in Chasm Falls when he felt the cell phone in his pocket vibrate.

"Mike? This is Tarin."

"Hey, you. I bet you're busy getting ready for the big day, aren't you?" He glanced at a calendar on the wall. "Let's see—looks like we're only a week away."

She didn't answer and Mike sensed something wasn't quite right. "You don't sound like an excited bride-to-be. What's up?"

"He's not dead, Mike."

"Who's not dead, Tarin?"

"You're going to think I'm crazy, but Scott Simmons isn't dead. He's here in San Diego

This wasn't the first time the officer had dealt with a victim's lingering fear and denial in the aftermath of a traumatic experience. "Tarin, you've been through a terrible ordeal, and it's normal to feel what you're feeling, but Scott died on that mountain in January. There's no way he can hurt anyone else ever again."

Her reply was adamant. "But what if he didn't die? The sheriff hasn't been able to find his body, has he?"

"True. But that's not uncommon when someone is lost during a blizzard. More than two feet of snow fell after Simmons was shot and the wind caused unbelievable drifting. We couldn't take the body out that night and by the time a crew could get up there, all the markings we'd left were obliterated. Normally we would have stationed an officer with the body overnight, but we couldn't risk the lives of any of our men in weather conditions like that."

"I've seen him, Mike."

He sat down and leaned back on a stool.

"Okay. Let's take it one step at a time. What makes you think you've seen him?"

"Jon and I went sailing on Nick's boat. It was the day Jon asked me to marry him." She paused to gather her thoughts. "After we brought the boat back and were leaving the marina, a man sitting at a table greeted Nick. When Jon asked Nick about it, he said the man had started a conversation with him while he was waiting for us."

"I don't see anything unusual about that."

"Nick said the man was scruffy looking and seemed to be homeless. During the conversation, the guy told Nick he'd been a Marine and served two tours in the Middle East."

"Tarin, thousands of men and women served in Iraq and Afghanistan and now, unfortunately, some of them find themselves homeless. What made this man different?"

"Finn."

"Finn? What in heaven's name does your dog have to do with it?"

"When we were on the way to the parking lot, Finn started growling and barking at the man. It was all I could do to keep control of him on his leash." She hesitated, "You know Finn. He's the gentlest dog in the world—nothing phases him. But he sensed there was something he didn't like about that man. If you remember, Finn bit Scott's leg during the boathouse burglary."

"That's true, but Scott was at your house many times after that and Finn didn't react to him."

"That's true, but when I started thinking about it, Finn was always outside in his kennel or at Jake's house whenever Scott was there."

Tarin paused. "That's not all, Mike. When the man looked at me, it sent chills through my entire body. I've seen those eyes before—it was Scott Simmons."

"Tarin—one of our deputies checked Scott's body for a pulse after he'd been shot. There was none. He was dead."

"But there was so much chaos at that point, could the officer have made a mistake? Jon told me when he found me in the cave, I didn't seem to have a pulse, either, but I'm alive. Scott had extensive survival training. He could have survived the storm against the odds. Didn't you tell me you covered his body with blankets and a tarp? That protection could have helped him make it through the night. Maybe he found my cave."

"Could you be reading too much into this? After what you've been through, I can understand it if you are."

"When the man was talking to Nick about being in the Marines, he said he'd been an MP, worked in security, and had been trained as a sniper.

"That still doesn't mean the guy Nick met was Scott Simmons. I don't suppose this homeless man happened to tell Nick his name."

"He did, but all Nick could remember was Sam something. He thinks the last name started with an 'S.' Nick also said he has a bum right arm and can hardly lift it. There's something else. He mentioned the man had a sterling silver butane lighter with a Marine Corps insignia on it. This Sam person said he'd gotten it to replace the one he carried while he was stationed overseas. He told Nick he'd lost the first one a few months ago."

"Have you shared any of this with Jon?"

"No. I didn't want to worry him."

"You should tell him—he needs to know. But okay, Tarin. I'll admit there are things about this guy that fit Scott's profile. But he died in that blizzard."

"I need to ask again—have they found his body? Because of the warm spring in Chasm Falls, much of the snow must have melted."

Mike shook his head. "No, they haven't, but his remains were probably mauled by scavengers. As gruesome as it may sound, hikers will probably find bones scattered all over that part of the mountain."

Tarin was silent.

"Maggie, the kids, and I are coming to the wedding." Against his better judgment, he continued, "What if I come to California a few days early to see if I can discover anything about this mystery man you saw?"

"You would do that?"

"Yes—if it will ease your mind. I'll let you know when I've got a flight. But you're going to need to explain why I'm coming before my family makes the trip. Tarin, Jon needs to know what's going on. You can't hide this from him. If you'd like, we can talk to him together when I get there."

"Thanks, Mike. I'm sure you think I'm crazy, but I know what I saw and what Finn sensed."

"Time will tell. See you soon."

CHAPTER 54

A Haunting Possibility

SITTING AT HIS DESK IN THE POLICE STATION, MIKE dialed the Granite County Sheriff. "Hi, Rick. Mike Wilson here. How's it going?"

"Good. What's new in Chasm Falls?"

"Nothing much. Hey—this is coming out of left field, but I have a question for you. Remember the case this winter when Scott Simmons kidnapped Tarin MacGyver and shot that private detective?"

"Of course, I do. That's an experience I may never forget. Why?"

"I'm not quite sure how to approach this, but Tarin called me earlier today. She's convinced Simmons is alive."

There was momentary silence at the other end of the line.

"Mike, there's no way he could have survived the blizzard after being shot."

"I know—at best it's a one-in-a-million longshot. But there are loose ends I need to investigate."

"Come on, Mike. That was an open and shut case. What grounds could you possibly have to reopen it?"

"Tarin swears she's seen Simmons in California."

"We both know he died on that mountain in January."

"I know, but she brings up a valid point. We still haven't found any trace of his body. Is there the slightest chance he could have survived the night?"

"My deputy checked, and Simmons had no pulse after he was shot."

"Is it possible his pulse may have been undetectable? Jon couldn't find Tarin's when he got to her in the cave."

"But Mike, what about the gunshot wound?"

"That I can't answer. We thought it was a chest wound, but maybe the bullet entered closer to his shoulder than we thought and missed vital organs. Since we believed Simmons was dead, we weren't checking for hospitals treating gunshot victims that night or the next day. While I have no idea how he could have made it to a nearby clinic, assumed an alias, and devised a plausible story about how he was shot, but we all know how resourceful Simmons can be. His mind may be twisted, but he's smart and knows how the system works. Then after being treated, he could have checked himself out of the hospital and disappeared."

"That's an imaginative scenario."

Mike continued. "Because of the damage Simmons has done to so many people, I want to believe he's dead. But I can't discount the possibility he's still out there somewhere. He could be devising another plan to hurt people I care about."

"What makes your friend think she saw him?"

"She was sailing with Jon Parker on a friend's boat. When they got back to the marina, Nick—the boat's owner—had been talking with a drifter. During the conversation, the guy told him he'd done two tours of duty in the Middle East with the Marines. Remember the lighter we found in Tarin's bedroom? This guy had one just like it. He said he'd lost his first one a while back and had to replace it. And then there's Finn."

"Who the heck is Finn?"

"Tarin's dog."

"You're losing me, Mike."

"Finn is Tarin's dog."

"Her dog?"

"Bear with me, Rick. The night Tarin's boathouse was broken into, Finn bit the burglar's leg while he was trying to get away. This week Finn was with Tarin and Jon at the marina. When they walked past the vagrant, the dog started growling. Tarin said she had to struggle to keep Finn from attacking the man. She said it was like he recognized him."

"Okay, Mike. I can tell there's nothing I can say to keep you from pursuing this. So, what can I do to help with this wild goose chase?"

"Tarin and Jon are getting married at his house in La Jolla next week. Maggie and I will be at the wedding. I told Tarin I'll come a few days early to see if I can track down the mystery man she believes is Simmons. In the meantime, it would be great if your staff could check nearby hospitals for anyone treated in the twenty-four hours after Simmons was shot."

"You got it. I'll keep you informed if we find anything. I don't suppose we happen to have a name for this homeless person?"

"Tarin said all Nick could remember was Sam something. But he did say the last name started with an 'S'. That would make his initials the same as Scott Simmons. There is one other thing that could be important. Nick said the guy's right arm is useless—it just hangs at his side. I'm not a doctor, but it's possible the damage could have been caused by a bullet. Scott's wound was on that side of his chest."

Mike contemplated his words. "Rick, I'm going on record saying I think Simmons is dead and we'll find his body on the mountain this spring. But Tarin's frightened. She said because the man at the marina was scruffy with long dirty hair and a full beard—she couldn't really see his face. But she said his eyes pierced through her and when he smiled it was more like an evil smirk. I can't let fear ruin what should be the happiest time of her life. Tomorrow I'm going back to the cabin and up the mountain to see if we missed anything last January."

"Now you've got me curious. What if I meet you there? Two sets of eyes are always better than one. Can you round up a couple of snowmobiles? We're going to need them?"

"That shouldn't be a problem, Rick. Why don't I meet you at Shuck's for lunch at noon and we can go from there?"

"Works for me. See you then, Mike."

"SORRY, I'M LATE. IT must be spring break because traffic was worse than usual." The sheriff slid into the booth across from Mike. "Are there any new developments in the case?"

"A few. After we talked yesterday, the military sent me Scott's service records."

"Did they contain anything new?"

"Not much, but the report did verify most of what we already knew. I'll fill you in, but what if we order and talk after we eat?"

Pushing the dishes aside forty-five minutes later, Mike began to share what he'd learned about Simmons' military history. "He was deployed to the Middle East twice, but before going overseas the first time he was accepted into the Marine Raiders Special Ops program. He trained for several months before washing out. Apparently, those in charge didn't feel he met the psychological criteria."

"Imagine that."

Mike continued, "He was sent back to his original base where he became an MP. But while he was trying to make the grade as a Raider he received specialized training in emergency medical procedures, sharpshooting, and survival skills."

"All training that could have helped him survive the blizzard."

"It's still a long shot," Mike said, "but I need to know one way or the other. It would be so much easier if his body would turn up."

"Ready to go?" Rick asked, tossing a tip on the table.

"Guess so. But I hope we find something on that mountain. I had a plow clear a path to the cabin, but we're going to need snowmobiles to get to the cave from there. Let's take my truck. I've got two snowmobiles on the trailer."

IT TOOK THE OFFICERS almost thirty minutes to navigate their way to the hunting cabin. The wind had shredded the crime tape on the front door, but a padlock still secured the handle. Cutting the lock, Mike pushed open the door.

"Well, the cabin looks like it did when we left it that night." Mike turned to Rick. "Did you bring any evidence bags? I have some but they're in my pack on the snowmobile."

"I brought a few inside." Walking toward the makeshift countertop, the sheriff put on a pair of latex gloves. "We'll find DNA, but I'm not seeing any blood evidence. If Simmons survived the blizzard, he didn't come back here. He probably couldn't get in because of the padlock."

Rick stepped toward one of the small windows. "His Jeep is still sitting where he left it. Has anyone bothered to check its interior since that night? He could have used the SUV for shelter once the deputies packed up and left."

Mike nodded. "Let's collect a few samples and start up the mountain. We can look at the Jeep on the way out."

Reaching the area where they believed Simmons had been shot, the two prepared to split up and continue their searches.

"The Park Service was right. This morning they told me that even though we're having a warm spring, there would still be several feet of snow in most places. There's no way I'll be able to locate a body without bringing in sophisticated scanning equipment. But I'm still going to look around and see if I can find anything."

"While you're doing that, I'll check the cave. I'm not sure how much attention the search team gave it after you got Tarin out and onto the snowcat." Rick connected his radio headset. "I'll call if there's anything out of the ordinary there."

"Gotcha," Mike replied, beginning to survey the wooded area.

Minutes later, he heard a transmission from the sheriff. "Mike, you need to come to the cave. I hate to tell you this, but your friend Tarin could be right. The blankets the deputies used to cover the body and the tarp are here. They've got a significant amount of blood on them. One of the blankets has been torn and several long strips are gone. Simmons may have used the wool for bandages."

"That's not what I wanted to hear. I'll be right there."

"I found something else, Mike. There's a spent bullet on the dirt floor. It looks like Simmons removed it himself before leaving the cave."

Back in the cabin, the two officers folded and wrapped the bloodied blankets in the tarp and prepared to load them onto Mike's snowmobile. The bullet was placed into an evidence bag and put in Rick's backpack for safekeeping.

Outside, Rick peered inside the Jeep. "I can't open the door because of the snowdrift, but there's a sleeping bag on the back seat and it looks like there might be blood on it."

"There's no way a tow truck will be able to pull this vehicle out to thoroughly investigate until we remove more of the snow, but this could be another place where Simmons found shelter from the storm."

"What's next?" Rick asked, securing the straps holding the snowmobiles to the trailer.

Mike shook his head. "I wish I knew. We need to have the blood tested to verify if it belongs to Simmons and double-check the DNA. There are more than enough samples to examine. We can do our own testing through the county, but the military can help us determine for certain if anything belongs to him. This is turning into a nightmare."

The sheriff shook his head and smiled. "Gotta thank you, Mike."

"Thank me for what?" Mike asked as they began the drive down the snow-covered lane back to town.

"Since everything took place in the county, you've just dumped the case back into my jurisdiction." He paused. "Got any ideas about how we're going to handle this in the media?"

"Can we put a gag order on it?"

"That's something I'd like to do for the time being since it's still speculation at this point, but I'll need to talk with the district attorney and probably a judge or two. What are you going to tell Tarin?"

"God, Rick—I don't have any idea. Jon and Tarin both need to know Simmons might still be out there. But this isn't the kind of thing you explain to someone in a phone call. I'll book a flight and make the trip to California tomorrow. I'd planned on going early anyway."

"While you're doing that, I'll do my best to expedite testing the samples. Because of the circumstances, I think we can be almost certain the results will lead us back to Simmons. But until we know for sure, I don't want to jump the gun."

Rick felt his cell phone vibrate and looked at the call coming in. "Hold that thought. It's one of my deputies." He held the phone to his ear. "Hey, what did you find out?"

After a short conversation, Rick ended the call and looked at Mike. "A small emergency clinic in Winter Park treated a gunshot victim after midnight on the night in question. A man was brought in by a snowplow driver who found him stumbling alongside the highway. The hospital staff called local authorities, but since the guy appeared to be homeless with no ID, there wasn't much they could do. The man said he had been robbed and shot. The investigating officers filed a report, but the alleged assailant couldn't be identified so it was pretty much a dead end."

Rick paused, "For the record, the clinic records note the bullet had been removed before he was admitted. Your scenario turned out to be spot on. Apparently after being treated, the guy checked himself out the next day and disappeared. Speaking of the bullet we found in the cave, we can have ballistics check it against the gun Jon used to shoot Simmons on the mountain."

"Now what?" Rick asked.

"I'll fly to San Diego to see what I can find.' "Mike glanced at the sheriff. "Any chance you could make a few calls to the police department there to see if they could help us with the investigation?"

"Unfortunately, our hands are tied until we get the tests back. Court records still show Scott Simmons is dead."

"I know, but I'm going with or without those results."

"Be careful. If he is still alive, we know what he's capable of doing. After being shot and left for dead, he'll be even more determined to dish out retribution."

"Before I go, I need to call Jon to let him know I'm coming. But I'll wait to fill him in completely until I get to La Jolla, and we need to be sure they have protection. There's no doubt in my mind if Simmons is alive, he'll go after them."

"HI, MIKE." STANDING BEHIND the bar at the Sip 'n Strike, Jake looked at his watch. You're in uniform and here early today. What's up?"

"Do you have Jon Parker's cell number?"

"Yeah, why?"

"I need to call him."

"Don't tell me he did something stupid again and the wedding's off."

"No, nothing like that. We just need to talk."

"We've been friends long enough for me to know when something's bothering you. Clue me in."

Mike was reluctant to speak. "Promise what I'm about to tell you will remain just between us?"

"Sure. So, talk. If it concerns my sister, I want to know."

"Tarin called yesterday. She's convinced she saw Scott Simmons in San Diego."

"But he's dead."

"You know that, and I know that. Well, at least I thought I did."

"What's that supposed to mean?"

"I can't go into details, but after her call, the county sheriff and I decided to take another look at the cabin where Simmons held her captive, the place where he was shot, and the cave where Tarin was rescued."

Jake sat down on a stool behind the bar.

"The blankets and tarp the deputies used to cover the body after he was shot were in the cave. They were bloodstained."

"Are you trying to tell me Simmons didn't die that night?"

"Wish I had an answer, but we're still waiting for tests on the blood and DNA to tell us if they're his." Mike looked forlorn. "He might still be out there, Jake, and Jon needs to know they could be in danger. Especially with their wedding a week away. It's the perfect time for Simmons to seek his revenge."

Jake slammed a glass onto the counter. "Will this ever end, Mike?"

"Not before Simmons is either buried or put behind bars for the rest of his life."

CHAPTER 55

The Manhunt Begins

JON MET MIKE AT THE AIRPORT AND DROVE HIM TO the hotel in La Jolla where the wedding guests would be staying. "You haven't said anything to Tarin, have you?"

"No. When we talked last night you asked me not to." Jon opened the trunk to retrieve Mike's luggage. "I'm still trying to digest what you told me."

"You and me both."

"Mike—I saw the bullet hit Simmons that night. He fell face-first into the snow and didn't move again. He can't still be alive."

"We want to believe he's dead, but for Tarin's sake, we need to be sure. Let's go inside and talk. I have a few questions and there are other things you need to know." Mike put his key card against the lock and opened the door to his room.

"What kind of questions?" Jon asked. He sat down at the room's small round table with Mike across from him.

"First of all, at the marina you saw the man your friend, Nick, had been talking with, right?"

"Briefly—I glanced at him when we walked by. He was sitting at a picnic table."

Mike pulled a small notepad and pen from his pocket.

Jon was puzzled. "You're going to take notes? You're buying into Tarin's paranoia, aren't you? Tommy is in jail and Scott's dead. We're trying to move on with our lives."

Mike nodded. "Don't call it paranoia. You're right—Tommy's in jail, but until we find that monster's body, she has every right to be concerned. We need to prove without a doubt that Simmons is dead. Jon, you didn't hear her voice on the phone when she called. She was trying not to show it, but I could tell she was terrified."

"I'm sorry, but she was finally coming to terms with Simmons and what he did. Now if this is true, everything will be brought to the surface again."

"Think back, Jon. Did you notice anything odd about the man at the marina? Let's see," Mike flipped through a few pages of his pad, "he was calling himself Sam something."

"Honestly, no. I mean he looked like he hadn't changed his clothes or taken a bath in weeks, but otherwise, there was nothing noteworthy. Nick told us a bunch of other stuff later, but I didn't think I saw anything sinister at the time."

"Did the man look at all like Scott?"

Jon shrugged. "He had a full beard and long shaggy hair so I couldn't see his face. Didn't Simmons have brown hair? This guy's hair was black."

"It sounds like you think Tarin is making something out of nothing."

Jon fidgeted in his chair. "She's been dealing with so much since January. I can't blame her for the way she's feeling."

Mike put his cell phone on the table. "I don't know if this will make any difference, but a message from Rick Harrington—the Granite County sheriff—was waiting for me when I got off the plane this afternoon. He called in a few favors and expedited the blood and DNA tests." He paused. "They're matches for Simmons."

"God. What does that mean?"

"The results confirm that your shot didn't kill him. Apparently, he was able to find refuge in the cave under the blankets and tarp the deputies used to cover his body. Unfortunately, even with the test results, we can't prove he got off the mountain. But a small clinic in Winter Park treated a man claiming to be homeless for a gunshot wound. We're waiting for the samples they sent to a lab to be analyzed. If they come back belonging to Scott, we'll know he made it out alive."

Jon leaned forward in his chair. "That means Tarin really could have seen him at the marina and he might be stalking us."

Mike tried to reassure him. "Jon, we don't know anything for sure, so don't overreact and jump to conclusions. Even more importantly, don't cause Tarin to worry more than she already does. You need to be calm and supportive."

When Jon stood to leave, Mike asked, "Could you take me to the marina tomorrow morning? There are a few things there I'd like to check out."

"No problem. I'll pick you up at ten o'clock."

"IS THIS THE TABLE?" Mike asked.

Jon nodded. "The guy was sitting on that side, facing the walkway." He pointed toward the docks. "Nick's boat is over there."

"Tarin told me the man gave Nick a beer and drank a couple himself. Did he happen to mention what brand it was?"

Jon shook his head while Mike walked toward the trash and recycle bins. "No but let me call and ask."

While Jon placed the call, Mike put gloves on and continued to survey the area.

"Nick said the beer was Bud Light. Why?"

Unfastening and lifting the receptacle lids, Mike commented, "I'm sure the maintenance crew has emptied these containers since you were here, but it's worth taking a look." He shook his head and closed them. "Just like I thought. There aren't any beer cans in either of them. If we'd been able to find one, it could have been tested for DNA."

Mike got down on his hands and knees to scrutinize the ground below the table.

Jon followed suit. "Now what are we looking for?"

Sitting up on his haunches, Mike explained, "Maybe the groundkeepers aren't as thorough under tables as they are in the open areas. Nick told Tarin about the cigarette lighter the man had. I'm sure that means he must have smoked while he was sitting here." He resumed the search, sweeping his fingers through the blades of grass. "If we could find just one butt, the DNA could prove whether or not the person we're looking for is Simmons."

Jon pointed to something near one of the table legs. "What's that, Mike?"

"You've got a good eye." Mike restrained Jon who was reaching for what appeared to be several discarded butts. "Let me get them—I'm wearing gloves. We can't risk contaminating anything."

"Will these help us figure out who the guy really is?"

Mike smiled. "You better believe it." He put the cigarettes in an evidence bag and stood. "My briefcase is at the hotel with all the case documentation. Could you drive me back to pick it up? Then I'll take a cab to the San Diego Police Department."

Jon shook his head. "No cab necessary, I'll drive you. The sooner we get this garbage tested, the sooner we'll know what—if anything— we're up against."

"Then let's go."

"SHERIFF HARRINGTON, I HAVE a call for you from Mike Wilson."

"Put him through, Peni." Rick picked up the receiver, "Mike, do you have anything new? I was going to call you this morning."

"We may have hit the jackpot. Jon took me to the marina where the alleged sighting took place, and we found cigarette butts that could have been left by Simmons."

The sheriff rifled through a stack of papers on his desk while he was talking. "Are they being tested for DNA?"

"We just dropped them off at the San Diego PD. I had a chance to show a captain named Noah Metzler the case documents. Due to the circumstances, he agreed to send the evidence through channels as quickly as possible. He also promised to assign two of his detectives to assist me if the DNA does belong to Simmons."

"You must have sweet-talked him, Mike."

He smiled. "Not really. It didn't take him long to realize this has the potential to become a high-profile case." Mike paused. "You mentioned you were going to call me. Any word on the results from the hospital samples?"

"Well, you can tell your new PD friend the tests confirm Simmons was the gunshot patient they treated. It's very possible Tarin's gut reaction was correct—she may have seen him in San Diego."

"That worries me, Rick. Simmons finding Jon, Tarin, and their friend at the marina couldn't have been an accident. He must be tracking them." Mike looked up when he heard footsteps in the hall. "Hey, I've got to go. The captain is coming my way. I'll keep you posted, and you do the same."

Mike stood when Captain Metzler approached.

"Officer Wilson—I just got off the phone with the commander in La Jolla and briefed him on your situation. He would like to meet with you if it turns out the samples you brought in today belong to the suspect in question. If this man—what's his name?"

"Simmons."

"If Simmons is as dangerous as the file indicates, we need to do everything in our power to get him off the street."

"I talked with the Granite County Sheriff a few minutes ago. It's been verified that Simmons was treated for a gunshot wound at a clinic in Winter Park, Colorado. He's alive and likely to be here in San Diego. The cigarettes we brought in today could provide the evidence we need to prove if it's true."

CAPTAIN METZLER CALLED MIKE early the next morning. The DNA results had come in overnight. They verified Scott Simmons and "Sam" were one and the same.

Honoring his pledge, the captain assigned two plainclothes detectives to the case.

After the call, Mike set out to see if Simmons had used his new identity to apply for any jobs at the port's six shipyards. To achieve credibility in the search, he was accompanied by a young detective, Anthony Maynes. The first five facilities provided no leads, but at the last one, the general manager vaguely remembered a man fitting Sam's description. In a pile of papers on his desk, he found a partially completed job application.

"I could tell he was down on his luck and the poor guy only had one arm he could use. He couldn't even provide a local address." The manager shrugged. "We didn't have any work for him, but I referred him to a homeless shelter a few blocks from here. It's called the Sunrise Center. I told him if nothing else he could get a hot meal, shower, and a bed there."

"Do you think I could look at the application?" Mike asked.

"Sure. In fact, you can have it because he didn't complete or sign the dang thing. I was about to shred it anyway."

"Thanks."

Mike had turned to walk away when the manager stopped him.

"Is this guy in some sort of trouble?"

"You could say that. There are state and felony warrants facing him in Colorado, including first-degree murder. Feel blessed that you didn't hire him." Mike reached into his pocket and handed the man a business card. "Give me a call if he should come back."

"Sure thing, sir."

Walking to the detective's unmarked car, Mike speculated, "Thanks to the application, we now know he's going by the name Sam Scofield. Are you familiar with the Sunrise Center?"

"It's one of the shelters in the city's homeless housing network. I help coach basketball with some of the kids that stay there, so I know a few members of the staff."

"Can you take me there?"

"Not a problem. It's not far from here."

THE OFFICERS WERE MET at Sunrise Center's front door by a volunteer.

"Good morning. Could you tell me if Director Barnes is in?" Detective Maynes flashed his badge, causing the volunteer to take a step back.

"Is there a problem, officer?"

"Not necessarily, but we are here on official business."

"I believe he's in his office, sir."

"Thanks—I know where that is."

Detective Maynes tapped on the open office door.

"Come on in."

The man behind the desk stood immediately to greet the detective. "Anthony—good to see you. What brings you in to see us this morning?"

Detective Maynes gestured toward Mike who was still standing in the doorway. "This is Mike Wilson. He's an officer with the Chasm Falls Police Department in Colorado. I'll let him explain why we're here. Mike, this is Sean Barnes. He's the shelter director."

Mike extended his hand. "Nice to meet you, Mr. Barnes."

"Please have a seat."

"We're trying to locate a fugitive we believe might be staying at the Sunrise Center."

"Does this man have a name?"

"He's been using the name Sam Scofield." Mike handed Barnes two pictures of Scott Simmons. "I'm sorry, these are old photos and we've been told he's altered his appearance. One of his most predominant features is that he's lost the use of his right arm. Does he look at all familiar?"

The director nodded. "But that's not the Sam that walked in here two or three days ago. He was unshaven with dirty black hair and had obviously been on the streets for a while. We gave him new clothes, a haircut, and now instead of a full beard he has a goatee. We did notice he has problems with one arm." He put the pictures on his desk. "Why do you ask?"

"He's wanted on several warrants in Colorado. Can you tell us if he's still staying here?" Mike asked.

"Why, yes. In fact, I saw him in the kitchen about fifteen minutes ago. He was helping reset something on an oven."

"Could you show us where that is?"

"Certainly."

The trio was leaving the director's office when Scott Simmons left the kitchen to go back to his space in the dormitory. Looking across the empty commons area, he changed directions when he saw Mike and Detective Maynes and hurried toward the front door. Mike began to sprint toward him.

"Stop, Scott! Don't try to get away."

But Simmons was already out the door.

Once outside, Mike glanced in both directions, but Simmons was nowhere to be seen.

Mike was out of breath when he finally gave up his fruitless pursuit and returned to the shelter. "We lost him, Mr. Barnes. Could we look at his bed and belongings? We might find a clue or two there."

"Of course, but what is he accused of doing?"

"The list is long, but it's topped by first-degree murder."

The director's face became troubled. "Follow me. He was staying in a dorm down the hall."

Driving to the PD, Mike sorted through the duffle bag Simmons had left behind.

"Did you find anything?" Detective Maynes asked.

"Not yet." Mike shook his head. "Shit, this isn't good." He held up a handful of .45 mm shells. That means he's gotten his hands on a gun."

"What's next?"

"You know, let's not go back to the station quite yet. I want you to meet the two people he's targeting and help us devise a plan to protect them."

"So where are we headed?"

"Camino De La Costa in La Jolla."

"JON, TARIN—THIS IS DETECTIVE Maynes. He's with the San Diego Police Department." Mike paused. "I wish I didn't have to tell you this, but Tarin's gut instincts were correct. Scott Simmons is not only alive but he's here in the city."

Tarin looked down at the floor and Jon wrapped his arm around her shoulders.

"What does that mean, Mike?" she asked.

"It means we need to do everything in our power to protect you both and put him behind bars once and for all," Mike replied.

Jon was searching for answers. "How did he know we would be at the marina that day?"

Mike shook his head. "It would seem he's been stalking you, making note of your daily routines—where you go, who you see, all of that."

"How can we find him, Mike? And what's he been living on?" Jon asked.

"We almost got him today. He's been hanging around the docks looking for work. One of the shipyard managers remembered him. While he didn't have a job for Simmons, he felt sympathy for the man he thought was a homeless veteran. The manager told him about a shelter where he could get hot meals and a place to sleep." Mike paused, "We decided to check it out, and sure enough, he's been staying there for several days."

He continued, "As for what he's been living on, the day he kidnapped you, Tarin, he closed his bank accounts in Chasm Falls and took everything out in cash. But since he's looking for work, he must be running low on money."

Still staring at the floor, Tarin asked softly, "Did you see him?"

"Yes. But unfortunately, he also saw us and ran for it. That means we have another problem."

"What's that?" Jon asked.

"Now he knows we're onto him and he'll be much more careful about his movements. Jon, you're going to need around-the-clock security here at your house. The police here will do what they can, but it won't be enough. With the wedding in three days, you're going to have delivery trucks, caterers, florists, and you name it coming and going. All the vendors and their employees need to be vetted. You'll also need security on the beach side of your house."

"I'll make sure we have whatever it takes, Mike." Jon turned to the detective. "Can you help steer me toward a reputable company as soon as possible?"

He nodded. "I've got a few good ones in mind."

Mike picked up his notepad and turned to leave. He did his best to reassure Tarin. "Hey, you. This time Simmons won't catch us by surprise. We know what he's up to and I promise we'll get him."

She sent a faint smile his way. "I hope so. Thanks to you both for what you're doing."

CHAPTER 56

A Guarded Situation

B Y NOON THE NEXT DAY, ARMED PERSONNEL WERE stationed in front of Jon's house monitoring arrivals and departures. They stood with clipboards verifying identities and reasons for the deliveries. They also had at their disposal an artist's sketch of what Simmons might look like with a goatee and black hair. In addition, two security men were positioned at the back of the house and two more were on the beach.

Simmons hadn't returned to the homeless shelter or the shipyards which left Mike and Detective Maynes grasping at straws.

Two days before the wedding, a caterer's van displaying a company logo pulled into the drive. The security guards were able to verify the company as legitimate, however, there was a problem with the driver. The clean-shaven blonde-haired man's name wasn't on the list of approved employees. But he was wearing a uniform, complete with a nametag.

The guard followed procedures and called the caterer to speak directly with its manager. After a short conversation, the woman apologized and told the guard that due to the size of the job, she'd needed to hire several additional employees at the last minute. Unfortunately, she hadn't had an opportunity to add them to the list. And yes, she had authorized this new driver to deliver serving pieces to Jon's home.

Satisfied, the security guard waved the van and its driver toward the house.

"LOOKING FOR THESE?"

Tarin felt her heart skip a beat when she saw Simmons sitting across from the shower holding her towel and bathrobe.

He smiled. "I don't know why you're trying to be so modest—I'm not seeing anything I didn't see in the cabin."

"How did you get in here?"

"It was easy. I got a job with the catering company you hired for the wedding. They thought they were hiring some guy named Jake Carpenter." He fingered the nametag on his khaki-colored shirt. "Nice name choice, huh? Your security goons called my boss. She verified I'm legit and that I'm driving one of the delivery vans. As far as they're concerned, I'm bringing serving dishes for this weekend's big event. An event that won't take place, I might add."

"But the guards have a sketch of you—"

"With black hair and a goatee." He smirked, running his fingers through short bleach-blonde hair. "Do you like my new look? I decided to get a makeover just for you."

"Get out of our house."

"Your house, is it? Oh, that's right. You're planning to marry Jonathan Parker in a few days." He reached into his pocket and pulled out a crumpled paper. "Look—I've got my own invitation."

"Where did you get that?"

"From the shop that printed them. You didn't see me, but I was there while you were picking out the invitations. After you left, I told the clerk my fiancée was supposed to meet me there but had a change of plans. I mentioned I was interested in the design you picked, but wondered what it would look like with text. Your order was still on his computer, and he was kind enough to print me a sample copy. Date, time, address—it's all right here."

Simmons gave her a moment to digest what he'd said. "I visited your florist, too, and you already know I connected with the caterer.

The only time I didn't follow you was when you and your friend went into the bridal shop."

"You're supposed to be dead, Scott."

"Oh, such antagonism." He tossed the towel and robe toward her. "Now get dressed. We've got places to go."

"You're sick."

"Think what you want, but you're not getting away from me this time. And don't bother waiting for your knight in shining armor to come to your rescue. I saw him leave the house about twenty minutes ago. We're alone."

Tarin looked toward the cell phone vibrating on the vanity.

"Don't answer that."

"If I don't, he'll worry."

"Okay but put it on speakerphone. Be careful what you say and how you say it."

Jon's voice was cheerful. "Hey, you—I'm coming back. I forgot to bring the song arrangement we've been working on and Nick wants to see it. I think I left the score on the piano. I'll see you soon."

Tarin stared at Simmons before blurting, "Jon, he's here—Scott's in the house. Call Mike!"

Simmons knocked the phone from her hand. "That was stupid, Tarin. When that lover boy of yours gets here, first I'll make him suffer and then I'll kill him while you watch." Simmons thrust her into the bedroom. "Now, I told you to get dressed."

JON WAS SPEEDING DOWN the road when Mike accepted his call. "Mike—Simmons got into the house. My god, I think he was in the room listening when I called Tarin a minute ago. He must have heard her tell me he was there and told me to call you."

"Stay calm, Jon. We're only a minute or two away. I'm in the lead car and there are two San Diego detectives behind me. I'll alert the security team. Hang tight. Don't try to take him on by yourself."

"But he's been alerted that you're coming and who knows what he'll do. I'm afraid he'll hurt her this time."

"Jon—" The connection ended abruptly. "Damn it. He won't wait if he gets there before we do."

Minutes later, Tarin heard the front door slam and footsteps on the stairway.

"Jon—don't come up! He's got a gun."

Simmons grabbed Tarin from behind with his left hand, his right arm dangling at his side. "Think you can take me, Parker? Even with one arm, I can handle you. You couldn't finish me off on that mountain at point-blank range. Now you're not even armed. What makes you think you can save your little damsel in distress this time?"

Jon stood at the bedroom door. "Let her go, Simmons. The police are right behind me and when they get here, there's no way you can escape."

"Maybe not, but it will give me great pleasure to shoot you a few times before they get to me."

"Go ahead and kill me if you want but let Tarin go."

Outside on the driveway, Mike and the officers were hastily designing their plan of attack with the security guards.

"Who's familiar with the house?" Mike asked.

One of the guards raised his hand. "I've been stationed at the back since we started the surveillance. There's a stairway leading to the bedroom deck. We could approach from there while your guys take the front."

Mike needed clarification. "I've only been in the house once or twice, but the master bedroom is near the top of the stairs, correct?"

A second guard nodded.

"I've got an idea. Isn't there a dog in the kennel on the veranda?" Mike asked.

"Yes—why?"

"Let's just say that dog has a history with Simmons. Take him with you on a leash when you go up to the deck. When you slide open the glass doors, let him loose. That should be more than enough distraction to get Simmons' attention and give us an opening to free Tarin and take him to the floor. Keep in mind her fiancée is in the room, too, and there's no love lost between those two men. Simmons can only use one arm, so we have an advantage. But he does have a gun. If possible, I want him taken alive."

Mike looked at his watch. "We'll give you five minutes to get to the back of the house and start up the stairs. Be as quiet as possible. Any questions?" Not hearing any, he took a big breath and moved forward. "Okay, let's go."

Opening the front door, Mike called, "We're coming up, Scott. Put down the gun and let both Tarin and Jon go. You must know there's no way you can escape this time."

"Why would I do that, Mike? You'd have me extradited to Colorado to face a murder rap, kidnapping, and all the other charges the DA will pile on. I think I'll use my hostages as bargaining chips instead."

Simmons sat down, holding Tarin on his lap and using his legs to secure his grasp around her. He managed to balance his almost lifeless right forearm on the wide upholstered arm of the chair and put the gun in that hand with a finger poised on the trigger. His back was to the sliding glass doors leading to the deck. "Come in if you dare, Mike. Just know Parker will be my first target. I owe him at least one bullet."

"Don't make this more difficult than it needs to be, Scott."

Suddenly, there was the sound of a chair being knocked over on the deck. At the same time, the glass doors slid open, allowing Finn to charge into the room. He was on target, instantly ripping into Simmons' leg without mercy. Scott dropped the gun, his right arm slipped off the chair, and Tarin fell to the floor.

"Get away from him, Tarin!" Mike shouted, but Jon was already at her side, helping her stand and kicking the gun across the floor.

With Finn biting, barking, and growling, the three security guards who had entered from the back of the house wrestled Simmons to the floor and secured handcuffs on his wrists.

"Call for backup, ASAP," Mike ordered.

Detective Maynes started down the stairs, "Yes, sir. I'll also have them tell the captain we've neutralized the suspect."

Lying in a prone position on the floor, Simmons began to laugh and then grumbled, "Damn dog."

"Get him out of here," Mike demanded, his emotions beginning to flare. "Take him downstairs and wait for backup. If anybody has shackles for his ankles, use them."

Mike turned to Jon and Tarin who were huddled in a corner of the room with Finn sitting at their feet. "We've got him in custody, Tarin, and I see at least one life sentence in his future." He paused, looking into Tarin's tear-filled eyes. "I'm going downstairs to supervise his transport to jail. Then I'll come back so we can sit down and talk. I'm also going to have the San Diego PD send a crisis advocate to help you both deal with what happened today. Is that okay?"

She nodded.

Moments later, Scott Simmons was forced into the back of a specially equipped prisoner van and taken to the San Diego County Jail.

SITTING AT A TABLE on the veranda, Mike appeared somber and apprehensive when he faced Tarin and Jon.

"Thanks for taking the time to talk with me. Today's given us a lot to absorb in a very short time. There's something you need to know that will affect you both," Mike began. "I'm the one who told the officers to take Scott alive. He was threatening you both with a gun, so using lethal force would have been justified. But for him that would have been the easy way out. Instead, I want him to be judged in court for what he's done and—as a fellow citizen—see him rot in jail for the rest of his life."

"Now that he's in custody, what happens next?" Jon asked.

"The authorities here will press charges against him for his actions today. Then he'll face extradition for murdering Dan Martin, kidnapping Tarin, attempted murder for shooting Jake, sexual assault, and anything else the DA decides to file."

Mike paused, almost afraid to continue. "There will be a trial and unfortunately, that means the two of you and Jake will need to testify against him. You'll have to relive everything that happened in Tarin's house, the cabin, and on the mountain."

She simply stared toward the ocean.

"I'm sorry, Tarin. We'll do our best to work with prosecutors to keep the most sensitive testimony out of the public eye, but the defense attorneys may have other ideas."

Jon was quick to object. "Hasn't she been through enough already??"

Tarin put her hand on Jon's arm before looking at Mike. "It's okay, Jon. I'll do whatever it takes to put that man behind bars." She did her best to smile. "I'm not going to let Scott ruin another day of our lives."

CHAPTER 57

―――

Hope for the Future

J ON BROUGHT TARIN A GLASS OF SPARKLING WATER
and sat in rattan chair next to her on the veranda.
"It's good to be home." He leaned over to massage their dog's ears, "I
really missed our guardian angel Finn."

It had been six months since Jon and Tarin were married in front
of an intimate gathering of friends and family on a sunny Southern
California day. After the wedding, their first decision was to take
time off—Jon from the recording studio and Tarin from her job with
the newspaper. It was a much-needed escape after what most would
consider a terrifying year. During the months away, the couple wrote
music together and traveled the world.

They returned to Paris, ventured to Fiji, took Jon's parents to
visit his mother's family in Italy, and Tarin helped Rachel and Alex
in Chasm Falls after their new baby was born. But now the time
had come to return to La Jolla before venturing back to Colorado
for Scott Simmons' trial. The impending court appearances haunted
them both.

"Tarin, I need to share something with you," Jon admitted.

She looked puzzled. "You're looking so serious. What's going on?"

He pressed his lips together and hesitated before continuing. "I've
done something, and I hope you'll be okay with it."

She took his hand. "Try me."

"Jake and I have been talking the past couple of weeks—"

"And? What kind of mischief has my brother gotten you into now?"

Jon turned his chair to sit at her side. "Well, you know Jake and Maria have moved into the new house by the barn, and when I called to congratulate them, we started talking about things."

She smiled. "What kind of things?"

"He told me how your friends miss having us around, and I have to admit, I miss them, too." He laughed, "Just don't let Jake know I said that because it would go to his head." Jon paused, formulating what he wanted to say next. "I understand why you decided to sell the house your grandparents built because of everything that happened there, but Ledge Lake and Chasm Falls are part of who you are. Jake and Maria have been telling me about a house on the other side of the lake that is much older, but a lot like yours. It's the one Dan talked about buying for Maria before he was killed. I guess it's a real fixer-upper but has great possibilities."

She squeezed his hand. "You bought it, didn't you?"

"Don't be angry. I should have talked with you first, but I was afraid you would say no." He stopped to try and decipher Tarin's reaction. "Please say something."

She smiled. "You are so sweet, but what about this house? We both love it here."

He nodded, "I know, and I don't think we should sell it. But Maria's sent me pictures of the other house and I already have so many ideas. There are plenty of bedrooms and bathrooms, a big kitchen, a floor-to-ceiling moss rock fireplace, an old-fashioned wrap-around porch, and lots of trees. There's also a small guest house facing the lake I could turn into a perfect recording studio. I can work there and then fly to LA whenever I need to check in with Nick and Paul."

Jon continued to plead his case. "You love your job and even though you can do everything from here, think how much easier it would be if you were closer to Maury and the newspaper office in Denver. Plus, all your furniture is still stored in Chasm Falls—even your grandfather's boat is in a warehouse there. We could have everything moved into the house when we take possession and build a new dock for the boat."

"Does this house happen to have green shag carpeting and avocado-colored appliances?"

He grinned, "How did you know?"

She shook her head and smiled. "Just an educated guess. I've been in that house a few times, and I do remember thinking it has lots of potential."

Jon glanced into the living room. "Do you hear something?" he asked. "Sounds like my cell phone. I'll be right back so we can continue this conversation. Don't go anywhere."

"I promise not to move an inch."

A few minutes later, Jon put his phone down on an end table and stood staring into space.

Tarin came in from the veranda and walked to his side. "Who was that?

He didn't respond.

"What is it, Jon? What's wrong?"

"Wrong? Right? I'm not sure which word to use. That was Mike."

"What did he want? Is Jake okay? Did something happen to someone we know?"

"No, everyone is fine." He paused, almost choking on his words. "Mike called to tell us Simmons isn't going to trial, Tarin. None of us will have to testify."

"I don't understand."

"The authorities in Colorado transferred him from the county jail to a larger facility while he was awaiting trial. Simmons apparently didn't make many friends there. Yesterday, he was in the exercise yard when a small group of inmates gathered around him in a remote corner. He was stabbed multiple times with a modified kitchen knife. The camera coverage was spotty at best, so officials don't know which prisoner attacked him and no one is talking. Scott is dead, Tarin."

She collapsed into his arms and the glass she had been holding shattered on the floor at her feet.

Jon carried her to the couch and discovered she was crying. Wiping the tears from her cheeks, he did his best to console her. "Hey, you. Why are you crying? This means Scott is truly out of our lives forever. There's no coming back this time."

Her voice was muffled, "I am thankful we won't have to relive everything that happened last January. But I can't celebrate when anyone—even someone like Scott—is killed that way."

"Come here." Jon held Tarin in his arms, combing his fingers through her hair. "Now we can concentrate on the future instead of the past."

Tarin gazed into her husband's eyes. "There's something I need to do and somewhere I need to go, Jon. Will you come with me?"

A WEEK LATER IN St. Peter, Minnesota, Jon and Tarin found themselves standing in front of a rose-colored granite marker in Calvary Cemetery. Tarin placed a bouquet of fresh flowers at its base.

"Why are we here, Tarin?"

"This grave belongs to Ashley Simmons, Scott's wife. He told me about her the one time he let his guard down while holding me prisoner. Ashley was the anchor in his life and when she turned to another man while he was overseas, it destroyed him. Between losing her and suffering from the effects of PTSD, he became the man who terrorized us in Chasm Falls."

"But the name on the marker is Ashley Kincade."

"That's her maiden name. Even though it was never proven, Ashley's parents were convinced Scott was responsible for her death and they refused to put her married name on the marker."

Tarin paused, her memories taking her back to the cabin.

"That's the only time I saw Scott show any remorse. He admitted he'd been drinking the night she died and knew his wife was with the other man. When Ashley left her lover's house, Scott followed her. At high speed on a precarious curve, he forced her car off the road and over an embankment. She died in the crash."

Tarin rested her hand on the cold stone. "In some strange way, Ashley and I will always be connected. I want her to know that now she can finally rest. While it won't erase the pain he caused, Scott paid with his life for what he did."

Walking back to the rental car, Tarin asked, "Jon, when we're living at Ledge Lake, can we buy a sailboat? Nothing huge, but something bigger than my Sunfish."

He was perplexed. "Of course, we can. But what made you think of that today?"

She paused. "I want our kids to experience everything I did growing up at the lake."

He smiled. "You know what, I just realized we haven't spent much time talking about if and when we want kids."

"True." Tarin smiled, "But even so, while the number is up for discussion, the when is now."

Jon stopped and turned to face his wife. "Wait a minute—are you trying to tell me I'm going to be a father?"

She nodded. "My doctor called with the test results the same day Mike told us about Scott's death."

He was dumbfounded. "Now I understand why you've been drinking sparkling water rather than wine." Jon rambled on. "Nick and Roxie just told us they're having a baby, so we're what—a few weeks behind them? Our kids will grow up together like Nick and I did."

"Hold on a minute. The two of you got into more than your share of trouble when you were growing up in New Jersey. But whether our babies are boys or girls, Roxie and I will keep close tabs on their antics—mischief that will probably be incited by you and Nick. God forbid if there's a boy and a girl. You two will start planning their wedding before they can even walk. Thank goodness there will be several states between them when we're at Ledge Lake."

Beaming, Jon hugged Tarin with all his strength. "Do you know how happy you've made me? Let's go back to La Jolla and start researching sailboats. We'll need to start planning nurseries for both houses, too, won't we? I've never changed a diaper and I'm not sure I want to, but will you teach me how? What about names?"

Tarin pressed an index finger against his lips, attempting to silence her husband's random chatter. "Jon, we don't need to decide everything right this minute. We'll start this new adventure together—diapers and all."

"Is there any chance we might have twins? I'd love to be one up on Nick."

"Stop, Jon." Tarin put her hand on his cheek and simply smiled. "Let's take whatever the future holds one day at a time. If there's one thing we've learned this past year, it's that we need to treasure every moment we're given."

Jon grasped her hand and kissed it before wrapping his arms around her. Then he held Tarin at arm's length. "What do you say we go home and begin planning for all of our tomorrows?"

"Which home?" she asked.

He hesitated before answering. "Are you trying to tell me you might be ready to visit Ledge Lake?"

She looked deeply into Jon's eyes before she spoke. "I think so—as long as you're at my side."

"Always and forever," he replied. "Always and forever."

THAT SAME NIGHT NEAR Chasm Falls, Colorado, a father and his young daughter sat on a white Adirondack-style bench overlooking Ledge Lake from what locals continue to call "The Point." She responded to his tickles with infectious giggles.

"Daddy, can we go fishing tomorrow?"

"You bet we can. Your grandpa is coming to live with us, and I know he'd love to tell you all about fish and fishing. He's bringing his boat and when you're a little older, I bet he'll teach you how to drive it." He gave her a quick hug. "Do you think your mom has the hot chocolate and cookies ready?"

"Let's go see. I'll get there first, Daddy!"

"Be careful, Emma," he called after his daughter who was running toward the house as fast as her short legs could carry her.

The man turned to look out over the rippling water. Dusk was falling and flickering lights were beginning to appear on the opposite shoreline. The night was calm with stars above and moonlight silhouetted the mountains. An owl hooted in the distance. It was a new beginning for this special place and the spirit world approved.

The end

Milton Keynes UK
Ingram Content Group UK Ltd.
UKHW010123280923
429520UK00012B/86/J